Sign up for our newsletter to hear
about new and upcoming releases.

www.ylva-publishing.com

FRAGILE

a novel

Eve
Francis

For T & K

CHAPTER 1

The shipment was late. Carly Rogers crouched down next to her coworker, who was nestled inside a bunch of knockoff Gucci sunglasses.

"Hi," Carly said. "I think the manager told me to help you until the truck gets here. What are we doing?"

"Hi. Um. I think we're mostly putting sensors on these sunglasses. Just loop it around, like this."

The woman demonstrated with the small device. She threaded the pointy end of the sensor through the nose of the Gucci sunglasses and then locked it into place with the ink pack on the other end.

"Then hang 'em up." The woman slotted the sunglasses onto plastic notches on the large board in front of them. In front of the woman's thin legs were two buckets, one of sunglasses and the other full of sensors.

Carly nodded. "Sounds easy enough."

The woman smiled and brushed a strand of brown hair away from her forehead. She wore a pink top with cinched sleeves and jeans. When Carly looked at the edges of her jeans, she noticed the quick hem job so they could fit over the woman's small body. Carly and the woman both wore their blue aprons for Marshalls, but the woman had pushed hers off to the side so she could sit down without dragging the apron over the dusty warehouse floor. Carly followed suit as she sat down next to her. She spotted the woman's nametag hanging off the side of the sunglasses display. *AMBER* read back at Carly.

"So, Amber," Carly said. "Are you a newbie too? Or have you been poached from another store?"

"No, I'm new. But I've been trying to get a job at Marshalls or Winners for the past few years. Makes it easier to buy baby clothing at a discount, especially when I don't like Walmart."

"I hear you there." Carly slipped a pair of sunglasses with red frames over the stand. Amber's small confession of kids made Carly pause, especially since this woman didn't look much older than Carly's twenty-four years. She barely looked as old as Carly's kid sister. But Carly was getting used to not trusting her first impressions, especially in a grand store opening like this.

Marshalls, the retail outlet that provided cheap and discount knockoff clothing to its patrons, was opening up in the new strip mall across from where Carly lived. It was going to be the biggest Marshalls store on the West Coast, so the company had started hiring early—and aggressively. Lots of signs, ads in the newspaper, and even takeaway application forms at all the other stores that T.J. Maxx owned in the area. Carly needed a job and her mother had been more than helpful in taking several application forms home to her and reminding her to complete them every other day.

Carly procrastinated with the whole thing, knowing that like with any minimum wage job, she would get it—so long as she took her college degree off her resume. So, for a while on paper, Carly Rogers had become just like any other high school graduate who had hopped around at minimum wage jobs, from coffee shops to waitressing, to being a phone person in a telemarketing place, and the seasonal help in her stepfather's law office. Carly received a call back the day after she handed in her application form for Marshalls. An interview later, the job was hers. *Surprise, surprise.*

The next two weeks were full of large conference halls where the T.J. Maxx and upcoming managers for the new store trained and talked to their new employees. Everything was being done on a mass scale, to the point where Carly could blend in and not respond to anything. So long as she handed in her banking information, signed a few forms, and showed up, no one bothered her. She clung to her red purse—filled with her cell phone, iPod, and a book—and was able to disappear.

Today was the first day of actual training inside the new store front. The near empty building was next to a Best Buy and down the street from a liquor store. A bus route passed through the strip mall and constantly made Carly jump each time the bus honked its horn. The new staff had been divided and allotted to separate areas. Carly should have been in women's wear along with a handful of other workers. They were supposed to get the racks filled with clothing and covered in plastic from the back, take them to the already labeled sections in the store, and put the clothing out.

But the shipment was late.

At first, Carly had been cleaning around the back dock as they all waited. She pulled out the broom and began to clean, trying to fight her way out of the boredom and tedium of minimum wage work. Most other people chatted with one another. When two hours had passed and there was still no truck, the day manager sighed between her gapped teeth and told them all to get out. The first truck had come earlier, so there was still work to be done. That was when Carly had been pulled away from her delightful solitude and forced to find someone else to work with. Carly had almost missed Amber entirely behind the large sunglasses rack, as she wandered around the store. But Carly figured that a small, girl-child would be the best bet to keep her company for another two hours, until she could go to lunch and hide again.

"And you?" Amber asked, tilting her head to the side. "Do you have kids?"

"Oh, no, no," Carly said, with a shake of her head. "I am just…between jobs at the moment."

"Oh, okay. Well, don't worry. They've been telling us that if we do well as sales associates, there is opportunity in management."

"Ah, yes. Management. Very important," Carly echoed, with a slight roll of her eyes.

The last job Carly had before this was at a used clothing store. She had been on the way to official sales manager status, when she pretty much threw in the towel and quit. There was more to life than sorting out donation bins and bickering over quarters from the patrons she had tried to tell herself and other people. She had only taken the job in desperation and didn't want to dwell on it too much more. There had been other reasons for her quitting, Carly knew in the back of her mind. But no one really wanted to hear that her boss made her uncomfortable and got too close during training sessions. It was much easier to tell people that Carly wanted a life with *meaning*.

"This is my second job," Amber commented, sliding a sensor onto another pair. "So I figure I'll have to settle for whatever they give me. But hey, there's always hope that something small here could lead to something good. That's the dream, right?"

"The American way, yes." Carly sighed, sliding on another sensor and putting the sunglasses on the rack. When she touched the next pair, the white frames and wide lenses pulled her in. Playfully, she slid them over her nose and turned to Amber.

"How do I look?"

"Good, good," Amber said, smiling and laughing in the same childlike way from before. "You know, I think we get some kind of discount on even this stuff. It's going to be pretty nice, for a while. Pretending, you know. I mean, why would I even need Gucci?"

"Yeah, I know." Carly slid a sensor on the white glasses and hung them up. "Pretending can be fun."

The two of them continued to work, diminishing half the bucket of sunglasses long before they reached the end of their bag of sensors. The entire rack was almost filled with sunglasses, top to bottom. Carly noted there were still nobs on the side of the rack, thicker, and definitely not meant to hold sunglasses.

"What's this for?"

"Scarves," Amber said, not needing to think about it. She turned around, regarded some of the boxes from the earlier shipment. She spotted a skid in the middle of the aisle with a small tip of a leopard fabric pointing out of it.

Carly nodded, understanding. "I'll grab it. Bring it over. Yeah?"

"Sure! Thanks."

Amber went back to work as Carly approached the skid that was taller than her. The box of leopard scarves was halfway up the tower and covered in plastic wrap. *How on earth am I going to get this down?* Carly glanced around the store. Other workers walked back and forth under the hot lights. The sales floor seemed crowded ever since half the staff was kicked out of the shipment room. The store, from shoes to men's ties, was still empty of merchandise and waiting for the shipment to come.

"Do you need some help?"

Carly turned around to see a woman with short hair. She stood with a similar apron around her thin frame and held an X-acto knife in front of her.

"Yes! That would be perfect. I need scarves from here."

"Let me get that for you, then. Probably easier since I have this." The woman held up her X-acto knife.

"Yeah, probably."

The woman took a step closer to Carly, their shoulders brushed. Carly tried to see the woman's name tag as she moved, but she was too fast, already cutting away the plastic wrap and freeing the boxes underneath. She stepped away from the skid after grabbing a box of scarves and handing them to Carly.

"Here you go."

"Thank you," Carly stated. "This is a relief."

"Not at all. It's nice to actually have some work."

Carly was about to ask the woman's name when she turned around. Her legs moved kinetically down the aisle and back into the shipment room. Carly walked back over to Amber, who had begun to organize a new pile of sensors for their next task. Each one now was a solid hoop, with a tiny ink pack attached.

"Has the new shipment come in?" Amber asked, noticing as a few more people moved to the back of the room.

"I have no idea." Carly placed the box of scarves down. Amber peeled back the old Scotch tape and began to take out the leopard print. She knotted the scarf around the loop before she hung it on the side of the rack. Carly tried to imitate, failing miserably her first few times. Amber tried to show her, looping in and out, and holding Carly's hands as she did it. Carly's face flushed and she tried to push any thoughts away. *This woman with kids*, she thought, *and probably with a husband at home.* The definition of unattainable.

Carly kept looping the scarves, finally getting the hang of it.

"Are you going to leave when the shipment comes in?" Amber asked. "I don't mind, because you gotta do your job, but it's been nice having someone around."

"Probably," Carly said. "But I like being out here too. Easy work, even if it is a bit dull."

"Yeah, exactly. Another person spices it up a bit," Amber said, with a playful wink.

Carly hung up another scarf. She watched as the employees moved around. One man was sweeping, pushing a large broom up and down the aisles. She spotted the woman with the box cutter again, moving around and taking stuff off other people's skids. Aside from the dull murmur of people talking, the pushing of brooms, and peeling back of tape, things were quiet. If a shipment was there, they would know. The beep-beep of trucks backing up would be almost deafening.

"Maybe the shipment will never come," Carly said aloud. "Maybe this is just like an odd, modernist play. We could be on stage, walking back and forth, and waiting for someone named Godot who would never show."

"What?" Amber asked. "What do you mean?"

Carly glanced down at the scarves, her cheeks slightly red as she laughed at herself. *Carly, your college is showing. Carly, your pretentious English major is showing. Forget Waiting for Godot for one moment. You and Amber are hardly Vladimir and Estragon, and the boy is hardly the butch woman with the X-acto knife.*

"Oh, nothing." Carly hung up another scarf and then unfolded the next one against her neck. "Just pretending to pass the time."

CHAPTER 2

Soon, it was lunch. No shipment had arrived yet. The manager got on over the loudspeaker and announced in a clear, calm voice. "Okay, Marshalls staff. We appreciate all the work you've done so far. They say Rome wasn't built in a day, but apparently, they never had shipment or traffic issues. The first half of the staff, I want you guys to take your lunches now. Forty-five minutes, be sure to clock out. The second half, you'll go as soon as they get back. And maybe, just maybe, we will have a shipment to unpack."

The woman's voice seemed shaky, as if she was holding together her positive attitude with nothing but the flimsy tape they had all been given in the back. Carly's stomach rumbled as soon as the prospect of lunch was offered. She got up, turning to Amber with a tilt of her head.

"You coming?"

Amber shook her head. "I'm technically in section B for my lunch hour. I'm still out here."

"Oh," Carly said. She could not help but feel slightly disappointed. She hoped it didn't show on her face. "How can you tell?"

"A-M is shift two, N-Z is shift one." She hung up a few more scarves, grasping the last at the bottom of the box. "It's a bit backward, but makes sense, I suppose."

"I'm an R," Carly said.

"Then go!" Amber waved her arms in a command, then flattened a cardboard box. "I'll hold down the sunglasses hut here. It won't be too long. But you should go before the lineup is too much."

"Right. Good point." Carly wanted to thank Amber for being an unofficial tour guide. It had been a long time since Carly was lost in the crowd, to the point where it was detrimental. She turned around suddenly, realizing the mass rush of people toward the back of the Marshalls storeroom. She left without a wave, passing by some of the larger men on staff who got out of her way as soon as she approached.

Not too bad, Carly figured when she arrived at the punch card system. There were only a few people ahead of her. Including, she thought she saw from the back of her head, the woman with the X-acto knife. The woman removed her blue apron, as soon as her card went through, and then double backed toward the bathroom. Her eyes caught Carly's once again, nodding slightly, with a careful grin, before she walked right by.

Inside the break room, Carly made a mad dash for her locker. She grabbed her red purse quickly and then tossed it in the closest seat. She was right next to the window, still covered with thick blinds that did not allow the spring sunshine to come through, far away from the kitchen microwave. Carly had learned long ago to always avoid that spot, unless you wanted a smorgasbord of unappetizing food stench around you at all times. Carly pulled out her phone and responded to a few messages from her sister and her friend, Landon, before she took out her book and hid her face. She nibbled on her bagged lunch between the pages. Generally, with enough concentration that she had honed with years of customer service, she could forget she was in the room at all.

There were enough people there so that every single spot was filled, including some of the stray chairs in the back of the locker room. A tall, black man with a weary gait sat next to Carly, seeming equally eager not to talk. A woman with salt and pepper hair sat to her right. Some people chatted with one another; most people minded their own business.

When the butch woman from before came in the room again, Carly didn't even have to lift her eyes from the page to see her. The woman's short hair, masculine clothing, and friendly attitude pulled Carly in. *Please be gay. Please, please.* But so many of these traits didn't necessarily signal any type of queerness. Carly had fallen for so many girls with pixie cuts and who wore ties only to find out that they were as straight as anything else. Carly knew that she couldn't assume—or else she would start to fall for women with children and the proverbial straight girl again. Using her book as a cover, Carly merely watched. The woman moved toward the fridge, pulled out a can of Coke, and swallowed some of it down in a quick gulp before glancing at the lunch room again.

Carly shifted her eyes back to her book. She read the same sentence again and again, trying to remember the world between the pages and not the hope in the back of her mind. *Besides—what else could I really do in Marshalls break room of all places? Forget about it. You are just pretending again.*

Carly finished her sandwich and threw the Ziploc back into her purse. She finished the current chapter she was on and then took a drink from her water bottle. Between the movements, the woman appeared again. She walked behind Carly, close to the window. She peered over the man who sat next to Carly and then straight at her.

Well, not quite at me, Carly realized. The woman was looking at the cover of her book.

"*The Edible Woman,* huh?" the woman said, smiling with one side of her mouth."

"Yeah. I like Margaret Atwood."

"You should try *The Handmaid's Tale,* then. I read it last year and liked it a fair bit."

Carly's shoulders relaxed. She realized she had braced herself for a slew of ignorant comments that she had heard at previous jobs about reading. But this woman was okay, definitely.

"I read that when I was in high school, actually," Carly answered. "I even saw the terrible movie version of it."

"Oh, really? I'll have to see that, then. I love bad book-to-movie translations. Like *Slaughterhouse-Five.* Have you seen that? Terrible, my God. It was just awful."

"The book was really good, though," Carly said. She folded *The Edible Woman* over her hands, using her fingers to mark her place. "Have you read that?"

"I've read most of Vonnegut, actually," the woman said. "Though most of my brothers made fun of me while I did it, since there were pictures in at least half of his books. They said I was reading kiddie books."

"I can see where they're coming from, but I doubt many kid books have tombstones drawn in them."

The woman laughed again—light and airy. Carly felt like she could listen to it for a long time. "*Catch-22,*" the woman added.

"What?"

"*Catch-22*. It's another book that's really good, but the movie comes up short," the woman remarked. "It's kind of not fair, though, you know. Since so many of what we're talking about are classics, and the movie industry just didn't have time to catch up."

"Good point."

That was another thing, Carly realized, about this whole conversation. They weren't talking about *The Hunger Games* translation from book to movie, not even something like *The Fault in Our Stars* or *The Perks of Being a Wallflower*. They were talking about classics and oldies, stuff that most people here would have no concept of unless they were forced to read it in high school or had jobs in libraries in the past. Carly had almost forgotten how much she liked to talk about books with someone who had a better grasp of them and their nuance than her sister, or even Landon, who tended to stick with how-tos or novel adaptations of *World of Warcraft*.

"I'm Carly," she said, her heart beating too fast.

"Very nice to meet you Carly." The woman stuck her hand out, waiting for a shake. "I'm Ashley."

Carly shook her hand. She noticed how warm and dry Ashely's fingers were from the dust and the unpacking the workers had been doing.

"Nice to meet you, too," Carly echoed. Before Ashely could respond, the man next to Carly got up from his seat and gathered up his lunch.

"Hey, sir," Ashley called. "Do you mind if I steal your seat?"

He waved his arm in the air. "Knock yourself out. I'm going out for a smoke, and maybe, just maybe, the truck will come."

"Good luck," Ashley said. "But a watched truck will never come."

The man didn't seem to notice the remark. Carly could not help but smile in spite of herself.

"The joke wasn't that bad, was it?" Ashley asked, squinting her eyes as she sat down.

"I've heard worse."

"Well, then, at least I'm not the worst." Ashley smiled before she nudged the book cover. "So tell me more about this book. Why is the woman edible?"

"Well, I'm not entirely sure yet. Atwood's stuff always takes a while to develop. So far, this woman just has a hard time eating when she starts to feel used by those around her. She feels exploited by her boyfriend and then suddenly she can't eat meat. I'm at the part where her friend is talking about pregnancy and now she can't eat eggs."

"Sounds heavy."

"Yeah," Carly agreed. Relief flooded her system that Ashely didn't make a joke about the title referencing eating a woman out. *Or maybe I want that kind of joke?* Carly brushed by the thought. "I picked it up from a pile of discards at the library. I paid like a quarter for it, nothing much."

"That sounds like a great deal. What library?" Ashley asked, with genuine interest. She pulled out her phone and began to scan through an app that pulled up a map of their city.

"The city library by Rolland Street. It's just by my house, actually."

"Oh. You have to be careful about who you give your address out to."

"I can't be too careful. You already know where I work."

"Hah. That I do." Ashley scrolled through the map on her phone, locating the library and marking it with a star on her interface. "I'm actually envious you live so close to the Marshalls. I have to wait through buses to get here—or beg rides."

Carly was struck by this for a second. She thought, judging from Ashley's tall physique and her energy, that she was older than Carly. Surely old enough to know how to drive, even if she didn't have a car. Then again, Carly didn't want to push asking for anyone's age, considering the mishap that had happened with Amber earlier.

"So, tell me more about books," Ashley requested. "What else do you like?"

"Um," Carly said. "I just honestly read whatever I find around the house."

"Not true. If you read whatever you found, I would spot some Harlequins."

Carly smiled wider. "Oh, when I was a kid. Didn't we all?"

Ashley raised her eyebrows and winked. "Until we found the good stuff."

The supervisor came in, holding up her hand, as she announced they only had ten minutes of their lunch left. "And then the second crew has to come in, guys. So let's leave this place somewhat clean for them. Remember to punch your cards when you go back on the clock, too."

The lunch room murmured. Some people left, freeing up more seats as they went to clean out their Tupperware containers. Carly was relieved when Ashley still remained seated next to her. She leaned in closely, sipping her Coke, but otherwise paying attention. Carly curled her fingers around the edge of her book. She looked for her bookmark and then settled for dog-earing the page. She watched as Ashley hissed with disapproval.

"What?"

"The book. You should be nicer to it. Even if you only paid a quarter."

"I don't have a bookmark."

Ashley held up her hand and then went to dig through her pockets. She pulled out a few receipts and then found an old stamp card for a coffee place. "Here," she said, passing it forward.

"But there are four out of five cups stamped. Don't you want this?"

"Nah, you keep it. Coffee makes me jittery. Besides," Ashley said. "I know where you work."

"And sort of where I live."

"Right. Maybe I'll see you at a library sale."

"Maybe." Carly grinned

The sudden screeching of chairs backing up and punch cards echoed inside the room. Ashley got to her feet, and Carly reluctantly followed. When Carly turned the corner to put her book back in her locker, along with her purse, she noticed Ashley lingering close by.

"Thanks again," Carly said.

Ashley nodded, still gazing around the room. "Where are you working?"

"In sunglasses. You?"

"In shoes. They seem to like putting me there. I was supposed to be helping to unload the truck, but it's looking like that's not going to happen at all today."

Carly nodded. A sudden thought came to her. "Hey, so… This probably sounds odd, but have you ever read *Waiting for Godot?*"

"Definitely," Ashley said with a smile. From the way she raised her brows and laughed a little, Carly could tell that Ashley got the reference.

"Well, I'll see you out there," Ashley stated. "Hopefully I won't have to wait too long."

"You too."

As she watched Ashley walk away, Carly felt her body tremble with excitement. She would make sure that the two of them had coffee and talked more about books, no matter the cost.

"You look happy," Amber remarked.

"Hmm?" Carly walked over toward the sunglasses rack, only to find Amber trying to take down a box at the top of the skid in the aisle. Carly helped unload another couple boxes of scarves, purses, and general accessories. In the time since she was gone, more white and silver racks had been added to Amber's work space for her to fill. She was in the middle of adding stuffing to each purse, puffing it out so it could display well, in addition to adding more anti-theft devices to them.

"I said you look happy." Amber undid the zipper on a lime-green Coach bag and threw in some brown paper. "Lunch always does a body good. Anytime my kids are mad for no reason, I give them a granola bar. Cheers them right up. Blood sugar does a lot."

"Yes, I guess it does."

Carly picked up a purse, only to watch as Amber grabbed another one too, seemingly unaware that she herself also needed lunch to improve her mood.

"You need to go," Carly chastised her. "Come on, I got this now."

Amber nodded, her small eyes revealing tiredness now that it was permitted. She undid her ponytail, running her hands through her thin hair to redo it.

"Thanks, sweetheart. You're great. Everything is easy right now, so I'm sure you'll do fine."

"Thanks for the vote of confidence."

With Amber gone, Carly stuffed the purses and appreciated the time to herself. She was about to wonder what Ashley was doing, and if she'd come over to see, when the recognizable beep-beep sound echoed from the back of the room. A small crowd of people, including Ashley, began to make their way to the back.

"The truck," Carly said, laughing a little under her breath. "I guess we're no longer waiting."

CHAPTER 3

"How was your first day at work, sweetheart?"

"It wasn't technically my first day," Carly corrected. "I'm getting paid for all those training sessions."

"Yes, but this was the first time in the store. Doing real work and not having to listen to people talk."

Carly rolled her eyes a bit, out of the range of her mother's vision. *If you had heard some of these people's voices, you would change your mind about real work.*

"It was fine, you know. It's retail."

"It's a job," Jillian corrected sternly. "And jobs are good. Even if it's only for the time being. But that doesn't mean I want you to quit—not like the last one. You were doing so well there…"

Jillian leaned into the mirror and checked her makeup as she trailed off.

"Well, considering I went from a used clothing store to an outlet type of mall, I guess I'm moving up in the world," Carly said, feeling uncomfortable. She hadn't bothered to tell her mother the real reason why she had quit her last job. Even if Jillian did know about the manager's awkward advances, she probably would have thought it was "harmless fun."

"Maybe soon you'll be in fashion boutiques."

"What a time to be alive," Carly quipped. "If only."

Jillian spotted Carly in the mirror and smiled at her with a strained glance. Though Carly was still silently angry at her mother's assumptions, she couldn't deny her mom's beauty. Jillian was barely fifty years old, but still able to turn heads. Her dark hair was curled behind her ears, and she wore a dark, burgundy top over her black, A-line skirt. Her makeup matched her dark clothing and was different than what she had worn to her law office in the morning.

"Well, thanks for giving me an update. I always like to know what's going on with you," Jillian said quickly, before moving on. "I'll be back soon. Tonight, I'm just seeing Richard at his place. Just dinner."

Carly nodded. "Don't worry. I can take care of myself."

"And Cynthia?"

"Cyn is getting old now, you know that, right?"

Jillian gave Carly a patronizing glance from the mirror again.

"Yeah, I'll look after Cyn, too. I'll also probably see Landon tonight," Carly added. Her voice went high at the end as if she asked a question. For a moment, she still felt like she was Cynthia's age and had to report for curfew.

Jillian nodded, though Carly could detect the slight veil of annoyance at the mention of Landon's name. Since Jillian was running out without much warning and without making dinner, Carly figured she would let this indiscretion pass. As much as Jillian liked to argue and meddle, she was a lawyer and she knew when to take her chances and when to back off. She turned from the mirror and folded her hands together in front of her body.

"Thank you, Carly. I really appreciate you taking care of stuff like this. Sometimes, I just don't know what I'd do without you."

"Yeah. Sure. No problem..." Carly waited, as her mother slid her leather purse strap around her shoulder. Jillian gave herself a final check in the mirror. She smiled, once more, through the pane of glass and then left.

After the door was shut, Carly let out a breath.

"Fuck," she said, to no one in particular. "Fucking fuck fuck."

Carly felt fifteen all over again, twisting and shouting words and hoping it was enough. Her mother angered her so much some days, but it was never enough to actually fight about. She understood her mother's want and need for free time. Her attractiveness, her success, and her ability to thrive with and without high-powered men in her life. Carly was even jealous of it some days, because she knew that secretly, it was what her mother wanted for her. Jillian wished that Carly could have an "easy life"—one where she could be loved and successful. But Jillian wanted that life for Carly *her* way, through *her* rules. And Carly knew that the life her mother had would never make her happy, even if she had been allowed to live it with high-powered women, instead of the many men Jillian courted. *And you're always so mad at her,* Carly chastised herself, *because you know she's disappointed.*

With another sigh, Carly moved back to the kitchen and looked inside the fridge. There were some packages from the Chinese place around the corner, left over from a few days ago. Old banana bread, some tuna salad, but nothing really that appetizing. Carly got down on her knees, digging through the bottom shelf, until she came across the whole wheat pitas and cheese.

"Hey, Cyn," she called upstairs to her sister. She listened closely as Cynthia's music was shut off. "How do you feel about pizza tonight?"

"Yes, please!" Cynthia shouted. Her music cranked back on at the end and was switched to a more celebratory song. Carly laughed when she realized it was the song "Gimme A Slice" by the Sand Witches, a riot grrrl band singing about pizza. *Of course. How appropriate.* Carly waited until the two minute song was over before asking Cynthia to come downstairs and help.

"It'll be pita pizzas tonight, so you can choose your own toppings."

"Sweet!" Thudding sounds came from the stairs and Cynthia barreled down. Carly began to take out all the things she could find for small pizzas, including the whole wheat pitas at the back, and laid them down on the counter.

In the last two years, ever since watching the film *Whip It* when she was thirteen, Cynthia had completely changed. She became the punk rock, feminist, Roller Derby wannabe Carly now saw on a regular basis. A week after watching the film, Cynthia cut her long hair into a sharp pixie cut that made Jillian swallow her gum when she first saw it. Cynthia's hair was curly, and the short styles made her hair curl even more, puffing into a near Afro. Since then, Cynthia allowed her dark hair to grow back, keeping it tamed by adding more barrettes and sometimes dying sections of her hair different colors. She listened to anything that Kathleen Hanna fronted, and read third-wave feminist zines that Landon brought her from the queer library he worked at one summer.

Those zines were really one of the first things that put Landon in the bad book with Carly's mother. The actual first straw, Carly knew, was the fact that Landon used to be Lisa, the small girl that Carly had grown up playing with at school.

The summer he was nineteen, Landon began his transition from female to male. While Carly—and especially Cynthia—accepted Landon, Carly knew her mother couldn't stand the change. It made her uncomfortable on the most visceral of levels. She never said bad things, not really, but Carly saw her twitch each time Landon was mentioned. This prejudice was always so bizarre to Carly. Her mother had accepted when Carly came out as gay when she was fifteen (though there was initial hope that it was going to be a phase). Nearly ten years later, Jillian had grown into the fact that her daughter was always, and only, going to bring home women to the kitchen table. That had been fine. She had learned to deal with that. But Landon was another creature to Jillian. Carly knew her mother's insults extremely well, even when they were silent.

Cynthia's footsteps knocked Carly out of her thoughts. She sat down at the kitchen island and smiled wide, baring one of her chipped teeth.

"Has Mom not fixed that yet?" Carly said, leaning in and looking at the small damage on the front tooth.

Cynthia shrugged. "I kind of like it. I think Mom told me she wasn't going to get it fixed until I stopped skating."

"So, you're going to be a toothless old woman by the time she gets around to doing it?"

"Yeah! "I think it's becoming."

"You know what? Good for you. Whatever makes you happy."

"At least someone thinks so."

Cynthia grabbed garlic and jalapeno peppers, and started to chop. It took Carly a moment to even register Cynthia's disappointment. Even if Jillian knew when to pick battles, she was still too cold for both of them. *Not just me.* Cynthia could cut her hair and dye it, wear ripped jeans, and skate all the time; while Carly could laze around the house, go to college for English, and date women. But there was always a small, unspoken antagonism inside the house. Carly was never quite sure what she could say or do to relieve it, so she got used to treading the fine line between approval and apathy.

"You know Mom," Carly said. "She says she'll be back tonight, later than usual, but she'll be here."

Cynthia nodded, eating some of the hot pepper without even thinking about it. When she gagged on it, she moved over toward the fridge and drank soy milk right out of the jug. Carly laughed, poking her sister in the side as she struggled to get her hot tongue under control. Carly shredded some more cheese and handed it off to her sister, who ate some sections of it slower than before.

"What will you be doing tonight?" Carly asked.

"Skating," Cynthia said, not raising her eyes from the cutting board. "The usual. You know."

"Done your homework?" Carly asked. It was late spring, and though the concept of having homework, or even classes to attend, seemed like a distant memory to Carly, she often tried to remember those days when she was around her sister.

"Yes, *mom*, I will do my homework. Jeez. I swear you ask me more than she does."

"I'm around more. And probably can actually help you with your homework if you did need it."

"Even trig?"

"I stand corrected." Carly added more toppings to her pizza, as Cynthia continued to make large red dots with the sauce.

"Well, I'm fine. It's only my junior year and most teachers there already think I'm smart. They grade on a curve, you know? So even though I know my answers are really shitty half the time, I've done the most work and put the most thought into most projects, so they let me get away with it."

"Well done. Play that curve. It will be the one way you survive."

"Even in college?"

"*Especially* in college," Carly emphasized with a laugh.

Often, Carly forgot that Cynthia was still just fifteen years old. She still seemed like a young girl, impressionable and very consumed with the movie that pretty much shaped her whole life so far. In their small city inside of Vermont, there wasn't much to do with the Roller Derby life that was pictured in the film. But that still hadn't stopped Cynthia from buying her first pair of Rollerblades and seeking out any place that was vacant enough to skate on, at all hours of the day. After a couple months of searching, Cynthia had found a local skateboarding park she'd often sneak out to visit, though Jillian always hated it. So long as Cynthia got good grades though, there was almost nothing Jillian could argue with. Cynthia seemed to know that point more than anything and had planned her success since the first day inside high school, analyzing the grading system and using it to her advantage. More time without homework meant more time outside. Now that spring was finally here again, Carly knew that Cynthia was itching to get out there again.

"I'm heading out with Landon tonight," Carly said.

"As ever."

"Well, true. Can you be back before I am? So that Mom doesn't get any ideas about your proclivities for tonight?"

Cynthia grinned as she ate another bit of cheese from their pizzas. "Of course, big Sis. Have I ever let you down before?"

"No," Carly said. "And you're about the only one who hasn't."

CHAPTER 4

When Landon knocked on the door, Cynthia was the first one to hear it. "I'll get it!"

Cynthia ran from the kitchen, her pizza only half-eaten in front of her, and opened while Carly was still getting to her feet.

"Hey, hey Cyn," Landon called out. He engulfed Cynthia in a hug in a matter of seconds. Landon was about six feet tall, and he had gotten much bulkier in the past four years he had been on testosterone. His large body seemed counterintuitive to his soft spoken and cheery nature, especially when he interacted with Cynthia.

Carly gathered up her plate and some of the extra napkins from the counter, before she made her way into the front hall. She could hear the slaps of high fives, along with the air whooshing past their grips, as Landon and Cynthia completed their secret handshakes. When she arrived, Landon was on his knees so he could look Cynthia in the eyes—and also see a killer bruise she was showcasing over her knee. Deep purple marked her already dark skin, spanning outward into browns and yellows. Carly made a face as Cynthia continued to laugh.

"Oh, God," Carly gasped.

"It doesn't even hurt, Car," Cynthia warned. "Don't worry. I'm tough."

"Indeed, you are. But careful or there will be nothing left of you to bruise. Hey, Lando. "You see her teeth, too?"

"Of course," Landon said, getting back to his feet again. "I'm still shocked she has some."

Cynthia guffawed, then chatted aimlessly to Landon, as he shifted from side to side. Not only did testosterone help Landon fill out his clothing, going from a men's medium to a large and extra-large overnight, but Carly was sure that his shoulders became broader and his hands bigger than before, too. Within the last six months, Landon had also had a mastectomy to remove his breasts. That surgery, hands down, was the best thing Carly had seen happen to him. He walked taller, talked louder, and was generally a much happier guy since healing from the operation.

Now, Landon seemed to take up the entire room with his energy. He wore a dark jacket, unbuttoned and overtop of a casual, plaid and black T-shirt. His jeans were big, loose, and finished off with a large belt and a Batman buckle.

"You ready?" he asked Carly, his keys jangling by his side.

"Yeah, just give me a moment to pack away a few more things in the kitchen."

"And you, little one?"

"Fuck off—I'm not little," Cynthia said, scolding Landon with a smile.

"Everyone is, compared to me. But on your skates, you've gotta be what, like five feet? Maybe even four seven?"

"Fuck off," Cynthia said again, though she still smiled. Carly wrapped up the leftovers in the kitchen, keeping an ear out to hear the kerfuffle in her front hall, as Landon and Cynthia tackled one another again.

"I swear to God, Lando," Carly called. "If you give her another bruise—"

"You'll tell your momma on me?"

"No, not at all," Carly said, appearing by the doorway with her purse over her shoulder again. "I will help you out. Now, come on. Hold her down for me while I tickle her without mercy."

Cynthia shrieked, as Carly and Landon both descended on her in a stream of giggles.

Landon drove a 2008 Dodge sedan, gray in color, and with a typical, pine air freshener hanging off the rearview mirror. Landon liked to joke that his car was gray to match his sexuality.

"What does gray mean again?" Carly asked, as she slid into the car and did up her belt. "You know, if the pride flag is rainbow colors, where do you fall in?"

"I'm a storm cloud, raining on your parade," Landon answered with a wink. "I'm a gray-a asexual."

"Can you really be asexual, though?"

"Yes!" Landon said. "Testosterone injections kind of make it hard, but for the most part, yes. I prefer the company of women, but I mostly like to cuddle."

"Aren't you just the big and wonderful bear I always thought you were," Carly teased. She rolled down the window of his car, allowing the light, spring breeze inside. She stuck her hand out the window as Landon backed up, feeling a bit like a small child on a road trip. "Where are we headed tonight?"

"I don't know yet. I figured we'd make up our minds when we get there."

Carly had gotten used to people picking her up and driving her around to places ever since high school. Usually, Landon had been her best companion on the road. He was one of the first people within their small group of friends in high school to drive, and Carly, of course, had been one of the last. Technically, she was still the last person to know how to drive, since she hadn't bothered to learn after a couple near-disastrous attempts with her mother as the teacher. Davis, Cynthia's biological father, had offered to teach Carly, but those plans never panned out—especially since he and Jillian divorced when Carly was barely in her teen years. Then Carly was in college and too far away to learn.

Carly had decided, out of necessity and a need to accept the world as it was given to her, that being a passenger was an okay life. It meant you got to watch as the houses went by, seeing who was up and awake at three in the morning when coming back from a concert. It meant that you got to see the stuff outside the window, looking at landmarks and committing them to memory. Usually, she also got to control the songs in Landon's car. After chasing the breeze a bit more with her hand, she slipped under the seat to grab the book of CDs Landon kept there. Since Landon's old car didn't have a docking system for iPods, he and Carly had pooled their old collection of CDs together.

"A bit like in high school, again," Carly commented, as she skimmed over the bands from their youth. She lingered over Fall Out Boy's *Folie à Deux* for a little too long, before she decided on a 1980s and '90s compilation album.

"Oh, God. Why?" Landon groaned, as he heard some of the familiar, one-hit wonders come through his speakers.

"This is *your* CD, Landon."

"Which you gave to me as a birthday present."

"And I know what's good for you." Carly smiled as Landon continued to squirm at "Cry, Little Sister" from *The Lost Boys*. "I like this stuff. Reminds me of when I was young and I didn't know any better."

"Hah, good point."

Carly slid down in her seat, bobbing along to the music and overly corny lyrics. The next song seemed to fall in line with a segment of birds in the sky. Landon began to loosen up and moved along to "Kiss Them for Me" by Siouxsie and the Banshees, as he continued to drive.

Often enough, all Carly and Landon would do when they hung out was drive around the small city they called home. They would crank the music, sing along to it really loud, and forget about deep conversations. Singing the same words over and over again—especially if it was Fall Out Boy—was all they needed to feel a connection to one another. This type of bonding had been especially necessary when Carly found out about his transition. She had supported him entirely with it, but the first few times they saw one another had been tense. Landon was nervous about how his family and friends would take his new self (not all of them had been good), and Carly struggled with her own expectations of her friend. Using music as a crutch, until those deep conversations came again, was all they had needed.

Landon fidgeted as he drove. *Something on his mind?* Carly wondered. She turned down the music after only a couple of songs.

"Thank *God*."

"Where are we headed?" Carly asked again. "Since you're not in the mood for music, there's gotta be something else we can do."

Sometimes, she and Landon went out to grab a coffee or to see a movie. Other times, they went to one of the parks they knew Cynthia would be at to watch her skate and then hiss awkwardly at every last fall Cynthia took. From the scenery they passed, Carly knew they were probably headed toward the far end of the city, maybe to a park—or just in circles again.

Landon was still quiet. His back was stiff as he held the wheel.

"Come on," Carly urged. "Stop driving in circles. I'm getting dizzy."

"I was thinking…"

"That's a shock."

Landon nudged her. He stopped at a stop sign, and Carly stuck her hand out the window again.

"I am going to teach you how to drive," Landon declared.

Carly laughed lightly under her breath. "I do believe that's a suicide mission."

"What? Why? Didn't you and I have the same driving instructor for a while in high school?"

Carly nodded, but then backtracked from her own statement. "High school was a long time ago, Landon. It's hard for me to really consider myself a driver anymore. I think there is just a peak year where you pretty much decide whether or not you're a pedestrian or you're a driver. I'm not sixteen, or even in my teens at all, anymore. I don't feel quite right claiming ownership over driving."

"I know you're kidding, but you *do* realize how ridiculous you sound, right?"

Carly shrugged.

"It's like saying to me that transition was ridiculous, because I had already missed that boat. Oh, no, raised a girl. Better luck next time," Landon said, with a slight bitter edge to his voice. "It's bullshit, Carly. You only have one life and you should use it for what you want. It's the same thing for you and women, too, you know. Just because there was that one guy back in high school, that doesn't negate the utter awakening you've had now."

Carly shoved Landon playfully. "Come on, come on. I know what you mean, Landon. But seriously? Driving doesn't matter that much. I have a bike. I should cut down on my carbon emissions anyway. Global warming and all that. You know."

Landon sighed overdramatically. Carly could tell from the changing scenery around them that they were headed toward the south end of the city, near the lake and the power plant, along with the city's university hospital called Left Bank. It was one of the few places in the small city that wasn't littered with subdivisions and parks for kids to play at with their mothers with twin strollers. Underneath the large bridge was a pavement pathway littered with graffiti and cigarette butts, though there had been a pretty substantial cleanup effort, on the part of the city, to make sure the space was more commuter friendly. The bridge was just by a dirt road, which Landon turned onto now, his stare determined.

"It's been a long time," Carly remarked, as Landon bumped over a few mounds of dirt and rocks.

"But it's never too late to come home. I think you've proved that substantially."

Landon parked the car under the overpass. "Are you ready to switch?"

Carly shook her head.

Landon got out of the car and walked around to her side. He opened her door and she sighed.

"What a gentleman," she said. "But I'm not driving."

"Fine—but humor me. Come for a walk. Sometimes it's nice to use our legs."

Carly eyed him, trying to decipher if this was a part in his plan. He held his large hands up, trying to signal that he was good to his word as always.

"Fine." Carly undid her belt. Landon extended his hand, which she took, as they began to walk under the bridge and into the night.

CHAPTER 5

Carly and Landon had grown up as next door neighbors and gone to the same elementary school. Carly was ostracized in school and so was Landon—both of them for being a bit too tomboyish and for being gay.

Looking back now, Carly was pretty sure that no kid in the second grade really knew what the term "gay" or "lesbo" meant. They just knew that, like the F word, it was something bad. Landon had always been tall for his age, big boned, and a bit chubby. When he wasn't called lesbo, it was something like fatso. Lesbo and fatso went together nicely, and Carly was pretty sure their friendship had been formed on this basis alone. They sat next to one another in the school lunch room, trading their sandwiches for better selection, and then walked home together. They protected one another from the insults thrown at them by simply being there. It was a lot easier to handle alienation when someone else was suffering through it, too. When things got a bit more hectic and violent, it was always Landon that stood up and protected Carly. His size alone was enough to scare away most bullies—of either gender.

For a long time, Carly was sure she was in love with Landon. At the time, of course, this would have been Lisa who caught Carly's eye. It was confusing a lot of the time, being friends with Landon when he was still Lisa. The lesbo insults they'd thrown at Carly proved correct by the time she got to high school. She fell in love with her math teacher, and then in her history class had learned that Lesbos was an island. From there, she pieced together who she really was.

But it was a lot harder for Landon to find the language he needed to express himself.

"I think I like women," Landon said when they were on Landon's parents' porch, up way past their curfews. They had just started high school, and Carly knew she'd get in trouble for showing up at home late, but she also knew that this conversation was well worth getting in trouble for. Landon kept starting and stopping, his hands balled into fists as he tried to articulate his precarious feelings. "I mean, I know I like women. And something more, something else, too. You know when we watched *Say Anything* together?"

"Uh-huh."

"I felt more like Lloyd than I did Diane. As in, I wanted to be *with* Diane, not be her, you know?"

"I do!" Carly said, her eyes wide. Her hands had been trembling, but she reached forward and grasped Landon's fingers in her own. "I'm a lesbian, too."

"Well, I don't know if I'd use that word, but yeah, I guess," Landon said. "I like women, so I guess if that's it..."

"It is," Carly said quickly. "We'll talk about this more—I'm sorry, I have to go!"

As Carly ran home, all she felt was relief. Finally, she could tell someone else about the isle of Lesbos and the other authors and poets she was discovering who also shared her proclivities. Over the summer and well into the next year, she and Landon would trade stories, talk about their girl crushes, and Carly was in heaven. They had even made out at a few sleepovers, just to try it out. But when Landon stopped responding to re-readings of *Annie on My Mind* and suddenly couldn't be around Carly, she thought it was personal. She thought she had screwed up.

"Why don't you want to hang out anymore?" Carly asked Landon their last year of high school, when his avoidance of her had been the worst.

"What do you mean? We're hanging out right now!"

"Yeah, because I found you hiding in the cafeteria and made you sit with me."

"Fair enough." Landon's eyes refused to meet hers; he barely touched his lunch.

"Do you still want to talk about our plans for prom?" Carly asked, hoping for a neutral change of topic. "I know it's extremely ridiculous and completely boring since every single straight couple does the same thing, but we can do it different, right? Make it gayer this time around and go as friends."

Landon smiled, but only a little. "Yeah. But I don't want to wear a dress. I just...can't."

"I know! I'll wear the dress. You can get…a pantsuit or something? I know there are things butch women can wear."

"Yeah, but I'd rather just wear a men's tux. I think it'd suit me better."

Carly giggled a little. "Yeah, but you're not exactly built that way. Even if you got a men's suit, you'd still need to take out the chest a little. It's just the way it is, you know?"

Landon pressed his lips together and didn't respond for quite some time. "Yeah. Whatever. I may just not go to prom. Why bother? Not like we're going to be remembered as King or Queen anyway."

"Yeah, but that's half the fun. We make our own memories. We can be Queen and Queen in our own world. Just you and me, Lisa."

"I'm…I'm still not sure."

"You don't want to go—or you just don't want to go with me?" Carly's chest tightened. This small disagreement, whatever it was, felt more like a breakup than anything she had ever experienced before. "I thought we were friends?"

"We are," Landon insisted. "I just…need to figure some things out."

"What do you mean? We can talk about it. Haven't we talked about it before?"

"We have. You're a good listener, Carly. But I'm just…really busy."

"Really busy with what? I'm getting sick of you hiding from me."

"Yeah, well, I'm getting pretty sick of hiding."

Before Carly could tell Landon anything else, he had picked up his stuff and left her in the cafeteria by herself. Carly threw out her prom plans the next day, deliberately buying concert tickets for herself and Cynthia on prom night instead.

At the end of high school, Carly had left for college and never really said good-bye. Two years later, when she returned during the summer, Lisa was Landon.

"Oh," Carly said, when Landon had called her and asked her to meet by their old school. He had shown up in his car, with a baggy hoodie over his body and wearing men's jeans. None of that looked particularly out of the ordinary—until Landon stepped out and she heard him speak for the first time. There was a depth to his voice that she hadn't heard before, and a new way he held his body. He was no longer cowering in the corner and attempting to hide himself, but presenting a stronger front.

"Yeah, oh is about the right response right now. So, can I introduce myself again?" Landon said, extending his hand. "I'm going by Landon now."

"Oh," she said again, involuntarily. "Well, I'm still Carly." Stepping forward, she took his hand. His palm was so, so warm—much warmer than she remembered as kids. But it was nice, Carly was sure of that.

Landon smiled and said, "Yeah, I figured you'd still be Carly."

She laughed in spite of herself.

"Not all of us go away for a summer and then come back new people. But I assure you," Landon insisted. "I'm really not that different. Come sit and talk? We can trade stories. I'm sure you have just as many as me."

"Pfft," Carly said, but got into his car anyway.

It was not exactly easy rebuilding a friendship after that. But Landon suddenly began to make way more sense than Lisa ever had. A new language of expression—and affection—cropped up between them as they sat together in Landon's car, pretending the heat didn't bother them, and discussed the years they had missed. Carly began to understand why their romance, or whatever she had wanted from those small kisses when they were young, could never happen.

"I want women," Carly said. "I like women."

"And I do too," Landon said, avoiding Carly's eyes. "But I can't like you. I can't be in a relationship with someone who's a lesbian, because it will make me feel like something I'm not. It's always made me feel like I'm something I'm not, as much as I loved you back then and still do now."

"You're straight," Carly said, nodding along and finally putting all the pieces together. "I know that."

"Yeah, exactly." Landon knitted his brows as if he was apologizing for something horrific. "I can't. I just want a woman. A woman who understands."

"I know, and you will, trust me," Carly said, touching Landon's shoulder. For once, the action wasn't knotted up with expectation and hopefulness. There was a tenderness to Carly's touch, and Carly hoped Landon felt the same way. "You know how people—usually guys—always give me shit for liking women? They say they like lesbians, but only if I make out with random girls at parties for their own enjoyment? I can't just be gay without somehow fulfilling someone else's expectation. I can't like what I like."

"Yeah, I remember that." Landon had fought off some ridiculous men for Carly over the years. From bullies with sand to men with big ideas in bars, Landon had always been there for Carly as a protector.

"Well, it's the same thing. I shouldn't owe anyone a free show or anything else for being a lesbian. Being a lesbian doesn't make me obsessed with boobs and vaginas, either. It makes me love women. And you, my dear Landon, are a man. You're my friend. And you don't owe me anything else."

Landon smiled, relief evident in his face. They continued to talk for a while longer in the car, sorting out the minutia of what this meant for their friendship. Landon also caught Carly up on his own relationships; he had been seeing a woman just before Carly came back home, but it had ended a little badly.

"All pear-shaped," Carly said. "I get it."

"Pear-shaped?"

"Something my great-aunt says. It makes devastating situations sound a little less so."

"I guess."

"Hey, it's her loss, okay? We will find you someone else. And then we'll find me someone, too. It will be a nice, fun dating game."

"Well all right," Landon said, then stuck out his hand. "You have a deal."

Their friendship had a few more bumps and hurdles after that. Carly knew it wasn't all going to change overnight. She still had a complicated history with Landon, who used to be the first girl she ever loved and first person she kissed. Now she was looking at Landon, the first man she had ever really been close with and the best friend she could ever have. When Carly started to think of Landon in the future and envision him with male pronouns, a new name, and new look—everything got easier. She grew excited about the possibilities to repair their friendship, and was able to leave the past as a memory and nothing more.

There were still occasionally slipups on both of their parts. Landon, as a new person, was someone who began existing when he was still in his twenties, when Carly and Landon's history together had spanned much longer than that. Whenever Carly slipped up with pronouns, it was always in memory. She worked at catching those instances, changing them, and moving on. Landon was grateful and patient, and Carly was still learning.

Each summer that Carly came back to her mother's place, Landon had changed a little bit more. More facial hair, different face shape, and then no more binding. He grew happier, too, which was really the best part about it all unfolding.

"You're beginning to catch up to me," Carly once said. "Your voice didn't crack the last time. It's like you're a real grown boy!"

"Hah. Very funny. I've had to go through two adolescences, while most people only get one. So be patient with me, as I finally reach your adult status, Car."

"Oh, please. I'm hardly an adult. At this rate, you'll get there faster than me. I think you already are there, actually. You're looking a lot better."

"Why, thank you."

"See? Soon enough, we'll just be remembering our teen years, instead of repeating them."

"I can only hope," Landon said with another small smile.

Landon walked around the concrete enclave, making his way toward a rickety bench, as Carly followed close behind. On the wall behind them was a large mural done Bansky-style, with a rat and a few stencils on it, alongside some tags from unknown gangs that were probably more show than anything. Carly sat on the bench cross-legged, holding her hands in her lap to keep them warm. The night air was cold, even though the summer was close by.

"How are you doing?" Landon asked.

"I'm fine," Carly said, tilting her head to the side. "Why?"

"You did start a new job today."

Carly shrugged. "It's just a retail gig. The store's going to open soon and it will be chaos, but then it will be same old, same old."

"Are you happy, though? I mean, it's retail and you have a degree."

"Most people in retail now have degrees. At least arts degrees. The person my mom gets Starbucks from pretty regularly was apparently a PhD candidate for Chaucer."

"Really? And what did your mom say to that?"

"Don't study Chaucer." Carly laughed, then sighed.

Landon nudged her again. "This is what I mean, Car. Are you okay? You don't seem like yourself lately."

"It's summer. Things always get better in the summer."

"That's not really an answer."

"I could ask you the same question, Landon," Carly said, putting on her best mental health worker's voice. "How are you doing? Are you happy? Finding meaning in your life?"

"Oh, man. You're sounding like my therapist now." He shook his head and gave his rote answer. "I'm fine. Thank you for asking."

"Really? What's new with you?"

"Nothing new. But I like my life right now. I have this great apartment, a nice new computer for my new job, and I feel set. I'm happy."

"Are you really? I mean, I get that your advertising job is wonderful, and you get to use your graphic design degree for something, but what about comics?"

"You mean the comics we planned on doing when we were younger?" Landon scratched a hand through his stubble contemplatively. "I remember that. It's been a long time, but I remember it."

"Right." Carly grinned. As kids, she had promised to do the writing for their pet project since she read so much and Landon would obviously illustrate. He had been a pro at drawing as a child, always coming up with amazing characters and zany colors. As soon as Landon completed his degree, he was snapped up and into the workforce. "I'm pretty sure, even with this new job, that I'd have time to write the comic—if you still have time to draw?"

"Maybe," Landon said. "But I'm really happy now."

"What about *meaning*, Landon? Does your job give you existential meaning—or angst?"

"It's not the best work. But I like it. I can still draw."

"Does it ever bother you, though? That you're not illustrating books, but designing ads instead?"

Landon shook his head. "It's not my dream, no. But it's close enough to it. For now, I'm really fine. As much meaning as I need."

Carly nodded. "You ever notice how parents always tell kids to pursue their dreams, but then they double back and are like, 'Wait no, not that one! That dream makes no money. Do something with money.' I think it's bullshit."

"Money is important," Landon said. "Contrary to popular belief, I think it can buy happiness as much as poorness causes unhappiness. But I know what you mean. Do I ever."

Landon's parents were still "coming around" to the idea of a son. Carly and Landon had already had several tearful and stoic conversations in the car about how his parents were still calling him by his old name and never considered pronouns to be a choice. Even as Landon began to change physically, his parents often seemed blind to it. Carly couldn't fathom that pain, and she was often struck mute when Landon spoke about it, even incidentally. He had told her it was merely enough to have her there as support and Carly had trusted him that it was.

Carly wondered if Landon's dreams had changed along with his body. Could he handle doing ad jobs the rest of his life, so long as he got to pick the body to do it in? Carly shrugged and figured it was none of her business. At least Landon was happy and successful.

Carly looked down at the concrete around her. She wished it was sand, so she could scribble something in the dirt with her shoe.

"What exactly do you want in life, dear Carly?" Landon asked airily.

"That's the problem," Carly said. "I really don't know."

"Then what makes you happy?"

Carly shrugged as she looked out at the setting sun. She was no longer filled with the same wonder of her college years, the same kind that made her read poetry and study English. She was about to tell Landon something cynical, when she turned and remembered Ashley, the woman from the store. Carly smiled, her cheeks going red as she looked down again.

"Oh my," Landon said. "Did we just have a breakthrough?"

"No..."

"Tell me! You're keeping something from me."

Carly blushed. "There was a nice woman at work today. I was reading my book and she stuck her nose right in the middle of it."

"Rude." Landon teased.

"No, it was nice. Sort of like someone seeing a band T-shirt that you and I would wear in high school and starting a conversation. Remember doing that?"

"Yeah, except no one ever wanted to get us talking about Fall Out Boy. We would have gone on for days. And you would have probably tried to show them your fanfic."

Carly laughed, louder than she meant to. "Hey. You wrote some too. I was particularly fond of your crossovers between Fall Out Boy and My Chemical Romance while on tour. Very interesting reading material."

"Ugh," Landon said, running a hand through his hair. "Don't remind me. Pretending to be Gerard Way online was the only way I could be a guy for a long, long time."

"Water under the bridge then," Carly laughed. "So, this woman..."

"Does she have a name?"

"Ashley. I was reading my new Atwood novel and she wanted to talk about it. To think! A discussion about Atwood by someone who's not Canadian. How rare is that? It was just so nice, you know. She even gave me a coffee punch card as a bookmark so I didn't dog-ear the pages."

"Ah, love," Landon said. "That's really what makes the world go round."

"It's not love, but maybe... Maybe whatever it is could be enough."

"Do you know what I heard?" Landon said as he drove Carly back home.

"What?" Carly looked back from the passenger window, no longer watching the lights in the houses go on and off or the TVs flickering through dark houses.

"There is a Roller Derby starting here."

"Really? Where? I thought those things were only for places like New York and...not Vermont."

"Come on," Landon said. "It's not that bad here."

"Pfft. I can't speak for the rest of Vermont. But here? This town? A little dull."

"Well, not all of us can aspire to Boston and go to fancy colleges."

"Please, Boston was hardly an aspiration. Or else I'd still be here."

Landon was quiet, having learned a long time ago to not poke at Boston—the same way that Carly didn't poke too much at the summer he officially became Landon.

"Well, there is a new league starting up. I saw their posters inside the queer library. I even had one of the skaters come in and talk to me about it. She tried to recruit me, actually."

"I take it you told her no, but informed her about Cyn instead?"

"Yeah, I figured it would be a good opportunity for her."

"You know, she can't actually skate there yet, right? Jillian would flip."

"Does she need Jillian, though?" Landon countered. "Couldn't you help out in that regard?"

"I think most leagues need you to be at least sixteen or eighteen. There is a lot of injury that comes from that sport and no one wants a lawsuit—especially from the skater's mom."

"Fair enough. But any kind of injury she'd get there, she's probably done to herself accidentally," Landon argued. "Have you seen that kid take a spill? My God. I thought she was going to break every bone in her body one day, but she just got up and laughed. Fucking *laughed*, Carly, while she was bleeding from her knees and nose. Jesus fucking Christ. It's like staring into the abyss when I watch her skate."

Carly laughed so hard she grabbed her stomach. "Oh trust me, I know. I watched that kid take so many tumbles as a toddler and get up and not be affected at all. I dropped her at a park once and she yelled, 'again!' I had to hide my face in shame from the stroller-mommas who were giving me dirty looks. She's a handful, but I love that kid's attitude. Something to strive for, I'll tell you."

"See?" Landon said. "This is exactly what I mean. Cyn deserves to be in a league."

"She's tough, yes. I don't even think my mom quite grasps how tough she is. But either way, my mom is still going to freak out. Cyn will always be her baby and all that other sentimental crap. Moreover, Cynthia is still so young—and she can tolerate hurting herself. It's a lot different when you have to hurt others or they hurt you. She's seen the movie, but the movie's not real life."

"No, that's not quite what I meant," Landon said, shifting in his seat. "I meant that you saw her as a toddler. You've pretty much raised this kid."

"I have not," Carly said, but wasn't really convinced. Jillian was really busy opening her own law firm when Cynthia was starting school. She didn't ignore the family, but Carly ended up spending a lot of time with her sister. Not because she became a proverbial mother figure—but because Carly and Landon had stopped speaking then, and she lacked other good friends. "I can't be Cynthia's guardian for a Roller Derby form, if that's what you're thinking. No one would believe I had her at ten."

"Maybe."

"Maybe," Carly echoed, thinking of Amber again. Amber looked to be about Cynthia's age from some angles, and she had kids. Maybe Carly could pass herself off as thirty years old and fake guardianship to get her sister to skate. "Even if I do that, there's still Jillian. There is always going to be Jillian."

"She can't be that bad. I mean, if it makes her kid happy..."

"Then why the hell is she so sad?" Carly rolled her eyes. "I don't know. Jillian is and always will be a mystery to me."

Landon nodded as both of them drew quiet. Carly scanned the neighborhood as they approached. She tried to see if she could spot Richard's Ford Civic or her mother's car on the road with them, but no luck. Not even Cynthia was around, skating down the sidewalks to get home. Carly hoped that Cynthia was already parked on the family couch watching reruns of *Daria,* since it was dark out now. Carly and Landon were another couple subdivisions away from Carly's place, and she didn't really want to deal with her mother finding Cynthia doing something she shouldn't.

"But still," Landon went on. "Cyn's a good kid. And something she loves is closer by now."

"How close?"

"About an hour away, near one of the universities inside a big stadium. It's good. Legit. Even if Cyn doesn't play, she can still watch. She can get close to something that she loves. I, personally, see no issue in just watching. The first game is Saturday, too. Just a practice, but it could be good for her to see the insides of it, without all the Hollywood flash."

Landon pulled the car into Carly's subdivision, as she thought about Landon's proposal. The driveway was empty, as Landon pulled in the car, cutting the engine. But the house was still dark, as if no one was home. Before Carly could panic, reflective tape from the back of Cynthia's jacket shone like a beacon from the sidewalk, close by. Cynthia pulled into their driveway just seconds after them. She was pushing her curfew, but as there was no sign of Jillian, Carly saw no reason to argue, especially as Cyn waved her hand joyfully from where she stood.

For a moment, Carly felt as if they were playing tag like she and Landon did when the two of them were younger. *Olly, olly oxen free. We are all home safe now.*

"Maybe, you're right," Carly said, turning to Landon as she undid her belt. "I mean, what's the harm in asking?"

CHAPTER 6

Cynthia practically buzzed with excitement when she found out about the news.

"Really? So close?" Cynthia asked, her eyes wide. "How do you know?"

"I was talking to someone who skates."

"Oh, God. What was her name?" Cynthia asked.

"Lizzie Whordon," Landon said with a wry smile.

Cynthia laughed with delight at the name, and even Carly found herself chuckling, though her arms were still folded stoically over her chest by the front door. She kept glancing back from the display with Landon and Cynthia to the driveway, watching out for her mother. It was only ten, ten-thirty. Not even late, really. Jillian probably wasn't coming home for another hour at least.

"Hey, jumpy," Landon said. "You're making this sound like a spy mission over there."

"It kind of is," Cynthia stated. "I like looking at this as a whole-night reconnaissance mission."

Cynthia said the last words with another singsong quality to her voice. Landon nodded his head, as if he recognized the tune. The two of them had probably exchanged more mixed CDs or emailed playlists on *8tracks.com*. Carly couldn't keep track anymore. She watched as the two of them slammed their hands together again, exchanging their secret handshake.

Carly stepped away from the door. "Sorry. I just get nervous."

"I know, Car. You're a bundle of nerves, sometimes. Which is why," Landon emphasized again, "you should come with us."

"To a derby?"

"Of course!" Cynthia said.

"I would hate to break up the double date," Carly joked. She glanced back again toward the driveway and saw another flash of light.

"Hey, hey," Landon said. "Your sister is a lady and can date whomever she wants."

Carly swallowed, realizing she had stepped over one of Landon's raw nerves again. It was bad enough that he got shit from Jillian about sometimes being "too close" with her other daughter; there was also the threat of Carly's queerness and what that meant for Cynthia.

Good role models, Carly always heard Jillian lament. *My daughters just need good role models.* Even though Carly was convinced that Cynthia had found the best role models inside a Roller Derby ring—and a true confidant in Landon—Jillian was still leery.

Carly was sure, from conversations she had had with Cynthia over the years, that she was straight. But Carly knew that Cynthia's interest in men could possibly extend to someone like Landon, because in Cynthia's eyes, he was just as much of a man—probably more—than most of the guys she went to school with. That potential terrified Jillian.

"Right now," Cynthia said. "I could care less about guys. That's one of the reasons *Whip It* was such a good movie."

"Why again?" Carly asked, though she had probably seen the film a dozen times.

"Ellen Page—and her character Bliss Cavendar. At the end, Bliss ends up alone. But it's not a bad thing. She realizes she doesn't need the guy to complete her life. She just sits atop the Piggy Diner she and her friend work at and watches the sunset. It's so utterly perfect."

Carly nodded, remembering the scene. It was the first romantic comedy she had seen that had more than three different types of women in it and an ending that was so counterintuitive to the romantic structure of film. It was a rare gem, really. And so good for Cynthia to see.

"Yeah, I agree." Landon put his arm around Cynthia in a friendly way. "I think she and I have a lot of business to attend to—and we don't need anyone stopping us. So, Carly, what do you say? Do you want to come with us and see if real life can hold up to the movies?"

Carly shifted. The headlights she thought she saw across the street were now working their way toward the driveway. Jillian was behind the wheel of the car, a slightly tired expression on her face. Even then, she still looked beautiful.

"I do, I do," Carly said. She took a step back from the door. "But we may need to run this by Mom before any of us move. Especially if we have to spend the night someplace else."

Landon nodded. His hand gripped Cynthia tightly before he let go and buried his hands in his jean pockets. "You all know that I have an air mattress and a futon if you need it. My apartment may be small, but it's versatile. And it's clean, too."

Carly nodded absent-mindedly. Her heart beat faster, as her mother approached. *I'm twenty-four. I'm not Cynthia's age. I'm an adult and I can do what I want.* And yet, Carly had still not convinced herself by the time Jillian got out of the car. She heard the familiar beeping of the lock and then Carly crumbled. All before she even stepped inside, Carly chastised herself. *Really? You're already scared?* She tried to take a deep breath, and felt Landon squeeze her shoulder briefly.

"Breathe, she's human, Car. Just breathe."

Carly nodded as the door opened up.

"Oh," Jillian said. She eyed everyone in the room, spending extra time on Landon and Cynthia. "Is everything okay?"

"Yeah, yeah," Carly said. Her hands sweated more than when she told her mother she was gay. She took another breath. "Just wanted to ask you something."

Jillian's face went down as she placed her purse on the side. She folded her arms over her chest, and then nodded. "Well, okay. Go on."

With another breath, Carly began.

Jillian stayed in the same place during the entire Roller Derby explanation. Occasionally, Cynthia cut in and added some details, along with Landon, but for the most part, all of this felt like the group projects Carly used to do in school. She only wished she had prepared a PowerPoint of the pros and cons of this mission.

Jillian barely moved or blinked. Carly knew that this really wasn't that out of the ordinary, especially since her entire explanation really only took a couple of minutes. But the pressure of her mother as an unmoving statue made Carly quake. She could feel Cynthia's eyes on the back of her neck and did all she could to fight through the sensation.

"And how will you get there?" Jillian asked, finally breaking the silence.

"Drive there," Carly said. "It's only an hour away. Around Chelsea."

Jillian raised an eyebrow. "Since when can you drive, Carly?"

Carly clenched her jaw, feeling her inadequacy come to the surface. "Well, there are other options."

"Like me?" Jillian said, raising her eyebrows and scoffed. "I don't know. I'm really busy on Fridays, and I can't just drop what I need to do. I'm not a taxi service."

"I know—I respect that."

"But," Cynthia added. "I have friends who could take me."

Jillian raised her gaze. "Who?"

"Lots of people," Cynthia said, flustered already. When Jillian still made no move, or anything, Cynthia began to grow desperate. "Come on, you used to commute farther to see my dad. I could even ask to see if he'll take me."

"I don't know. We can talk about it later. You know he's busy too."

"Too busy to see his darling daughter?" Cynthia said, smiling and displaying her chipped tooth. "And his stepdaughter, Carly?"

"Former stepdaughter," Jillian said. "But I see your point."

"You'll let me go?"

"I'll let you ask. I highly doubt he'll say yes, Cynthia. He's busy. After a long week at work, most adults make other plans…"

"Landon can take me," Cynthia cut in.

Landon nodded, taking in a deep breath as he stepped forward. "I would love to take Cynthia. I know the person who's running the Roller Derby that night, and I know where the stadium is, so I can be sure to have both Carly and Cynthia home at a reasonable time. Or if you're worried about being disturbed, the two of them can stay at my apartment. Whatever is easiest for you, honestly. There is always lots of room at my place, and it wouldn't be any trouble at all."

Jillian's eyes flashed. Carly dreaded the expression; the disapproval was silent, but it was there.

"I think it's late right now," Jillian declared. "It's best to talk about this later. In the morning, after we've all had time to sleep on it.

"Okay, that is reasonable. Thank you for your time." Landon's voice had a different quality to it; almost as if he was speaking to a doctor or a psychiatrist, someone who he wanted to impress, but he knew he would be in a losing battle with.

As Landon left, he nodded to Carly and Cynthia, before grabbing his keys from the front hall. Jillian moved back, away from Landon, as if he was contagious. This was something that Jillian had done before—but Carly had always thought no one else could see it, since they weren't looking for it. This time, Landon blinked. He saw the movement and his crushing disappointment rippled through his face.

"Goodnight, guys," he said, his voice more somber.

Carly waved along with Cynthia.

The entire energy of the room had been deflated. As soon as the door was shut and she heard his car pull away, Carly allowed the anger to replace the awkwardness.

"Well, that's a relief. Let's all just go to bed now," Jillian said. "Is there leftover dinner?"

"We made pizzas," Cynthia said.

Jillian shot a look to Carly as if to disapprove of the meal she had no guidance for whatsoever.

"Well, it's something. Vegetarian, at least."

"Mom," Carly said, before she could turn into the kitchen.

Jillian stopped, raising a manicured brow. "Yes?"

"What was that?"

"What was what?"

"Landon. Why did you make him feel so shitty?"

"I did no such thing. I merely stated the parameters of my daughters' lives as a parent. He thinks he's doing something good, but it's just stirring up trouble. I had to deflect the situation before it became too hostile."

Jillian seemed to forget that Cynthia was in the room. She blinked slowly under the sudden argument and with a skill she had learned from the divorce years earlier, walked up the stairs without making a sound. She left Carly and Jillian in the front hall, still standing stock-still under the hall light.

"Why do you assume that Landon will be hostile? He's one of the nicest men I've ever met."

Jillian gave Carly a look as if to say, *Really? But he's not even a man.*

"Of course you think that. Landon is your friend. I find it odd that he hangs around with Cynthia."

"Why? He's not contagious. There's nothing wrong with him."

"I never said there was."

It was Carly's turn to look at her mother with a *Come on, really?* expression.

"It's just not right," Jillian said with a sigh. "He had no right to come in here and ask to whisk you all away. And expect it, too! It's just too much entitlement. I can't handle that. I see it every day, and I don't want it. Just because he thinks he's a man now doesn't mean he can be like that."

Jillian raised her hands, as if to push away the situation all together. She began to walk into the kitchen, the loud thwack of her shoes against the tile floor ringing in Carly's ear.

"It's just Landon," Carly argued. "He's not that bad. You should know him. He was our neighbor for years. You know he's not like that. You *know* Landon."

"I knew *Lisa*." Jillian moved into the kitchen, opening the fridge. She pulled out one of the leftover pizzas and slid off the plastic wrap and placed it into the microwave. "I knew the little girl that used to sleep over and play Barbies with you. I knew the little girl with blonde pigtails and a dress that never fit her right. That's the person I knew. I don't know who *Landon* is. He's completely changed."

"That's kind of the point of being transgender," Carly said. "You change."

"Then I don't like who he's become. He's not the same person."

"Mom. Don't be a dick about this just because Landon doesn't have one."

Jillian sighed. "Even if I knew Landon like I knew Lisa, then I still don't think it excuses the past."

"Forget the born this way shit," Carly said. "Landon's past shouldn't have any bearing on who he is now. Because he is a he. And he wants to help us with

Cynthia. He wants to take both of us out. I can't drive—but I would like to go. So here he is, saving us the trouble. You know how much of a huge favor that is?"

"It's not a favor if he put the idea in her head first."

"No one is putting ideas in anyone's head," Carly said. "Cynthia makes her own decisions."

Carly paused, worried about her volume. Another trick that Cynthia had learned from the divorce was how to hear arguments through vents. Carly didn't want to make her feel bad, as if she was in the middle of yet another fight. Carly just hoped, through years of listening, that Cynthia knew when the fight was *for* her and not *about* her.

"No, that's not what I mean," Jillian said, her voice terse. "I mean that Landon or Lisa, whoever, has always been a difficult child. And I don't want *that* kind of influence around Cynthia, confusing her."

"Mom, being a teenager is confusing. We could keep Cyn in a box and she'd still be confused. It just happens. Just let her be happy and don't make a big deal out of it."

Jillian's red lips were thin, dark, and held tight across her mouth in a look of disagreement. "Don't tell me about being a teenager. I know how hard it is. But Cynthia is not like that. She does not have to be *that* way."

Carly folded her arms across her chest. She knew that her mother was including her in her grab bag of things that could go wrong. Just because Landon was trans, and Carly was gay, didn't mean that Cynthia had to turn out *that way*, too. Carly always balked under her mother when her own past was mentioned. She could fight for Landon, fight for Cynthia, but herself? She still felt shame deep inside of her. She still felt immovable, immobile. She felt four feet tall in front of her mother, the giant, and she fell silent.

"Just go to bed for now, honey. We will talk about this later. I mean, I haven't even said yes or no yet. I just want time to think—and moreover, I just want Cynthia to stay with people she can trust. For now, I can only trust you."

"What if I found someone else to drive us?"

Jillian tilted her head.

"What if," Carly asked again, "I found someone to drive us and I stayed with Cynthia and I made sure the whole thing was safe? It's just watching the derby. We wouldn't be putting her into it. Just…let me find someone to take her. I can do that, right?"

"We will talk about it later. If you are good to your word, that is."

Carly sighed. She knew that was the best she could get out of her mother this late at night. Jillian waited, holding her pizza up with a stern expression on her face.

"Well?" she asked in her professional, lawyer's tone. "Have we decided on something?"

"Yeah. Sure. Sounds good. We'll talk later."

Jillian gave another nod and left Carly alone in the kitchen. Aside from the small clicks of her mother's heels, Carly could hear the soft murmur of crying—or laughing—coming from the vents.

"Maybe, Cyn," Carly whispered. "Just maybe."

CHAPTER 7

When Cynthia was a kid, she used to crawl into Carly's room at night. At first, it had been just so the two of them could talk late into the night without getting into too much trouble. Then, as small arguments became larger ones between Davis and Jillian, and the threat of divorce loomed, Cynthia needed Carly more than ever before. Carly had already lived through a divorce; she could tell Cynthia what would happen next and who would most likely live with whom. It was all easy to Carly at that point.

Jordan was Carly's father. It was his divorce from Jillian that started Carly's fascination with books. Anytime she heard fights starting, she hid behind books and read until the middle of the night. She'd sometimes wake up when she was younger, hear murmuring, or the closing of doors and starting of cars, and pull out a book. Her mom would often find her in the morning, covered in pages and words from worlds that did not belong to her. Whenever her mother took the books away, Carly bought new ones. There were always books, she had learned at a young age, even when her mother was often distant.

So when Cynthia started to crawl into Carly's bed again, during the middle of a bad fight, Carly knew exactly what to do. They pulled out *The Hobbit* and began to read the series from the beginning. By the time they had reached *The Return of the King*, it was all over. All done with. Davis, the tall black guy with a southern accent, Jillian's second husband, and Cynthia's father was gone. He was a dentist with a lucrative practice, which he eventually transferred to the other side of Vermont when he moved out. Cynthia still visited him, every other weekend and holidays, that type of thing. Davis was a nice man, and for a time, Carly did consider him her father too. That divorce had been amicable, really. The best of all of them.

Jillian had only married one other time. This was to Steven, an insurance salesman who had really bad teeth. Carly always figured it was some type of rebound, because that relationship had not lasted long at all. Three years, in and out. The divorce barely affected either of them, since there was no other child to throw into the mix, and they were already used to it.

Richard was Jillian's current boyfriend. She had sworn off getting married and moving in, but with the amount of time she spent with Richard adding up, Carly figured it was only a matter of time before she was suffering through more family get-togethers and fumbling over stepfather stuff. Davis was really the only person she still called Dad without worrying too much.

After the argument with her mother, Carly had gone back to her room. She angrily brushed her teeth, combed her long, dark hair back over her shoulders and into a loose ponytail. She texted Landon with a couple of furious apologies, before she headed into her room. She spotted her purse, on the small chair by her window, and dug out her book from inside. Since Carly was nearly done with *The Edible Woman*, she decided to go back to page one. Read it over a couple more times, trying to grasp the nuance of Atwood's writing, until she calmed down.

Soon, Atwood's dense prose was replaced by Ashley's face in her mind. Carly calmed down. Most of Landon's text messages had not been upset at all.

I get the overprotective mother stuff, he wrote. *Really. We'll get Cyn out eventually.*

Carly didn't quite know how to convey just how *unnecessary* the overprotective stuff was, especially when most of Jillian's worry stemmed from Landon being Landon, and not Lisa. But bringing that up to Landon would only make both him and Carly sad, so Carly ignored it for now. Landon was fine, in spite of the tension. Carly, for the most part, was fine too. She had even begun to grow sleepy, nodding off from the long day she'd had, when there was a knock on her door.

"Yeah," Carly said, her voice quiet. She knew who it was before Cynthia poked her head into the room. In her oversized Bikini Kill T-shirt and her long boxer shorts, Cynthia looked like the small love child of someone from the late '90s. Which really, wasn't far off, even if her parents had not quite been the cultural revolutionaries that Cynthia dreamed herself to be.

"Can I come in?"

"Of course, Cyn." Carly moved over on her bed, peeling back the sheets. She put down the book on her bedside table. Though Cynthia seemed hesitant to crawl onto the bed, she moved quickly next to Carly's body when the space was provided for her.

Carly held Cynthia close to her. An arm slipped under Cynthia's waist, clasping her hand. Carly's free hand went to Cynthia's dark, curly hair. Carly absent-mindedly combed her fingers through the curls.

"I'm sorry about before," Carly said. "Don't pay attention to Mom."

"It's kind of hard not to. She's kind of the boss around here."

"Temporary. Technicality. Remember what I told you?"

"Three more years. Three more years then I'm gone."

"Yeah," Carly said, her voice weak. "Only three more years. And really, it's nearly two right now."

The room grew quiet after that. Carly was flustered. The three year statement wasn't *quite* a lie, she knew. In three (really, two and a half) years, Cynthia could do whatever she wanted as far as being in a derby went. She would be, on paper, an adult. But Carly looked at her own life and the trajectory it had taken. Sure, she left the house when she was about eighteen, went to school, and was able to live on her own. But at twenty-four, nearly ten years older than Cynthia, she was *still* stuck in this house. Carly had almost gotten used to being rocked back and forth, between childhood and adulthood, without really finding a place.

"What happened at school?" Cynthia asked, as if tapping into Cyn's anxieties.

"Oh, a lot of things," Carly said. "Don't worry about it."

"You always tell me not to worry, but that doesn't really help. I still do."

"I know. I'm sorry."

"Don't be sorry. You know that whatever happened is probably not your fault, right?"

"Probably is key word there, Cyn."

"You know what I mean. Just because you're the older sister doesn't mean you have to shut up all the time. Doesn't mean that you have to fight my battles."

"Yes, it does. That's what being a sister is for. I'm supposed to protect you."

"And who exactly protects you? Landon?"

"Sure, that's good. He and I try to protect one another."

Cynthia shook her head. "Try being the key word there."

Carly could tell that Cynthia wanted to argue more, but she didn't press on. Maybe she didn't want to look down the rabbit hole of responsibility. If this person took care of this person, then this person, by this person... It was too much for a teenager to handle. An early teenager too, one with her own goals and problems.

Or maybe, Landon's name brought the argument back to the surface. Cynthia shifted in the bed, running her hands through her curly hair. She pulled on the white shirt she wore, the black outline of a record player and the name Bikini Kill written in thick, block letter font; the entire shirt had become a symbol for the riot grrrl culture that had passed Cynthia by and that she was still trying to recapture.

"I really want to go," Cynthia said, her voice quiet. "I know it's not fair of me to expect it. I know it's not fair for Landon. But I really want to."

"I know," Carly said. "And I don't ever want you to feel bad for wanting something, okay? Ever. Because that's all Mom is doing. She's not making a great political or moral statement. She's just making Landon feel bad for wanting something, for wanting to be himself."

"He can't help it though, can he? I thought that was the point?"

"Most of us can't help what we like," Carly said. She sighed, thinking about her mother's expectations. They were almost always there, nagging at Carly, like a bruise. "It's just harder, Cyn, when you're older."

"Why, though?"

"Because you think you've been told you will have a dream life, but no one allows you to sleep."

Cynthia turned her head and cocked an eyebrow. "You're being weird again."

Carly pushed her sister. "I know. I'm just tired and upset."

"Me too."

"Cyn," Carly said, a moment later. Cynthia moved, grabbing her sister's hand again.

"Yeah?"

"Don't worry. I'll think of something."

CHAPTER 8

"Carly Rogers?"

"Yes?"

Carly sat at the tables near the front of the break room. Most people who had been called into the store today had barely had enough time to knot their blue aprons at the top—and they looked beyond tired. Carly hadn't been surprised to get the sudden call this morning, since she realized how ridiculously understaffed the store was the last time she was at work. And since she only had to walk the fifteen minutes on foot to get here, she didn't look too worse for the wear.

As soon as Carly stepped inside the front doors, the overnight manager, Christina, swooped her up, along with a handful of other bleary-eyed employees, and took them to the back to wait for their specific instructions. Carly was relieved to see that Ashley was one of the unlucky people called in. She was stuck in the middle of a display at the front, but she smiled to Carly as they passed by.

"We want to train a few more people on cash," the day manager, Suzanne, now explained. Her bracelets shook against the clipboard as she went down the names of new recruits. "Carly Rogers, Samantha Peyton, and Daniel DaSilva, you're the first in the shift for training. Then Markus Cooper, David Jenkins, and Maura Reed, I would like to train you for the afternoon shift. The rest of you will be working in the back and putting stock away at the front. Most people trained on cash now will not always be required to work there. We just need as many as we can for opening day. Marshalls is a big deal, remember. It will be a hectic week. But then it will get better, I swear."

Carly nodded, and the rest of the crowd murmured. Suzanne had a few more words of encouragement before the rest of the group was divided. Carly headed to the front, but looked over her shoulder in time to see Ashley smile and wave. She mouthed something, but Carly couldn't quite make it out. It almost seemed like Ashley was murmuring, "*Catch 22.*"

The worker's dilemma. Buy this car to go to work, go to work to pay for this car. She stood at her till and began to go through the morning routine, one that she knew would soon become second nature.

Carly was on the second lunch shift this time around. This meant that she got to eat with most of her cash counterparts, like Samantha Peyton and Maura Reed. The two of them seemed to know one another from high school with the amount that they talked and traded their bejeweled phones so they could see one another's photos. Carly moved to the back spot, where the blinds were now open and warm sun filled the break room. She sat with her sandwich and book, prepared to ignore the world.

Until Ashley came in again.

Right. So Ashley's name starts in the second half of the alphabet. She is a second shift person. Ashley nodded to Carly from the table, a grin on her face, before she popped into the fridge for another one of her Cokes. She drank from it slowly, before she dug into the back of the fridge, pulling out her lunch bag.

"I have something for you," Ashley said, walking over toward Carly. There was no introduction, no small talk. She went right toward Carly's table, holding her arms behind her back as if to obscure something. Carly sat up immediately, forgetting Atwood and her lunch.

"Really?" Carly said. "Is this a gift exchange I didn't get the memo about?"

"Like this early morning shift?"

"So what is it? What do you have for me?"

"Well, Carly Rogers, I have a book." Ashley moved her hands from behind her back, holding up an old, beat-up copy of *The Sun Also Rises*. The cover was painted like a water color, the sun a yellow and orange blob in the corner. Carly knew better than to call the cover an impressionistic piece, but it had soft edges like their work. She couldn't figure out if this was an homage to an already famous painting, or if it merely looked familiar in the same way that all paintings of suns and landscape do.

"It's beautiful," Carly said. She reached out a hand to touch it before Ashley pulled away.

"Ah, ah. Have you read it, though? I know it's beautiful, but things that are beautiful can only do so much. You should know not to judge a book by its cover."

"Well, it's a good book, though. One of Hemingway's best."

"Damn," Ashley cursed, still playful. "So you have read it?"

Carly nodded, biting her lip awkwardly. "I don't own it, though. I got it from the library when I was a kid."

"You read this when you were a *kid*?"

"Yes, and I liked it. I could always read it again. And I don't own it, so I appreciate the gift. If this is a gift for me...?"

"Yes, of course." Ashley looked back toward the counter, where her lunch still remained next to the coffee maker. She tilted her head. "Can I get you anything else?"

"You mean other than the book?"

Carly watched as Ashley went back to pick up her lunch bag again. She raised her eyebrows, and extended her hand overdramatically, as if to offer up a cornucopia of treasures, when all that was there was merely generic coffee, a few packets of saltines, and a work fridge that was already starting to smell, though the store had not even officially opened yet.

"Maybe some coffee," Carly said, though it felt as if she was asking for too much. "If you can't hold it all, let me..."

Ashley held up her hand. She slid the strap of her lunch bag around her broad shoulder, as she made a small cup of coffee, all with the novel under one arm. When the novel proved to be too much, she stuck it in the back pocket of her pants, the tall cover sticking up against the blue Marshalls apron. Carly could tell from the worn edges that the book was already used, so Ashley's slight mistreatment didn't alarm her.

"Black? Sugar?"

"Sugar is fine," Carly answered. She usually took cream, but she could tell from her seat that there was nothing there. Ashley nodded, finding some small packets at the side of the counter and adding a few to her cup. Ashley stirred it and then brought the paper cup to Carly with a grin on her face.

"This okay?"

"Perfect." Carly noticed that Ashley hadn't made anything for herself. She still had an open Coke with her lunch, so Carly didn't mention it.

"All right now," Ashley said, when they were both seated again. "You must be careful with this."

Ashley passed the book across the table, allowing Carly to finally touch it. The book felt even rougher in her hands, its spine cracked and worn. Many of the pages were dog-eared and slightly brown around the edges. Some of the pages were so fragile that Carly thought they would break off if she was too hard with the spine. But the book's cover still blew her away.

"I love it. Seriously."

"Good, I'm glad. I wanted to indulge on that library book sale you told me about. I was worried it would be completely picked over, but I found this gem."

"Thank you. Didn't you get anything for yourself?"

"I did, I did." Ashley nodded. She pulled out a copy of Hemingway's *The Old Man and The Sea.* "Now, let me guess; you've also read that one?"

"Yeah. Hemingway was always a fast read for me."

"Yes, well, you'll have to let some of us catch up, Carly Rogers. We all can't be as fast as you."

Carly narrowed her eyes, taking a small sip from her cup of coffee. "Why are you saying my whole name like that?"

"Like what, Carly Rogers?"

Carly's eyes widened. "Like *that.* What are you doing?"

"I like your name. I didn't realize your last name was Rogers before."

"And now you're saying it like it's…" Carly trailed off, taking another sip of coffee and trying to place the tone. *Excitement? Mocking? No, mocking is too mean.* But this was a type of coy tease, a type of poke that kids gave one another in the school yard. This was like Ashley coming up from behind and pulling on the long dark strands of Carly's hair to show that she liked her.

Wait. Carly eyed Ashley up and down. *Is this flirting?*

"I think Carly Rogers kind of sounds like Jolly Roger," Ashley explained. "It makes me think you're a pirate. Already, you're ten times cooler than anyone here."

Carly laughed. "I have to say, in all my years of grade school, I've never heard that."

"Those kids didn't have game. I always won stuff like that."

"I bet you did. It helps when you read."

"Indeed." Ashley smiled, her sharp cheekbones making Carly melt in her place. Each time she sipped her coffee, her butterflies got worse. *Yes. This has to be flirting.*

"What's your last name?" Carly asked. "Can I return the favor?"

Ashley sighed. She touched her forehead, running her hands through her hair as if it used to be much longer. "Promise not to laugh?"

"I can't. It wouldn't be in my pirate's nature."

The joke was bad, but Ashley still smiled. She folded her hands on the table and said in a lamentable voice. "Poindexter. My last name is Poindexter."

Carly's eyes went wide again. "That's a last name? I thought that was what kids called one another on a playground."

"Exactly. I have been learning how to master comebacks from a very young age. I've had to, with my name disability and all."

"Huh. Makes sense then." Carly nodded, impressed. "Don't worry, Ashley Poindexter, I will be kind."

"I would hope so, Carly Rogers, especially since you still owe me a coffee."

"And a book now, apparently." Carly traced her fingers on the rim of her coffee cup. She remembered the bookmark in *The Edible Woman*, and realized she was close to thirty pages from finishing it, even after starting it all over again. Now she could start *The Sun Also Rises*, or maybe something else. "I thought you didn't like coffee?"

"I don't, but I could get decaf. Or tea," Ashley said. "There was one cup left on that card, right?"

Carly nodded. "I believe so."

"Okay, then. I have to buy one more to get a free one for you. How about tonight, after work? If we both got called in at the same time, I'd reason they'd be letting us go the same time, too."

Carly smiled, stirring the idea over in her mind. Then she remembered Landon, her sister, and the fight from a few days ago.

"As much as I would like that, and as much as I'd like to pay you back for this book..."

Ashley's face dropped. She held up her hands. "Not a big deal. We can reschedule. Work was sprung on you last minute, but that doesn't mean I have to be as well."

"No. It's more complicated than that. I just..." Carly paused, a sudden idea coming over her. "Can you drive?"

Ashley's face fell again. "I can't. Technically, anyway."

The phrasing made Carly pause. She tried to rephrase her question. "I have a car, if you need one?"

"No, I actually don't have a license. It was taken away from me." Ashley must have seen Carly's face drop, because she clarified shortly after, moving her hands. "Not for a DUI or anything bad like that. I just had a few...medical issues."

"Oh, I'm sorry to hear that."

"Don't worry. It's a long story. I just needed to give my license up in the process. In truth, I can drive perfectly fine, I just...shouldn't. If I get caught in a car, I can get fined. Why? Are you planning on running away, Jolly Rogers?"

"Oh, no. Nothing like that," Carly said, a small laugh in her voice. "Though the thought of running away from here is tempting."

Ashley smiled again, brushing some of the hair out of her eyes with a subtle head tilt. Another round of workers came into the break room and tried to start the coffee machine. Carly knew their break was almost over, so she pushed on, determined she knew she could solve this.

"What do you say we make a deal? A trade?"

"I'm listening," Ashley said.

"Good." Carly smiled, relieved, and then began to talk.

CHAPTER 9

This was the plan; in order to get Cynthia to a derby over an hour away, they needed someone to drive. Landon was the only person in this entire scenario, which now involved Ashley, who knew how to do that—legally, at least. Which meant that Cynthia could *only* go with Landon. In the meantime, Ashley and Carly would appeal to Jillian as the designated drivers. As soon as Jillian was convinced, Ashley would get in the car and drive everyone down the block, where Landon would be waiting. Landon would take the car, along with Cynthia, and go to the derby by themselves, while Ashley and Carly would be left alone, on foot.

"We could have coffee then," Carly said. "After this whole bait and switch. I know it sounds completely ridiculous and over the top, but—"

"I'm in," Ashley said, before Carly could finish her plea.

"Really? Are you sure?"

"Definitely," Ashley said. When Carly's brows were still furrowed, Ashley seemed to notice and elaborated a bit more. "First off, I love plans like this. The more convoluted, the better, so I feel like I'm in a heist film. Though, this isn't even that complicated if we plan it out just right. So I'm definitely into it. Also, a Roller Derby? Your sister wants to play in a derby?"

"Yeah, I know. It's a bit ridiculous, and she's pretty hard-core right now. She saw *Whip It* when she was thirteen."

"No," Ashley said, cutting in again. "Don't just write it off as a *Whip It* phase. Even if it is, that's downright badass. Out of all the things your sister could want to break the rules for, this is a pretty good reason. I'm in love with this plan, basically. Also, if we can help your best friend and your sister while simultaneously saying fuck you, quietly, to an adult who still needs to evolve a bit as far as gender and family goes, then I'm for it. No disrespect to your mom, of course."

Carly shrugged. "Of course. I love her, she's my mom, but she sometimes makes me want to scratch my nails on a chalkboard."

"Don't worry. I think you're doing the right thing."

"Really?"

"Yeah. You're making sure that your mom gets what she wants, which is peace of mind that her daughter is safe. Yes, she has an outdated idea of what safe is, but you're still providing it to her by doing the switch. I'm driving, but I'm not driving. It works. It's perfect."

"You're very…enthusiastic," Carly said with a smile. "I really do appreciate it."

"Hey, it's the least I can do. It keeps this place looking interesting, for one," Ashley said, referring to the walls of the Marshalls break room. "Speaking of which, we'd better get back before they realize we're gone. Or else, people will think we're planning way too many conspiracies."

"Right," Carly said.

Both of them gathered their lunches quickly and got ready to head back out to work. Carly had been given instructions to go and help someone with their clothing duties after she had been trained on the cash.

"Do you mind if I stay with you?" Carly asked, sticking by Ashley's side. "I'm done with cash for what I hope to be my last time."

"Are you kidding me?" Ashley asked with a small laugh. Carly watched as Ashley swung down the aisle for women's wear and grabbed a large rack full of swimsuits and lingerie. She eyed Carly from under the haze of women's clothing and lace. "I need help getting through all of this. I have no idea how to make out the sizes."

"I don't know how much more help I'll be…"

"Two heads are better than one," Ashley countered. "Trust me. You're probably better at this than you give yourself credit for."

Carly smiled, blushing slightly. She took a few steps forward and began to throw herself into the task. Her year of working at a used clothing place ended up being more informative than Carly once gave it credit for. She gave Ashley quick instructions on how to hang, where to categorize, and at what ends of the typical store layout that they had been shown earlier to hang stuff.

"You are a lifesaver," Ashley said, taking the swim bottoms and putting them with the other tankinis.

"And so are you."

"Then we're even." Ashley grinned. "There is another set of women's clothing in the back. Full of dresses and skirts, I think? Power suits? I don't know, maybe some things with shoulder pads."

"I should hope not. It's not the 1980s anymore."

Ashley shrugged. "They should put me in men's. I would know more."

"Maybe you could ask?"

Ashley shrugged again. She moved toward the back to get the final rack of clothing. In the time until she came back out again, Carly turned a few things over in her mind. If Ashley was flirting, what if she wasn't flirting for the right reasons? What if Ashley was like Landon, and was thinking of transitioning? She was pretty butch, but that could mean a lot of things. And Ashley could be a unisex name. Carly felt her stomach sink.

"And here we are. Wonderful styles that I have no idea how to pronounce," Ashley said when she dropped off the metal rack. She smiled, slightly flushed in her face, proud of herself. "I saw Suzanne in the back and told her where you were. She said it was okay to stay and help me, since you were already trained for cash."

"Okay, good." Carly sorted through the items again and give Ashley quick directions. Ashley took the hangers and walked around for a while, following orders. This rack went particularly fast, and Carly wondered if they could finish and take a break early, plan out a few other things.

And maybe I could ask her what she really wants, Carly thought, dreading the inevitable conversation. *No*, she corrected herself. If she wanted any clarity on what they meant to one another, she would have to wait until Cynthia was at the derby.

"Oh, Carly Rogers," Ashley said, after hanging up a couple skirts. "There is something on your mind."

"No, no. I'm fine."

Ashley leaned against the rack. "Come on. I've seen enough people have that expression. It's like suddenly being lost in something you once thought was familiar. What's up? Am I too eager to break your sister out of her makeshift jail?"

"No, I just..." Carly ran her fingers at the end of her hair. She tried to remember the advice Landon had given her in this type of situation. "I was just wondering what your preferred pronouns were?"

The question felt weak and stilted when it came out of her mouth, but she also felt immensely better for asking it.

"Ah." Ashley nodded, running a hand through her short hair. "Well, I identify as a woman. I'm not exactly the most feminine creature, but I'm not like Landon, if that's what you were curious about. I'm okay with who I am—not that he isn't. But you know what I mean."

"It would be okay if you were, you know," Carly said. "Like Landon."

"I know it would. But I'm not. She/her/whatever feminine pronouns for me are good," Ashley insisted. When she smiled, Carly felt another weight lift off her chest and went back to work, sorting through some of the fabric.

"But," Ashley said, considering something else with the tilt of her head. Carly looked back, a blank expression of anticipation on her face. Ashley's cheeks seemed flushed still, from all the running back and forth.

"I am gay," Ashley continued. "Most people I know don't have a problem with this, but if I'm going to be the responsible one picking up your sister, is my sexuality something your mom would take issue with?"

Carly tried not to, but she laughed. Ashley grinned as she nodded along.

"Ah, okay, then. I take it you and I are on the same page."

"Oh, definitely." Carly touched Ashley's arm, as she hung onto the side of the rack. Their eyes met one another with the same thrill from the break room. Carly smiled. "My mom is fine with gay people, about as much as she can be. I'm gay."

"Okay. Good to know." Ashley picked up another pair of women's jeans, and turned away from their conversation.

"Wait. Wait," Carly cried out. "So we're still okay for Friday?"

"Oh, of course, Carly Rogers," Ashley said, as she waltzed into the aisle. "Consider it a date."

CHAPTER 10

Ashley showed up at quarter to seven, ready to go. She wore a leather jacket, which Cynthia eyed eagerly from the hallway. Underneath, Carly spotted a familiar, collared, green shirt that she knew Ashley had put away a few days ago, when she was in men's wear. No doubt, Ashley was already using her employee discount and updating her wardrobe. The shoulder patches on the jacket and the knees of her jeans made them look worn, but well loved. Her short hair was damp and slightly darker than the blonde it normally was when dry.

She looks so good. Carly smiled as Ashley stepped forward into the small hallway. Jillian came down the stairs, still in her work clothing, a purple skirt and a small suit jacket. Her diamond earrings sparkled in the hall light as she moved. Cynthia hid by the living room; she was still visible to Carly and Ashley by the door, but hidden from Jillian. Carly figured that was the best bet for everyone involved.

When Jillian reached the bottom step, Carly took a step forward as she began the introductions.

"Mom, this is Ashley. Ashley this is my mom, Jillian. Ashley and I work together at the Marshalls store. The one that's opening."

"Yes, of course. Nice to meet you, Ashley."

"Very nice to meet you, Mrs. Rogers."

"Call me Jillian, please. I change my last name so much it's just easier to say my first," she said, sticking out her hand.

"Nice to meet you, then, Jillian." Ashley clasped Carly's mother's hand, shaking it with a thin smile on her face.

"Thank you, so much, for taking Cynthia out. I really appreciate this."

"Not at all, Carly and I were probably going to talk books while it was all going on."

"Really? Carly was an English major. I'm glad she's using that education."

Carly's stomach sank to the bottom of her shoes. She looked away from her mother, trying to not let the thinly-veiled criticism hit her.

Ashley nodded and stepped to the side, in between Carly and her mother. *She's blocking the view*, Carly realized. Ashley was strategically placing herself between mother and daughter, as if to dissipate the tension. Cynthia noticed, cocked her head to the side, and then smiled at Carly. Carly did her best to smile back.

"What time," Ashley asked, "should I bring them home by?"

"Midnight or as close to it as possible, since it's Friday. Carly, make sure you sleep when you can. You have to see Dorothy tomorrow. I arranged for Richard to pick you up early."

"I know, Mom. Okay," Carly said, her voice tense. Ashley shifted again, deflecting the energy. Ashley narrowed her eyes down to Cynthia, who beamed at the sudden attention.

"You must be Cynthia. You look fantastic, by the way. I love your shirt."

Cynthia looked down, as if forgetting what she was wearing. Her face beamed when she realized she had on her Sublime shirt.

"You like them?"

"Are you kidding me? I'm pretty sure Sublime got me out of a pretty bad time about a year or two ago. Music is good that way. You can listen to it and then have no more troubles. At least, for a while."

Cynthia nodded, echoing the sentiment with the same singsong quality to her voice. From the way Ashley laughed, Carly figured they were exchanging lyrics. Carly knew most of the bands that Cynthia listened to, but they seemed to have missed directions on what genre to fall under. Cynthia, as ever, was more into the punk, ska, riot grrrl scene from the past—whereas, Landon and Carly had both grown up under pop punk and still held pop punk in high regard. Carly imagined, for a brief moment, how Landon and Cynthia would argue for music on their hour drive.

"You're going to give me directions?" Ashley asked. "And then you'll have to explain to me everything you're doing, okay? I'm so out of the loop with derbies, it's not even funny."

"Don't worry," Cynthia said with a subtle nod of her head. "You're smart. You'll get it all down like it's nothing."

"You think I'm smart already, huh?" Ashley stated.

"Well, you have good music taste. So you can't be far off."

Ashley laughed. "Fair enough."

"Thanks again," Jillian stated, before she went up the stairs. "I wish I could have more time to talk, but I'm seeing Richard tonight, and I have to clean this place. I would like to get to know you more Ashley, but when the time is right."

Ashley nodded, her demeanor changing from addressing Cynthia to addressing Jillian. Carly had seen this before, if only peripherally, while at work. Ashley was extremely professional when she wanted or needed to be. This fact alone probably made Jillian's worry dissipate.

"Not at all, Jillian. Have a wonderful night," Ashley said.

"You too." Jillian smiled again, her face mercurial and hard to read. Carly still felt a tiny, fractured nerve in the bottom of her spine, as if she was leaning up against a bed of nails. She waited for her mother, like all the after-school specials, to scrutinize the new guest in the house with cross-questioning. Carly even anticipated Jillian asking to see Ashley's license. In that regard, they were going to bluff with Ashley's old one. It had expired three years ago, but Carly just prayed that Jillian would not turn the license over.

But there was nothing. Carly watched as her mother nodded to them all again before moving up the large twisting staircase of their house. When her bedroom door closed, everyone in the room's shoulders dropped. Carly let out a breath.

"Okay," Ashley said, rubbing her hands together. "Let's bait and switch."

"I think that works as a name," Cynthia declared when they got into the car.

"What exactly?" Carly tilted her head back so she could see Cynthia and gave her a quick smile before she felt her phone buzz in her pocket. This was no doubt a text from Landon, who was around the block and under a tree.

Their code word for the entire night had been "night reconnaissance." If he was there and ready to go, that was what he was supposed to text. If things had gone "pear-shaped"—that was the next code word. Carly fumbled with her hands into her jacket pocket, pulling out the phone.

Night Reconasa...shit I need spell check. But yes, I'm here, Landon wrote.

You know, Carly typed. *A code word doesn't really work if you elaborate everything anyway.*

Whatever, whatever, Landon texted back. *I'm just so tired of living in a closet. Come and get me now.*

Carly could hear Landon's booming voice in her mind as she read the texts. Carly shoved her phone into her pocket and placed her hands on her lap. *One issue out of the way. Now to deal with the second.*

Jillian had come back downstairs soon after they all left, her clothing changed. She stood in the front window, her arms akimbo as she waited to see them pull out. Carly waved to her mother, hoping that would allow her some relief. Jillian didn't seem to see. Carly told herself it was just the car, the setting sun in the background, and the shadows that everything cast.

"Bait N. Switch," Cynthia said.

"What?"

"Bait N. Switch. That's what I want my Roller Derby name to be."

Carly laughed. "You know, we actually have to get there scot-free before we can start celebrating."

"Oh, come on," Cynthia said. She raised her arm and waved to Jillian in the front hall. Finally, Jillian waved back and turned around into the house. "We're *fine*. And I'm calling myself Bait."

"You are a certain kind of bait," Carly joked. "But you may not want to broadcast that."

"Landon will like my name. You just wait and see."

"Oh, I don't doubt that. He's waiting, by the way."

"Good."

They pulled out of the driveway, now that everyone had been accounted for and all belts were done up. Ashley had her hands on the wheel casually, a smile on her face. "Man, I have missed this so, so much."

"You can't actually drive?" Cynthia asked.

"No, I can," Ashley said. "It's just been a while. Don't worry, you're in good hands. See, you can even check my license if you wish."

Ashley dug into the front pocket of her leather jacket. She tossed a leather wallet back to Cynthia, who caught it with a quick grasp of her hands.

"You still kept it?" Carly asked

"Yeah. For sentimental reasons. It's not like they took it from me completely at the DMV and cut it up in front of my face. Sometimes they put stickers over it so that cops and overprotective mothers will know I'm not supposed to be in a car. But my case isn't quite like a DUI. I'm a medical removal. So I can't renew it anymore without my name being flagged."

"You look...different." Cynthia held the card in her hands by the edges, as if she was touching a relic. She eyed Ashley and then looked back at the license. "You with long hair is really odd to see."

"I know, right?" Ashley chuckled under her breath. "Cutting off all my hair was the first thing I did after my license was taken away from me. Utterly cathartic, really, to chop it all off like that."

"I know," Cynthia said. "I did it a few years ago, but everyone freaked out."

"I personally like the look you have going on right now. The pink at the side? Amazing."

Cynthia smiled, then clasped the pink curl by her left temple. "It's an extension. Not real."

"Well, that license is also not real, but it still gets the job done."

"True, true." Cynthia passed the wallet back up to Carly, since Ashley was still in the middle of driving.

"Can I take a peak?" Carly asked.

"Yeah, go ahead. See me through the looking glass. I got to spy your baby pictures on some of those walls, so it's only fair."

Carly closed her eyes, her cheeks crimson. She knew the exact photos that Ashley was referring to. Just before the hardwood floors turned into the living area, there was practically a shrine to Carly and Cynthia. There were baby pictures, graduation photos, and even some stuff with Carly holding this little tiny creature that was Cynthia at one week old. There was nothing of Carly past high school, though—which always made Carly feel as if the photos on the wall weren't really her. They were a past image of her, before school and before too many girlfriends went bad. Before living at home again. The first week back in her mother's house, Carly had practically hissed at the images as she walked by each morning. Now, they had become common place—so much so she had no idea that Ashley could spy on her former life.

"My God, I totally forgot these were up. Ignore them from now on. They're not me."

"You have a secret twin, Carly Rogers?"

"Not any more than you do," Carly said, pulling out the old license photo. Ashley's light brown, almost blonde hair was draped around her shoulders. It was much, much longer that the near crew cut she had right now, so long that her hair seemed to spill out of the photo itself. She had not smiled in the photo, but her eyes were the same. When Carly scanned the other details, she discovered Ashley's birthday.

"I just missed it," she said. "I apologize. Happy belated birthday."

Cynthia echoed the sentiment from the backseat.

"So that makes you…" Carly wondered aloud. "What? Thirty? Wait… Thirty-two?"

"Twenty-nine! *Wow*," Ashley teased. "No wonder you're an English major."

"I'll have to get better at math if they stick me at cash again." Carly slid the license back into her wallet and then held onto it.

Though they had not gone far in the car, Carly could tell that Ashley was a good driver. She had a bit of a shaky start backing out of their driveway and around the roundabout, but that was from a few years of no practice. They were now down the second side street that they had planned to meet on.

Carly spotted Landon right away. He had a backpack over one shoulder, loosely hanging off, with Cynthia's Rollerblades sticking out of the back. There was no promise of skating at the derby, and Jillian had forbid her to even consider doing so. It was one of the many conditions of the night; look, but don't touch.

Luckily enough, Landon and Cynthia had always had a backup plan anytime her blades were forbidden. There was pretty much another set of materials in Landon's small apartment for her. The stadium probably still had a better practice area, and once everyone was gone, Landon was probably going to take her around.

"I'm probably going to have to clean those wheels," Cynthia remarked as she saw Landon emerge. "But they're good. Excellent, really."

Cynthia grinned at the two of them in the front seat, before she began to roll down the window of the car to wave to Landon.

"Quiet, this is a secret mission," Carly chastised. She soon relaxed, as Ashley pulled up to Landon. They were there. And really, unless Jillian was absolutely paranoid and followed them around the block, she would not see any of this. They were home free.

"And we're here," Ashley said, pulling the car up and putting it in park. "And no one is dead. I'm really starting to think the DMV was overreacting."

"Three, four hours tops," Carly said, reminding everyone in the car. "And then we'll meet back here again."

"Yeah, yeah," Cynthia said. "You really worry too much."

"Probably." Carly turned to Ashley, who leaned forward and grabbed her wallet from Carly's lap.

"Thank you so much," Carly said, undoing her belt. She moved quickly, throwing it around her shoulder. Ashley got out of the car, extending her hand to Landon.

"Landon, what a pleasure," Ashley said. "So good to meet you. Have fun tonight."

Landon smiled, in his big and dopey way, taking Ashley's hand in his.

"Thank you," he said, "for being the bait."

"And switch!" Cynthia added. She moved up to the front seat, zooming past Carly. Landon nodded and made his way to the driver's side

"We'd better head out, to make your time line."

Carly took a step back from the curb. When she realized she was holding her hands akimbo—the same way Jillian had—Carly moved to wave instead.

"Drive safe."

Landon nodded with his arm outside the window again. It was only another few moments before the sound of The Buggles came out the driver's side window, followed by Cynthia's laugh.

"Well, now we have the night," Ashley remarked as soon as the car had disappeared. "What do you want to do?"

"A bookstore," Carly said. "Naturally. Come on, they always make me feel better."

CHAPTER 11

"So where is this place?" Carly asked, flipping the coffee punch card that had been her bookmark for the past week over. "I've never been."

"Just around the corner from Powell's, actually. It's been a while since I've been there, too." Ashley extended her arm, pointing in the direction of one of the many strip malls around Carly's house. "Don't worry," Ashley said quickly, noting Carly's sudden reservation. "It's not in the same lot as Marshalls. We will be able to get away for a bit."

"Ah, okay then. Lead the way."

They walked slowly. Though Carly most likely knew her way around better than Ashley, she enjoyed the slower pace and relinquishing some control of the situation. Carly often speed-walked most places, since she was heading there on foot instead of driving. Ashley sauntered, her eyes going over the elementary school they passed, and a few gas stations, before they reached a large cross walk that would lead them to the strip mall. They waited for the walking man to appear on the right side; if Carly and Ashley had been heading to Marshalls, they would have crossed on the left. As they walked away from their work, Carly could sense both herself and Ashley relaxing around one another a little more.

"I have to say," Ashley mentioned. "I'm completely jealous of your mom's house."

"What? Why?"

"It's so close to everything. You're pretty much in the middle of the city. It makes life on foot a lot easier."

"For the most part, I guess." Carly's place was in a subdivision just alongside one of the city's main roads. They weren't quite downtown, but they weren't in the middle of nowhere, either. The city had been developed around the time of WWII, but it was never actually planned. There was just a lot of buildings, a hospital, a school, laid out for the soldiers as they came through, thinking it was going to be a temporary space. Carly's subdivision was referred to as "the war houses" and each street and crescent name was for a battleship in the US Navy. When the town's population began to grow after WWII, so did the amount of stores and outlet malls until the biggest Marshalls was finally announced.

"I guess that's really why I never bothered to drive," she added. "I could just walk to school and to work for such a long time."

Ashley pressed her lips together, as if she wanted to ask for more information. But instead, she pointed toward a small park close to the outlet mall, and insisted they cut through there so they could stumble on the strip mall from the back and find the coffee house right away.

"Oh, this place," Carly said as soon as they arrived. "I used to come here as a kid... But it was a dentist office then."

"It's much nicer now, trust me."

The door jangled as they stepped inside. A few people with thick-rimmed glasses and laptop computers sat near the back, no doubt penning the next great American novel. There was a mother with her young kids in front of Carly and Ashley as they got in line. A baby was asleep in a carriage, and a two year old boy plastered his face against the small display of croissants and muffins. When it was finally their turn, Ashley stepped forward first and ordered a cocoa.

"What do you want?" Ashley asked, turning to Carly. "It's the free mark on the card, so don't worry, okay?"

"Large coffee," Carly stated. "Thanks."

"Don't mention it."

With their orders placed, they waited at the end of the counter, near the window area. Carly could already see the Powell's book store, which made her feel much better. Talking with Ashley had been so easy before, when they had the backdrop of work and the short clock between breaks. Even when they were out on the floor together, they were always focused on a task that they could default to when the silence became too much. *Sort the bathing suits and complain about time. Simple.*

Now that they were inside a small café, Carly felt all the topics that she knew about before fall out of her head. She had no idea how to go forward, especially for the four hours that they could spend together.

Ashley seemed nervous too, but she hid it a lot better. She smiled as she tapped her fingers against the counter, while Carly glanced furtively toward Powell's and back.

"They aren't Starbucks, so sometimes they take longer than they need for a simple order. But I'm used to this, I guess. I feel as if I'm always waiting, you know?" Ashley finally declared. It was clear that she did not just mean coffee.

"Okay," Carly said. "How so?"

"I live on the other side of the city, in one of the more recent developments. And that's probably why I never met you before; we went to different high schools."

"You're also older than me. You would have just gotten out of high school by the time I was there."

"True. But it still feels like I'm far away from everything over there. We need a car to get everywhere."

"We?" Carly blushed. *What if this is a complete misunderstanding, and Ashley's already in a relationship. What if she's married?* "Who do you mean?"

"My dad. Don't worry, no one special," Ashley said quickly. "But I think you and I are the perfect example of quarter-life-crisis kids."

"What now?"

"It's something one of my brothers calls people like you and me."

"What is that?"

"You know, the kind of kids that used to be independent and live on their own, but for whatever reason, usually financial stress, they are forced to move back in with mommy and daddy again. Sometimes, parents understand the stress because of the way the economy has changed. But not all parents do. A lot of the time, it's difficult and no one can really see that. Like, take my dad," Ashley said. "He went to school for about three years at a college. Maybe paid a fraction of what we would now. He got a job within three months of graduation. Paid off his debts within a couple years. Bought a car, bought a house. Got a wife. Had three kids."

"Just like that, huh?" Carly said, sighing. She sometimes forgot that people had nuclear families and that they had straight, solid trajectories from one home to another. That they didn't bounce around like she did with her mother and Cynthia.

"And now," Ashley went on. She grabbed Carly's coffee from the barista, handing it to her and nodding thanks before she picked up her own cocoa. "You have kids like us who are only a quarter of the way through our lives and we're already having identity crises. We go away and get a degree, then suddenly find out it's useless and end up working shitty jobs. Even my brother Darren is somewhere in the middle. He's not quite quarter-life, but he's under thirty-five. He has a good job as a computer software guy, and sort of lives with his girlfriend."

"Sort of?"

"He technically lives with us. But he's over there so much that he may as well be."

"Okay," Carly said, nodding. She stirred her coffee to do something with her hands. "I guess that makes sense."

"Then there is Alex."

"Oh? And what about Alex?"

"He's the exception that proves this quarter-life crisis to be a rule. He's old enough to not have this affect him. He got a good job right out of school, is now married, and has a kid on the way. He is my father, through and through."

Carly nodded. She liked hearing these small details about Ashley. She could tell from the way she held herself as she talked, her grand hand motions, and the smile on her face that she took great pride in her family.

"What about your mom?"

The corners of Ashley's mouth fell. "She died a little while ago. Maybe five, six years?"

"I'm sorry," Carly said. "I didn't mean to bring it up."

"No, it's a natural question. Not a lot of kids stay with their father. It's always mothers that get kids in custody battles."

"Oh, yeah. My mom fought tooth and nail for us. For both of us."

"Somehow, I kind of figured that."

"Yeah, my mom's pretty intimidating and usually gets her way. *Usually.* When Cynthia was born, her last name was hyphenated so Rogers could be part of it in some way. So her full name is technically Cynthia Alexandra Carlisle-Rogers, but she just goes by Rogers now, especially since Davis is on the other side of Vermont."

"Oh, thank God," Ashley said dramatically, with a hand over her chest. "Everyone needs to have Rogers as their last name. Especially in your family."

Carly gave her a sidelong glance. Then she sighed. "Oh, right. Pirates."

Ashley smiled, again, and then looked around at the coffee shop as the Friday night rush came in.

"Should we sit down?" Ashley asked. "Before we can't anymore?"

"How about we just go to Powell's?" Carly said. "I feel like being around books rather than people."

"Except for me?"

"Right," Carly said. "You're the exception that proves the rule."

Ashley laughed again, light and airy. The sound made Carly's stomach flip. "Sounds good, Carly Rogers."

"This is kind of like high school all over again," Carly remarked once they were inside. "I can't go out without lying to my parents, and I'm still stuck in the same area. How humiliating."

"Yes, but it's only humiliating, really, if you had it taken away from you."

"Maybe," Carly said.

Once the two of them bypassed the front sales tables full of bestsellers or mass ordered books, Carly led them toward an area she knew quite well, literary fiction. Unfortunately, Carly couldn't spot any Hemingway or even Faulkner on display. Everything that was face out to them was some new incarnation of a literary giant, like David Foster Wallace or Jonathan Franzen. Both works she had read, but she found both men to be insufferable—almost as much as the twenty-something guys who carried their works around as if they were Bibles.

"So Carly Rogers," Ashley stated, her tone shifting dramatically as she turned to grin at Carly. "You're an English major."

"Oh. Um. Yes, I was, at least."

"Why do you say you were? Most English majors I meet get all sentimental about books, trying to smell them at every last instant. I'm actually surprised you haven't done that right now."

Carly laughed. "I don't really like these books. They're all done by so-called literary giants who have yet to face the sands of time."

"There's that literary snob I knew was in there," Ashley said with a smile. "I was waiting for her to come out."

"No! All I mean is that there isn't really a thing as "literature." I'm actually trying to be the *opposite* of snobby right now. I think the only books we can consider lit are the ones that have been passed down enough times to be considered something memorable. All literature is really just made up of old books that we still talk about."

"Okay, fair enough. I like that definition a bit more. But I swear, most English majors I know get *this close* to jumping on desks and yelling about Walt Whitman."

Carly chuckled. "Nicely done, knowing that it was Whitman who said 'O Captain! my Captain!'"

"Ah, yes. It was one of the many pieces of knowledge that was passed down to me," Ashley said, holding up her cocoa as if it were a mic. "But be careful before you start to think I'm an astute student. I could have just watched *Dead Poets Society* a lot. Which I did. Darren used to study English too and get all sentimental about changing young minds. He wanted to be a high school teacher—then he discovered computer software and sold his soul for money. I can't say I blame him, really. Anyway, that's my story."

Carly smiled. "Very riveting. You should adapt it for the stage."

"I'm actually holding out for movie rights."

Carly laughed again. "I don't really think I'm that different from you. I mean, you've read Atwood and you knew who Godot was. You've done a lot of reading."

"I'm not an English major, though. I don't know the symbolism or what the author had for breakfast before he wrote his big scene."

"Fair enough."

"But maybe Godot can be our thing," Ashley added. "Vladimir and Estragon end up together, right?"

Carly blushed. "Yeah, but they were waiting for something that never came."

"Hmm. I think we should adapt a new version, then. No more waiting for nothing."

"Yeah. Maybe." Carly's heart fluttered as they strolled past the literary works and moved onto the genre-heavy aisles.

"Why have you read so much? If you're not an English major?"

"Hospitals." Ashley touched the edge of a new book, with a bright yellow cover, neither one of them seemed to have heard about before. "They give you a lot of time to wait. You need to find some way to pass the time."

"Ah, okay." Carly nodded, as if this was a good enough reason. She still felt uncomfortable prying into that aspect of Ashley's life. She was forthcoming with it—she admitted that she had medical problems—but she was also cold and distant with it, too. She only said as much as she needed to get her point across. It was in the same way that Carly had watched kids from Cynthia's grade react to all the kids who suddenly had deathly peanut allergies. They carried around their epipens and informed people of their illness. But that was it; everything else was closed for discussion and they went on their way. They had probably had to deal with so many doctors, worry from their parents, that there was no need to discuss their illness as if it were a plot point. Carly figured she should do the same thing.

"Did hospitals really have things like *The Great Gatsby*?" Carly pointed to a cover of the famous novel, this time with Leonardo DiCaprio on the cover, making the classic hip again.

"Maybe, if they had this cover," Ashley said. "But you're right. Hospitals aren't exactly a breeding ground for culture. The first few books I read there were what the nurses could find in the hallways and in waiting rooms. People leave their books behind in hospitals as much as patients leave their flowers behind."

"Really?"

"Yeah. I guess the thing you read by your mother's deathbed has some pretty negative associations with it, and you kind of want to forget about it."

"Or you don't get to finish the book." The thought brought chills to Carly's back. She absolutely hated to not finish a novel. It felt worse than a death, but like a literary suicide, giving up on something that could have had potential. She always had to get to the end, even if the characters were annoying or the writing was dry. Carly had gotten through *Moby Dick* for the same reason, and usually by the ending, she was glad she had.

"The first few things I read were romance novels," Ashley said. Moving through mystery and horror, Ashley led the way to the romance section in the store, as if to illustrate her point. They hovered around the covers of the Regency romances as Ashley pawed through the pile to find the best, most clichéd, one.

"Yeah," she said, holding up someone with half a shirt on. "Something like this. Definitely. Romance novels are a dime a dozen in hospitals."

"Did you like it?"

"It was something to read. I was so bored when I first got there, because they kept me in for observation. For tests. I read the first book in a day and thought it was stupid and completely problematic. It talked way too much about guys I had no interest in, but I still found myself wanting more. *So* much more. The books kept me...focused on something else, you know?"

"I get that. It makes a lot of sense." Carly paused, taking a sip from her cup of coffee. "I use to read a lot of Russian novels for that reason. I just wanted someone that I could read that would always be there. It takes forever to finish something like that."

"Totally. Anyway, my brother got me an e-reader for one of my longer visits in the hospital, so I could still have something when I got back. I had to step down from my job around this time, too, so I really needed another outlet. I kept reading—I even found lesbian romance online, too. Now, *that* was fantastic. Then, from there I read stuff by Sarah Waters and other lesbian fiction. Then just fiction. Soon, I managed to stumble onto Hemingway and other authors that I could use to impress people like you at work."

Carly smiled with the attention suddenly turned toward her. "You don't need to read Hemingway to impress me."

"What do I need to do?"

Carly bit her lip. "Tell me more about these lesbian romances. And maybe, you'll have something."

The two of them continued their discussion, wandering around the bookstore. They ended up in the old classics section last, standing in front of a huge sale.

"It's because all their copyrights have passed. They can literally package a book like this for nearly nothing at all." Carly picked up copies of *The Secret Garden* and *Jane Eyre*, flipping them over so she could see where their cover images came from. "I think it's another image out of copyright too. This is the easiest thing to produce in the world."

"And they are still making a killing." Ashley gestured toward a couple who were talking in animated terms over *Tess of d'Urbervilles* and *Wuthering Heights*.

"If the story is there," Ashley added, "then it's good to tell it again."

"I guess so."

"You know, if all of this is so cheap," Ashley said. "Then the two of us should start a book club."

"Really now? What about the library sale?"

"They're cheap too. A couple quarters or a couple dollars. It's the only book club people like us can afford. The quarter-life-crisis club. Come on, it would be fun."

Carly glanced back down toward *Wuthering Heights* and the couple kissing on the cover. A book club would be pretty steeped with romance and nostalgia. It seemed like the perfect thing for someone like them to do. Not to mention all the time they would have to spend together afterward, discussing whatever they read.

"Really, though," Carly corrected. "We're kind of talking about a minimum wage book club. I used to always hide inside my novels whenever I was at work, pretending I wasn't there."

"Really? I hadn't noticed."

"It could be good though. So long as the book is less than what we would make an hour, we can read it. How does that sound?"

"I like that. I think it works perfectly."

"Okay. Are we starting with *The Sun Also Rises?*"

"No, that's not fair. You've already read it. And there is no cheesy movie for it."

"Ah. I'm understanding the new parameters a little better now."

The two of them took another few steps down the shelf, only to cry out with excitement as soon as they reached the classic kid's section. The covers of *Alice's Adventures in Wonderland* and *The Secret Garden* were even more captivating than the old renditions of *Wuthering Heights* or anything by Dickens. Carly's hand grazed Ashley's as they reached for the covers of *Little Women* and *Treasure Island*.

"Okay, this, this is what I was looking for," Ashley said. "I think we need to choose from here. This makes the minimum wage book club essential."

"Not that I'm disagreeing with you, but why?"

"Because book clubs and English majors are so snooty and don't pay attention to the kid's books. The real classics. Books like these pretty much raised me and my brothers. We needed guidance in fictional characters and large set pieces from these worlds to help structure our games, you know?'"

"Okay, so…do we start with *Little Women* or *Treasure Island?*"

"Why those two?"

"This way, we can watch a really bad movie adaptation afterward."

"Okay, but are we talking about the old timey *Treasure Island* or the animated *Treasure Planet?*" Ashley asked. "This is important."

"I'm sure it is," Carly said. "I was thinking the old timey one with the full on Long John Silver and pirates. Also, I was thinking the Claire Danes version of *Little Women*, because come on, Claire Danes."

"Naturally," Ashley said. "I like the specifics so far."

The two of them stared at both book covers, Ashley placing a hand to her chin. Carly tugged on the ends of her dark hair, struggling to remember some of the plots of these stories. She had only read the abridged versions as a kid. Most people, she figured, knew the plots in the same way that everyone knew the basic plot of Grimm's fairy tales or the Bible. With enough references and jokes, the whole thing could be pieced together.

"As much as I'm all for coming of age women, and especially like girls named Jo," Ashley said, holding her cocoa out as if it was a speaking stick, "I have to go with pirates. For your sake."

"For my sake?"

"Come on, now, Carly Rogers. You sound so much like a pirate that I can't help but think of you swashbuckling."

'"Oh, you're ridiculous." Each time she heard her name said aloud, in full, Carly's heart stopped. She eyed Ashley in front of her, eyebrows narrowed playfully.

"But do you accept my challenge?" Ashley said.

"I guess I have no choice but to say, you have a deal Ashley Poindexter."

"Ah, yes," Ashley said. "That's my name, please, my dear, wear it out."

CHAPTER 12

With their copies of *Treasure Island* under their arms, Carly and Ashley both headed out of Powell's bookstore. Carly checked her phone, noticing no new text messages from either her mother or Landon and Cynthia.

"How are things going?"

"Um. Good. I think." Carly looked up and tried to smile at Ashley. The sun had already set behind them, leaving a small chill in the air. Most of the stores, including the coffee shop across the street, were closing now that it was past nine at night. There weren't too many places for them to go, aside from walk around the subdivisions and play more back and forth questions about their favorite books and their lives.

"Are you okay?" Ashley asked.

"Yeah, I'm just…tired, surprisingly. I don't think I've talked this much in a long time."

Ashley smiled. "Well, we don't have to talk. I'm enjoying your company. And I think we have a lot in common."

"Other than books? And Marshalls?"

"Yes, I do. You know those people that you can just be around without stressing too much about it?"

"Sure, for the most part."

"You two can sit in a room and barely exchange a word, but it doesn't feel awkward or stressed?"

"Yeah, sometimes."

"Who is that for you?"

Carly thought for a while, wondering whether or not to reveal it. "You heard my mom mention Dorothy before, right?"

"Yeah."

"She's my great-aunt. One of my great-grandmother's sisters. She lives about an hour or two from here. We take care of her."

"And tomorrow is your weekend to see her?" Ashley asked.

"Yeah, it is. It's nothing much, really, to take care of her. She has arthritis pretty bad and sometimes has a hard time moving around. But she's all there upstairs still and in relative good health for being eighty years old. It's usually difficult for her to clean her house alone now, so that's what we do. My mom, Cynthia, and I will go up and stay for a weekend, clean and cook while we visit, and then come back."

The two of them walked through the strip mall, hiding under the awnings and against buildings from the breeze. Carly shivered a bit, so Ashley shifted closer to her, acting as a windbreaker from the cold.

"She sounds like an interesting woman," Ashley remarked. "How often is it just you with her?"

"More recently. I've just had the time."

They were quiet again, but Carly still thought it was strained. She wanted it to be the type of quiet that needed no excuse or explanation to fill the air. She really did. But she still didn't know Ashley well enough yet to allow herself to relax. She still wanted to talk about their pasts and what music they liked. Like high school all over again, Carly just wanted to talk for the sake of talking, to fill the air, and to hopefully find a connection therein.

"So can I ask," Carly said carefully. "How exactly did your license get taken away?"

"Medical issues," Ashley repeated. "But I suppose that's not the answer you were looking for?"

Carly nodded and then averted her eyes. "Maybe I shouldn't really ask that. It's not quite polite."

"No, I get it. It just is what it is. I mean, the staff at Marshalls know. They have to—since they're liable if I have a seizure there." Ashley paused, pushing her hands into her pockets again. "So, yeah. There you have it. Seizures."

Carly nodded. From the amount of cancer books they passed by in Powell's, she had already built up the fake case history for Ashley inside her head. Cancer would have made a lot of sense, especially because of the long medical trips Ashley had described, along with losing her job. Carly didn't really know anything about seizures, and she found herself at a loss to relate in anyway.

"I'm sorry to hear that."

"No, you're not," Ashley said.

"What?"

"Don't be like that with me."

"Like what?"

"You're all stiff and awkward again. I was just getting to know you, about your family and your life, and now you pull back as if I'm another patient in a room."

"I'm sorry," Carly repeated. "I just…I don't have much experience with medical issues."

"Sure you do. You have Dorothy. Do you treat her like she's sick?"

"No," Carly said suddenly, shaking her head. "No, not at all."

"And that's probably why you like going there. You have fun with her because she relaxes around you. You can have a very calming presence, but not when you're constantly worried about breaking me by taking me out like this."

"Well, okay then. I'll try more."

"So, yes, anyway," Ashley went on. "I just had a really bad seizure one day that no one could figure out. No one can still figure it out, but they've been easing up on the amount of tests."

"Epilepsy, maybe?"

"That's the most common cause, yeah. But I don't have a lot of the other issues and most of my MRIs were inconclusive. So, I just have to be careful. And I definitely can't drive. I can't live alone, either, or have that high stress of a job."

Carly bit her lip from saying sorry again. "What did you do before?"

"I was a contractor, mostly. I moved around in agencies and companies, fixing things and planning stuff. I was taking night courses, for a while, to become an engineer. But then I got sick, and I kept missing my classes. My contracting business that I wanted to open became a far off dream. So I started to read books about Fabio instead."

"I…" Carly started again and then doubled back. "I'm sure that Marshalls will give you something. I mean, I think they're going to hire managers soon too."

"Yeah I heard that too. I'm moving up in the world. Truthfully, I haven't had a seizure in over a year, and I was bored, so I got a job. I'm hoping that I can prove to people that I can still handle the real world, you know?"

"I do. At least as much as I can."

They crossed the large intersection and turned back toward Carly's street.

"So, now it's your story time," Ashley declared.

"What?"

"What happened with you? Why are you living with your mom when that clearly doesn't make you happy?"

Carly was struck by how forthcoming the words were. Ashley did this, Carly had already noticed. She flitted between jokes and flirting, between high energy and fun comments to sudden, cutting acerbic remarks. Inside every single sarcastic joke, Landon used to tell Carly, was an idealist weeping at the sentiment. Carly had never really grasped that idea until now. Each one of Ashley's laughs seemed to stem from something much deeper and cast a shadow much further.

"I don't really think I have much of a story," Carly said. "I decided on a major that had no jobs that could make me enough money. And the economy, and stuff."

"And *stuff*," Ashley teased her. "That's your mom's idea of what happened. What do you think?"

Carly couldn't really put into words something that so often felt like an emptiness inside of her, a blankness that she spanned over her time in Boston. Carly had always believed she had gotten a degree and then come back home to be around her sister. To have a small vacation. Only her small vacation turned into two years, and she was suddenly doing the same thing every day without variation or hope of change. Carly had never really thought of herself as unhappy before. She had all she needed; a roof over her head, food, and Cynthia. But as she and Ashley walked, Carly felt the sudden bitterness on her tongue. The low-grade anger she kept brewing toward her mother and her time in Boston.

"Maybe, I got into a routine." Carly brushed a hand through her hair and tried to stay upbeat. "Maybe, I decided I liked looking after Cynthia because I had done it my whole life. Dorothy started to get really bad when I finished up school, too. So I wanted to stay with her."

Ashley nodded; that seemed to be enough of an explanation to suit her. The two of them turned a corner and began to walk down the same side street, by the elementary school they had passed on their way to the mall. No cars were on the road around them, save for the occasional city bus.

"Can I ask," Ashley said a few moments later, "why you can't drive?"

"Long story. I kind of already hinted at most of it. We're in the middle of everything." Carly gestured with her hands. "There was no reason for me to."

"Humor me. That's an excuse you find afterward."

"I just never learned. Never saw the need."

Ashley looked as if she was about to open her mouth to ask something else, when Carly's phone buzzed in her pocket.

"Sorry," she apologized, scrunching up her face. "Just give me one second."

Ashley nodded, almost cordially, and took a step back from Carly to give her privacy.

"Ah, they're on their way back now," Carly said, after she read the message.

"So how was the derby?"

"You know; I didn't even think to ask. I think I was so relieved it was all over and done with, and so far, there have been no angry calls from my mom."

Carly typed a quick response, asking how the actual show went. She read Landon's response aloud a few moments later, ushering Ashley's body close to her again.

"The show was good. Interesting, really. Bait N. Switch here got to talk to Lizzie Whorden. They hit it off. Alas, she is still too young to try out, but she's already been initiated as like a child prodigy. She got invited to the first official stadium show in about two months or so."

"That's good, right?" Ashley asked. "It sounds promising."

"I think so…" Carly said. She texted Landon with the same question of Ashley's. He responded almost immediately.

Yeah, yeah, all is good on the western front. Have plans on your end worked out so far?

Carly could see the smile on Landon's face as he typed that message. He had already been sending her probing questions about who Ashley was and how they had met earlier in the week, most of which Carly ignored. Landon had promised that he would hold off on the big brother dialogue with Ashley for now, but if things developed past tonight, then Landon wanted to know. Carly smiled as she held the phone in her hand, eyeing Ashley over the screen.

Yeah, Carly wrote. *I think the plan has gone off without a hitch.*

"So should we head back now?" Ashley asked, when Carly put her phone away.

"Nah, we have maybe an hour or two before they get back. Possibly less, since there won't be too many people on the road." Carly paused, placing her hands over her purse again. "But maybe we should head to the curb where they dropped us off."

"Okay, sounds good," Ashley said. "I think there's a streetlight there."

"Yeah," Carly answered, tilting her head to the side. "Why is that important?"

"We can start our book club, if you want." Ashley held up her copy of *Treasure Island* with a large grin on her face. Without waiting for a response, she opened to the first page and began to ready the story aloud. "You okay with that?" Ashley asked, breaking away from the narration quickly. "We can sit under the light and read aloud until they come back?"

Carly smiled. She hadn't been read to since she was a child. "Yeah, actually. Is that how you want to do the club?"

"Reading outside?"

"No, well, yeah, that could be nice." Carly suddenly had visions of spring, of more than mud puddles and chilly night air. Outside of Marshalls, she and Ashley could go toward some of the park benches on their breaks and lunch hours, take out the adventures of Long John Silver, and sit there and read to one another as the flowers bloomed outside. It was so saccharine, so romantic and cliché, but it made Carly's heart stop, nonetheless.

"I mean, we could read aloud," Carly went on. "So we're a little different from other book clubs. They scramble to get the book done and then drink as they gossip. I'm not really a big fan of that."

"Or we could pretend we were in an English class, and try to find symbolism in nothing."

"Yeah. I am very familiar with that."

Ashley read a few more lines before she put the book under her arm to cross the road. When both of them got to the streetlamp, they sat down on the curb. Ashley took off her jacket and spread it out, allowing for them both to have some type of cushion. *The whole thing really does feel like high school. The nerves, the awkwardness, cheap dates that could be paid for in under twenty dollars, and then waiting for someone to pick us up and not being sure what to do with the time.* As Ashley read aloud again, inflecting whenever she got to dialogue, Carly felt as if the two of them were doing homework.

And just like high school, their hands had gotten so close to touching—without actually doing it. They had not kissed one another or even drawn attention to the fact that this was a date. Carly eyed Ashley's body as she read, wanting to nudge closer to her. To put her hand on her knee, but it was late. And Carly didn't know when Landon would soon come around the corner.

"Man, I'm tired," Ashley said. "I suddenly appreciate voice actors ten times more now."

"You can stop, if you want. We'll have to save something for next time."

"Yeah. I'd like that. Especially since," Ashley leaned around Carly, assessing the highway, "it seems as if the adventure is now over."

Carly spotted her mother's car with Landon behind the wheel. She and Ashley stood and waited for the car to come around.

"Well," Carly said. "Landon can give you a ride home. We'll hop in again and then…I'll see you at work."

Ashley nodded, her features soft and caring. "Yes, Carly Rogers. I had a good time tonight."

"Me too, Ashley Poindexter. Me too."

CHAPTER 13

Dorothy Thibodaux was the oldest sister in a family of three girls. The youngest was Sally, who married without finishing high school and then went on to have five kids. The middle sister, Mabel, finished high school and married her then boyfriend around the same time that Sally had her first baby. Their wedding and baby showers were a month apart, both spring affairs. When Carly looked at the photos of their weddings, Dorothy was wearing the same blue dress as when she acted as maid of honor.

Mabel had waited to have lots of kids, but when she did, she only had two. A boy named Robert was followed by a daughter, Lauren. Lauren went onto have three kids, one of whom was Jillian. Her brothers were Christopher, a soldier who died during the Vietnam War, and Matthew, who had died in a car crash when Jillian was only seven. In her own way, Jillian had always been an only child.

Dorothy never married, but she stayed close to the family, eventually inheriting her parents' large, historic house when they died. The house was three stories tall, the third one mostly used as an attic and storage area. The first and second floors were all hardwood, and filled with antique furniture, and photos of the family along the walls. Over the years, Dorothy had updated some of the technology. There was a telephone line, a television with cable, and even a computer, though the internet was still of the dial-up variety. The property had a large backyard that was closed off by a chain link fence, just before a rock quarry. She and her neighbors were separated by acres, and Dorothy liked it that way. The quiet house, along with her inheritance, gave her ample time to study early on in her life, and she became the first person in the family to obtain a university degree.

Of course, Jillian and some of her cousins from Sally's marriage had gone on and gotten degrees. Jillian had a bachelors in economics and then her law degree. There were also some engineers, a pharmacist, and a few psychologists on the other side of the family. But Dorothy had been the first—and she was still, from what Carly could tell—the only female science major inside the family.

One of the things that Carly loved about Dorothy was that she never really did anything with her degree. She completed a bachelors while studying mathematics, organic chemistry, and biology, but she never went beyond it. Sometimes, she studied graduate courses in her free time, but she audited those. She never used her knowledge for a job in the STEM area. Instead, she kept her job at the local library, going back and forth from this large Victorian house, and reading in her spare time. She had no need to strive much beyond that, not really. She already had a house, already had a sizable amount of money from her parents' death, and she didn't have kids. Since she never married, she allowed herself the freedom to continue this lifestyle.

"It just seems wasteful," Jillian once told Carly. "Why bother getting all of that education and then doing nothing with it? Why bother being the first person in the family to try if you stop before you get anywhere?"

Carly always wanted to speak back to her mother's snap judgements about Dorothy's life. She didn't owe the world anything, Carly wanted to say. Dorothy had no attachments, no one depending on her, and she was able to pursue what she wanted. Wasn't that the real American Dream? Liberty and the pursuit of happiness? For some people, that meant doing great things, but for others, like Dorothy—and Carly included herself in this—it meant reading in their rooms, getting up in the morning, and continuing with a simple life.

Carly couldn't exactly tell her mother that, like Dorothy, she had no measurable goals. It sounded bad when it came from her mouth, so she remained silent and nodded along, so her mother wouldn't get suspicious. When Carly went to college in Boston, she tried to imagine how Dorothy would have handled herself on campus. If you didn't think of your entire future as depending on this tiny piece of paper, then the simple joy of learning came back. Learning became fun again. Carly took English classes, walking back and forth from her dorm room to the library, with vague hopes of being just like Dorothy when she grew up.

Carly thought back to the conversation she and Landon had had a few weeks ago. *What exactly do you want in life, dear Carly?* She had found herself lacking any real response to the question that night. But that didn't mean that Carly was an empty vessel, or a freeloader, like her mother surely thought she was. It just meant Carly was beginning to understand that her definition of success and happiness didn't quite have a language yet. She hoped, as Richard drove her to her aunt's in the morning, that Dorothy could help her find that language. And if not, then she could understand Carly's quandary with silent support.

"So, your mom tells me you have a new job," Richard said, glancing over to Carly in the passenger seat. "Where is it, again? Walmart?"

"Close. Just as blue with their logo. I work at Marshalls now."

"That place that's opening in a few days?"

"Yep. I will be there opening day, bright and early."

"Oh. Sorry to hear about that, then. I know you hate crowds."

Richard said shifted his hands on the wheel. He drove his old truck, with the snow tires still on it and snow gear still in the back, along with Carly's large duffel bag. In her lap, she held her purse. It was too early in the morning for Landon, or even Cynthia, to text her, but she clasped it tightly in case she missed out from anyone else.

Richard was a chiropractor, and like most of his clients, he seemed to love snowboarding an obscene amount. He had been dating Jillian for the past year and a half. Carly liked him, as much as she could. She was polite and cordial, but she was used to her mom always being with him, and neither one of them hanging out at the house anymore. Everything Carly knew about Richard was second hand information, like she figured most of what he knew about her was. It was kind of like talking to a reference book or Google, unsure how to type in the exact phrase in order to get the correct result.

"I should stop by. With Jillian, too. We could get some new clothing, nicer stuff, right?"

"Yes, nicer than Walmart. Don't worry," Carly said. Richard, in spite of his rugged truck and outdoorsman hobbies, dressed immaculately. She even figured Marshalls would be too downscale for him. It was one of the benefits of having a good job, but no children this far in his life. He practically sat on stacks of money and could buy Gucci or Armani anything, whenever he wanted.

"There will be a lot of people there opening day," Carly warned him. "So enter at your own risk."

"Well, we will still stop by, just to see you," Richard said. "How are you liking it so far? Good?"

"Yeah, I mean. My coworkers are nice."

He nodded. From his silence after the answer, Carly figured her mom had not mentioned Ashley. Unlike her mother, Richard was usually not afraid to ask questions about Carly's dating life. The few times the two of them had had conversations that lasted beyond small talk, they were discussing women.

"Is this what you want to do?" Richard asked a few moments later.

"In life?" Carly asked with a slight sarcastic drawl. "Did my mom make you ask?"

Richard laughed and Carly knew it was genuine. His cheeks dimpled, even against his stubble from the morning. "No, no, don't worry. She does think about that a lot, but this is me asking, mostly. Is retail what you want to do?"

"I think retail sort of just happens to people."

"So does being a chiropractor."

Carly raised her eyes. "Oh really? Don't you need a degree for that, or are you a snake oil salesman?"

He smiled again. "No, but most people sort of fall into their jobs, Carly. They don't really mean to. They just follow one lead to the next, especially now, in this economy. Then you kind of wake up and realize that it's your career now."

Carly nodded and shifted in her seat uncomfortably. "You ever watched the show *Daria*?"

"Um," Richard said, slightly thrown off guard. "Not really. It's kind of old, though, right? Like *Beavis and Butt-Head*?"

Carly nodded, impressed. "Yeah, both shows had the same animators. What you just said reminded me of something Daria said in an episode. She was telling a school auditorium about how we wake up one day and we realize we're forty, working a job we never anticipated, because we were forced to choose a life goal when we were in high school."

"Yeah," Richard said. "I suppose it's something like that."

Carly nodded, pressing her lips together. She didn't add that in the show Daria presented this as a nightmare scenario, not as something that was just part of everyday life. Carly looked out the window, watching as the houses changed from the suburban sprawl she was used to into the long acres of nothing but land and the occasional house. They'd left the highway maybe fifteen minutes ago and were now making the long and arduous trek down a narrow road to Dorothy's place.

"All I mean to say, Carly," Richard added, perhaps sensing a small tension in the silence. "Is that you should be happy."

"I am," Carly said. "About as much as I can be."

"Well, good."

She didn't tell Richard that she didn't think that the type of happiness she had—or wanted for her future—was the kind that her mother had in mind for her. Especially given Jillian's reaction to Dorothy's life so far. Carly thought of Dorothy's science degree, and how it hung on the wall next to pictures of Jillian and her brothers as kids, just as much of a piece of nostalgia as the childhood photographs.

When Carly leaned forward to change the radio station, Richard nodded his approval. *Good. One less thing to discuss.* As "No Rain" by BLind MeLon came on, Carly pushed her hand out the window, allowing it to trail along in the wind until they arrived.

CHAPTER 14

When Richard dropped Carly off, there were a few minutes of the standard, "good-bye, thank you, your mother will pick you up on Sunday with some more groceries for Dorothy," and then they stood and looked at one another awkwardly until Richard got in the car. They had yet to breach past the handshake stage and only ever hugged the one Christmas that Richard spent at their place. Carly thanked him for the ride, grabbed her duffel bag, and then headed inside the house. When she touched the doorknob, she smiled to find it open.

"Hello, Dorothy. I'm here."

Right away, Carly heard the sighing of the floorboards from the living room. The rocking chair, probably Dorothy's most prized possession, swayed back and forth like the pendulum in the grandfather clock. Carly rested her bag against the staircase and turned the corner into the living room.

"Morning, dear." Dorothy was dressed in a blue sweater with long sleeves, and black slacks. Usually, Dorothy favored dresses since they allowed her to bend her hips and knees easier with the medical braces she sometimes wore. Carly took this change of outfit as a good sign.

"You need to lock the doors," Carly teased. "I could have been a crazy person ready to take all of your doilies and antique lamps."

"I was watching," Dorothy said, pointing through her curtains. The rocking chair was always placed in front of the window, rather than near the TV at the end of the room. Her gray couch took that spot in front of an old wide-back television. Even when Dorothy did put on the TV to have some background noise, Carly was pretty sure that the rocking chair would always face the window. Nature, to Dorothy, always had the better show. She was a biologist, technically, and had studied bugs from underneath the very porch Carly had walked on, drawing diagrams in her childhood notebooks and labeling them with crayons.

"How was the drive?" Dorothy asked.

"Same old, same old. Richard drove me."

"And yet he hasn't come in to see me? Rude," Dorothy teased.

"He's afraid of you, naturally," Carly said. "You're pretty much Mom's mother. And when you get to dating in your forties, you tend to think that you no longer have to worry about meeting parents."

Dorothy smiled coyly. "He should *want* to see me. I'm a testament to how attractive your mother is going to look when she gets to be my age."

"And for me, too, I guess. I do appreciate you letting me study."

"Not at all, dear."

Dorothy curled her hands over her hair, which was tied up into a bun. Small strands of gray filtered down near the back, which gave away the true length of her hair. For someone in her eighties, Dorothy looked really good. Her face was clear, full of color, and if not for the wrinkles that marked her eyes and the corners of her mouth, she wouldn't look over fifty.

"Now. Stop talking like you have some place to be." Dorothy pointed to the doorway, where Carly was still leaning against the frame. Carly noticed a small twinge of pain when she moved her wrist. "Come and sit, stay a while, and tell me about your life."

"Okay, but before I do, can I get you anything? Tea?"

"Medication?" Dorothy asked with a raised eyebrow, half-mocking. "All you guys want to do is pump me full of meds."

"Yes, of course. I will get you that, too. But I think tea is good as well, don't you?"

Dorothy smiled, a wry grin on her face. "Couldn't sound better."

One of Carly's first duties at Dorothy's was usually making food. While she put the kettle on for tea, she scanned the fridge to see what was there. Some old turkey had been taken down from the freezer and some of the Tupperware containers on the top rack had been labeled with a black, felt tip pen in fancy writing. There was definitely enough for a small lunch along with their tea. Carly would have to make dinner, but she was used to that by now. Dorothy almost always had enough dry goods for Carly to make something quick with the vegetables from the freezer to add to it.

Though the land was no longer a farm, pecan and plum trees still grew in the backyard. Carly looked out of the small window over the sink to notice the blooms on each of them, ready to prepare for the summer. Along one of the fences were some tomato plants that Dorothy insisted on, along with some potatoes and green beans. They were usually the easiest vegetables to plant and didn't require too much work. Some days, Dorothy could get up and go on with her daily routine as if nothing was wrong. Others, she would be so overwhelmed by pain she could not leave her bedroom. On those days, she often called her friends or Jillian to come by and help her with her meals.

When Carly brought the tea in, she had a handful of pills on the side of the plate. Most of them were already ordered inside the pill keepers that Dorothy had on the side of the counter. The big pills, ones that couldn't ever fit inside the small daily containers, often made Carly gag just to look at them. But Dorothy never seemed to mind. She didn't even flinch as she took the first handful with a sip of water.

"Is this okay?" Dorothy asked, pointing to a chair close by.

"Yes, yes," Carly said. "Don't worry about me. Anywhere is fine."

Carly placed down their food on a small TV tray between Dorothy's rocker and the small arm chair. Once she sat down, and their tea had been properly sugared, Dorothy smiled, and Carly let herself relax. The sun came through the small window and the slow, chirping sounds of bugs echoed in Carly's ear. There was no sign of traffic, no close next door neighbor. It felt utterly perfect.

"So, tell me," Dorothy stated. This was all Dorothy would normally say whenever Carly came by. There wasn't as much pussyfooting around personal information as there was with Richard, or even her mother sometimes. Their attention always felt fractured to Carly, as if her mother always felt as if she should remember details of Carly's life, but didn't. Dorothy, on the other hand, knew she was missing details of Carly's life, and instead of guessing or filling in the blanks about them, merely asked. Carly always wondered if these differences in attention spans had anything to do with the fact that Dorothy hadn't a Facebook account and never texted. Dorothy knew that she had to depend on the person for their own updates when they were sitting with her in the flesh. "So, tell me" to Dorothy was as direct and more memorable than any Facebook status update. And Carly appreciated the direct approach.

Carly told Dorothy about her new job at Marshalls, along with Landon and Cynthia's trouble with the derby.

"Keep it between us?" Carly asked when she got to the bait and switch plan of the night before.

"Oh, come on. Even if I did tell Jillian something she wouldn't believe me. Senile. I must have gotten confused."

"Fair point." Carly told Dorothy about the derby, Cynthia's new derby name, and everything that came with it. Dorothy was good with most things to do with the modern age. She even accepted Landon's status as a transgender man—and surprisingly fast.

"Say it to me one more time," Dorothy had asked only once when Landon, and not Lisa, had been brought up. Then she sat back in her chair and nodded. "He's just like a parrot fish, then, changing genders to survive. I studied those fish when I was in school."

When Dorothy found out that Carly was gay, it was another easy conversation. She brought up homosexuality in other species and then said she didn't care.

"So long as you're happy." Normally, Carly hated that response to her sexuality. *As long as you're happy* still felt as if she was getting in trouble in some way. She still felt aberrant, outside of the normal lines. It was like, *well, damn you're different and weird, but I guess that's okay if you're happy while doing it.* When Dorothy said it though, she spoke about it as if it was a normal circumstance that some women fell in love with women. It didn't matter to her. Dorothy's nod to happiness seemed a lot more genuine, given how Dorothy had lived her life in quiet solitude.

"And how have you been?" Carly asked, feeling a bit red in the face after talking so much about Landon and Cynthia. "I say a lot about myself sometimes, sorry."

"I asked, dear. And your chatter was more about your sister and her troubles than yourself. Should I be calling Cynthia, Bait N. Switch now? Is that like Landon's name change?"

"No, not quite. Still female pronouns for Cynthia. Bait N. Switch is mostly a stage name for her now, and really, she won't get to be on that stage until she's eighteen."

"No time like the present to practice, though," Dorothy said. "Good for her."

"How have you been?" Carly asked again.

Dorothy gave a so-so wave of her hand. "I can't complain, really."

"What have you been up to?"

"Reading, mostly. I've been looking into the work of P. K. Page."

"Never heard of her. Should I have?"

"Well, she's a terrible poet. It's utterly baffling really how she got so famous."

"Then why read her?"

"She has some interesting metaphors about math. About geometry. I like it. Reminds me why I studied it for so long."

Carly nodded, a small smile on her face. That was another thing about Dorothy that always stuck with Carly. She loved poems. Absolutely, more than anything in the world. They were just like math to her, just like solving an equation. The two of them talked a bit more about the merits of P. K. Page, with Dorothy even offering to give Carly a collected version of her work for the weekend to glance over.

"Really, glancing is all you can do. Some of the poems are terrible. Some of them, like I said, have an okay metaphor here and there. Try 'After Rain'. You may like it."

"It's okay," Carly said. "I will give it a glance, but I think I have enough to read."

"Always do," Dorothy said. "Always prepared."

Dorothy folded her hands over her waist, leaning back as she rocked in her chair. Carly was about to collect up the dishes and maybe put on *Whip It* to show Dorothy the more complex nuances of Roller Derby, when she caught another look in her great-aunt's eye. She seemed to stifle a smile, her eyes squinting as she leaned back and examined Carly. Carly felt her face flush under the sudden scrutiny and turned away.

Dorothy always seemed to know when Carly was hiding something. Not like her mother. Her mother could tell when Carly was lying, when she was avoiding certain tasks and responsibility. But Dorothy could tell when Carly cut herself short, speaking in platitudes and niceties rather than real words.

"Something is new," Dorothy stated. "And while I respect your privacy, you have to know that I'm a curious woman who is often alone. I always want gossip, especially if it's good gossip and it comes right from you. So tell, me— what's *really* new with you, Carly?"

"Just the job," Carly said, still blushing. "I only started a few weeks ago, so it's been keeping me busy. It's boring, but consistent. There's been no time for anything else, really."

Dorothy nodded, slowly. "Uh, huh. I bet. I'm sure that's not the only reason you're busy, though."

"*Maybe.*"

"Just as I thought. Do you love anyone yet, dear?"

"Oh, I like a lot of people," Carly said with a roll of her eyes. She got up from her seat and began to collect their dishes. "The world is my oyster, dear Dorothy. I love everyone under the sky."

"As you should." Dorothy rocked back and forth in her chair, her hands pinned to her stomach as Carly continued to collect their lunch plates. "But don't let your love of the world turn things all pear-shaped."

"What do you mean?"

"Don't fall for ideals, my dear. Fall for bodies. Bodies are good." She sighed, looking down at her own two feet and knees that probably hurt more than Carly could fathom. She seemed tired then, for more than a blink. Carly didn't linger on the thought and neither, it seemed, did Dorothy. She began to speak again, with a small smile. "Even when bodies break down, bodies are still the one thing you fight for. Okay, dear?"

"I'll try."

"One more thing," Dorothy added, before Carly could leave the room. Carly turned around by the doorway, her dark brown hair bouncing at her shoulders and forks clinking against the plate. "Bring her home to see me. You know, while there's still time. I like to meet new people."

"I will." Carly tried to smile, but she knew it came out awkwardly. Promises, especially to Dorothy, always made her stomach twist into anxious knots. What if she couldn't deliver on her end? Words had to mean something between them, especially since they were poets together, and if she didn't deliver, Carly never liked to think about the outcome. She and Ashley were hardly an item, so how could she promise to bring her over? *And what if...?* Carly stopped her thoughts before they finished. Dorothy may not have a lot of time left, but that didn't mean that Carly had to anticipate the ending.

"I'll try to bring her by," Carly said again. "We're not quite...official yet. But soon. I hope—and trust me, you'll be one of the first people to know."

Dorothy nodded in her chair, pleased by the answer. "Good."

CHAPTER 15

After Dorothy was in bed that night, Carly began her cleaning duties. She did the easy stuff first; took out the garbage from the kitchen and upstairs bathroom, along with dumping the small compost bin into a fertilizing area at the back of the property. The mulch was still stiff and frozen in some places, but otherwise good.

Carly washed the dishes from dinner next, soaping them in warm water before she dug underneath Dorothy's sink to find sponges. When she crouched down, she noticed a small leak from one of the pipes. She peered under for only a moment, assessing the situation before deciding it was beyond her reach. She placed a small bucket underneath to catch the drip and made a mental note in her series of tasks to empty it and check in on the leak in another few days. Maybe she'd need to call the plumber, though she would probably have to run that by Jillian first.

After the dishes, Carly put away some leftovers and small meals for the days to come. She labeled most of them, letting Dorothy know the date the food should be eaten by. Her handwriting wasn't as neat as Dorothy's, and it made Carly smile to see her writing and Dorothy's side by side.

When Carly opened the cupboard to put the dishes away, she found a poem written on a cue card stuck inside a tea mug. She read it under the fading sunlight of the spring day.

The birds talk at four am,
When the sun still has not come out.
In darkness, they do not know anything of morning
But a pattern and a hope,
That what they knew yesterday

Is still true for today.
If only human minds
Could be as trusting
As birds and their instincts. We hear
Garbage trucks and alarm clocks
And fear that we are too late.

Carly pondered for a moment about how to continue the poem. Then, she wrote down her response.

Humans are drawn to human-made voices
Even inside small mechanical motors.
We recognize ourselves inside shiny new parts,
In the machine-like beats of our hearts. We have
Lasted as long as we have,
Evolved far more than we thought
Because we have learned from our mistakes
And long to trust others
Who show us that if we move just right
We can hit the snooze button, and
Buy ear plugs so we don't hear
The garbage truck. We have come so far
And learned to love
Sleeping late as our reward.

Carly sighed before she hung the poem back up again. Part of her wished that Dorothy was online more, or at least had a cell phone, so she and Carly could continue this round robin poetry game even longer than just the weekend. Carly often wanted to text Dorothy with stray lines from the book she was reading or even more lines of poems that often came into her mind in the middle of work.

The dull drudgery of minimum wage is the perfect place for poetry. For great literature, even. It was one of the reasons why she clung onto the idea of *Waiting for Godot* as much as she did when the truck shipment hadn't come or when one of her supervisors was missing. *We spend so much of our lives waiting,* Carly thought, *that the real poetry or meaning of everyday life came from those moments where seconds slip by us.* She felt, a lot of the time, that it was her duty to try and make those fleeting moments that felt like wasted time something good again. This was probably Dorothy's influence over her more than anyone else, other than maybe Ashley. Though their relationship was still too new to tell.

For a while, as Carly swept the front walkway of Dorothy's house, she thought of Ashley's body. She was supposed to fall for that, wasn't she? In the words of Dorothy, at least. She knew that her aunt had meant something more than mere physicality. When Dorothy had told Carly she should fall in love with bodies, and not ideals, she was advocating for the opposite of the manic, pixie, dream-girl syndrome Carly had watched take over half the Boston campus while she was in school. Dorothy wanted Carly to fall in love with the way a person really was. From their flaws to the way they laughed— and not the illusion of romance or a dream girl.

Sure, physicality was part of that promise Carly had made. And it was one of many things that kept crossing Carly's mind about Ashley.

Ashley had strong shoulders, in spite of her skinny frame. She wore loose clothing, in addition to the blue smock the store insisted they wear, but underneath Carly knew that Ashley's body had to be great. Carly imagined pale skin and light colored nipples that went taut with the faintest touch. She imagined her sex with a crown of pale hair, unmanicured, growing naturally between her legs. The women Carly had fallen for in the past were never as skinny as Ashley, but there was something about the way Ashley carried herself that made Carly see past what normally didn't excite her. Ashley was not delicate, in spite of looking like the wind would take her away. She demanded physical labor, demanded to be treated like one of the men in the back. She fought and talked in loud voices, and she wore her clothing outside of work like a loud statement too. It was something that made Carly pay attention and want to know more than just her first and last name, and her book preference. She wanted to know what was inside of her clothing, under all that skin, and inside her heart.

By the time Carly had finished with most of her tasks, she had broken into a small sweat. She ditched her oversized hoodie and sat down in the wooden chairs in the kitchen to catch her breath. Dorothy never minded that she had music on as she worked, but Carly turned it down when it was no longer white noise as she cleaned. Carly reached into her bag and found her phone. Almost ten messages now, most of which were from Cynthia and Landon, keeping her up to date on life back in the city.

Cyn and I are going to see a movie. Cyn had to lie, of course, so tell your mom that Cynthia's new friend Angela is totally awesome and safe, right? Apparently that's my code name now.

Sounds good, guys, Carly texted back. *Have fun! And let me know if the movie's worth seeing.*

It doesn't involve reading... You probably won't like it, Landon teased a couple minutes later.

Carly was about to put her phone away again and head in for the night, when it buzzed in her hand. Ashley's number came across the screen, and Carly was suddenly wide awake again.

I had a lot of fun with you the night before. I was going to tell you to bring your new book with you to work next, but I think the next time we see one another is opening day.

Carly looked up at the calendar on the wall. May was still there, when it had been June now for a few days. After Carly changed it to June, she realized Ashley's claims were right. The next time she worked was Tuesday, the glorious opening day—and a ten hour shift. It would be a ten hour shift with Ashley, but it was a small victory, especially since there would be as many people as a Black Friday gathering. They probably wouldn't be able to see one another through the crowds.

Go figure, Carly typed. *Time certainly flies. You're working right now, aren't you? How is that going?*

Busy. Annoying. I miss you. I think you're the only intelligent person here.

Carly was struck by the frankness in Ashley's texts. She wasn't sure how to respond to the claim of *I miss you*, which seemed to have its own weight, so she went for the easy stuff.

Perhaps I am. But you shouldn't be so quick to judge others. People have different types of intelligence. It matters, but I understand, it's hard.

Blah blah blah, Ashley texted back with a small smiley face. *Way to take away from the compliment I was giving you, Carly Rogers. I think you respond better when I call you a scurvy-riddled pirate.*

Hey, Carly responded. *I resent the scurvy diagnosis. Everything else is fine.*

Okay, I'm glad we've reached this understanding. But...I have to get back soon, Ashley wrote next. *I know, I could text in the aisles, but I'd like to keep this job. I hope to see you on Tuesday.*

Counting down the days, Ashley Poindexter, Carly wrote with another smile. Again, their words seemed much to frank on the screen. She couldn't walk away from it or make a joke like she could if they were face to face, even though they tried using emoticons. She tried to imagine Ashley's smile, her sharp cheekbones, and the way she had looked at her as they browsed the aisles at Powell's.

Until then, Carly added, *I have my Treasure Island to keep me company. Hopefully you don't mind if I read too much without you?*

Not too much, Ashley responded. *And so long as you think of me as you do.*

Of course. I wouldn't have it any other way.

Good. I wouldn't, either.

CHAPTER 16

The first person Carly saw the day of the store opening was Amber through the store windows. She looked even smaller than before; her thin brown hair was tied back in a loose ponytail, and her blue apron hung off her small hips and waist. She stood at the front of the store, along the lines of cash registers, in preparation for their hectic day. The store wasn't even opened yet, since it was seven. Christina, the night manager, let Carly in after Carly held up her employee badge.

"Thanks," Christina said. "I knew it was you, but as protocol for today, no one gets anywhere important without those badges."

Carly didn't respond, and Christina wasn't exactly looking for small talk. As soon as she opened the door for Carly, she moved right to the back to talk with Suzanne.

"I'm on cash," Amber said, before Carly could move very far. Amber's thin eyebrows furrowed.

"Yeah, most people are today," Carly said briskly. She moved to her locker, throwing in her purse and book before grabbing her own apron. As she tied it across her waist, she realized hers was much too small. She walked back toward the front of the store, where Amber had not moved. Her eyes were still wide, as if caught in headlights.

"Do you want to switch?" Carly offered.

"Shifts? I think we're kind of late for that now," Amber said.

"No, do you want to switch uniforms? I think this will fit you better."

"Oh," Amber said. She began to undo her apron before saying yes or no.

They swapped their uniforms just as Suzanne approached them. "Come on, ladies. Clock in and get the party started."

A group of workers, most men, moved past Amber and Carly at the clock-in station. They held large Tupperware and plastic containers with dips, vegetables, and even some pizza and brownies to the side.

"What the?"

"We're getting free lunch," Amber expanded. "Since we're working longer shifts."

Carly's stomach rumbled instinctively, and she nodded, relieved.

"So long as it's better than the coffee we have now, I'm pleased."

Amber was a lot less frazzled with a uniform that fit her, but her eyes were still wide. More people trained on cash came up and set up their registers. Maura and Devon were two of them; Carly recognized them from her training earlier. Everyone else was a blur. Carly knew that Ashley would come in later, most likely to clean up the displays after the crowds of people had dismantled them. At that moment, Amber was the only person that Carly knew beyond first names, and even then, she didn't know her that well.

"So...are you ready?" Carly asked, struggling to make small talk. "Are your kids going to see you today, during the opening?"

Amber shrugged. "Maybe. But I don't think we're allowed to use our discounts."

"Right," Carly said, nodding. "Fair enough."

The silence between them stretched on, even as the commotion in the back became louder. Carly began to set up her register, hoping that keeping herself busy would make the awkwardness between them dissipate. By the time she had finished, Carly noted that Amber's machine wasn't even on.

"You may want to set up," Carly stated. "We're probably going to open soon—maybe even sooner if Suzanne gets her way. I swear, she'd like everyone inside so long as they bought something."

A lineup had already formed around the small patch of sidewalk, from Marshalls blue logo to the beginning of a liquor store. People near the front continuously checked their watches and then swayed from side to side, talking to the person beside them with angry expression on their faces. A van pulled up and let out more people, and that's when Carly realized a line of cars were also waiting to add their passengers to the ever-growing line up.

Okay, that's unsettling. This wasn't going to be quite Black Friday, but Carly was already a little worried. She had never worked on one of those dreadful days, but she had driven around with Landon one time and watched the chaos unfold. Jillian was never into sales or second hand stuff at all. The only other person who dared to go to sales or second hand stores was Cynthia, so she could make skating costumes. Even then, Cynthia could handle the crowds. Carly even believed that she derived some strange sense of satisfaction from the whole thing. Though it was the beginning of summer now, and not even close to the holiday season, Carly could anticipate the same amount of chaos at their store today.

Suzanne's brown eyes widened at the oncoming masses, her hands rubbing together. She walked to the front of the store and narrowed her eyes as she inspected the cashiers.

"Hurry, hurry," she chastised. "Time is money."

When she walked away again, getting ready to open the doors, Carly glanced at Amber. She still hadn't moved.

"Are you okay?" Carly asked. She extended her arm, finding the black button on the side and flipping it up. "You just turn the machine on here…"

"Thanks. But…I don't think you quite understand," Amber said.

"What?" Carly turned around and watched as Suzanne walked outside. She still hadn't opened the door yet, but she began to pass out coupons to the first twenty or so people in line. Carly felt dread mount in her stomach. Coupons were the worst. "Are you ready?" she asked again, turning to Amber. "This is about to get insane."

"I've never been trained," Amber blurted out.

"On cash?"

"Yeah, no one ever did. I was called into work one day to train, but they didn't get around to me. I ended up being in shoes for the entire time. I don't think they saw me over the displays."

Carly was about to raise her voice and ask why Amber hadn't spoken up. *That's the logical thing to do, right? Why didn't she do that?* But just as Carly opened her mouth, Carly saw how small Amber was. Underneath the too-large clothing and the slightly better blue apron was someone who slipped under the radar, almost completely. Even if she had brought up that she had been skipped over, there was no guarantee that someone would listen to her. And so long as she was still getting paid for the time she was here, Amber was not going to cause a fuss.

"Okay," Carly said, trying to remain stoic. "I can help."

She walked over a few feet to Amber's station. She began to program in their codes and employee numbers (which Amber thankfully had on her badge) as the machine whirred to life.

"This is how it works..." Carly trailed off, giving her the condensed 101 show, just as the doors to the store were opened.

Amber caught onto cash easily. It was much better, from what Carly had seen in her years of customer service, to get the basics for a machine and then put it into practice right away. A good balance of theory and practice was what had been missing from most of Carly's college courses, too, she thought. In order to understand English, she and other students were told to read books. But Carly could only handle so many concepts, themes, and definitions without losing track of the reason why she was there. Theory needed practice to back it up. While Carly didn't think that every single English major should have to write a novel in order to understand how one worked, transcribing one from start to finish really did illuminate how words were put together. Carly had typed out the entirety of a Hemingway book one summer just to see how it worked and the process had changed the way she looked at novels. Similarly, Carly hadn't thought about poetry much at all until Dorothy started to write it with her. Then, Carly slowly realized the mechanical and almost methodical purpose behind each line.

As Carly continuously scanned items and made change, she kept that mathematical precision to poetry in mind. She tried to drown out the slamming of machines and murmuring of voices. The store seemed to get so loud in a matter of minutes, the songs over the Muzak completely disappeared. Occasionally, she'd look over to her side and make sure Amber was okay. She only stalled a couple times, when an item didn't have a tag or when someone tried to use a coupon. But she was good—a smart and fast learner. Carly wished she could have boasted about her to someone else higher up, but that would have given away the initial failure. So Carly went back to scanning and waited. This shift was going to be ten hours long, with two meal breaks. Carly was an early bird, as ever, but she knew that she would not be alone for much longer in this sea of people and discounts.

Finally, three hours in, Carly spotted the green collared shirt and short cropped hair that belonged to Ashley. She pushed her way in through the front door, a large backpack over one shoulder. One of the managers, Tim, waved her over to him, so Ashley paused. She looked back toward Carly, who smiled and waved.

"Ma'am, ma'am," Carly's customer said. "I need a price check for this."

Carly looked back down. "Oh, right. Give me a second."

Carly grabbed one of the scanning guns from the back counter. As she worked, she tried to spot Ashley in the crowd again. *No such luck.*

"Your jeans are twenty-two dollars," Carly answered her customer. "Plus tax."

The woman grumbled, but agreed that that was an okay rate. She piled the rest of her clothing onto the counter and Carly went through them, getting back into a rhythm. She was surprised when she saw Ashley move back and forth along the front of the lines.

"What are you doing here?" Carly whispered soon after her customer left. Ashley had bent down in front of her cash register, retrieving something from the ground. "Are you here to help me out? Rescue me?"

"No, but I do wish I could," Ashley said with a smile. "People dropped their socks and their shirts right here, but no one can see it. They also knock over displays. I'm merely attempting to clean the storefront before any manager sticks me in one area."

"Really now?"

"Yes. And I can see you this way, so there are benefits."

"I enjoy a friendly face. Especially when they're not asking me for a price check."

"I do what I can," Ashley said. She paused in front of Carly's register, a couple of balled up socks tucked under her arm.

"So where are you working today?" Carly asked.

"Men's wear, mostly."

"Good." Carly grinned wryly. From the cash area, she had a good view of the men's section.

"And how long do you work for?" Ashley asked.

"Until about five tonight."

"Really now?" Ashley smiled.

"Yeah, why?"

"No reason. I just wanted to make sure that you, Carly Rogers, are ready for this madness to really begin."

"Oh, Ashley Poindexter. It's even worse than you could imagine."

Just before Ashley could say another word, a man wearing a track suit plopped down a pile of business wear in front of Carly's cashier, knocking down some of the display that Ashley just finished fixing.

"I believe I'm next," he stated. His pugnacious face broke out into a grin just as Carly sighed.

"Of course, sir." She began to ring up some of his items just as Ashley walked away. Before she disappeared completely in the crowd, she gave Carly one last smile and mouthed, "Good luck, Carly Rogers," as she moved.

It wasn't much, but Carly hoped this small interaction would be enough to get her through until five, when there would be more.

Way too many people asked Carly about the same cross-stitched Tommy Hilfiger jackets and blue oxford shirts. Both had been mislabeled before they were put out on the floor, so someone on staff had started to tear away the price tags entirely. This made it even harder to get an accurate price check. By the time Ashley walked up with the same items in her hands, Carly had already seen them at least ten times.

"No," Carly said, her voice quick. There was still a slight playful edge to it, so Ashley merely laughed instead of balked away like many of the high school students who worked the shift had done when they had approached Carly the same way.

"What's up?"

"That fucking shirt. Too many. Price checks. I'm dying."

Ashley laughed. She moved to the back, found the pricing gun, and began to affix new price tags from the packages the store kept at the back.

"I know. I am here to fix all of your problems now."

"You are a saint, Ashley Poindexter."

"Yeah, that's actually a good and flashy name for a saint. I can imagine a prayer card with my face."

Ashley held her hands, with a pricing gun in her left, in a prayer pose. Carly had time to utter a few quick laughs, before another customer came to her till. She worked as fast as she could, uttering her inane script for each customer, with Ashley's presence behind her acting as a slight comfort. Carly got through a large group of shoppers before the line slowed, and she spotted Ashley walking around the counter again.

"Leaving so soon?"

"I must. Gotta hang these shirts back where they belong."

Carly nodded, her eyes down. She was about to usher the next person in line to her, when Ashley walked back over. She took her red sign that said "sorry next till" and placed it over Carly's work space.

"Since we were so rudely interrupted last time," Ashley explained.

"What now?" Carly asked, before pointing to the sign. "If Suzanne sees this, she's going to kill you."

"Nonsense. You're showing me something to do with Tommy Hilfiger. Or I am showing you. Either way, this is a business meeting."

"Okay. I'm listening."

"You should come by my place tonight."

"Oh, should I?" Carly asked playfully.

"Yes, if you're free, that is."

"I booked off the whole day for this affair. I really don't have much else going for me, other than this menagerie of affordable clothing."

"Excellent. And you finish at five?"

Carly nodded, her face blushing slightly. She looked down at the tile floor and noticed the lineup getting clogged up again. Ashley noticed it too and did her best to position her back toward the crowd. One of the first things you learn in minimum wage work is to make sure the customers never see your eyes. If they can't meet your gaze, they can't yell at you. It's a BAND-AID solution, and in this case, Carly knew it would only work for a time.

"Good. I now finish at five, too."

"Now?" Carly asked.

"Yes. They didn't bother scheduling me for a long shift today, which I was surprised about. But I spoke with Suzanne and pleaded my case. I said that this place was ridiculous and that I'd stay another hour, just to make things fair. You know, between us."

"You sacrifice so much for me," Carly joked. Ashley nodded her head back into a pious pose, overplaying it.

"My dad is going to pick me up," Ashley added. "I know, I know, this is kind of lame, kind of like high school all over again."

"He won't mind?" Carly asked. "If I come along, I mean."

"No, he'll be glad I'm out playing with the neighborhood kids." Ashley ran a hand through her hair, peeking at the growing crowd before murmuring to Carly again. "What do you say? We already did the coffee and bookstore routine, and I'm sure you don't exactly want to sit around and discuss the major themes and motifs in *Treasure Island*, but I do have a lot of bad movies lying around. After this day, it could be nice to get off our feet."

"Yes," Carly said. "Yes, I think I'd like that very much, Ashley Poindexter."

Ashley grinned. "And that is how I know you're serious, Carly Rogers. A pirate's oath."

"Sure. I solemnly swear."

"Good. Me too."

On Carly's second break, she texted Landon.

Ashley invited me out again. This time not as a bait and switch for Cynthia and not for a larger, external cause.

External cause? Landon texted back. *Is this a fancy English major thing? A literary reference I'm not getting?*

Pfft. You know what I mean. Before, it was just like a scheme. It was a con. We were bonded together for a greater good of Roller Derbies and liberating younger sisters. But now, this is just an invitation to come over and maybe watch bad movies. I don't know how to read it.

Carly waited, biting her fingernails slightly for Landon to reply. She picked up the phone again before he had the chance and wrote a short addendum.

I mean, maybe we're just bonding over this stupid Marshalls opening day bullshit. I read ages ago that trauma bonds people together. This is pretty traumatic. Worse than Black Friday. We could just be sticking together because we'll now both have war-flashbacks to this opening day. But I think it's more than that. Could it be more than that?

She placed the phone down again. She bit the other finger. She was about to type again when Landon replied.

It's opening day? Aren't there like, special types of discounts now?

Yes, but I swear to God if you ask me another question about men's wear I'm going to snap. Carly hit send and then wrote a more gentle follow-up text. *Sorry. Lots of customers today. It's kind of like herding cats.*

Ah, got yah. Pear-shaped.

Something like that.

Look, Landon wrote. *First of all, this isn't Vietnam, and you don't have PTSD from working a cash register.*

Are you invalidating my identity, dear Landon?

Hush. Landon was quiet for a time after this. Carly couldn't quite grasp if he was upset with her or if he was wording the next part carefully. Carly ate some of the free food at the lunch tables, as she waited for Landon's message to come in.

You will be fine. Customers are just people with wants and needs that you can sometimes satisfy with your superior sales knowledge. And you know, Ashley is the same way, too. She has wants and needs, just like you. I don't have much work in the relationship business, but this is what I know: You don't even agree to a larger, external cause with a complete stranger unless you're interested in them. You also don't ask them out after a big opening day, when you're probably exhausted yourself, unless you're into that person.

So... Carly texted with one hand as she ate a baby carrot with dip. *What are you saying? Yes or no? I just need to be sure.*

You're not a mistake, Landon texted. *You're not an outlier. She likes you. I saw the way she looked at you.*

For five minutes, you saw. The rest of the time, you were away and I couldn't verify those stares.

Stop this!!! Landon texted. Carly could practically hear his loud voice in her ear. *You are, at the end of the day, someone's first choice. You need to let good things happen to you, or else you'll be completely overwhelmed by the bad.*

Carly nodded, though she knew that Landon could not see her. A couple more people streamed into the break room, turning over the egg salad sandwiches and the hummus the company had gotten for the snack table. Carly spent the rest of her break rereading Landon's words. She tried to make herself believe in them. She thought of Aunt Dorothy again and her small, but persistent, mantra in her mind.

Fall for bodies, not ideals.

Carly sighed as she began to text again. *Okay, Lando. I know you're right. I'll try. But I also have to go now. Break over.*

Thank God, Landon texted her back. *Not that your break is over. But that you're listening. I love you and all, Car, but I didn't know how much more Doctor Phil I could do. Now, go back to work before you lose your job. Good luck!*

Carly smiled at her phone. She sent a quick emoticon to convey her last message, before she adjusted her uniform again. As she left the break room, she glanced at the clock. *Another three more hours—and freedom.*

This time, Carly headed back to cash with a genuine smile on her face.

CHAPTER 17

Ashley's dad was a tall man with gray, wiry hair and a moustache that was sharply trimmed at the corners. Ashley hopped in the backseat of the car, right along with Carly.

"Sorry to taxicab you, daddy dearest," Ashley said.

"Not at all. Where are we off to?"

"Home."

Ashley's dad narrowed his eyes in the rearview mirror. "Does your friend need a special stop?"

"No, if that's okay."

Her father shrugged, holding his hands up in a mock expression of exasperation. "As ever, Miss Daisy, my wish is your command."

"It's nice to meet you, Mr. Poindexter," Carly said, once the quick back and forth was over.

"Oh. Please. Call me Mike."

"It's nice to meet you, Mike."

"And you too…?"

"Carly."

"Carly Rogers," Ashley corrected. "This is my pirate friend I was telling you about."

Carly beamed. *She's been talking about me. Maybe Landon was right.*

"You'll have to forgive my daughter," Mike said, as they turned onto the road and out of the strip mall. "She has so many playmates sometimes I can't keep track of all their names. Regardless, it's nice to meet you, Carly."

"You too," Carly said, eyeing Ashley with a grin.

The rest of the drive was slow, bumper to bumper traffic in the downtown area. Mike asked a few questions about the store opening and what it was like, most of which were answered by Ashley using her quick wit and delightful back and forth banter between the two of them. She recanted a long and laborious story about working the lingerie section and being utterly appalled by how many of the pairs fall all over the ground, into the dust and whatever else is in the back, and then onto the store room floor.

"The protective shields or whatever the hell they put in women's underwear were all torn off by the end of it," Ashley said, motioning with her hands. "And yet, all these women were taking armfuls—I'm telling you, *armfuls*—of this stuff into the changing room. Like it's nothing!"

"I think you need to do some kind of Pictures of Walmart thing, but for Marshalls," Mike suggested. "Partly so other people can enjoy these stories and not as much onus is put on me."

"We should start a Facebook group," Ashley said. "Or I should write an op-ed piece."

"That was a quick escalation. How is *The Huffington Post* going to hear about this? What angle are you marketing—and what is your pitch?"

"Misogyny," Ashley said with a playful smile. "All the men's underwear is wrapped in plastic, protecting it. The women's underwear is downright abused and mishandled. It's clearly inequality at work."

Carly stifled her laughter with a hand over her mouth. Mike groaned as they moved a bit faster through the traffic.

"I hope she's not a handful for you, Carly," he said.

"No, not at all. I like it. Keeps me on my toes."

"That's not all I'll do," Ashley said.

Carly's eyes widened, surprised by such an obvious flirtation. Mike only laughed and then playfully hit his steering wheel when he was stuck in traffic again.

Finally, they pulled into a nice, semidetached house on the opposite side of town, no more than twenty minutes from where Carly and Landon had gone under the bridge. From the store on a good day, Ashley would need at least a thirty minute drive. With the traffic they had sat through, the trip had been almost an hour ordeal. The time had passed quickly, because of the conversations, but Carly could not imagine someone driving this route every day or for every shift.

"So what made you pick Marshalls?" Carly asked as they stepped out. "Surely there were other stores around that you could work for?"

"I was drawn in by the underwear."

Carly snickered. After Mike got out of the car, he went into the trunk to pull out his leather briefcase. From snippets of their conversation in the car, Carly had put together that Mike was in advertising, though he seemed to also have a journalism background. Mike walked ahead of both Carly and Ashley, who got caught up in more conversations as Carly admired the house in between jokes.

The house's front lawn was green, though there were patches in some areas that were brown, filled with dead grass and dirt. The garage door was closed and Mike parked outside of it, not bothering to open it or pull the car inside. The door itself was painted gray, the same color as the bricks and window shutters on the house. Carly noticed that the paint was chipped when she stepped closer, and there were many cracks and potholes in the driveway and front steps. The screen door was closed to the house, but the larger door, with a brass deadbolt, was open.

When a dog barked, Carly turned toward the screen door and saw a small dog—definitely a mutt—peering out between the mesh paneling. Mike tried to worm his way past the dog as he opened the door, but was only met with even more loud barking.

"You okay with animals?" Mike asked back, holding the dog by his collar.

"Yeah, I'm fine. I wish I had a dog growing up."

"Why didn't you?" Ashley asked, almost balking under the admission.

"Dogs tear apart the furniture and require too much attention," Carly said, mimicking her mother's voice before she could stop herself.

"Pfft. Bad dogs tear up the furniture. And all living creatures demand attention."

"Not cats," Carly said. "But we had to get rid of our cat after Cyn was born. Allergies."

"Ah, well, good riddance," Ashley said. "Cats are jerks."

"They can be nice. The one we had was raised around a dog, so it was pretty much a friendly animal."

"See?" Ashley said. She walked onto the porch and took over handling the dog's collar from her father with a nod. The dog, tan and black in color, growled at Carly but then relented when Ashley began to pet behind its ears. "Dogs were probably why your cat was so good before."

"Probably." Carly put her bag down on the porch and then sat on one of the steps. "Is it okay if I pet him?"

"Of course, why else would we get a dog?" Ashley said in a jovial voice. "He's shy, and protective of us, but he'll like you. You have a good demeanor about you."

"Then why did he growl a minute ago?"

"Stress. He could tell you were anxious. And since most people who are anxious when walking up to a house are probably going to rob it, he got scared."

"Oh, I see…" Carly hadn't realized how easily her nerves gave herself away, even to animals. Carly still had to text her mom and Cynthia to let them know where she had gone to. And possibly cancel plans with Landon tomorrow, depending on how much rest she needed after today. Sometimes, when she worked more than six hours in a row, it took her that much time, and more, to have her own thoughts back, and not the repetitive loops of cashier noises and small talk.

The dog soon came over to Carly, his eyes and nose darting around to examine her. She held out her hand first, palm up, so the dog could sniff around her wrist. She tried not to move too quickly and to relax. She smiled up at Ashley when the dog moved his mouth and nose over to her lap, allowing her to pet his head.

"See?" Ashley said. "You're a natural."

"I really do wish we had a dog growing up. It would have been nice to get out of the house every so often to walk him and have an excuse to leave."

"You don't need an excuse to leave, do you?" Ashley asked, cocking an eyebrow. Her tone was inquisitive, not accusatory, but it still made Carly pause under it.

"No, I suppose not. But where am I going to go? I don't have a car. I feel like a crazy person if I just walk around the block and then go back home."

"You wouldn't look crazy. But you could also go someplace. A coffee house, perhaps? Read your books?"

"Going out costs money. And I don't exactly have a lot of it right now."

"Who does? I believe that's why people go into credit card debt."

"Because they don't have enough money?"

"Because they're lonely."

"Huh. Never thought of it like that." Carly ran her hands around the dog's neck, over his small shoulders, and then to his tail which continued to wag. He looked up at her, his small head still on her lap, and then rolled over to show his belly full of tan fur, speckled with black spots.

"See?" Ashley said, rubbing the dog's stomach too. "He definitely likes you."

"What's his name?" Carly asked.

"Pizza," Ashley laughed. "See the spots on his belly? We figured those were pepperoni and his tan fur was the cheese. He's also a mutt, so he's really a mix of everything."

"That's…awesome." Carly rubbed his belly again, eliciting a few pleased murmurs.

"Pizza the Hut, technically," Ashley said. "As a proper homage to the *Star Wars* film franchise and our favorite food."

"Pizza Hut?"

"Oh, no." Ashley made a face. "God no. Pizza the Hut, as a dog, helps to redeem the terrible franchise that is Pizza Hut. We're just talking about pizza in general with his name. You know?"

"Oh yeah," Carly said.

When Mike walked across the hallway, Pizza flipped up and onto his feet again, running after Mike into the house. Both Carly and Ashley got up, ready to follow.

"Speaking of which," Ashley said, leading Carly into the house more. "I think there is a pizza in here. Not from the hut, thankfully. Is that okay for dinner?"

Ashley held open the door for Carly as she smiled. The singsong words of Cynthia filtered through her head, and Carly couldn't help but mimic them. "Definitely. Pizza's great."

"So what do you want to do?" Ashley asked after dinner.

They were huddled around her small living room table, with stacks of newspapers and magazines near the china hutch. At one point, Carly could tell that the small house had been furnished with an acquired taste and keen eye. Now the furniture was all still there, but it had been added to over the years with small trinkets, keepsakes, and a lot of newspapers and bill envelopes. The house wasn't quite as bad as a hoarder's, but Carly could see the beginning roots of a problem developing. There was a kind of stagnation in the living room that spilled into the kitchen, along with letters with red stamps on them declaring that stuff was overdue. Ashley walked around the house like she knew what she was doing, as if she had allowed the clutter to blend into the walls around her. Carly could appreciate that—especially since Ashley made no apology for it.

Carly bunched up her napkin and set it down on her paper plate.

"How about we start that book?" Carly suggested. "I'm dying to get back to my pirate roots."

"Sounds perfect." Ashley picked up both of their paper plates and threw out the mess, before she wiped her hands on some more paper towel and added it to the tall garbage in the corner of the kitchen.

"And in that case, do you want to head to my bedroom? It's probably like half the size of yours at home, but there is enough space that we don't disturb Darren with our loud and uproarious reading."

Carly froze, barely nodding her head. Darren, Ashley's brother, had returned home about fifteen minutes ago, giving both of the women a quick hello. He disappeared into the family room after grabbing a piece of pizza and turned on a game right away. From the theme music and the amount of shots fired, Carly guessed it was one of the 007 video games.

"Yeah," Carly said, her voice only a little shaky. "That sounds really good."

"Great. Just let me clean quickly before I invite you up, okay?"

"Sure."

Ashley gave another quick smile before she ran up the stairs, taking them two by two. Carly folded her hands at the living room table, her gaze fixated on the small knot in the wood. Carly could tell from the way Ashley talked; there were no ulterior motives in her voice. She wanted to get Carly alone, maybe, but to only read a book. *Not to fool around, not really. Is that bad?* Ashley joked about a lot of things, but Carly had gotten used to that. This really was a time for reading, for their hackneyed, minimum wage book club. Carly supposed that now was as good as time as any to begin.

Then why am I so afraid? Or is that disappointment? Carly was about to get her phone, to reread the encouraging text message that Landon had sent, before Ashley came back into the room.

"Okay. Much cleaner now. You ready to go?"

"Sure. Lead the way."

CHAPTER 18

Ashley was right—her room was at least half the size of Carly's. It reminded Carly of her dorm room first year, with only enough space for a small chair in one corner, a bed that was barely a twin size mattress, and a bookshelf jammed full with books and trinkets. Her closet was to the side of the bookshelf, closed tightly. From the stray corner of a T-shirt that stuck out, Carly guessed that Ashley had jammed everything in there for storage in her small attempt to clean. The bed had also been made. She eyed the posters tacked up on the wall over the bed. Some were for *Scarface* and others for *The Dark Knight* trilogy.

"So," Ashley said, extending an arm. "Take a pick of where you want to sit."

Since there was only one chair in the room, Carly made her way over to it. She sat down inside the basket-like cushion and felt herself almost go off balance.

"It's adjustable…" Ashley said with a small laugh. "It was a bad trend from the '90s. I really do apologize for my room. This is pretty much sixteen-year-old me you're looking at right now."

"I don't mind," Carly stated. "You'd see the same thing at my place, only less movies and more bands. We all have homes and high school pasts."

"Oooh," Ashley said, flopping down on the bed. "I think I'd like to see your secret, high school past. And the bands you listened to."

"It's really not that revelatory."

"I beg to differ."

"Then Fall Out Boy. They'll always have a place in my teenaged heart."

Ashley laughed before she hummed the first few bars of their big hit in 2005.

"See?" Carly said. "Not that surprising."

"It's not what you like. It's how you liked it."

"Sure. I'll have to keep that in mind."

"I used to have a place to myself," Ashley said after a few moments. "I had an amazing apartment with real adult furniture and real adult art on the wall. Only one or two pictures from *Scarface*, I swear."

Carly laughed lightly at the joke. "Where did you live before this?"

"Doesn't matter, really, since I'm not there anymore." Ashley glanced behind her, past Joe Montegna and his machine gun, and reached back under her pillow to pull out her copy of *Treasure Island*. "I think it's better we travel over the seas right now, don't you think?"

"Sure," Carly said. "I'm looking forward to it."

Ashley nodded, giving another smile, before she began to read aloud. Her voice was strong, solid. Carly didn't know what to do with her hands at first when the reading started. She folded them over her chest, played with the zipper on her purse, before she finally just relaxed enough to allow the story to overtake the room.

Ashley was a good reader, and Carly was relieved she didn't have to keep talking for the rest of the night. She was so sick of asking how someone was and struggling to make conversation, so Carly allowed herself to listen. She allowed for her past thoughts of the rush on the store to be replaced by something better, something more poetic than she could ever imagine for a boys' book about pirates. Ashley continued to read, only stopping once to grab a glass of water from the bathroom. When she returned, she lay down on the bed, her head on the pillow and held the book above her. Carly remained in the chair, though she sloped down lower as the night went on, and she began to grow tired.

When there was a knock at the door, Ashley folded the book over her chest. Carly sat up straight and fumbled with her hands again, as if they had been caught in the act. Ashley leaned behind her bedpost where the doorknob was located and opened up without moving from her lying down position. Her father poked his head into the room, a pair of old reading glasses at the edge of his nose.

"Hello, daddy dearest."

"Ashley, hi. And Carly. Do you need me for a ride later?"

"No, Jeeves, I think that will be all." She beamed up at him. When he nodded quietly, Ashley pressed further. "Are you headed to bed?"

"Yes, I think so." He sighed. The lower light from the hallway made all of the creases on his face appear deeper.

Ashley turned to Carly. "You okay getting a ride with Darren later?"

"Yeah, yeah. That's fine. Not an issue."

"Goodnight, then, ladies." Mike lifted his hand very briefly, before he shut the door again.

"Man," Ashley said when Mike's door shut. "I forget how much older he looks some nights. Dressing up really does take the age away from the face. Maybe I should wear more suits, too."

"I think you look fine now."

"Pfft, that doesn't mean much. Even you said I was in my thirties when you saw my license. That's bad."

"Hey," Carly said. "That was bad math. Not because you looked old."

"I know. But it's easy for you to say. You're practically a baby."

"*Hey*," Carly repeated, still smiling. "I'm an adult."

"That's the problem. Your early twenties are hard. You're not old enough to be taken seriously but you're also too young to feel bad for. Just like the quarter-life-crisis stuff my dad told me. And now, I think I respect his opinion on aging a lot more."

Carly considered this. She certainly felt the lack of pity from her mother on occasion. But Mike didn't seem like the type of guy to pity Ashley, in spite of what had happened to her. He seemed relieved, almost, that she was back at home again.

"Tell me more about your apartment," Carly requested. "You know, from before."

"Why?" Ashley held the book up, almost obscuring her face. "Surely my treasure back then is less interesting than the booty here."

Carly chuckled. "I know, but the book is far away. You're right here. I'm curious to know more about you."

"The book's not that far away," Ashley said. "Come sit on the bed with me and you'll be closer to it."

And closer to you, Carly thought with another belly flip of nerves. "I meant that more figuratively. Characters in books always seem so far away, because the act of reading about them distances them."

"That sounds too smart," Ashley said. "But we're supposed to be reading the book, not analyzing it like an English major."

Carly feigned a laugh, putting her hand to her head. "But I cannot help what I am."

"Maybe," Ashley said, laughing now. "But I still think you should come over here."

Carly raised her eyebrow, trying to figure out how serious Ashley was. When Ashley's gaze didn't waver, Carly swallowed. She placed her purse on the floor and moved toward the bed, as Ashley shifted closer to the wall to allow for more space.

"Ah, much better," Ashley said. "Now, I don't have to project my voice as far."

"You don't have to keep reading," Carly said.

"You'll take over?"

"Well…I can. But I want to hear more about you," Carly said. This close to Ashley, she felt her courage soar. She pushed further. "I know some stuff, but it's all surface details. I'm curious about more."

"You know, I barely know anything about you, either. I thought we respected our differences."

Carly nodded. She held the book in her hand now, and locked eyes with the boy on the cover that was supposed to be Jim Hawkins. She recalled his story, about how his mother had died and really the only thing going for him was sailing ships with criminals.

"My father died when I was pretty young. About nine or so," Carly stated. "Sort of like Jim. I know, at least a little, what it's like to lose a parent."

"Ah. I think that's mostly different for everyone," Ashley said. Her brows creased in her forehead, and she looked away, up at her posters for *Scarface*. Carly could sense something in Ashley's expression, possibly about her mother, but she knew it would be dangerous to push too far.

"I'm sorry," Carly said. "I didn't mean to bring anything up. I was just…"

"It's okay. Really. We all have our issues. My mom, when she was around, was one of mine. I think that's a common thing, though, for most moms and daughters."

"Really?"

"Oh yeah, especially if they're gay."

"Why, do you think?"

Ashley shrugged. "I pretty much spend a lot of my time deliberately *not* thinking about this... But I guess, the fact that a daughter is gay means that suddenly, they are no longer going to follow the same life trajectory. They aren't going to get married and have a baby, at least, in the same way. It presents a sudden difference. That's a lot of disparity to handle, especially when a lot of moms latch onto daughters like they're the fucking Da Vinci code and a missing link to whatever life they thought they could have, but didn't."

Carly had never heard Ashley swear before—at least, not in this way. Carly could see and sense the deep seated issues underneath the surface. *But what does it matter?* Carly's father was exactly the same as Ashley's mother, a parental figure that had disappeared, leaving nothing but illusions and an empty space in their wake. There were a few good memories, a couple bad ones, and a lifetime that she and Ashley could spend trading sob stories. For a moment, Carly understood Ashley's blasé attitude and her jokes. It was a way to cope, a different way to see the world. She deliberately didn't think about her problems. Not because they weren't there, but because everyone had them. They didn't make you special. *Unless you're Jim Hawkins on a pirate ship, your problems don't win you millions. They only cause more.*

"Do you mind?" Ashley asked after a few moments. She pointed to the book. "I think I'm more interested in Jim's issues than my own."

"Yeah," Carly said. "Me too."

Carly continued to read, though her voice was not as animated as Ashley's. After an hour or so, she found herself whispering more and more as she struggled to stay awake. The only clock inside of Ashley's room was behind the bed, and Carly couldn't bring herself to look. She enjoyed how close she and Ashley were, mere inches from one another. The bed was so small and her voice so quiet, they pretty much had to be that close in order to listen. While Carly read, Ashley fidgeted with her hands before she propped them behind her head as a pillow. She even appeared to fall asleep once, herself, and only perked up when Carly stopped reading aloud.

"Hey," she said. "That was a cliffhanger. I want to know more. Don't leave me like this."

"You know, cliffhangers started to be called that because one author actually had someone hanging off the edge of a cliff when he wrote serial fiction, to get people to come back next week."

"Less facts and more story, sweetheart," Ashley joked. She looked at Carly with another wry smile. "I'm kidding. That's actually really neat."

"I'm good for something, even if it's random lit facts."

They were only about another fifty or so pages from the end, now. Carly wanted to slow it down all of a sudden, just to hang onto the book a little longer. She was about to suggest a pause when there was a slam from downstairs.

"What was that?"

"Shit." Ashley sprung to her feet and rushed toward her bedroom window. She swore under her breath again and balled her fingers into a fist. Carly got up from the bed and peered out the same window as Ashley. She watched as a black car from the other side of the street backed up and pulled away.

"That was Darren," Ashley explained, "and now he's gone for the night."

"Oh, that's not a big deal. Is it?" Carly asked. She yawned, in spite of herself. She noticed it was nearly one on the clock. Her eyes went wide just as Ashley laughed.

"Well, it's only a problem if you wanted to get home. Since I can't drive and all…"

"Oh, I can text…Landon, maybe?"

Carly pulled out her phone and realized she had two messages from Landon saying that he was working late that night and a couple more from Cynthia who said that mom had gone to Richard's. Again.

Which means I get to listen to music all night. I guess you're gone too? If so, no biggie. I can eat all the food and walk around naked. Have fun, whatever you're doing, as I'm sure being naked is involved.

"Shit," Carly said. It was too late now to call any of them and wake them up—even if they had been free. "I have...no one to call."

"And I'm not waking my dad up. He will be less than civil."

Carly stayed silent, her limbs paralyzed. "I could call a cab?"

Or walk even, she thought. It couldn't be that far. She had done worse in the past, but she had always walked those long distances during the day. Not in the middle of the night and near the downtown area.

"Why? Is it really that bad being trapped with me?" Ashley grinned, playfully.

"No, not really. But I don't want to be a burden on anyone."

"You're not. Consider it a sign from...whoever is in control of these things."

Carly laughed. Could this have been deliberately set up by Ashley? This could be a test. Did she really want to go home, or would she prefer to be trapped? Did she want the place of comfort or the adventures on the high seas?

"What's wrong? It looks as if you're planning something."

"I don't have any pajamas," Carly said with a smile.

"Oh, well, if that's your only worry..." Ashley walked over to a small dresser and pulled out some gym shorts and another boxy, oversized T-shirt. "Then I've got you covered."

"Okay," Carly said. "Then I guess I'll stay."

"Perfect." Ashley flopped down on her bed again. She picked up the book and noticed how many pages they had left with a raise of her eyebrows. "Not too bad. Now, where were we exactly?"

"You're not too tired to continue?"

"Nah." Ashley held the book this time, like she was going to take over. "If I really wanted to, I could go all night." Ashley nudged Carly's shoulder with a gleeful smile.

"Yeah," Carly said. "Me too."

They began to read again, but Carly didn't hear a single word.

CHAPTER 19

In spite of her boasts, Ashley started to fall asleep while reading, too.

"Okay, I give up." She folded the book on her chest. "I'm done for the night."

"Yeah, same here." Carly suppressed a yawn. With the book now out of the way, she waited, with butterflies in her stomach, for their next move. Ashley only grinned deviously at Carly.

This is it, Carly thought. *She's going to finally kiss me now.*

"I'll take the bedroom," Ashley stated, "if you want the bathroom to change?"

"Oh." Carly tried to hide her disappointment. "Okay, I guess."

"Great. It's just down the hallway to the left. Just by the overflowing laundry hamper. Pay no attention to it."

"Sure." Carly rose from the bed, gathering the gym shorts and T-shirt Ashley had given her earlier. She lingered by the doorway for only a moment before she left. She could hear Mike snoring from his room as she passed by, but soon her thoughts overwhelmed her.

The whole situation still felt a little odd, as if they were having a sleepover in high school rather than… *What, exactly?* They still hadn't even kissed yet. She thought of it several times while they were reading aloud, especially as Ashley's head bobbed so close to her own. But there was never a good moment, never a good time. Even when they did get close, Ashley didn't even try.

You can always kiss her. Carly knew that was a good option. More often than not, she was the person who initiated relationships. She could never stand the awkward silences or the second-guessing. Though most of her attempts had been rebuffed, Carly was always relieved when she made them. If she kissed a woman at a club or study group, and it didn't work out, then she'd most likely never see them again, anyway. No harm done. But Carly knew Ashley now. They worked together. The more she thought about kissing her, the harder it became to act upon because she was too invested. A job, a book club…so many things could be destroyed if they were misread. That thought was terrifying.

Just change, she told herself. *Change into clothing that, hopefully, you can take off again.* She washed her face while she was in the bathroom and did her best to find some type of mint or gum at the bottom of her purse—just in case. When she got back to the room, Ashley was already dressed in long, plaid pants and a black T-shirt.

"Is it okay if I take the aisle seat?" Ashley asked, shifting on the bed.

"Um. Sure. Doesn't really matter to me. I'll take the wall."

The covers had already been peeled back, so all Carly needed to do was slide in and move over. The mesh fabric of the gym shorts felt odd against her legs, and part of her wished she had shaved before work this morning. She moved right to the edge and then waited for Ashley with a hitch in her breath. She came in next, turning her body toward the desk light close by.

"You okay if I turn this off?" she asked.

"Yeah."

"We'll get someone to drive you home tomorrow. Do you have anywhere to be?"

"No," Carly said. "No, not really."

"Then we can sleep in," Ashley said. "I'm not going to set an alarm. After today…I need it."

"Me too." Carly felt the sudden ache in her bones from standing all day, from reading aloud for hours. Each moment of stress seemed to stich itself into her skin. She shifted again under the covers. She waited in the darkness for Ashley to reach out her hand to Carly in comfort. If they were both tired and achy, then they could help ease one another into sleep.

Right? That is why this has happened, Right?

"All right… Well, goodnight," Ashley said after a few moments. She leaned over to her side of the bed again, turning away from Carly.

"Yeah, goodnight."

There was no more response, no more back and forth. No joke or flirtation. That was it for the night.

When she heard Ashley's breathing change, Carly tried to turn toward the wall. Then on her back, so she could make out the window in the dark. *This bed is too damn small for two people—especially if we're not touching. Why aren't we touching?* Carly racked her brain, replaying their conversation and trying to figure out where they had gone wrong. Where she had gone wrong. Why didn't this end the way Landon seemed to think it would? Why didn't she roll onto her side, press their lips together, and make out? Wasn't this the best trope in all of the romantic films she had ever seen? You fall into bed with your crush, after flirting heavily, and you wake up again, together, tangled and euphoric.

But, instead, this day had been long and tiring. That's all it was—that was why they hadn't made out. *Maybe.* As Carly turned over, taking some of the blanket with her, she faced the wall, and she didn't think so. She wanted to text Landon or Cynthia, but her phone was across the room, and Ashley was at the edge of the bed. There was no way out.

So like in other troubled times, Carly began to tell herself stories to help herself sleep, and she began to remember things that she often wished to forget.

Never fall in love with a straight girl. That was the golden rule to Carly as far as relationships went. That was what *The L Word* tried to impart, and that was what *Orange Is the New Black* often echoed with its dramatic and heart wrenching Alex and Piper situation. Never fall for a straight girl. Know better. But it was so hard, Carly knew, when you still did it anyway. When the girl was so beautiful it didn't matter and so perfect that it seemed as if, by will or fate, it would work out, somehow.

When Carly went to school in Boston, she met Brooklyn Fuller. Brooklyn was in Carly's photography class. Really, it was a "media theory class" that talked about the proliferation of images and the way in which culture changes them. They talked a lot about civil rights photography, like the boy with the dog that circulated during the Birmingham riots, along with the work done by

Dorothea Lange during the depression. The professor begged them to explore how an entire world view could be changed with a single image.

Carly had been taking the course for a simple credit. She just needed something else in media studies that was not English based in order to get her degree. She thought the class would be her easy credit that semester, since so much literary theory could often be applied to any media text. But when Brooklyn sat down, Carly knew she was done for. The image of Brooklyn with short, dark hair, purple eye shadow, black nail polish, and wearing a men's tie was pretty much seared into her brain that first class, along with the professor's rant about the image as mythology. Brooklyn's face was sharp, her nose angular. Her skin was pale, her body thin and androgynous. She was just Carly's type—and moreover, she was completely into the course. One of the smartest people in the room. Carly found herself gravitating toward her for extra insight on photography that she probably could have figured out for herself, but always sounded so much better coming out of Brooklyn's mouth.

"Hi," Carly said, after they had suffered through a long and dry lecture on Roland Barthes.

"Hi there." Brooklyn's voice was light, as if they had always been friends, and she smiled that way, too.

"Have you ever seen that documentary by Slavoj Zizek that was mentioned in the essay?"

"No, actually," Brooklyn said. When she raised her eyebrow, Carly noticed a small scar, just above her eyebrow, from an old piercing.

"I have it," Carly said. "I actually haven't seen it either, because I thought it would be boring. You should watch it with me."

It had been the most forceful Carly had ever been with a woman. She was usually used to some vague flirting before she tried to make a move. But there was something about Brooklyn that made her lunge forward, toward it. She wanted to grab it before anyone else did.

"Sure," she said, "that actually sounds great."

They began to see one another, mostly for movies and to proofread papers. Carly didn't even think that Brooklyn was gay when they first met. But Carly found her feelings wandering in that direction, anyway. She just wanted to be her friend if she couldn't be her girlfriend, but even that became a hard endeavor. Her stomach seemed to drop each and every time Brooklyn called out to her, said her name, invited her out for movie night, or sent her an email with a small attachment that said *Thought of you. Like?*

Slowly, their friendship grew closer. Over the summer, when Carly had gone home and found out about Landon's transition, Brooklyn was the first person she told. The two of them worked out Carly's feelings for her new friend, all the while still talking about photography.

Have you ever heard of Loren Cameron? Brooklyn asked over texts.

No, why?

He's a transgender model. Landon may have heard of him. He's a trans man, then got into body building. There's actually a lot of books on transgender photography. I can send you the names or pdf files of some? I learned about it all in my Gender in Popular Culture class. It may be helpful?

Yeah, sure. That would be great.

When Carly woke up the next morning, she had a couple new emails from Brooklyn, all with attachments for e-books. Up until this point, Brooklyn had never seemed to veer one way or the other as far as boys or girls went. But this sharing of incidental queerness began to give Carly hope.

Thank you so much for this, Carly wrote back. *I will spend most of today reading, no doubt.*

She did, too. It was really partly thanks to Brooklyn's informal syllabus on art and transgender issues that Carly came around to Landon so quickly. He had his own reading list for her, too, but by that point, Carly had already grasped as much as she could about transgender people, without really transitioning herself, from Brooklyn's information.

For the rest of that summer, Carly and Brooklyn spoke daily. Even if it was only a small text to say "hi" or "have a good day"—they were never far from one another's minds.

I'm going overseas, Brooklyn wrote one day near the end of summer. *I finally heard back about my application to study in London. Someone backed out last minute, so my waitlist came through! I was accepted. To think, I'll be so close to so much culture. France is pretty much a train ride away, along with Berlin. It's going to go into my final media project.*

Oh. Nice. Congrats! Carly wrote back. She was relieved, so very much, that they were not talking on Skype when they had this conversation. Carly could use many exclamation points or happy faces to disguise her feelings this way. Carly knew words, from all her years of reading. She could control them and temper her response. She was devastated, but also happy for her friend.

We should have a going away party, Brooklyn stated.

Okay, Carly wrote back. *I hate parties, well, people really. But I'll come for you.*

I mean just the two of us. At the café. Sound good?

Carly replied three hours later, so she didn't look too desperate. In the interim, she had gone out to a bookstore to help herself calm down. She wandered down the aisles, just pausing, breathing, and waiting for her heart to stop pounding. When she opened her eyes, she was inside the literature section, near the foreign novels. She picked up two copies of *Anna Karenina*—one for herself, and the other for Brooklyn.

Yes, sure, the café. I will be there. I have something for you, too.

When Brooklyn left for school in London, she took *Anna Karenina* with her.

"Maybe we can read it together," she suggested. "You know. To keep us together."

"That was the plan," Carly told her, trying to even out her words. They hugged good-bye and promised to keep in touch. Carly didn't expect to hear from her aside from small Facebook posts where Carly was tagged.

But when Carly got home, she found an email waiting. Brooklyn confessed her feelings, while still on the plane and flying over the ocean.

I don't know what I'm doing, the first part said. *But I think I'm in love with you.*

Carly had to read the email several times before she was sure she understood what was going on. Brooklyn had liked her, as a friend, for a year now. But only when the prospect of distance was placed between them did she feel as if those feelings of affection were something more.

I think I really am in love with you, Brooklyn wrote again. *In the same way that Anna is in love with Alexei in the book. Thank you, by the way. I read a lot of it on the plane, and I think it helped to clarify my feelings. I think.*

Carly tried not to be afraid of all the "I think"s and "I'm pretty sure"s in the email. If she had Landon read it, or even Cynthia, they would have seen the nervousness in each line. The hesitancy. It was not about being gay or bisexual—Brooklyn's worry wasn't even about the difficulties of being in love with your best friend. Brooklyn was declaring love because she really missed her home. She was viewing Carly the same way she viewed a country, her mother's house, and Boston. She wasn't in love with someone she thought she couldn't have; she was homesick, and the only way she knew how to express it was through declarative acts of love over an email, gifts sent through snail mail, and long conversations over Skype.

To Brooklyn, Carly was Boston. But to Carly, Brooklyn was her first real head-over-heals love. With Brooklyn, Carly finally allowed all of her walls to come down and her feelings to overflow.

After reading the email, there was another three hour gap and a bookstore trip before Carly replied.

Of course, she wrote. *Of course. I love you too.*

They had decided to start dating then, as much as they could, online. Brooklyn was going to be gone for nearly a year, both school semesters, with no chance of coming back home during any of the breaks. Carly had known that going into the relationship, and while it seemed like such a long time without seeing one another, she was okay. Brooklyn was too. She had wanted to make use of her semester abroad and fully appreciate the culture. But each night, just after Carly's dinner and just before Brooklyn went to bed, they talked. They talked until Carly thought she didn't have any more secrets to tell or books to recommend. They both lay out on their beds, reciting books and poems when they thought they had nothing else to say. They watched movies over Skype chat when they became too tired of talking. Then, as the relationship began to cool down, Carly and Brooklyn started to count the days left in London. From about sixty to thirty left, Carly had thought everything was still fine. Then the emails became less urgent, and their conversations online less animated. Even before her plane touched down, Brooklyn pulled away from Carly. But Carly had never given up, not even once. She had figured Brooklyn was saying good-bye to the friends she had met in London or was busy with her final projects. Carly had made a million excuses for Brooklyn's reservation, but once asked why she sometimes looked sad late at night when they talked.

Carly knew then, in the quiet way that people know when something is over, that she should have done more to save it. But she was also very young, and she thought, very much in love. She just wanted to get Brooklyn home again, so she could kiss her for real.

Just one kiss, Carly told herself often at night. *Then I don't care what else happens.*

Carly only told a few people about Brooklyn, mostly her friends at school who also knew her. But she never told her own family. She wanted to wait until Brooklyn was back and they were living together, so everything could be figured out first. At only twenty-one, Carly felt so sure of herself, so proud of her sexuality. But until Brooklyn could be around in person, the relationship was kept inside a box and treated as if it was so fragile that the sheer notion or concept of love itself would break if touched or questioned. Carly wanted it to work with Brooklyn so badly, so she could show her mother what a good person she had really become those years away from home.

When Brooklyn's plane finally landed in Boston, Carly was waiting at the gate. Though the two hugged almost instantly, Carly could tell how tired Brooklyn was. She was practically weak.

"Are you okay?" Carly whispered in her ear.

"Just jetlag," she said, trying to smile and avoid Carly's sharp gaze. "Just let me catch up on about a million hours of sleep, and I'll be okay again."

"I hope it's not as much as a million."

"No. But you never know."

They had parted ways in the airport with another quick hug. While Brooklyn slept in her old one-bedroom place, Carly crashed with her laptop and phone in her bed, just in case she called.

But the relationship was already done. When Carly finally got Brooklyn on Skype again, their once sweet words suddenly turned accusatory.

"I feel like you're avoiding me," Carly started.

Brooklyn sighed. "I only want space. Why can't you give me space?"

"I haven't seen you in a year," Carly argued.

"You're not the only one. I'm just trying to catch up... I spent a lot of time with you online, Carly. I just need to step away."

Suddenly, Brooklyn began to backtrack her initial feelings, casting doubt on her declarative "I love you"s and chaste kisses they had once shared on Skype.

"I was upset," Brooklyn said, her eyes downcast. "You were a good friend."

"I thought I was more than that," Carly said. She shook her head. "I can't *believe* this. You make me pine for you for over a year, you tell me you love me—"

"I didn't make you do anything."

"But you said you loved me. I thought we were more than just friends."

"You were, for a time. But now, I don't think I feel that way. I don't think I'm gay."

"You don't have to be gay. You could be bisexual."

She made a face, as if that was worse. She ran her hands through her hair, trying to flatten the frizzy bits over her ear. "I just think I was wrong."

"About me? So, you never loved me?"

"I did, it's just…not like that."

"You say that as if it's a bad thing."

"It's a bad thing if only one person feels it."

Carly huffed. She couldn't believe this was happening. She couldn't believe after the care and time she had taken, that this was what was happening. After nearly a year of waiting, it was all for nothing. They hadn't even kissed, for fuck's sake. Carly had been so hurt by that fact more than any other. She and Brooklyn fought in the following weeks.

"You shouldn't have led me on."

"You shouldn't think I owed you something. I don't."

"Of course you don't," Carly said. "But you said you loved me. And then you disappeared."

"I love all my friends."

"You never said it like that."

Brooklyn rolled her eyes again. Those blue eyes captivated Carly, along with her dark, pixie cut hair.

My God, Carly realized then. She felt her guilt and anger become one inside her body as they fought. Brooklyn really was the manic, pixie, dream girl. Everyone's perfect dream, everyone's wonderful cause. And Carly had fallen for it.

Carly stopped fighting with Brooklyn then. She knew it wasn't her fault—it was no one's fault, really. People were allowed to change their minds. People were allowed to feel hurt about it. But it didn't make sense to continue to fight over Skype or continue to feel anger well up inside of her anytime they passed across campus. After another short visit to a bookstore, Carly had bought some Vonnegut so she could laugh at the world again. She deleted Brooklyn from Skype, but still kept her on her phone. She tried to cut her losses and move on.

But it was never that simple. Carly soon realized there were so many places you can spot one another in the same campus. So many places that you can always run into one another, sharing coffee with another date. A different friend, another guy. Carly kept running into Brooklyn during her final year, until she finally stopped going to classes. She bombed that last year, because she couldn't stand to see the girl she had waited for and who still had not yet come home.

Carly's grades were so poor that last year, but still good enough to graduate. And she comforted herself with the fact that it never actually said on the diploma that *Carly Rogers was a perfect student until the end. Man, what a fuck up.* It was just a piece of paper that said she had graduated, something to frame and stare at later.

But even when her mother took her out for a nice dinner when she graduated, Carly couldn't get excited. Boston felt as if it never happened. In a lot of ways, she still felt as if she was twenty-one. She had spent so much time waiting, reading long Russian novels, ones that have a fifty-page description of someone sleeping, that it felt like no time had passed at all. The degree was never hung up and instead sat under a pile of boxes. She had no real job to show from the degree, no real relationships, and no real money. She lived at home with her mother, in her room, ate her food, and worked shitty jobs. The only good things in Carly's life were Landon and Cynthia—and even they seemed to have more shit figured out than she did.

"Never fall in love with a straight girl," Landon told her when she had finally dared to mention Brooklyn. Landon had shaken his head, looking critical. "Come on. I thought you already knew that?"

Carly thought of the advice now, years later and in bed with the girl she had fallen for so hard already. But Ashley wasn't straight, and because of that, Carly worried that her subtle rejection tonight had hurt her more than Brooklyn's before. Carly knew that she was wrong there, too. This pain was more than just being gay or straight.

Never fall in love with an image, she told herself. That was where the first problem always started. That was where the first myth always began.

Carly turned over in bed and did her best to fall asleep.

CHAPTER 20

"Fuck this," Carly said. She shifted on the concrete slab under the bridge, turning to Landon who sat on the bench. Carly stood, her arms akimbo. "I can't take this anymore. I hate living at home."

"You have to do something else, though," Landon said. "You can't just sit there and complain. Or…stand and stare at me aggressively."

"Ugh, I know. I'm sorry—this is not about you. But what exactly do I do? Move to Paris? Go to school again?" Carly asked, her hands in the air. "All of that takes money. Money I don't have. I'm knee deep in people's underwear and clothes hangers and receipts working at Marshalls. I don't have the wherewithal to pack up my stuff and leave. I want to, but I can't."

"What is this really about? I mean, I understand that's a shitty predicament, but I have a feeling there is more depth to the issue."

"Maybe. Maybe not."

As Landon raised one of his eyebrows, Carly just sighed.

Carly had called him about an hour ago, begging to go out, claiming that she was just *so bored*. Landon was skeptical, since Carly almost never got bored. Being an only child for the first ten years of her life meant that she got really good at keeping herself amused. She learned to build whole imaginary worlds in her mind and then read about other ones when she couldn't fill up the time herself.

About halfway through Sunday afternoon, Carly realized that books weren't going to cut it anymore. Her thoughts were already going a mile a minute. She could barely sit still without her mind replaying every last detail from spending the night with Ashley. Carly had tried to shrug off the fact that nothing happened. She could handle just being friends, right? But when she went into work and checked the next schedule, she realized that they would not have a shift together until another week or so.

As much as Carly was relieved that she wouldn't have to confront the terrible, confusing feelings inside of her, she was nervous. What if their friendship petered out in that time? Would there be an excuse to text one another without a job acting as an anchor? Carly tried to pass the time by talking to Cynthia and listening to way too much music from high school. Now she turned to Landon for comfort, only to complain about her mother instead of what really bugged her.

"I just don't want my mom to marry Richard," Carly said. "That's all. She's been at his place for the past week and it gets on my nerves."

"Why? You said he wasn't too bad."

"He's fine… I think he even wants to get married. He seems way too eager to please all of us, so that usually means he's on good behavior, which usually means men are thinking about marriage."

Landon laughed.

"Most men born before 1980, anyway," Carly corrected. "You know what I mean. I've just seen this pattern repeated so many times before. I don't want to deal with it again."

"Is being eager to please really a bad thing, though? Doesn't that show good social skills?"

"You're missing the point, Landon."

"Am I?" he asked, cocking another eyebrow. "I don't think you have a point. You're jumpy and weird. You've been weird since the opening day."

"Shut up. I haven't."

Landon nodded, his lips pressed together. "That confirms it, then. This isn't about Richard, as much as your concerns there seem valid on the surface. This is about opening day. Something at work."

Carly crossed her arms over her chest. She was quiet a long time. "*No.*"

"*Yes.* You sound like a kid sometimes. I almost forget I'm older than you."

"Barely," Carly said with a scoff. "By what, two months?"

"It matters, Carly. I have always been the more mature one." Landon touched his hand to his chin, stroking whatever small bits of hair he had there. He tilted his head to the other side as a thought caught him off guard. "Wait.

Does the fact that I've only been Landon for five years change anything? Am I really a preschooler, then?"

"Yes," Carly said, laughing. "Yes, that means I am older than you, Landon Harold Wilson."

"Oh, you broke out the Harold on me. This must be bad."

Carly chuckled. She remembered when Landon chose that middle name. Landon had been easy; he had kept it in the back of his mind ever since he first heard it. As much as there was a cliché with changing the birth name to the similar sounding masculine name (like Steven to Stephanie or Michelle to Michael), he had figured that Landon was different enough from Lisa to suffice. His mom also didn't have to get rid of all the things with L on it or her kids' initials. But middle names were hard and involved more thought. He had racked his brain for weeks before he opened up an old name book and then picked the first thing he saw. It also helped, Carly figured, that somewhere in Landon's family tree there was also a Harold.

"So you really should be worried then," Landon continued. "If I'm only five and more mature than you. Come on. What's bugging you? This is basic psychology 101 stuff. You're lashing out, projecting. I think Freud said something like jokes hide our true pathologies."

"And Freud has been discredited by most psychologists."

"Yeah. He may have been wrong about Oedipus, but where there is smoke, there is fire. I'm not saying that your mom isn't an issue, but that's something for another session. It's way beyond my pay grade. But this—whatever it is now—I'm sure I can handle. So tell me. What is The Issue of the Day?"

"Ashley," Carly confessed after a few moments. "I slept over at her place after the opening."

Landon leaned forward on his legs, his green eyes wide. "Did you get into her pants?"

"More or less, but I mean that literally," Carly said.

"What now?"

"We got stuck there after her brother left and her dad went to bed. So she told me to stay the night and gave me her pajamas to wear."

"That's a lot less sexy than I thought."

"I know, right? I mean, I could buy that her brother just forgot about us. That it was an accident. But we just slept in the same bed. And still—nothing happened."

"Nothing? I thought she was mega-hard-core flirting with you."

"I thought so too. But maybe the whole book club thing really was just that. A book club so we don't lose our minds at work."

"Have you ever seen a romantic comedy?" Landon asked, shaking his head.

"Have *you*?"

Landon laughed and then folded his hands across his chest. "Fair enough, but you have to know *The Jane Austen Book Club*, right? Doesn't your mom always have that on when she's cooking?"

"Yes, thereabouts. There's usually a glass of wine involved too."

"Well, that movie is about a book club—and it's a romance."

"There are lesbians too."

"See? Basically, a book club is a more sophisticated form of sending texts with your junk attached. It's a different version of I'll show you mine if you show me yours. Tastes, that is. She wants to know more about you, so she's recommending books to you."

Carly sat down on the bench next to Landon. "She calls me Carly Rogers."

"What?"

"Carly Rogers, my full name. Every time she sees me, it's hello Carly Rogers. How are you Carly Rogers?"

Landon raised his brow.

"I know, it's odd. But she said it was because my name reminded her of Jolly Roger. Like pirates. So we went to the bookstore and got *Treasure Island* to read together. We laid out on her bed and read it to one another, out loud. We pretty much fell asleep while doing it too, leaning in, our lips ever so close... But nothing came of it, and now I'm here."

"What do you call her?" Landon asked.

"Her full name too. Ashley Poindexter."

Landon chuckled. "Oh, no. You're in too deep."

"Yeah, I know. But it's become a pet name. I thought we were flirting. We also had a literary couple equivalent."

"A what now?"

"It's silly when I say it now, but you know *Waiting for Godot*?" Carly moved on when Landon didn't nod. She knew she had mentioned this play a least a dozen times around him, but sometimes her references were hard to place. She understood that. "So it's this play about two people who wait for Godot, but Godot never comes. We joked about it on our first day, because our shipment truck never came in. Or at least, I did, and she knew what I was talking about."

"Just because she gets your reference doesn't mean she's into you, but I will say that no one uses full names like that without flirting."

Carly sighed. "So I'm getting some pretty mixed signals, then. I don't know what happened. She didn't say or do anything. She knows I'm gay, and I know she's gay. We talked about it when we went on that first date, if it was a date."

Landon was quiet as he considered Carly's position for a few moments. "You said she was sick, right?"

"Well, not really. She has a condition, or maybe just stray seizures? She doesn't like to talk about it, so I don't push it. No one really knows what's wrong with her, but that's why she's living at home. She had to get her license taken away, because she kept having seizures no one could figure out. She lost her other job. It's only been within the last year that she's been strong enough to go and do work."

"And even then, it's at Marshalls, and it's part-time."

"Yes," Carly said. "What do you mean?"

Landon eyed Carly, as if it was obvious. "She doesn't want to feel broken."

"But she's not. I don't think she is."

"Doesn't matter. She's had enough people tell her that something is wrong with her, and she doesn't want to get anyone close involved."

"Then why flirt with me?"

"Flirting is harmless. The heart wants what it wants…" Landon sighed as he trailed away for a few moments. "I flirt all the time, but when was the last time you saw me take a girl home?"

Carly was quiet. She had always figured that Landon didn't always want to share his dating life, whether or not that was because it was too difficult explaining the whole transgender thing to people, Carly didn't ask. She figured it wasn't easy, per se, but there were so many online alternatives like OkCupid where Landon could be himself and have the awkward conversation, before he went out with someone.

But that's the thing, Carly reminded herself. She was always thinking of the transgender stuff as an awkward conversation to have. As something to explain to another party. Carly knew Landon was who he was, and he shouldn't have to explain it to anyone, but that wasn't how the world often worked. There would always be questions, always hospital visits, and medical tests that had made Landon feel like shit for most of his adult life. Even though he was fine with himself, and most other people around him were, there were still flare-ups of doubt. And that doubt had led enough people away from Landon. There had been no news on the dating front, not because Landon wanted to stay private, but because there was nothing there.

"Well, you're also asexual," Carly said. "I thought not dating came with the territory?"

"Not necessarily. Just because I'm ace doesn't mean I'm not a romantic. I don't want to have a lot of sex. But cuddling? Yes, I definitely want that. If I take someone home, we're watching a movie and touching. But not fucking. Honestly, your date with her sounds perfect. It's something I would want."

"Could she be asexual?"

"Possibly—but probably not. It's relatively rare. And if you've already had the "I'm gay" conversation, then she probably would have also told you she was asexual, too. Either way, I think she likes you, but she hasn't done anything because she is afraid. Her actions speak to fear more than abstract preference."

"Hmm. I'm sorry. I should have considered that—and you—more. I just…"

"No," Landon said, holding out a hand. "That is exactly it. Don't feel sorry for me."

"What?"

"Don't feel sorry for me. That's half the shit I deal with right now. Everyone is either angry I'm trans or sorry I'm trans. That's not the case."

"I'm…uh… I don't know what to say."

"You're fine, Car. I know you are. But do you see what I mean? I get these looks all the time. Even when I'm not afraid for my life or safety, I'm made into a pity party."

Landon sighed again, while Carly stayed silent. Carly sometimes felt as if she was doing this whole lesbian thing wrong. That she had missed an important seminar on dating and spent too much time pining after a straight girl that she messed up her entire queer cred. Landon was a saint, as far as Carly was concerned, for dealing with her—even after all the shit the both of them had been through, and for Carly's mom.

"Ashley's most likely been made to feel inferior through doctors. She lost her license. She lost her car and her ability to live alone, Carly. She wants what she wants, and I do think that she does want you. But when she goes to grab it, she stops herself. She can't see anyone wanting her in the state she's in."

"But I do. I really do want her," Carly said. The emotion gripped her voice, surprising her. She leaned forward on her legs, her tight jeans and T-shirt feeling too thin in a sudden gust of wind.

"You want her now," Landon said. "She's worried you won't when she's sick."

"It's been over a year since her last seizure. That was why she can work."

"And she's always waiting for the next one. She's anticipating it. She wants to know that you'll still want her when it happens."

"I will," Carly said, but her voice shook again.

When Carly had fallen for other people, especially Brooklyn, she had assumed that she would always want them. Sickness and in health, she reminded herself, wasn't that the point of commitment? Carly didn't just fall for the good parts of people. When she fell for someone, Carly wanted them so completely, so fully, that sometimes Carly was afraid by her own emotions. She couldn't imagine not wanting Ashley in the same way.

But her voice shook when that motive was cross-examined. With all her other relationships, health had been obvious, unspoken. Now it needed to be discussed. It needed to be planned for, and other people needed to be involved. Hell, both of them needed to call someone else in order to drive them places because of their health. This was something different than Carly had dealt with before, and Landon's scrutiny made her question her motives. But only long enough to make her reconsider—and still come up with the same response. She took a deep breath.

"No, Landon, no. I want her. I'm afraid, but I'm always afraid of shit like this. It's why I didn't kiss her last night."

"Do you need her?" Landon asked. "Want her?"

"Yes, of course."

"Then go tell her. I think. If I'm as good as an observer as I like to think myself to be, then she will want to hear it. Anyone wants to hear it, really."

"But it depends on whether or not she'll act?" Carly asked, biting the nail on her pinkie finger.

"Yeah, yeah. That is always the risk, right? She may still say no, even if she's really flattered. But really, Carly, how bad can it be to tell someone your feelings? That you think they're awesome and would like to do more things with them, especially naked things. It's the feeling that matters, Carly, and you should tell her."

"Okay, yes," Carly said, feeling her conviction grow. "Thanks, Landon."

"No problem." He sighed as he rose to his feet, extending his hand to Carly to lift her up. "Should I drive you to her place now?"

"In just a minute, okay?"

Landon nodded, but he was caught off guard when Carly threw her arms around him in a large hug.

"Thank you, Lando. You're a wonderful man, a better person, and I don't know where I'd be without you. No matter what anyone ever says, I love you. Okay? I always, always will."

Landon's arms stayed at his sides for some time. His breathed in and out, slowly, as if he was trying to calm down. Then, Carly felt him place his chin over the crown of her head. His arms moved around her shoulders, then up and down her back. They hugged like they used to do when they were kids.

"Thanks, Car," he said. "Now, enough sentimental crap. Let's go."

CHAPTER 21

Landon dropped Carly off at Ashley's house fifteen minutes later.

"Call or text me whenever you need a ride back," Landon said when he pulled into the driveway. Carly could see Pizza jump up at the screen door, barking at the unknown car. "Or, if everything goes well, and you don't need a ride back, still text me, okay, Car?"

"Okay. Thanks again."

Carly closed the door slowly and took a few steps back. Landon gave her a small wave before he drove off.

She wondered, vaguely, if she should have texted Ashley before coming here. She knew Ashley didn't have to work, but it was a pretty big risk to just assume she was homebound. Pizza's presence near the open door signaled that someone was home, and without looking in the garage, Carly couldn't be sure if Mike's car was there or not.

Pizza growled as Carly took the steps, but he calmed down as soon as Darren appeared close by. Carly waved to him, and he nodded, holding the dog back as he tried to take another running start. Carly was about to open her mouth to ask if Ashley was home when Darren pointed to the left.

"She's in the garage," he stated, pointing again. Pizza barked, as if to confirm.

"Oh. Okay. Thanks. Should I just...?" Carly turned to the side, noticing a small sliver of light from underneath the slightly askew garage door. She wasn't quite sure how to enter the garage, so she knocked on the metal siding.

"Hey, hey?" Carly heard Ashley's voice. There was some shuffling before the garage door was pushed open, and Ashley emerged in the space. She wore gray work pants with holes and paint marks down one side, and a large oversized shirt from a jujitsu class that probably belonged to Darren. As soon as Ashley realized it was Carly, she smiled and folded her arms in front of her chest.

"Well, well. Good afternoon Carly Rogers." Ashley motioned with her hand for Carly to step inside. "To what do I owe this surprise?"

Carly walked a few tentative paces inside. On one bench, models were set up. At first Carly thought they were tiny toy soldiers, but as she got closer, she began to realize that underneath the half-painted armor were unearthly creatures. Like something from a Tolkien novel, only outside of Carly's grasp. Ashley sat back down on a wooden bench with a cushion glued to the top. She leaned forward on her knees, her eyes attentive, before she picked up a model again.

"Don't mind me." Ashley picked up a paintbrush in her other hand, and dabbed the brush in her mouth before putting paint on it. "Do you mind if I continue, before you fill me in?"

"Not at all. What are you doing, though?" Carly asked. "I don't think I've ever seen anything like this before."

"No doubt. It's not exactly an easy hobby to trek around. Especially to Marshalls. Though I did consider bringing my mobile paint with me to work one day, just to have something to do during breaks. But I guess that's what books are for."

Ashley motioned toward a small white table that reminded Carly of a craft table for kids. There were tiny bottles of paints in small, cutout holes, along with a few tools like pliers and metal tools.

"Is that why you're here?" Ashley asked.

"Hmm"

"Are you here to have a meeting of our book club? I have to say, I forgot *Treasure Island* inside, so it will be…"

"No. No. I came on my own. I wanted to see you."

"Ah." Ashley continued to add gold highlights to the uniform on the small model.

"But you never answered my question," Carly stated, feeling playful—yet still very evasive and scared. "What is all of this?"

Ashley motioned with her chin toward a lawn chair. Carly sat down, her eyes not moving far from the display in front of her.

"This is something called *Warmachine*. It's pretty much what it looks like, toy soldiers on a chessboard. I buy these little kits from the store, which is really just a bunch of tiny pewter pieces. Then I sit out here and put them together and start painting. Eventually, I play games with them, but really this is the best part. I like building."

"I can see that..."

Inside the cramped garage, the small piles of metal took on new form. She saw pieces of arms and legs, swords, and wolves, that all needed to be pieced together. She grew quiet as Ashley continued to speak.

"I did this a lot when I got sick—especially painting. Darren used to give me his old models that he had already based to paint, since he had a job and couldn't always finish the fine detail work. It also gave me something to do, which I desperately needed—outside of my Fabio fascination. Obviously."

"Obviously," Carly repeated with a smile.

"I tried to play a few games too, since I thought it was only fair, once I learned what was going on. The games were often far away, though, and Darren didn't always go. So, I read the game books, the world building ones, and then finally the novels. Darren and Alex both brought me all the books they read in high school, including a dozen or so Halo or *Warmachine* kind. Sometimes, I play games with the two of them, but our dad hates it when we do."

"Why?"

"Because, we fight over this more than anything else," Ashley said. "Well, maybe video games. But video game rage is never really at your brother and sister, more like their avatar."

"They seem nice, though."

"Oh yeah, they are. Gaming just changes people." Ashley leaned in, painting fine detail on the sword of a fighter. "Do you want to see?"

"Yes," Carly said. Ashley passed her a small model.

"This is really neat. I have no idea how to play chess, let alone something like this. But it's neat. Very...consuming."

"Yes, in a way," Ashley said. She put down her paintbrush and folded her arms over her work clothes. "Did you just tell me you can't play chess?"

Carly blushed. "Maybe."

"Oh no. We cannot have that."

"It's not my fault," Carly argued. "I was an only child until I was ten, and my mother hated games. I learned to amuse myself by myself."

"Through reading books?"

"More or less. I also wrote poems for a while. Drew pictures. Went on walks. Not really a game person."

"What a sensitive child you must have been," Ashley teased.

Carly huffed. She picked up another model that she took to be a villain with big goggles and zany hair. Ashley had painted the outfit purple and gold, with red on the goggles and in the barrettes of the woman's hair.

"I'll teach you," Ashley said, after a moment's consideration. "Chess, anyway. And if you like that, then it couldn't hurt to have another person here playing armies with me. Especially when Darren runs away like Alex and gets married."

Carly put down the figure. "I'd like that."

"Really?"

"Yeah? I mean, why not? It would give me something to do at break in work."

"But only with me," Ashley said with a wry smile. "Only I can be your chess buddy."

"And book club buddy."

Ashley leaned back in her chair, balancing her foot on the edge of the work table. She kicked the chair back on two legs, leaning so precariously Carly was worried she'd fall over.

"So what brings you here? I don't think you answered that. I answered your question about the models, and surely you have learned a lot. Now, enlighten me."

Carly shifted in her seat. She wished her purse was close by for something to hold and fidget with.

"I wanted to talk to you."

"All good conversations start that way," Ashley joked. She dropped the chair back down to all four legs, making a loud thudding sound and kicking up some dirt and metal shavings. "Go on."

"I wanted to talk about a few nights ago."

"What about it?"

"I wanted to know…why we didn't do anything."

Ashley was silent.

"I mean… I should start again. I just think I'm getting some mixed signals. I thought we were into one another. I thought we have been going on dates. But maybe I've been misunderstood?" Though Carly asked the last part like a question, she could not raise her eyes from the garage floor to see Ashley's response. "I could definitely have missed a mark there. I tend to live in my head a lot, so maybe I just built up something that wasn't there. I just want to make sure we're on the same page, before I get my hopes up again. Make sense?"

When she braved a look at Ashley, Carly was surprised to find her just as contemplative as she felt. Her hands rested over her chest, folded. She fidgeted briefly with her thumb and index finger, as she looked around her garage, at her models, and then at Carly.

"I come out here because this is my space. Alone. I don't have to answer to anyone."

"I get that," Carly said, indulging in Ashley's sudden digression. "We all need a place like that."

"But I'm never really alone here. The garage is always half-open on their insistence, and Darren or Alex or my dad are almost always here. If they're too far into the house or not around, then they usually send Pizza to come in and sit with me. I love that dog, but I always worry he'll screw things up here."

"Always?" Carly asked. "They're always around?"

Ashley nodded, eyes wide. "If I were to tell them this, they'd deny it. Just say they wanted to be at home. But I know. I know it's because of me. They want to make sure I don't hurt myself, and if I do, that someone else is around."

"I see." Normally, Carly would have said something like "that's nice" but she could tell from the way Ashley's face twisted that a simple platitude or compliment would not go far to describe the complexity of the situation.

"I love my family. I would be nowhere without them, and I'm eternally grateful. But it's all *overwhelming*. It's so overwhelming, and sometimes I just want space to myself."

"I get it. I really do," Carly said. "And I'm sorry. Do you want me to leave you be?"

"No." Ashley leaned against her legs, propping herself up with her elbows now. "No, that's the thing. I definitely do not want you to leave me alone."

"Good," Carly said after a moment. "I like that idea."

Ashley's face soon fell. "It's just hard sometimes to be around someone like you. After I got sick, I was with a lot of women. I made sure never to tell them what had happened. Most of them just thought I was a freeloader from living the way I was, not that I was sick. But that was worse, you know? Eventually, they would notice that they were almost always being watched, to a certain degree, when they were with me. There was this weird miasma that followed us—that followed me. And the relationships never lasted long after that. I got used to flings and not something permanent. I got used to living in the garage, almost like a secret."

Carly nodded. She watched as Ashley picked up one of her models and began to twirl it in her hand. She spoke about it in a fluid and elegant voice.

"This is Connie. Well, her full name in the game is Constance Blaize, knight of the prophet. She's part of the Cygnar faction in the *Warmachine* armies. I'm utterly convinced that if there were to ever be a movie of this game, Gillian Anderson would play her. She would have such a great face and voice for it. Sorry," Ashley apologized suddenly and placed it back down. "I talk about them when I don't know what else to say. When I feel as if I'm taking my sob story too seriously, and I want to break away."

"It's okay," Carly said. "I get it. I know I've been saying that a lot...but I do. I may not be able to relate entirely, but I'm good at looking at things from others points of view. It's kind of the point of reading, right?"

Ashley raised her eyebrows a bit, skeptically. Carly leaned forward again, determined to not be written off.

"I like you," she said. "I do. A lot."

"I like you too, Carly. It's hard not to."

"Then why can't we do something about it?"

"We work together, for one."

"Usually on different shifts. Different departments. I'm on cash for the next month, and they've been putting you in shoes."

"That's true," Ashley said. "But still. I don't want to hurt you."

"You won't."

"I will."

"No, well, even if you did, I understand. I don't care."

"You will care," Ashley said. She took another breath, as if trying to calm herself. Carly had gotten so used to seeing Ashley composed or jovial; watching her struggle to control herself—and the topic—took Carly by surprise.

Ashley picked up another model. A smaller one this time, one that looked like a steampunk version of R2-D2.

"This is a pawn," she declared, holding him between her thumb and finger. "You have to be aware of losing some pawns when you play this game. I'm aware that in my life there are a lot of battles I just cannot win. I accept the surveillance. I accept feeling sick. I even accept living at home and taking a shitty job."

"But," Carly said. "But?"

"Love and dating, sex and whatever, they're harder. I can't always plan for that. It's too difficult. It's like taking a risk and losing a king. Sorry about the chess metaphor, but—"

"No, I get it. But you can't go on in life without being hurt," Carly said. "Without being upset. If Cyn has taught me anything from Roller Derbies, it's that you're going to scrape a few elbows and maybe even break a few bones. But do you stop playing the game? Hell no."

Ashley laughed. "Cyn is a smart kid."

"You should see her skate."

"I'd like to, actually. More girls need to do stuff like that."

"I agree. I'm really proud to be her older sister. Sometimes I worry what the hell I could really do, because I'm such a general fuck up, and she seems to always have her shit together."

"You're not a fuck up."

"You don't know that for sure." Carly leaned in closer, trying to get Ashley to see the parallels between their two plights. "I may be the worst fuck up ever, but I hide it well. You may be the biggest fuck up ever, too."

"Except, I don't hide it that well."

"I don't know about that. This garage cave thing you have is a pretty nice hideout. But my basic point still remains the same. We could both be fuck ups. Huge, astronomical fuck ups, but I don't think that matters. We will fuck up together, then."

Ashley smiled. Her eyes still stayed on the ground or fixated on her models, but Carly could tell she was getting somewhere.

"I want you, Ashley. I want to try something. I don't care what happens. Well, I do care a little bit. But I care only insomuch as I hope we will both be there."

"Oh, how noble of you. Are you sure you haven't read too many romance novels?" Ashley asked, her breath sharp.

Carly didn't say anything in response, but she watched Ashley carefully. She went to reach into the pile of her models again, but instead held her hand out. She made a small come here motion with her fingers until Carly got the message. She extended her hand, so they both linked across the table.

"I don't want just sex," Ashley said, as she traced a finger over Carly's skin. "I did that so often and it's just not worth it. One night stands only work for so long."

"I never really did one night stands. I always pined from afar."

"Oh, there's a story there." Ashley raised her eyebrows, a comical grin on her face. Carly blushed as thoughts of Brooklyn came back. She looked away.

"Never mind," Ashley said. "I'm sure you'll tell me that one later."

"I will. I want to."

Ashley nodded. Her strong, sharp cheekbones seemed more delicate now, under the garage light. Carly squeezed her hand, liking how the long fingers gripped hers. Ashley was into this, Carly knew, but there were still roadblocks. There would always be something like that, even if they weren't working together and there wasn't this strange illness between them. There would still be their midtwenties and all the drama that came from that. *Really*, Carly thought, *I would kill for the normal high school-like drama. Maybe.*

"When do you work next?" Ashley asked suddenly.

Carly closed her eyes, dreading the answer. "Ugh, Seven thirty tomorrow morning. I almost forgot."

"I come in at eight," Ashley said.

"Really? I thought you didn't work until Wednesday?"

Ashley gave Carly a small look. "Stalking me?"

"Merely wondering when was the best day to have this conversation," Carly said.

Ashley squeezed her hand again. "Suzanne called me yesterday and asked me to take someone's shift. I was all over it. But you're still on cash, so you're the early bird."

"Yes, but you'll be there tomorrow. So my day has already gotten better," Carly said. The cheesy statement made part of Carly cringe, but another part of her delight in it. She liked this feeling of new love—or even just the small butterflies of lust. She wanted to keep it as long as possible, and to tell Ashley how much she liked it.

Instead, all Carly did was squeeze her hand and feel Ashley squeeze back.

"Stay," Ashley declared.

"What?"

"Stay with me again," Ashley said. She rubbed her thumb over the soft places in Carly's hand as she squeezed her fingers tighter. "Darren can give us a ride in the morning."

"You'll come in early?"

"It will be a small sacrifice," Ashley said with another smile. "But stay with me tonight. Have dinner with me."

"And?"

"And we'll talk. We'll talk and get things figured out. We'll go…slow, okay? I don't want to say yes to anything yet."

"Sure," Carly said. Her heart hammered.

"Really?"

"Yes, of course. I'll stay and go slow and whatever. "I'll even let you teach me chess if you want."

Ashley laughed heartily and leaned back. "Oh, in that case, Carly Rogers. You have got yourself a deal."

CHAPTER 22

Ashley pulled out a couple more slices of pizza from her family's overcrowded fridge.

"I apologize," she said, sniffing one of the slices. "I swear these are completely fine, but you can never be too careful with my family."

"I don't mind, really."

Things moved slowly from there on out. They ate together, vaguely watching a movie that Darren had on in the living room from their spots in the kitchen. Mike, Ashley's father, came back from a business meeting and said hi before grabbing some leftovers, after a quick-witted exchange with his daughter. Then he was gone, and Darren fell asleep with the movie's credits running, and Carly and Ashley were alone again.

"How about chess?" Ashley asked.

Carly could only say yes. Ashley set up a board that looked as if it had been around for a couple decades. The paint was chipped on the corners, and one of the pawns had been replaced with a cheaper, plastic model. Carly nodded as Ashley explained the rules, but it didn't do much. Chess was a game of strategy, and Carly's brain felt like swiss cheese. She knew she looked utterly pitiful, as Ashley won each round but didn't boast or brag. It took Carly a long time, about their fifth game, to realize that as Carly plotted out her next move, Ashley kept staring at her.

"You go," Carly said once, when Ashley had seemed much more distracted than usual. Ashley nodded, but still kept her eyes on Carly.

"It's getting pretty late," she said. "How about we call this one your game?"

Carly wanted to argue that it wouldn't be fair. But she slid her piece next to Ashley's queen, and smiled.

"Sure."

When the game was put away again, Ashley headed toward the stairs, and Carly followed easily. Darren caught them just before they went inside her bedroom.

"Ash?" he called from the kitchen. "Does anyone need a ride?"

"Nope. Thank you," Ashley called back down to him. It took Carly another moment again to realize Ashley didn't joke with him. She was nervous, too.

"So, uh, again, you don't have pajamas," Ashley stated once they were inside. She hadn't bothered to hide any mess this time around. Carly noted a plate with crumbs on it, on top of the bookshelf, and a few socks and T-shirts on the ground. Ashley picked up her gym shorts and another T-shirt from the bottom drawer.

"They've been cleaned, but are these okay again?"

Carly nodded, now mute. She spotted the basket chair in the corner and had to fight the urge to sit there, out of the way. She tossed her purse on it.

"We have a couple more pages of *Treasure Island*," Ashley remarked. "What do you say to reading?"

"I'd like to savor it, I think," Carly said.

"You do that a lot, don't you?"

"Savor things?"

"Avoid them."

"Maybe."

Ashley laughed. When she sat on her bed, she patted the place next to her. Carly sat down and felt the inches between them disappear. Ashley's hand linked in hers again. Their lips were so close to one another, so close that Carly could almost feel Ashley's breath.

"I should call Cyn," Carly said, suddenly turning away. She reached down toward the basket chair where her purse lay. "I at least need to tell Landon where I am."

"Okay. Sure," Ashley said, letting go of her hand. She placed her palm on the small of Carly's back, rubbing in small circles as Carly texted them both.

"Better?" Ashley asked when the messages were sent.

"Yes. But I still need to wait for their responses."

"Ah. Well, that makes sense."

"I'm sorry. I know it's neurotic."

"No worries. Trust me. I said I wanted to go slow, so, here we are. Taking forever. But at least we're good to our words." Ashley folded her arms behind her head and laid down on her bed.

"Ugh." Carly closed her eyes, then ran a hand through her dark hair. "I'm terrible at this."

"No. You're just nervous, whereas I'm careful. It's a small difference, but don't worry. I still think you're cute."

"Well, that's…" Carly's phone buzzed. She looked down and saw Landon's name appear.

Good! So glad. Now get what you want!

Jillian texted her next, making Carly's sudden smile disappear.

Well, so long as you don't lose your job. Get there on time.

Carly sighed. She folded her phone back in her purse, not wanting to see anymore.

"Now that everyone is safe," Ashley began, "how about you join me here?"

Carly lay next to Ashley on the bed, careful to leave at least an inch between their torsos. Ashley was bolder, and slipped her hand around the nape of Carly's neck and ran fingers through her hair.

"This used to relax me when I had long hair," Ashley explained as she combed her fingers through the strands. "Does it help with you?"

Carly closed her eyes. She took a deep breath in. "Yeah."

"Good." Ashley kept her hands in Carly's hair as her body inched closer. Carly's body flushed with arousal and anticipation. *All I ever wanted from Brooklyn was a kiss.* Now, as Ashley's hands moved from Carly's hair to her chin, pulling her face close to hers, Carly knew that her wait with Ashley would soon be over. But Carly was still afraid.

"Are you sure?" Carly felt her lips move so close to Ashley's and Ashley's breath against her skin. Ashley's nose rubbed hers as she nodded.

"I am," Ashley said. "Are you sure?"

Carly nodded. The act of nodding itself brought their lips together, grazing one another. That should have been enough to make Carly feel better. But she recoiled, just slightly, until Ashley inched closer yet again. Soon, they were going to fall off the bed with this constant shifting. So Carly made herself stay in one place—and accepted Ashley's lips against her own.

Ashley laughed into the embrace as soon as Carly kissed back. The laughter opened her mouth, allowing her tongue to slide forward to coax Carly a little more. Carly looped a hand behind Ashley's neck. There wasn't as much hair to comb with her fingers, but Carly worked her fingers through the short mane. Ashley's tongue touched her own and their bodies pressed together, deeper and tighter. From the first meek peck, they were now making out.

Now that Carly finally had what she wanted, part of her waited for it to be taken away. *There has to be a catch, a caveat, a footnote to something I didn't anticipate.* Like her mother's backhanded compliments, Carly knew that there was a price to pay for getting what she wanted. But Ashley was silent aside from small moans. She was content to hold Carly just like this with only their bodies communicating.

And it was all too much. Carly pulled away from the embrace, murmuring an apology as she did.

"Shush," Ashley whispered. She wrapped an arm around Carly, pulling her closer with a sigh. Her fingers combed through her hair again, calming and pleasant. "Oh, what happened to you, Carly Rogers, that made you so worried about a simple kiss?"

"You really want to hear that story now?"

"Now is as good a time as any. And if it prevents you from kissing me like you had been, then yes, let me hear it. So we can get back to normal."

Carly smiled and then sighed again. "I fell in love with a straight girl."

Instead of giving her a kiss to heal the wound, Ashley asked, "And?"

"And. Um. Uh." Carly felt a prickle of embarrassment under Ashley's gaze. "I guess I was just sad, disappointed."

"But she was straight. If you knew that, then why get yourself hopelessly involved in an issue you can't change?"

"I know. I just. Love is more complex than that."

"I have to disagree," Ashley said. Her grip was still tight on Carly, but she was no longer tracing her fingers through her hair. "I think selfish love is like that."

"Selfish love?"

"The type of love that most books by Nicholas Sparks are based on. That most films like *500 Days of Summer* are like, too. The woman has no agency. She is meant to be wanted, to be looked at. It seems like romance, but it's really…consumption. Not all romance novels do it, which is why I had to have a delicate screening process when I read them. I like love stories. Love stories are great. But both people have to love the flaws and not just the surface, you know?"

"I know, I know," Carly said, closing her eyes in embarassment. "I really fell in love with an image instead of a person."

"Yes. And that will definitely get you hurt."

"I know."

"But I can't say I blame you. It's easier to love an image than a person. Especially when you've been rejected most of your life."

Carly tilted her head slightly, looking up at Ashley. "What do you mean?"

"Emotional abandonment sucks. That's all I mean."

"I haven't been… I mean…I have Cyn and Landon."

"But you don't have your mom. Not always, anyway. I don't want to sound like Oedipus or anything, and maybe all lesbians have mommy issues, but your mom was distant. She's still distant. Our parents teach us how to love people. And if you don't get a first swing at it in your own house, it's hard to love people outside of it. It's easier to love images, because they don't change."

"Huh. But Brooklyn still screwed me over."

"Because she was a person. Perhaps a misguided one—I don't know the full story. But what I do know is that when I was in the hospital, I read a lot of romances. And then, when I got out, I slept with a lot of women."

"You know, that's the second time you've mentioned that," Carly said, cutting in. "It almost sounds like you're bragging."

"Hah. I'm not. Trust me. All of that sex was meaningless, and I realized what I was doing because I had read about it so much. I was trying to fix my own illness and failure with other women. And while that may sometimes work on the pages of Harlequin with big strapping young men, that's just not how it works in real life. You can't fill up a life that way… Gah," Ashley said, suddenly losing her focus. "I know I sound a bit corny right now, but hear me out. You wanted to love this girl, Brooklyn. You wanted her so much, right?"

"Yes," Carly said. "Of course."

"Did she love you back?"

"Yes, she told me so. She sent me emails, we talked on Skype." Carly sighed now. "Can I just tell you what happened? The whole story is useful to know. I feel like the bad guy unless I tell you what happened."

"Context is good, sure," Ashley said. "But I don't know if it will help much. The myth of the straight girl and how it's her fault that lesbians get their hearts broken… I just hate it. It's falling in love with an image and actually has nothing to do with sexuality. We're all guilty of it—trust me, I've done the same thing. I was trying to do that after my illness, trying to find the best person to help me escape without opening up myself. But I had to realize that my own dream girl or straight girl was not mine to love. She was a person, with her own will and desires, and I had to respect that. Even if she said she loved me back. Some people express love in many different ways. It's just…difficult."

"Tell me about it." Carly pulled herself up into a sitting position in the bed, along with Ashley.

"You can tell me," Ashley said. "I didn't want to shut you up. I just wanted to let you know that even backstories don't always excuse behavior. It's just something we need to learn from."

"I know. So. This is what happened, more or less…" Carly spoke of Brooklyn in broken phrases, out of order, stepping in with relationships and explanations. It felt bad, like a shitty story that had a hackneyed editor, worse than Kerouac's ramblings about Mary Lou and the open road.

"I know Kerouac is a lost cause, and I should grow up," Carly said. "But Brooklyn was mine. This wasn't some white guy longing for a woman he couldn't have. This was me, and I had waited so much of my life to find someone I thought would make me whole. And then she just ran away. This is my story, even if it had been told a million times before by white men with bigger publishing contracts."

"That's your first problem, though," Ashley said after a few moments. "You want someone to make you whole."

"Isn't that...isn't that what love is about?"

"Yes, in books," Ashley said. "In books it's about soul mates and fixing yourself. Fixing another person."

"Yes. And..."

"And you shouldn't fix someone," Ashley said. "You should be whole by yourself. I mean—look at Cynthia."

"What about her?"

"Do you think she believes in fairy tales? That the prince or princess is going to save her?"

"No, she'd probably kick any guy in the nuts with her blades on if he tried that."

"Exactly. She is much more willing to be Bliss Cavendar at the end of *Whip It* than anything else."

"Right, I know. She has her shit together," Carly said. "So the new fairy tale is to wind up alone?"

"No, the fairy tale is to leave the person who tries to fix you. To ignore the person who tries to save you, because you can save yourself. Find the person, if you want, that *helps* you. Not people who think you're broken and need to be whole, but fall for the person who hangs out with you because they *like* you."

Ashley nudged toward her on the bed. She smiled a little as she did. Flirtatious, but still willing to discuss this point. "You need to find a partner. That's what I learned after my brief sojourn from the hospital to the hallways of women I barely knew. I didn't want love, and I didn't want sex. I wanted something in between."

"What's that?"

"A partner, like I said. I've always liked that term, because you never quite know if a partner is a dating partner, or if you rob banks together, or if you're cops. It's ambiguous and multifaceted, like a relationship should be. I don't want someone to fix me. To try and heal me. I'm fine. Even if I am sick, I am not this fragile creature that needs to be protected."

Carly swallowed hard. Ashley was moving closer and closer to her, their hands linked in between their bodies on the bed.

"I understand," Carly said. "I'm sorry. I know things with Brooklyn were half my fault. I was just so angry."

"And so young. She was your first love. You're allowed to be a dick for your first love. So long as you learn from it."

Carly nodded. Her throat felt tight. She watched as Ashley's blue eyes moved, looking at her up and down.

"I have learned," Carly added.

"Good. Is that what you want again? Something like Brooklyn?"

"Oh, God no. Not at all."

"Okay," Ashley said, her face close to Carly's now, and her voice a whisper. "What do you want?"

"What you described."

"And what is that? "Come on, use your words."

"I want a partner. I don't want to fix you. And I don't want to be fixed," Carly said, gaining conviction. As Ashley nodded, she got closer and closer. Their noses touched once again, but their lips still remained too far apart.

"I want you," Carly said.

"I want you too," Ashley said, whispering now. "And I don't want to hurt or fix anyone. I want to help."

"Okay," Carly said. "Then will you be my partner?"

"Yes, Carly Rogers." Ashley said with a small breathy laugh that Carly felt on her lips. "I thought that was obvious?"

CHAPTER 23

When Ashley brought her lips to Carly's, she didn't flinch. *This is it. For real now. Don't back down.* Carly opened her mouth to progress the kiss; Ashley took the hint, and soon they were making out on the bed. Faster than before, but still careful and tentative—Carly could feel the passion in Ashley's touches.

"The light?" Ashley asked after a moment. "Can we do this in the dark?"

Carly thought of a Fall Out Boy lyric she hadn't heard in ages and let out a laugh. "Yeah, yeah. The dark is good. Don't worry. I'm good."

Ashley gave her a wry grin before plunging them into black. "You'll have to tell me about that joke later." Her whispered words vibrated against Carly's neck and collarbone, while Ashley's hands found her waist. She tugged and twisted Carly's shirt, only exposing an inch of skin at a time to touch.

"Oh," Carly let out a breathy moan. This was all going too slow—and too fast—at the same time. The Fall Out Boy song still played in her mind; Carly swore it matched the rhythm of their breathing. *Just like high school, only now I know what I'm doing. Kind of.* Ashley's number of girlfriends and one night stands piled up in Carly's mind. Carly had only been with a handful of people for sex, and only one of them was a long-term relationship. *What if I don't know what I'm doing?* Fall Out Boy faded away, and Carly's hands shook as her kisses grew more frantic.

"Hey, hey." Ashley grabbed Carly's fingers. She kissed each knuckle, then placed Carly's palms over her chest. At first, Carly thought Ashley just wanted her to feel her breasts. But, as Ashley held Carly in place, she realized Ashley wanted Carly to feel her heart beat.

"See?" Ashley confirmed. "Just as scared as you."

"So should we wait?"

"Hah," Ashley said. "Only if you're not ready. But being scared isn't always a reason to stop."

Carly thought about this. Ashley's body warmed under her palms. When Carly kissed Ashley again, she felt Ashley's heartbeat rise.

"Yeah, now is good." Carly bit her own lip, before she kissed Ashley's neck. Ashley hummed from her throat. She didn't say anything for quite some time. When Carly's hands moved over Ashley's breasts, her nipples grew hard. Carly slid her hands under fabric, onto bare skin, and heart rates rose again.

Carly lost her clothing in a matter of minutes, followed by Ashley. In only bras and underwear, they returned to the bed and continued to kiss. Ashley's hands were urgent, but kind. Each time she caressed Carly's breasts or thighs, she hummed to her as she kissed. When the Fall Out Boy song from before returned to Carly's mind, she knew she was ready.

"Can I?" Carly asked, sinking lower over Ashley's body. She held the rim of Ashley's boxers briefs in her fingers, tugging lightly.

"Oh yeah. Definitely."

In another flash, they were naked. Carly hovered between Ashley's legs and their mouths met again. She traced a finger over Ashley's folds and felt wetness right away. *Wow.* Carly pressed her thumb around Ashley's clit, eliciting a shuddered moan. Ashley's hand clamped down on Carly's arm.

"Good?" Carly hovered above Ashley's lips. She moved her thumb around her clit again.

"Yeah," Ashley said. Even in the dark, Carly could still see Ashley's smile. *The smile that I caused.* Carly swirled her thumb again, before she kissed down Ashley's collarbones to her breasts. She sucked a nipple into her mouth as she slid two fingers inside.

For a while, this was all they did. Ashley moaned and guided Carly, encouraging her with shudders of pleasure and kisses when she could. Carly soon grew bolder, more daring than she remembered herself being. She sunk down between Ashley's legs, kissing her thighs. Ashley opened willingly to the embrace.

"Fuck, Carly Rogers," Ashley said through a shuddered breath.

Carly tried to hold back her giggles. "Really? Right here? Right before I'm about to go down on you, and you use that nickname?"

Ashley started to laugh too. "What? I guess I never excelled at dirty talk."

"Yeah, well, me neither, Ashley Poindexter."

"Oh. I like hearing my name like this. With you between my thighs." Ashley closed her legs a bit, playfully squeezing Carly between them. "Come here? I want to kiss you again."

Carly did as she was asked. When their lips met, Carly was taken aback by the sudden urgency. Ashley held Carly's chin, then pressed their foreheads together. When the embrace was done, Carly was relieved to slide back between Ashley's thighs. *Almost as if we both needed a moment. To remember that this isn't really that big of a deal after all.* Carly kissed another line over Ashley's thighs, before she drew along Ashley's folds. She was so warm and wet, Carly lost herself for a good couple moments, tasting Ashley with no real goal. When Ashley moaned, though, Carly grew focused.

"Oh, G—" Ashley ran her fingers along Carly's hair. Urgent, but considerate. "Like that."

Carly repeated the same motion with her tongue. She wrapped her hands around Ashley, steadying herself as she moved. When Ashley came, Carly's heart skipped to hear her name inside her mouth.

"Carly, Carly, Carly…." Ashley panted. Constant and musical, like a charm or a spell. Ashley pulled Carly up for a kiss, which soon turned into a heated embrace.

"Now," Ashley whispered, sending chills up Carly's back. "It's your turn."

Carly allowed Ashley to slide next to her in the dark, feeling no fear as they went forward.

"Can I show you something?" Carly asked.

"Yeah, sure. Though I don't know how much longer I'll be awake. I get kinda drowsy after I come."

"You were certainly energetic a minute ago." Carly chuckled, as she snuggled close to Ashley. They were in bras and underwear again, but only out of necessity rather than desire. Since the only bathroom was down the hall, and the house was still shared by others, it was an unfortunate reality that they couldn't sleep naked. As much as Ashley apparently wanted to. With Carly so close, Ashley slid a hand under Carly's underwear to caress her bare skin.

"Seriously," Carly said after kissing Ashley. "I just want to show you something small. I promise."

When Ashley relented, Carly rolled out of the bed. She found her iPod in her purse, then came back under the covers. The screen lit up the room, as she browsed her music. She had to focus on the iPod—and not use its light to stare at Ashley and the small marks she had left on Ashley's skin. "Here it is," Carly said, selecting a song. "Listen to this."

"Oh wow. Fall Out Boy. This takes me back," Ashley teased, then put in the headphone. She bobbed along to the music. "I don't know this song."

"It's one of their later ones. After their big album that made them famous. What do you think?" Carly bit her lip as she waited for Ashley's response.

"Not bad. Why did you want to show me? Not that I mind, of course."

"Of course," Carly parroted. When the song was over, she slid away the iPod with a sigh. "No reason. I just…thought of this song. While we…were…"

"Really?" Ashley grinned.

"Yeah. Is that weird?"

"Not really. I mean, there are worse things to think of while fucking."

"Not while we were fucking," Carly said, exasperated. Even with this minor frustration, Carly couldn't stop smiling. "Just before. When I was nervous."

"Oh. I see." Ashley ran a hand over Carly's hip, then her thighs. Carly shuddered, remembering the feel of Ashley against her skin. She wondered if they had time to go again. How much recovery did they really need? And how long was the night going to last? *We waited so long for this, we may as…*

"You thinking what I'm thinking?" Ashley asked. She stuck a finger under the edge of Carly's panties. When she caressed Carly's clit, she shuddered. A bit sensitive, but totally doable.

"If you go slow…"

"Go slow and listen to music?" Ashley suggested.

"Yeah." Carly laughed. "I like that a lot."

"Good." Ashley reached for the iPod, then cranked the volume. Listening through headphones on the floor wasn't the same as speakers, and certainly wasn't the most romantic song Carly could think of…but she liked it. It made her feel safe. As soon as Ashley slipped between her legs again, she knew she could definitely grow to love all of this.

CHAPTER 24

Everything inside the stadium was drenched in neon colors. The banner across the large entryway said, in gold and glitter: *Women's Roller Derby—Game #1*. The track was an old hockey rink, without the ice, and a few long wooden ramps added to the edges. The start and finish lines were painted green. A few patches of orange and red were also around the rink, though Carly could not quite decipher what those colored lines meant. The referee and MC were to stand inside the center of the circle with a large mic that reminded Carly of one of those 1950s crooner type stands.

The referee was the only one in the rink at that moment, measuring the lines and making sure everything stood up to the community's standards. He wore black and yellow, instead of the traditional black and white garb; he was also referred to as the "referbee" by the few people who passed by Carly. They moved through the front gates, and punk music played on high volume.

Tonight, there were only two entry fees; five dollars and a can of food for a local drive to help support the LGBTQ community center.

"That was my idea," Landon boasted after they dropped off their money into a small mason jar and some cans of beans into a bin. A woman with a labret piercing nodded to him, as if they knew one another. "When Lizzie Whordon came around and asked to drop off her publicity fliers, she said she wanted to include something else for their first games to help the community. We decided that this was the best bet."

"Very nice," Carly said. "Was that her?"

"Nah," Landon said. "Lizzie's probably still warming up. That was just one of the other people who used to work at the zine library. You should read her stuff, too. She's contributed to almost every issue of *Hoax*, and we have them all there."

"I will keep it in mind."

"You should," Ashley said, as she took her hand. She had donated a box of mac and cheese, and then paid her entry fee in rolls of quarters. "It could give us something new to read at night."

"There will be time for more, I hope," Carly said, squeezing Ashley's hand, before the murmur of the crowds became too much. Cynthia followed with Landon, as they made their way inside.

From the outside, the small stadium looked so unassuming. Aside from Cyndi Lauper being blasted from one of the old-style convertibles in the parking lot, it looked like your average Friday night in the middle of summer. But now that Carly had stepped inside, her mind had changed. She could sense the energy, the tension, and the pure glee in most people's voices here.

Everyone took their seats. A woman with blonde hair and a tiger tattoo on her arm, and another woman with black hair and dark skin, waved to Cynthia and Landon from the bench.

"That would be Lizzie Whordon," Landon explained. "The one with the tiger tattoo. The other woman is…um…"

"Jackie Ripper," Cynthia said, her eyes wide. "One of my favs."

"Very nice," Carly said with a smile.

"So," Ashley said. "Help the uninitiated to this wonderful event. What's going on tonight?"

"Just the first game in the series. The ones we've been going to before have been warm-ups and tryouts."

"They all as exciting and neon colored as this?"

Landon shook his head. "Nah, but I think the tryouts are way more violent. The team is way worse to one another when they're preparing. Just in case."

A tall woman stretched to pull her leg up to her chest, as another teammate skated over and nudged her to the sidelines. Both tumbled together with a roar of laughter. The team leader, designated by a large clipboard and a whistle, raised her hand in the air and called the two of them back like children with smiles on their red faces.

"They don't seem too bad to each other," Carly said. "Especially when everyone else seems to be having fun. And I'm definitely excited."

The lights and music dimmed, as the MC emerged from the sidelines. She was a butch woman with a crew cut and wearing a blue paisley suit. She tapped her microphone a couple times, before she moved her large sunglasses to the top of her head and smiled at the crowd.

"Welcome ladies, gentlemen, and everyone in between," she began. "We are here to start one of the first games of the season. Please, welcome our two teams tonight: the Serious Killers from the home state of Vermont, and the Pluto Cats from New Jersey."

There was a roar of applause, as the two teams funneled into the ring from opposite ends. They skated around one another, each team holding their teammates hands, until they reached the end of the track. As they faced the new team, they bowed, before setting up for the first race.

Carly figured out fast enough that Lizzie Whordon and Jackie Ripper were part of the Serious Killers. Their group name was stitched onto their outfits of lime green and bright orange, along with a lightning bolt logo crossed with an axe made from glitter. Along with Lizzie Whordon and Jackie Ripper, there was Aileen Rollerous, and a bunch of other infamous female killers. The Pluto Cats were dressed in purple and baby-blue uniforms, with a blind lady justice and scales on the backs of their uniforms. All of their names were after local, female senators, with a couple famous twists, like Eliz Warren and Hilary Clit.

Carly knew nothing of the game, but as the first round progressed, it was easy enough to figure out. Those who knocked down the most people seemed to win. The stadium was a blur of color and movement for each round, sometimes descending into a cacophony if anyone fell over much too brutally. The referbee came in every once in a while, to call a play, but for the most part, he was someone who took up the background. The woman in the blue suit, whose name turned out to be Connie aka Baby Blue, was the person who recapped certain plays and lauded certain players, while chastising others. Music blasted over the speakers.

Cynthia, of course, was in heaven.

When Cynthia was not singing along with whatever song blasted over the speakers, she was calling the shots right alongside Baby Blue. She was able to announce the plays before they happened, along with predicting what woman would come ahead in the match. Even Landon began to grow impressed by Cynthia's skill, and he had watched most of them develop.

"You know, young grasshopper," Landon remarked, "if this whole derby thing doesn't work out, you have a career in sports announcing."

"Why wouldn't this work out?"

Just then, a woman with a cherry blossom tattoo across her lower back was slammed into the wall. Blood spurted from her mouth, staining the wood and some of the windows around the stadium. The referbee walked over to her, only to have the skater shove her arm out. She waited as a surge of women skated by and then got back into the ring. Though she was technically on the Pluto Cats, Carly was still impressed.

"Well, there are your teeth for one thing," Carly joked, turning back to Cynthia. "Do you really want to keep them? Will you even have any left by the time you try out here?"

"Some girls are just idiotic and don't wear mouth guards. I don't intend on letting that happen."

"At least you're safe," Landon said. "But seriously, consider sports announcing. I could easily listen to you all day."

"Leave the little protégé alone," Ashley teased. "She has plenty of time to decide what she wants to do. And until then, we may as well enjoy the show."

Ashley slid an arm around Carly's shoulders. Carly smiled, moving into the touch. They kissed briefly, but didn't want to ruin the mood too much with their casual affection. They were ushered from their seats when the crowd did the wave, then settled right back into holding hands.

"How many rounds are there?" Carly asked.

"Enough," Landon said. "I actually don't know, and I think Bait over here is a bit too into the game to even come out for a moment and let us know."

Cynthia remained plastered to one of the windows, cheering and booing when stuff did not go her way. Carly shrugged with a smile. She slid her arm over Ashley's knee and tried to tap along with the beat.

The Serious Killers won the game. This meant that in another week or so, they would be traveling across state lines for the next round, which would hopefully bring them closer to the championship.

"From here on out," Baby Blue said into her mic. "Those Serious Killers are taking their game to the road and perhaps, will become another I-95 menace."

The Serious Killers skated around the rink again, holding their hands until they reached the end, where they bowed toward the crowd. Before everyone left, there was a final lap around the rink with both sides to be sure there were no hard feelings. Many people across both teams slapped high fives instead of shaking hands. Carly was amused when two women on opposite teams, maybe even Hilary Clit and Bee Tee Kay, held hands and then skated off together to make out on a team bench.

"Well," Landon said, when the crowd began to shuffle out of the stadium. "What did you think?"

"Not exactly like *Whip It*," Carly said. "A little more gore than that and a lot more brightly colored."

"But what did you *think*?" Landon said. "Comparing it to a previous image will only leave you feeling disappointed."

"No, no," Carly insisted. "I liked it way more than the movie, because it was so real. The movie had this whole kind of…Fox Entertainment quality to it. At the end of the day, it had to be about a girl and her life, not about the sport itself."

"Not to mention that Bliss, in the movie, is forced to forgive her parents. Why can't we just have one movie where the parents are actually bad people, and it's good to get away from them, and they're not just misunderstood?" Though Landon tried to play off his remark like he was joking, Carly could see the slight creases around his eyes.

"*Matilda*," Ashley said.

"What?"

"*Matilda* has that kind of ending. She leaves with Miss Honey and everyone is happy. We are meant to see her family as bad for her—and Miss Honey's too. Hey," Ashley said, turning toward Carly. "Maybe we should read that at our next book club meeting?"

"Maybe! I had forgotten about that book—and movie, too. At least the film adaptation was good. What do you think, Landon? Does that work for you?"

"Well, though I'm not in your book club, I do agree. *Matilda* does have what I'm saying. Perhaps I should reread it, too. But on my own." Landon gave them a small wink, before he looked back at Cynthia. "You know *Whip It* was a book, too? Cyn's been reading it nonstop since she found out. I got it at the queer library for her."

"You're a sweetheart," Ashley said.

"He is. Sometimes I feel as if you're the better older sibling than I am, Landon."

Landon held up his hand, shaking his head. "Impossible. There is no correlation. I'm the cool, older friend that seems to have everything because I have an apartment."

"How is your place, by the way?" Ashley asked. "Carly told me you just moved in."

"At the end of winter, yeah," Landon said, a large smile on his face. "It's a good building. Very small—but I don't have much. All I need is my computer for work and I'm set."

"You work from home, right?" Ashley asked. "Man, I wish I could swing something like that."

"It has its advantages and disadvantages. I get to stay in pajamas all day. But then again, staying in pajamas all day makes you feel kind of lazy, you know?"

"Like being in a hospital. You're not allowed to do anything, but you feel as if you're missing out, even if it's on just going to a shitty job."

"Yeah. Exactly like that."

Carly was pleased that her best friend and girlfriend were getting along so well. At first, she worried that they would have nothing in common and Landon would feel like a third wheel whenever Cyn wasn't around to balance him out. But both Ashley and Landon knew what hospitals were like, even if Landon was only in one for about a week after he had his mastectomy.

"Where'd Cyn go?" Carly scanned the grounds and found the bright flash of pink hair she still kept near her curls. Cynthia was on the track now, talking animatedly to Baby Blue and Lizzie Whordon. Lizzie grinned and nodded along, but she looked tense. Tired. Cynthia was probably taxing her every last nerve, especially after that gigantic spill Lizzie took in the last round.

"I'll go see her," Carly said.

"I'll come too," Ashley added.

"Nah, you and Landon stay here. I'm a big girl and I can go by myself."

"If that's the case, I will wait gallantly for your return." Ashley kissed Carly's hand playfully, before letting her go.

Much of the crowd had left for the parking lot. Landon mentioned earlier about the prospect of going to the after party for something like this, but Carly didn't think they would. The drive out there had been long enough, and Carly didn't want to push her mother's temperament by coming home late with Cynthia still riled up from the game and partying with her heroes.

"Hey, hey," Carly said, approaching the conversation between Lizzie and Cynthia with caution. "Mind if I step in?"

"No, go ahead," Lizzie said. She surveyed Carly with a quick glance. "Bait's sister?"

"Yeah. Good eye. No one ever realizes we're related half the time."

"It's easy," Lizzie said, with a wave of her hand. "You both have the same eyes and nose. The green really stands out against the dark hair. Bait also talks about you a lot. Are you thinking of skating?"

"Oh, no. No. I would fall down and utterly destroy myself."

"Everyone falls down," Lizzie said. "But it takes a lot more than a simple spill to destroy yourself. Even then, there is always the hospital. And you can build yourself back up again, ten times as strong."

Cynthia bounced eagerly on her foot, somewhat annoyed that the attention had been moved away from her. "When can I skate?"

"Not until your mom lets you. I know, it's ridiculous. Totally counterintuitive to the team's mission statement. But that's the sad fact about life. Telling the truth about your age usually gets you into trouble, and no matter where you go, people will still try to shove rules down your throat. Even here, where it seems like a utopia."

"I hear that." Carly chuckled. "Do you know what utopia actually means?"

Lizzie shook her head. "No, what?"

"It translates into no place. So really, utopias never exist."

"See?" Lizzie glanced at Cynthia. "Your sister has it. It's a bitch of a catch-22 here, too. You need to have a parent in order to be free. Sorry, kiddo. We've been burned too much in the past."

Though Cynthia nodded, she also pouted. Carly felt a lump rise in her throat. "I could sign for her, couldn't I?"

Lizzie shook her head again. "Sisters are all well and good, and you should love and respect them, but you're not her mom."

"She practically is," Cynthia said, her voice sharp and acerbic.

"Oh, trust me, I can tell, but still a no go I'm afraid." Lizzie crossed her arms over her chest. She flinched slightly, as if she felt a wound deep inside.

"You okay?" Carly asked.

"Yeah, hazard of the job. Speaking of which—I actually have to go wait tables now and get my ass grabbed by jerky men."

"Eh," Carly said. "And I thought my job was bad."

"All jobs kind of are. But they pay the bills. This place," Lizzie said, indicating the stadium, "is the only way I get through it."

"How am I going to get through it?" Cynthia asked.

"Keep skating," Lizzie said. "And you won't have to ever wait tables if you don't want to."

"High school is like waiting tables, only it will never stop for another three years."

Carly could hear the anger and disappointment in Cynthia's voice. She swapped long and strained eye contact with Lizzie. They wanted to help Cynthia, but they were both powerless to do it. They could both fight for so much and give Cynthia so much, but the last signature, the last parental right, was always going to be taken away at the last moment.

"Things will get better," Lizzie said, crouching down to be eye level with Cynthia. "I know that dick, Dan Savage, says that all the time, and it seems like he's lying, but trust me; age not only adds experience, it adds distance to your feelings. Stuff that seems overwhelming right now soon won't. You'll be able to deal."

"I wish I was an adult," Cynthia said, kicking the ground.

"Adulthood is a myth, Bait. Really. The only thing you gain is experience. You face a situation and don't think, *I'm an adult, I can handle this.* Instead you think, *okay, I've done this before and know how to fix it.* All that matters is experience. So keep skating, get that experience, and you won't let anything stop you."

Lizzie rose to her feet, then gave them all a small wave. "I gotta head out. Drive safe, you guys."

Carly waved back, but Cynthia didn't. She still looked distraught. Another lump rose in Carly's throat. She hadn't been able to deal with this kind of loss before, this type of anger or frustration. But she knew the only way to solve it was to stare at it head on.

"I'll be right back," Carly told Cynthia, touching her shoulder. "Just stay here."

Carly walked quickly back over to Lizzie, who was now undoing her skates by a bench.

"This is déjà vu," Lizzie said.

"I know, I'm sorry I'm bugging you again, but what if we just pretended?" Carly asked. "What if we just say I'm her mother? Even if only you knew, what would it matter? We do look alike—we have the same eyes and nose, right? I'd take full responsibility if anyone found out."

"I want to, but the league is getting ridiculous about this. Bait will get hurt. And when she comes into the hospital enough times with broken ribs or sprained wrists, then it's going to come down on us. We can't be the ones at fault."

"Even if I say in the hospital that it was an accident?"

"Accidents," Lizzie said, using her fingers for air quotes, "on a kid like that look suspicious. You're going to get children's aid involved. They will find out that you're not her mom. And things will go sour. I can't have that."

"Okay. Right. I didn't think of that."

"Just wait it out," Lizzie said again. "We all had to pay that price of time, right? Just another three more years."

"Right," Carly said, her voice weak. Lizzie gave another sympathetic smile, before she disappeared into the change room at the back of the rink. Since there were two teams, Baby Blue had divided up the men's and women's change rooms into team units instead. When Lizzie opened the door, Carly saw the urinals inside their room and a sign that said *The Serious Killers* had been taped over the men's symbol.

Three more years. But three more years at Cynthia's age was a life time. All she had was this sport. And the fact that she had to wait until she could really participate made Carly angry.

"I'm her sister," Carly murmured. The commotion outside was loud enough that she wasn't worried about people hearing her. "Why the fuck can't I just be her mother, too?"

"Hey, hey." Ashley appeared at her side. She placed a hand on her shoulder, startling Carly at first.

"Hey. I didn't hear you come over."

"You were gone a while, and I have cat-like skills to track you down," Ashley joked. Her face softened. "Are you okay?"

"Yeah, yeah," Carly said. "I'm fine. I just want to go home."

"So let's go." Ashley held out her hand. When Carly took it, she already felt better.

CHAPTER 25

Cynthia didn't want to leave just yet.

"It's almost eleven, Cyn," Carly said, trying to sound as firm as she could. "It's late and we still have to drive home."

"I *know* that. But we also won't be coming here for a long time."

"What do you mean?" Carly asked.

"The next game is in another state. We won't drive there. I know we won't."

Carly and Landon both exchanged looks. The deadpan expression from Landon confirmed what Carly already knew. Swinging this escape had already been hard enough, and they were still only an hour or so away. Leaving Vermont would be absolutely impossible.

"We can still come back here to skate," Landon said, stepping in. "I'm pretty sure Lizzie Whordon told me that the Killers were still going to use this place to practice."

"It's nothing when compared to the real game."

"And real games will come through here," Landon said. "I'm sure they will. It may not be the Serious Killers or even the Pluto Cats again, but someone will come by. And until then, we can come here and practice."

They walked through the stadium doors and out into the parking lot. Most of the other cars had left. Carly struggled to follow after Landon's strides, as they walked away from his car and toward the skate park.

"Like right here," Landon pointed to a ramp. "And here and here. There are lots of places for you to hang out on. You don't need a game, not always. Just keep practicing."

"Yeah," Carly added. "Think of what Lizzie said. Gain experience and nothing else will matter."

"I know. But it's not the same. Not the same as the game and the music and just, ahhh," Cynthia said, clutching her chest. "I just don't want to go right now. Please? Can I stay—just for a little bit. Just some small practice, so I don't totally feel like I'm missing out."

Carly exchanged a look with Ashley and Landon.

"Don't look at me," Ashley said, holding up her hands. "I am a mere passenger in this endeavor."

"And you're driving, Landon. What do you say? Just some practice?"

"I may be driving, but she's your sister, so I default permission to you."

Cynthia's gaze was already on Carly. And though Carly knew she would get into trouble for keeping everyone out this late, she didn't care. This was the one thing she could say yes to and hope that it counted for something more.

"Of course, Cyn. Knock yourself out."

While Cynthia skated, Landon, Carly, and Ashley all sat down on the curb just outside of the stadium. The echoes of Cynthia's skates up and down the wooden and concrete structures, along with the huffing of her breath as she pushed herself harder, soon became white noise, like water dripping in a tap.

"Should we check up on her?" Carly asked when Cynthia began coughing after taking a spill. "She sounds pretty hard-core over there."

"Let her be," Landon said. "She's got some demons to work out. And really, we should just give her space. Let her come to her senses that way."

"I agree," Ashley said. "I think all of us need that time to just get angry without guilt for a little while."

Carly nodded. "You're right, I know. So, let's move on. You guys want anything to eat?"

"From where?" Ashley asked, looking around. "I think most venues are closed."

"Yeah, but Landon's a walking snack cart, usually." Carly laughed. Testosterone had made Landon's appetite come back with a vengeance when he had started to transition. He pretty much always had some type of snack with him at all times.

"What exactly do you have?" Ashley asked.

"Don't get your hopes up too high." Landon pulled out a backpack from the trunk of his car. "I'm more likely to be a den mother bringing juice boxes to a soccer game than I am to have a bunch of booze in the back."

As Landon sat down, he began to pass around a small bag of trail mix and pretzels, along with a couple cans of Coke. Ashley's eyes lit up as she grabbed one, cracking it open right away.

"This is better, anyway," Ashley said. "I would have had to decline the alcohol, otherwise. And no one likes a party pooper."

"Not much of a drinker?" Landon asked.

"Nah."

"Really?" Carly said, tilting her head. "I figured most people had a rebellious period when they were young and longed to sneak sips of beer."

"Except for Cyn," Landon added.

"Yeah, she merely wishes to skate into the horizon." Carly opened one of the Cokes and took a sip, somewhat saddened by the remark. She turned around and watched, as Cynthia did a loop with her skating, going backward as she came up to a ramp.

"Well, partying used to be my scene, and drinking too," Ashley said. "But time changes everything."

"How so?" Landon asked.

"It's rather complicated…" Ashley said, "but I suppose my prohibition on drinking is more of a precaution than anything. When I first got sick, I went out to bars a lot. And the first thing doctors tell you to do is to stop all types of extreme behavior." Ashley rolled her eyes a bit as she took another sip of Coke. "They wanted to make sure I was clean and sober for most of their tests. But even then, they still didn't find anything. So maybe I should start drinking again."

Ashley held up her drink in a mocking cheer, which Landon and Carly also did.

"Do you mind if I ask what it was?" Landon said a few moments later. "You can totally plead the fifth on it, but I'm curious."

"It's nothing, really. Had a seizure and people freaked out. Then I had some more."

"Epilepsy?"

"That's what everyone told me. But none of my tests panned out. I'm an anomaly. A medical mystery."

"I hear that," Landon said. "I have been to so many doctors in the past five years that I think I've filled my quotient. I won't ever need to go again."

Ashley chuckled. "Exactly. Sometimes, I wonder if I should have studied to become a doctor. That way I could just treat myself at home, and we could save so much money on gas and ambulances."

"What made you stop?" Carly asked.

"Other than the ridiculous amount of school I'd need for a career in medicine?"

"Oh, that would never stop you. You like learning," Carly said with a wink.

"Truthfully, I stopped wanting to be a doctor after I saw so many and realized none of them knew what they were talking about. Yes, they have gone to school and treat a lot of people and do it really well. But they only know that from years of other people's research and years of guessing right. Everything with doctors is guessing. And when presented with a case as wonderful and weird as mine…the guess work becomes tedious."

"Yeah." Landon nodded along with wide eyes. "The body is a wonderful and terrifying mystery."

"Well, now I feel odd," Carly said.

"Don't," Ashley chastised. For a moment, Carly thought Ashley was going to say something else, but she merely leaned close for comfort. Landon was also quiet. All that any of them heard was the slow whir as Cynthia moved on her skates.

"You know," Ashley began slowly, after she turned around and watched Cynthia skate, "I wish I had a rebellious period when I was young."

"You didn't?" Landon asked. "What was all that talk about partying, then?"

"That was when I was older, already in my twenties. Before then, I used to have long hair and a good job and was completely quiet."

"No," Landon said. "You? Quiet and not full of sass?"

"Again, I know it's hard to believe. But I used to be just like…well, your mom. Quite frankly."

"What do you mean?" Carly said. "And why do I suddenly feel like Oedipus?"

Landon laughed. "That doesn't quite work, you know."

"Freud doesn't really work. Not anymore. Anyway," Ashley said, carrying on. "I *was* like Jillian in a lot of ways. I dressed very well, suited for my job. I went to work every day and was quiet. I didn't try to stir up much trouble. I had long hair and even wore makeup."

Carly tilted her head to the side, as if trying to decipher this. Even Carly didn't wear makeup, not really, unless lip gloss counted. Cynthia wore more than her on a regular basis. But that was a mere style preference for Cynthia, whereas Carly knew her choices were merely lazy. She couldn't be bothered with makeup—same with her hair. That was another reason why it was so long. She couldn't be bothered getting it cut.

"Yeah," Ashley added. "I had great makeup, long hair. The whole packaged deal."

"What changed?" Landon asked. "If you don't mind me asking again? I don't want to make you feel like you're seeing a shrink."

"Nah, I'm used to it. And shrink or not, there is nothing like passing out at your desk at work, then waking up inside a hospital room, to change your perspective with what you want out of life. I cut my hair when they finally let me out of the hospital, because I was so sick of staring at my split ends. I had stopped wearing makeup in the hospital, so I figured why bother keeping up with it. I just…went out into the world a different person. Well," Ashley said, changing her story slightly. "I don't like that whole reborn stuff like the evangelists used. I was the same person. Just less afraid, I guess. Just more…"

"Yourself?" Landon suggested.

"Yeah, sure," Ashley said, nodding along. "I was just so sick of the bullshit. I had only dressed that way because I thought it was expected of me. But if was going to wake up again and not remember how I got someplace, I wanted it to be a more fun experience. I didn't want my entire life up until that point to feel like some strange dream. So I figured I would do what I wanted, and I would get better. As if my first seizure was from stress." Ashley laughed a bit before her face fell. "Little did I know that the seizures would get worse, and I really would be waking up and not knowing how I got to a lot of places."

"What happened?" Carly asked. "After that?"

"After I was sick?" Ashley asked and Carly nodded. "There is no real 'after' for when you're sick. It's more like, when things are quiet, calm. In some ways, I'll always be sick, because there is always the threat of something new. I get that. I hate that, but I get it. After I cut my hair, I stopped going into that job. I got a new one. Then I had to quit that, sell my car, and focus on getting better. When there was no one left around me, I found myself changing. You learn to focus on little things to get you through the day."

"I kind of get that," Landon expressed. "You're never really done with transition, either. But soon, you learn to think of something different."

Carly nodded, but she didn't know what to say. She had always been healthy her whole life, never so much as a broken bone or stitches. She had no idea what it was like to know her body, not as a tool that brought her pleasure, but as something foreign and fragile that caused her pain and confusion.

Carly wanted there to be a more definitive ending to Ashley's story, but she knew it wouldn't come. They munched on more trail mix, sipping their drinks, as a sudden crash from behind them caught their attention.

"Mother fucker," Cynthia hissed.

Landon and Carly both rose to their feet.

"Cyn?" Carly said. "Cyn, you okay?"

"Fine. I'm fine—fuck," she hissed again. "Go away. I'm fine."

Carly jogged toward the skate park in time to hear Cynthia hiss again.

"Go away, I'm fine. Jesus fucking Christ. I may be hurt, but at least I'm not like you guys moping over there."

"You heard that?" Landon asked, guffawing.

"Yeah, I could hear everything. You sometimes forget I'm here."

"No," Ashley said. "But we feel close to you, Cyn. That's all."

She rolled her eyes and tried to skate backward. Carly saw the reddish bruise forming on her leg and tried not to gawk at the sight of it. When Cynthia fell again, this time tripping backward, Carly took a step forward.

"Stop it. I am fine."

"You are not," Carly said. "We should go home before anyone gets too hurt."

"Fuck off," Cynthia said.

"Hey, hey," Ashley said. "I know you're fine, but I'm still coming over. I have brothers, so trust me, I've seen it all."

Though Cynthia got to her feet again and tried to skate away, she didn't call out or swear when Ashley approached. Ashley seemed to take this as a good sign and approached. Cynthia sat on the edge of the ramp and pressed her knee into her hands. Ashley lowered herself to sit by her, but didn't immediately put her hands on the injury. She looked around first, admiring the tunnel that Cynthia had been skating through.

"This is nice," Ashley commented. "I wish I could have skated through something like this as a kid."

"You still could," Cynthia said, her voice changing slightly when pain shot through her leg. "I mean, it's not like you're dead. Even if all the doctors tell you you're sick. Don't listen to them. It's how I got this far."

Ashley chuckled. "I suppose, you make a good point."

"I could teach you how to skate," Cynthia said. "I'm good at it now."

"Even if you fall a lot?"

"That's half the fun."

Ashley nodded, considering it. "I may take you up on that later. First, let me look at what you have here, okay?"

"I just scraped it," Cynthia said with a hiss of a breath, her hands still pressed into her knee. "It's nothing."

"Right, I figured as much. You've scraped it before, haven't you?" Ashley asked, her voice strong. She wasn't coddling Cynthia, which Carly knew from experience didn't work at all. But she was treating her with a different attitude that Carly hadn't seen before and had a hard time placing. "You're pretty much made of scars and bruises now, aren't you?"

"Yeah, pretty much."

"You could definitely beat us all up, especially when we're waxing poetic over there, right?"

"Totally, I mean, you guys are old."

"Hey," Landon said. "Technically, if we count my life as how long I've been Landon, then I'm like five."

"See what I mean?" Ashley said. "You could totally give us a run for our money."

"Obviously," Cynthia said.

"So what's up?" Ashley asked, looking down at her leg again. "What's made you extra hurt?"

Cynthia looked around, from Landon, to Carly, and then the stadium they had just come from. She looked back at her legs again and then frowned, just barely.

"I wanted to play. That's all. I don't ask for much, really. I mean, so many kids at my school bitch for iPhones or concert tickets, but I don't care about that. I just want to skate. But I *still* don't have it."

"Ah," Ashley said, nodding sagely. "So this is pride that hurts more than a flesh wound?"

Cynthia huffed and rolled her eyes. "Maybe. But like I care what they think? I can just start my own skate league if I wanted to. I could crash their parties, do my own thing. That's the heart of the revolution or whatever, right? Do it yourself. I don't care about them. I have me."

"I would care," Ashley said. "If I wanted to be a big star, I would definitely care what the stars thought of me."

"Really?" Cynthia thought for a moment about this. When she tried to get up from her seat, she reached out to Ashley for balance.

"Yes, I totally would care about what they thought," Ashley went on. "Because they do know something, even if part of their logic is flawed. It's not Lizzie Whordon who is preventing you from skating. It's a league, the abstract rules. I would care what they thought, use their experience to help me, and then figure out a way to break those rules—on my own terms."

"What do you mean?"

"It's the first rule of strategy, of playing chess, or any type of game really."

"But skating isn't really a game like that. Right now, at least, it's more about me auditioning."

"Right, but you can't just play for yourself. You have to know the terms." Ashley put an arm around Cynthia's and then motioned toward the ramps. "You cannot fight a battle on your terms in their home, the stadium, because they'll win. But what you can do is wow them and make them change those rules."

"I can't be on the league unless I'm over eighteen."

"Maybe, but you may get them to make a loophole. Like parental consent," Ashley said. Cynthia gave her a sidelong glance.

"I could tell my mom I'm going to driving school, and I need to get her consent to learn with a driver's ed instructor. Like that? I could cover the form at the top, make it seem legit?"

"Now you're thinking!" Ashley said, clapping Cynthia on the back again. "You have to wow the team with your skills—both on and off the court. You can't fight the system, but you can make them think they came to the conclusion to change their minds all on their own."

"I like it," Cynthia declared. Letting go of Ashley's hand, she skated a few feet ahead of them all, doing a small loop. Carly hissed at the sight of blood on her leg, but Cynthia didn't seem to notice. When she nearly tripped, she looked down and caught her balance. When she reached the edge of the ramp and then swerved back to Ashley, she finished it all off with a small bow.

"Feeling better?" Ashley asked.

"Much better! Thank you," Cynthia said. She prepared herself for another large takeoff. Carly followed Cynthia's prepared trajectory and realized she was gearing up toward the biggest ramp in the practice area.

"Cyn," Carly called. She was surprised when she felt Ashley's hand against hers, holding her aside.

"And those same rules of strategy apply to you too."

"What do you mean? I just wanted to warn her..."

"That's exactly what I mean," Ashley stated, cutting her off. "You can't let Cyn think that this is dangerous, or the more she'll want to do it. But if you let her think it's her idea, then, well," Ashley turned her attention toward Cynthia. Carly followed, and watched as she approached the ramp with speed, only to double back.

"Nah," Cynthia said. "I'll wait."

"Aw, really?" Ashley said. "I could have sworn you could have done it."

"Later," Cynthia said. "I've gotta save my moves."

"Nice work, kiddo," Landon said. "You show them."

Carly nodded. Okay, maybe Ashley knew what she was doing. "Thank you," she murmured.

"Not at all. Now, come on, Cyn. Make good use of the rest of your time here."

"Yeah," Carly added. "Come on, Cyn."

Cynthia gave them all a devious grin, before she geared herself up for another round on the ramps. Even when she fell down, she got back up again. All like it was nothing at all.

And maybe it was. When Carly wasn't cheering Cyn on, she held Ashley's hand and watched as her sister excelled. And for a while, all nagging doubts were gone.

Everyone was all packed up to go, when Landon cursed under his breath.

"What's up, Lando?" Ashley said.

Landon didn't remove his eyes from his cell phone. His brow knit with worry Carly hadn't seen on him in quite some time.

"What's wrong?" Carly asked. "Is everyone okay?"

"That was Magda," Landon said, not looking up.

"Magda?" Ashley asked.

"She's your next door neighbor, right?" Carly asked. "The trans woman?"

"Across the street, yeah. She runs the clothing store on weekends. She just sent me the strangest text."

Landon handed the phone over the Carly.

Sweetie, your stuff's on the porch. The landlord was shouting about something, but I couldn't hear. I recognized your computer on the ground because it had paint all over it. Smart move, kiddo. The bright yellow made it easy to spot in the dark. I gathered it up for you, before anyone else could. If I were you, I would come home, see what's going on...and if you got a lawyer friend, bring 'em.

"What the fuck?" Ashley peered over Carly's shoulder and read the message. A knot formed in Carly's stomach. *Oh no. No, no, no.* Cynthia grabbed the cell phone before it fell on the ground as Carly moved toward Landon.

"Is this what I think it is?" Carly said. "Landon?"

Landon shrugged. His face was placid, as if he was still too shocked to react. When he lifted his gaze to Carly, though, she noticed the glassy appearance of his eyes. He was on the verge of tears.

"Do you guys mind if we make a detour to my place before dropping you off? I have a strong feeling I'm going to need as many hands as possible, since it looks like I've just been kicked out."

CHAPTER 26

Carly tried to drop Cynthia off at home before going to Landon's, but she was having none of it.

"I want to come—even if you think I'll be in the way. I'm coming. I want to help."

"Sure, fine. Okay," Carly said. "We'll be quick, because Mom…"

"Mom, Mom, Mom," Cynthia said, rolling her eyes. "Blah, blah, blah. I don't care. I call shotgun."

Cynthia jogged to the passenger side door and did up her belt in seconds. Carly and Ashley took to the backseat, while Landon did up his belt. When Landon remained quiet through the drive, Cynthia shifted closer to him and playfully punched him in the arm.

"C'mon. I know this sucks, but we can fix it. Right? That's the whole point about the zines you've been giving me." When Landon still didn't respond, she went on. "I've been training, too. I could tackle your landlord. Circle them like a vulture."

Landon cracked a smile then and muttered "thanks" under his breath. Cynthia elaborated her plan more, knowing somewhere it was a fiction to keep Landon from breaking down behind the wheel. Carly was so relieved for her sister in that moment, because she had no idea what else to say.

The four of them met Magda on the street. Her light colored hair was pulled back in a tight ponytail, and she wore heals with her jeans. She turned around as his car approached, but she only relaxed her stance as soon as Landon got out.

"I'm so sorry, sugar," she said. "I should have been watching more."

"You got my stuff before someone stole it," Landon said. "And considering there was an expensive computer there, and all of my clothing, I'm so grateful."

At first, Carly was confused as to why Landon put his clothing in the same category as his three thousand dollar computer. Then, it hit her; almost all of Landon's masculinity was expressed through his clothing. From his boxer shorts to his suit jackets, Landon was a man of clothing—and a man of software. They were the two things that made him who he was, and he needed to keep them as close as he could. And preferably, not scattered all over someone's front lawn.

Carly had only been to Landon's apartment a handful of times. His building was a large, gray building with roughly five floors. Landon was on the third, facing the street where Magda's clothing store stood. The two of them had met in group therapy for transition and formed a closer friendship as soon as Landon realized her place was across from him. They often went to the clinic together, though there was easily a thirty year age gap between them. Magda was an old drag queen from NYC, who had come to Vermont when gay marriage was legal, only to decide when she got here, and away from the ball scene, that she missed it—more than normal. She and Landon transitioned around the same time, and in the same way that high school friends stick together, they had done the same.

"I put most of your stuff that I could carry in my place," Magda said. "It's hard, though. I just don't have the strength that I used to."

"I know. It's okay, M," Landon said. He surveyed what was still on the ground in front of Magda's store. The couch, a bedframe, mattress, and a couple of dressers too large for someone to carry by themselves were still by the building's front lawn, whereas Magda had emptied much of the shelves and kept the books and other trinkets in boxes by her feet. She assured them that the computer and clothing were already indoors. Carly marvelled at how much stuff was there. Landon's place had been small and there had still been tons of space leftover once he had set up, but she wouldn't have guessed that judging by the amount on this lawn. It looked like it could fill an entire house.

"Is this all yours?" Carly asked. "Was anyone else kicked out?"

"I don't think so," Magda answered. "It's not the beginning of the month, so no one is moving in or out—and they're not evicting people. This just seemed like you, dear. And again, I'm so sorry."

"No time for apologies," Landon said. "Let's get this together."

Cynthia and Ashley teamed up with one another to gather the larger stuff from across the street, like the bedframe and smaller items they could carry together. Carly was compelled to go and help, but she was still trying to piece together the mystery. She was so upset, so angry—but mostly at why Magda and Landon seemed unmoved by all of this.

"What's next?" Carly asked. "I mean, does the building manager know about this? Was stuff just tossed because you didn't pay rent or...?"

"No, I gave them all postdated checks."

Okay, good start. Landon was always good with money. He had to learn to budget when he had to save for surgery. "Then, shouldn't they have given you some type of notice? Surely, they can't just go up and toss the place like you're a criminal. What do they even expect you to do, move back in?"

"Most likely, my key won't work," Landon answered. He eyed Magda, who nodded.

"Thought I saw the maintenance man earlier, when I was grabbing stuff. He probably changed locks."

"That...um..." Carly said, still unsure what to say. She turned around and watched, as Ashley and Cynthia laughed as they tried to balance a glass coffee table and move it across the road. It almost looked like a cartoon sketch, and she half expected someone to run into the glass plate and break it into a million pieces.

"This seems to be the lay of the land," Magda said with a sigh. "People will accept you when they think they know you. Then they freak out when you violate an unspoken rule. I just don't get cissies sometimes. Or straight people. But it gives me too many wrinkles to get angry." Magda gazed at the stuff on her lawn and shook her head. "But you're going to do something about this, right, sugar?"

Landon shrugged. "What can I do?"

"Sue him. He violated your lease."

"He could say that I'm a fraud," Landon said. "That I misrepresented myself."

"Isn't that discrimination?" Ashley asked. She and Cynthia set the coffee table down.

"Yeah. Aren't there protections for LGBT people? There have to be," Carly reiterated. "I mean, if you get a good lawyer who knows the law around gender issues, then there has to be something better than this. It doesn't matter if you misrepresented yourself if you are who you say you are. You're just a trans man—not a con man."

"I wish other people would see it that way," Landon said. "I think if I was a con man, I'd have more rights than the LGB variety."

"What about the T?" Cynthia asked. "There's usually a T in there."

"That's the thing. With a lot of laws and liaison groups, everything but the T is represented. There is no law in this state for the T."

"There are never laws for the Ts," Magda said with a sigh. "That's why I watch out."

Carly's mouth hung open. She looked away from the small conversation and back toward the pile of clothing. This whole situation felt like her mother's disapproval all over again, only on a larger scale. Gay and lesbians were okay. Bisexuals seemed to be a myth or used as the butt of a joke. But transgender people? They got their stuff thrown out and were completely invisible. No one fought for their rights. Everyone just cared if Neil Patrick Harris could get married, but not if Chaz Bono changed his mind about who he was.

Carly sat on the curb and began to fold some of the towels and bedding, before placing them in some of the stray boxes, as the conversation and chatter continued around her.

"That...doesn't make any sense," Ashley said. "You can't have selective equality. That defeats the purpose."

"Well, c'est la vie," Magda said. "I still think you should do something, Landon. Maybe not necessary the legal way, but you can't let him get away with it."

"What do I do, M? Take out a hit?"

"Maybe not that drastic," she said with a sly smile. "But I know people. Let me take care of it?"

Landon huffed. He grabbed some of the boxes of books by Magda's feet and began to toss them into the trunk of his car. He sighed, each movement caught between anger and fear. There was only so much space inside his sedan. And at nearly two in the morning, no way a U-Haul place would be open.

"You know," Landon remarked. "I may be considering that hit right now."

Magda laughed, the dry kind that came from years of smoking. "Well, it's like I always say: Let those without sin cast the first stone. I'll add a bunch of stones to his pile and wait to see if he throws."

Landon laughed a little, in spite of himself. He picked up another couple of bags and continued to add them to the trunk of his car.

"Most of this stuff," Magda stated, stepping forward and grabbing a bag or two, "can stay at my place overnight. A few days, even. I'll just separate it from the stuff I need to sell, so you can get organized."

"Really, M?" Landon asked.

"Of course. Someone has to look out for you. That's what I'm here for. And the rest of these wonderful people."

Magda extended her hand, smiling at all of them as she did. When she glanced back at the building, and the rest of the furniture that was still stuck on the other side, she let out a belabored sigh. "Silly straight people. Now, who is going to help an old queen with the couch?"

"I'll go," Ashley said. She extended a hand to Magda, who took it with a smile.

"Such manners," Magda said, as the two of them crossed the street. Carly kept folding, trying to give Landon some encouraging smiles, when Cynthia ran over to him and threw her arms around him.

"Hey, hey, Cyn," Landon said, grasping her shoulders. They both spun slightly from the sudden aggression of the act. "What's up?"

"You're staying with us tonight," Cynthia said. "I don't even care what my mom says."

Landon patted her back and sighed. "Thanks, sweetheart. But I don't know."

"No," Carly said. "Cyn is right. You're staying with us and fuck my mom."

Some snickering followed from Magda and Ashley, as they crossed the street.

"I'm serious," Carly reiterated. "I want you to stay with us. We'll find you a better place in the morning and get you properly moved."

"With what money?" Landon said, his voice catching. Magda stepped forward, placing a hand on his shoulder.

"I have people. I know them. We'll find you a place to stay, a better one in a good neighborhood with people just like you."

"All that easy, huh?"

"It is when you have people looking out for you," Magda said. "It took me years to build up a network, Lando, but once I did, they are indispensable."

"Thank you," Landon said. "I don't know what I'd do without you."

"You would be playing *World of Warcraft*," Cynthia said. "But now, you're going to amuse me and tell me stories all night, instead."

"Okay," Landon laughed. His eyes caught Carly's from across his pile of stuff. "Okay? Can I stay with you tonight? Just one night, I will be out as soon as..."

"Yes!" Carly said. "Yes, of course, Landon. Yes."

After another round of thanks and a couple more hugs, they all went back to work. Carly focused on folding and organizing Landon's stuff into boxes, while Cynthia dragged most of them to the back of Magda's store or into Landon's car. Landon and Ashley, with occasional help from Magda, worked on bringing the couch and mattress, along with other furniture items, into the back, too. It only took another hour and a half, before all of Landon's life had been packed up again.

"I don't think there's much room left in here," Landon said, peering into his car. "I can maybe take one person to Carly's place. I should have planned this out more."

"Don't worry," Cynthia said. "I was the one who packed that. I knew we wouldn't all fit there. I can skate, though. Yeah?" She glanced toward Carly. "We're not that far from home."

"Um," Carly said. Ashley linked hands with her, and stepped toward Cynthia.

"Only if we can follow along, right, Car?" Ashley asked. "If we walk, and your sister skates, that would leave Landon with more room in his car for another box of comics. Very vital."

"Come on," Landon said, laughing. "I don't have that many issues of Spiderman."

"Wouldn't matter if you did," Ashley said again, before turning to Carly. "How does that sound?"

"Good, actually. It's not that far of a walk for us to tow Cyn around," Carly teased.

"Pfft. More like I'd be pulling you," Cynthia said.

"Okay," Landon laughed. "Well, in that case, I may stop off and get some money out of the bank, cancel some checks. But I'll be at your place…" He looked down at the clock on his dashboard, his eyes wide. "Before three, for sure. Sound good?"

"Yes," Carly said. "Come home, Landon. I can't wait to see you."

"It'll be good to be back, I'm sure," Landon said, as he slipped behind the wheel.

Carly's keys jangled in her hand. Everything they did seemed to make too much noise. Each time the key scraped against the lock, the sound seared itself into Carly's brain. Ashley shifted behind her, looking around for Landon and helping Cynthia take off her Rollerblades. As soon as her foot came out of the blade, Carly gasped at the blood around her white sock.

"Don't worry," she said, holding her hand up before Carly could even respond. "I'm fine. Just a few blisters. I skated a lot tonight."

Cynthia said the last part with a wry smile, full of pride. As Carly finally slipped the right key into the door, she heard the house shift. The door opened, wood expanded, and then she waited for the next sounds; footsteps, followed by the flicking of lights. A rush of movements toward the stairs and the hiss of bitter indignation from her mother.

In all of her years of high school, Carly never once had to sneak out or stay out past curfew. She never really went out at all. But she had heard horror stories from other kids who had parents with tight curfews and liked to ground them. Carly knew they were three hours later than they had sworn to be. She anticipated every motion of her mother, every scorned look, every heated word. Carly had never acted out as a young kid, so this sudden and final rebellion when she was twenty-four—now almost twenty-five—was a strike against her pride as well as herself.

"Carly," Jillian announced from the top of the stairs. She folded her arms over her chest, her dark eyes as piercing as a knife. "Where on earth have you been?"

"I'm sorry, Mom. There was a bit of an issue tonight."

Jillian walked down the stairs slowly, her gaze fixed solely on Carly. A bathrobe in mint green hung over her body, with Lululemon pants and an old varsity shirt underneath. Her brown hair was pulled back in a clip, some of her long curls down her shoulders.

Her silence became a heavy weight in the room. Her stare communicated all the anger that Carly had worried about. She had to look away before her mother even reached the bottom of the stairs.

"I'm sorry we were out so long, but something came up."

"Yes." Ashley stepped in. She put an arm around her waist, pulling her close.

"I apologize, Jillian. That was mostly my fault."

Jillian ignored Ashley. She walked down the rest of the stairs, her eyes now jumping from Cynthia to Carly.

"I don't care whose fault it was. It was still someone's responsibility to text me to let me know what's going on. Do you know how late it is? I was *this close* to calling Richard."

Carly worked hard to stifle her laughter. It seemed too perverse to even find the situation funny, but she couldn't help it. What on earth was Richard going to do? Use his chiropractor skills to locate them? Why not get the cops or even call Landon's parents? It was clear that Jillian didn't think something was wrong, by calling Richard she merely wanted someone to comfort her in this time of need. She wasn't really worried about her girls. She knew that they were probably fine, with someone who could drive and take care of them. It was the fact that they had ignored her, not answering any texts, and implied that there was something else that deserved their attention.

"Well, don't worry," Carly said. "We're here. Everyone is fine."

"Cynthia looks more scraped up than usual," Jillian observed. She stood on the bottom of the steps, her eyes moving toward her bloodstained socks.

"Should I be worried about any Roller Derby people calling me and telling me my daughter was injured?"

"No," Carly said harshly. She always hated it when her mother talked about Cynthia without addressing her. It was the same way that some of the bosses at work did not address people in the room by their names, but instead talked around them, as if they were not there at all. It was removing Cynthia from the situation entirely. That was when Carly knew that her mom wanted to fight with her like an adult. *At least I'm not a kid anymore this way.*

"Are you okay, Cyn?" Carly asked and gestured toward Cynthia.

"Yeah, I'm fine. I'm tough, remember?"

"Yeah, well, it's late," Jillian said. "You're covered in scars and the children's aid is going to start asking questions. Get into bed and don't do this again."

She was about to turn around, when another car appeared in the driveway. When Landon stepped out, Jillian's eyes followed him as he moved up the driveway with a bag over his shoulder.

"What is...?" Jillian never finished.

"Mom, can Landon stay?" Cynthia said. "Please? He's having a hard time. Just for the night."

"He got kicked out, Mom," Carly added. "The landlord pulled a terrible trick on him."

"Did Landon apply as a man or as a woman?" Jillian's voice was calm and even, though her eyes betrayed the same casual hatred that always came across them when Landon was mentioned.

"That doesn't matter," Carly insisted.

"Yes, it does. And from that omission I'm going to say that there is no case there. Landon should have been more honest."

Carly clenched her jaw. She knew she was not going to win this battle. "Okay, fine. Whatever. Landon isn't going to pursue a case anyway, because he knows there is no way he can, unfortunately. But he is going to stay here until he gets things sorted out. That's why we were late. We were helping him move. All of his stuff was in the middle of the street. He was kicked to the curb, Mom, literally. I don't care what you think about him, but please have a heart."

"I do have a heart," Jillian said, turning her callous gaze toward Carly. "I do. Don't ever say that I don't."

"Okay," Carly said. "I'm sorry. Can he stay, then?"

"Not with Cynthia around."

"I'm right here," Cynthia cried.

Jillian turned toward Cynthia so quickly that Cynthia flinched. "In that case, I want you to go to bed. Now."

Cynthia, no matter how much she wanted to rebel, crumbled under those words. She flung her Rollerblades over her shoulder and then walked up the stairs, two by two. She slammed her door, playing up her exit. As Jillian turned her attention back toward Carly and Ashley, Cynthia tiptoed back out of her room. She lay down on the landing, peering out of the posts like a small child. Before Jillian started to chastise again, Landon came through the door. He nodded to Cynthia's small waving hand, just before his gaze fell.

"I apologize for bringing the girls home so late, Jillian. I take full responsibility for that. We had everything packed and ready to go, when I found out about my housing situation."

"We just finished informing her," Carly said. "But I don't think she cares."

Jillian stared at Carly dismissively. "I understand that life can be hard, Landon. Carly is an adult and can do what she wants. Often, she does just that. But Cynthia is still young. Do not involve her in your problems."

Landon was about to open his mouth to apologize again, when Carly held up a hand. "Don't. Mom, Landon's problems are hardly his fault. He is…"

Ashley took a step forward, placing a hand on Carly's back. She cut her off midsentence, even as Carly's eyes pleaded with her to not bother trying. *It's not worth it,* she wanted to scream at Ashley. *It's just not.*

"I understand your concern, Jillian," Ashley said quietly. "But I really think you should be proud."

"What?"

"Of Cynthia, I mean. She's one of the most intelligent and caring people I've met. The fact that she was willing to give up her Friday night to help out a friend of a friend, in spite of these odds, is incredible."

Jillian remained stock-still. She didn't yell or talk back to Ashley, something that only happened because Carly had worked so hard at keeping both of them apart over the past few months. Jillian had only met Ashley once or twice, approving of her each time. They only knew one another peripherally, and therefore, Jillian had no ammunition, no reason to think that Ashley was deluded by something, like Cynthia, or a menace, like Landon.

"Do you know what I was doing at fifteen?" Ashley asked. She didn't wait long to respond. "I was playing video games. I was pretty much failing most of my high school classes. I didn't care about anyone else."

"And this is supposed to make me feel better?" Jillian asked, raising an eyebrow.

"Yes, because that is normal, fifteen-year-old stuff. That's rebellion that doesn't help anyone else. But look at Cynthia. She spent tonight at a Roller Derby for something she loves, talking to some of those women after the show, because they are her role models. And when her friend gets thrown out of his house, she doesn't ignore him. She helps him. It doesn't matter who you are, you do not deserve to get kicked to the curb. Cynthia knows that, and she fights for those people, no matter who they are."

The room was silent. Carly felt the tension shoot over her like a pinched nerve in her back. She waited, feeling as if she was on the edge of a cliff, for something bad to happen.

Jillian sighed, running a hand through her hair. "I understand the good that was supposed to come out of the situation, no matter how misguided. But I am still *very* upset. I am still livid because it is late. But that's just the thing, it is late. There is nothing we can do now. Landon. Stay. But leave Cynthia out of this."

"No problem—"

"How about," Carly said, cutting in. "We talk more about that issue later."

Jillian shrugged. "Whatever. Both of you seem determined to do whatever you want anyway. I guess I may as well face the fact that I can't stop it. Only another three years."

"Yeah," Carly said. She let out a low breath, as Jillian turned toward the stairs. Cynthia jumped up from her place on the ground and ran into the hall bathroom, seemingly unnoticed.

"Goodnight. And don't forget," Jillian said, looking at Carly. "You're with Dorothy tomorrow. Richard is going to come bright and early. I suggest you get some sleep."

Carly let out a breath, as soon as she heard Jillian's door close. The room slowly eased with tension, and they all let out an uneasy laugh.

"Well, that was new," Carly said.

"Yeah," Landon agreed. "Can we count that as a win for the night?"

"Definitely," Carly said, with another laugh. "Now, come on. Let's go to bed."

CHAPTER 27

Carly flicked on her bedroom light. Landon and Ashley set down their bags and Carly peered in the closet, calling for Cynthia.

"Well, that's odd," Landon said. "I figured Cyn would be one of the few of us who didn't need a closet to hide in."

"Very funny," Carly said, rolling her eyes. "Cyn used to hide in here when she wanted to talk at night and didn't want Mom to see. Either the closet or under my bed, but that's been a no go option for a while now."

Curious, Ashley got on her knees to peer under the bed. She laughed as she drew back the bedding, exposing piles and piles of books. "Nice collection you have here. I should just come to your place instead of a library."

"What can I say? I'm sentimental. I like to keep my books after I read them, or else give them as presents."

Cynthia appeared by the doorway. She was dressed in her pajamas, her naturally curly hair bouncing at the sides, and her pink extension no longer visible.

"Hey, you!" When Carly peeked into the hallway, she saw no light under Jillian's door. *Safe now.* "We were just talking about you."

"Yeah, you and everyone else." Cynthia walked into Carly's room without invitation, flopping down on her bed. "Who knew I'd be so popular?"

"It's not bad, Cyn," Landon said, sitting next to her on Carly's bed. "It means a lot of people care."

"Are you kidding me?" Cynthia said. "I wasn't complaining. I mean, Mom can be annoying, but I'd much rather be popular if it gets me out of trouble. And thanks for pretty much being my defensive league. We are kind of like a league, right?"

"For Roller Derby or debate?" Landon asked. "Because Ashley wins at debate, hands down."

Ashley placed a hand over her chest, nodding and smiling as she bowed.

"Both, maybe," Cynthia said.

"Well, I still think it's dangerous cavorting here like this," Carly stated. "Even if Mom's asleep, we can't tempt fate. You should go back to your room. I just wanted to be sure you were okay for now."

"I am. And forget going back to my room. How much longer can she ground me for? Three years? Well, it's going to take me that long to get into Roller Derby anyway. I'm only going to be free when I'm eighteen. I may as well do whatever the fuck I want now, because there is nothing she can take away from me."

"And failing that," Landon added. "Just read in your room like Miss Librarian over here."

"Oh yeah," Carly said. "Because that allows you to go far in life."

Carly grabbed blankets from her closet, handing them out to everyone in her bedroom. She paused on Ashley.

"I guess you're staying?"

"I should hope so after that," Landon said.

Ashley nodded. "You got trapped with me, and now I'm trapped with you."

"I can find you a ride if you want, seriously," Carly said.

"Nah, I like it here. It's way too late to call Darren or my dad. I texted them while I was at the derby, anyway. So, I think I'll stay."

"Well, good. I like some positive news after tonight." Carly spread out a few blankets on the floor, while she peeled back the comforter on her bed.

"So, we all need spots to sleep…" Carly wasn't sure where to put anyone anymore. Her room had suddenly shrunk to half the size with so many bodies in it. As much as Carly wanted Ashley in bed with her, she didn't really think it would be fair to Landon. Or Cynthia for that matter. As long as she could remember, it had been she and Cyn in her bed during sleepovers.

"Don't worry," Landon said. "I'll take the floor. You and Ashley take the bed and Cyn, I'm sure, will be fine by herself."

"No fair," Cynthia said. "After all this talk about having a league, and you're already outing me?"

Carly exchanged a look with Ashley. She wasn't quite sure how to fit all three of them in the bed, or…

Cynthia turned to Landon, her gazed fixed on him. "You're coming to my room."

"Um," Landon said.

"Um," Carly echoed.

"On the floor, don't worry," Cynthia said. "But if you're staying, and it's going to be the floor no matter where you are, you should just come in my room."

"I'm okay with it if you are, Carly," Landon said.

"Should we really tempt fate like this? After all Mom said…?"

"By following her orders blindly, you only give her power," Cynthia argued. "A floor is a floor. Just sleep with me, with the doors closed, and we'll survive."

"You know," Carly said. "With that attitude, I almost believe it."

"Good!" Cynthia walked over to Landon and grabbed his hand. "Because you're coming with me right now…"

After a few aggressive pulls for showman effect, Cynthia and Landon laughed. Carly sorted some of the pillows and blankets from the pile, and tossed them to Landon. "Well, if she'll have you, then so be it. Who am I to get in the way?"

"Thanks Car," Landon said, taking the pillows. He stepped closer to her and then placed a hand on her shoulder. "I'm sorry, by the way. I wouldn't have wanted this to happen."

"Me too. But it happened. It sucks, but I know we can move on from this."

Landon nodded, considering this for a second. "I know, I know. I'm not going to pretend to be this brave solider, because I'm not. I may be a guy, but remember, I don't have any nuts…"

Landon's joke fell flat on everyone's ears. Carly wanted to tell him what she always did when he got like this: *Bravery is not a body part. You cannot get a transplant. You either have it, or you don't.* He had it.

"I'm just…so grateful to have friends like you," Landon said. "I am, even if I may not seem like a cuddly teddy bear of joy right now."

"You shouldn't be."

"But I *will* be," Landon insisted. "I just need to sleep. I need to shut away from the world for a while, get some rest, and decide what I need to do in the morning."

"Take your time, there's no rush," Carly said. "And if you ever want to talk more, just knock on our door and we will wake up and…"

Cynthia stepped forward, holding her hands up. "Okay, we're stopping the sentimental train right now. I'm tired and have had enough sob stories. I want to go to bed. You want to go to bed. Everyone in a bed. Now."

"Okay, sounds good," Ashley said. "Goodnight everyone."

"Goodnight!" Cynthia bumped her hip against Landon's large frame. Carly wanted to reach out and tell her to stop, to try and be nice to Landon, but she didn't. Landon picked Cynthia up, muttering under his breath, and began to tickle her for her trespasses.

And that's when Carly understood. Cynthia never treated Landon like he was different, like he was made of glass and should be treated carefully. So Landon could always tolerate her being a little younger, a little more naïve. He treated her back the same way, like she would not break either.

Ashley squeezed Carly's hand. "You ready?"

"Yes," Carly said, turning to Ashley with a weak smile. "Yes."

Carly worked in what felt like slow motion, as she set up their bed. She added a couple more pillows to her queen-sized mattress and then decided to throw a couple more blankets on too.

"I like to steal them in the night," she explained.

"I had noticed," Ashley countered. Her eyes were glued to her phone, clearly texting someone.

"Who's up so late?" Carly asked.

"I just wanted to ask Darren something quickly," Ashley explained.

"I want you to stay."

"I know." Ashley smiled and moved to the bed so she could hold Carly's hand. "But you still need to see your aunt tomorrow."

"Yes, I do. I figured Landon could drive us. Or shit, Richard is supposed to come, right? I'm sure Mom would just love me stealing him from her. Fuck."

Ashley squeezed Carly's hand, trying to get her to calm down. "Tell Richard to stay with your mom. She will need it after her so-called ordeal. Landon will be busy moving, but Darren can drive. I'm sure of it. We'll just give him some gas money."

"Okay," Carly said after some thought. "I like the sound of that."

"Good," Ashley said. She placed her phone on the nightstand so she could change. Once in her standard T-shirt and boxer briefs, and Carly in her own plaid pj pants and T-shirt, there was nothing left to do but get into the bed.

As soon as it was dark, Ashley put an arm around Carly and held her close. "Will you come with us on the drive?"

"Of course," Ashley said. "I have the weekend off. I was hoping I could come. The drive sounds really nice, actually. I like that part of Vermont."

"I think you want more than a drive."

"I do look forward to car rides now that I'm an invalid. Sometimes, even Darren lets me sit in his car without the engine on and go vroom, vroom."

Carly laughed. "Nice, but I meant something else."

"Oh, I know exactly what you meant, Carly Rogers." Ashley shifted in bed to lock their legs together. Ashley ran her hands across Carly's body, lightly trailing her fingers. The action felt more of comfort than desire. They were both drained from the day they had—and each touch brought back a feeling of serenity that had been lost between them. Carly grabbed Ashley's hand, kissing the fingers, before Ashley leaned down to kiss her.

"Aside from tonight, and this whole ordeal, I'm pretty sure my mom likes you," Carly remarked between kisses.

Ashley raised her eyebrows. "I should be nicer to your family."

"You're great with Cyn."

"That's because she's easy. She's an utter joy, actually. I wish my siblings had been that cool."

"It helps that there's a lot of years between us. She was never someone to compete with. She was just kind of there, and since she was my half sibling, I sort of felt like she was a friend. A friend that I had to take care of a lot of the time, but a friend. Once we progressed past middle school, things were easy."

"I fought a lot with my brothers. But it's true, things do even out once puberty and high school politics are over.

"But your mom, she's hard. Very difficult."

"I know."

"I don't want to make fun or make an already difficult situation more difficult, but it matters more to me that Cyn likes me than your mom."

"She does. Cyn, I mean. I can tell she thinks you're funny."

"My mission in life," Ashley said. "Then why do you care if your mom likes me? I mean, why mention it at all?"

"Because…" Carly paused, still not finding the right words for some time. "I feel as if I owe her something, maybe?"

"Why?"

"Because," Carly said. "Don't all good daughters want to please their parents?"

Ashley shrugged. "Maybe. But there is something more than that, here."

"Oh, really? Are you sure you weren't a shrink instead of a contractor?"

Ashley laughed, but she also squeezed her hand, encouraging Carly to think. Ever since coming back home after graduating college, Carly had been acutely aware of how much of a failure she felt in front of her mother. She managed to get a degree, but living back at home again took its toll. Ever since Brooklyn, and even a little before that, Carly had always felt as if she needed to catch up to people, like she was falling behind. She couldn't drive. She couldn't live on her own. She barely had any savings. She was so dependent on her mother that the small things, like her girlfriend, choice of friends, or even taste in clothing, mattered. She wanted her mother to be proud, because it felt like so often she wasn't.

"I just, I feel bad sometimes, I guess," Carly said.

"Why?"

"I can't give her grandkids."

"That's ridiculous."

"I know."

"First off, it shouldn't matter whether or not you can produce babies," Ashley said, scoffing. "You're not her broodmare."

"I know, I know. I got so angry when I told her I was gay and the first thing that came out of her mouth was, 'But what about grandkids?'" Carly shuddered then at the memory. "She would have never asked that if I had been dating a guy, because it would be assumed. And I don't like assumptions. I've always hated them."

Ashley nodded. "Do you even want kids? You don't have to have them because she feels as if they will be missing in her life if you don't. And if you did want to have kids, you don't have to feel like you did it just to fill up the void in her life. It's your decision, whether or not you want to."

Carly nodded. "I know that. But I honestly don't know if I want them or not. I've been told so many things that now I'm just confused, you know? It's the ideal, right? White picket fence and two point five kids. But it doesn't seem possible anymore, at all, gay or straight. The money, the job, owning property. Life is not like that anymore."

Ashley held Carly as their minds wandered. Carly thought of Amber, the young mother she worked with at Marshalls. She didn't know how someone who looked like Cynthia's age could ever have kids. She didn't know how she could afford it. And the act of having kids, who gobbled up money more than food, seemed to be utterly impossible given her hourly wage, not to mention health insurance, and housing. It just wasn't feasible, not with Carly's own income. Moreover, Carly didn't even know when that would look up.

"When there are two people," Ashley began, "*that* helps with raising kids. Two incomes help a lot. But I know. I understand what you mean. Sometimes, that lifestyle seems out of date."

"But?" Carly asked, nudging her shoulder. "There is something else there."

"But I still want it," Ashley said. "It may be completely unreal of me, especially given my health, but I like to dream. I would go crazy otherwise."

Carly nodded. She thought of the way Ashley had talked to Cynthia tonight, and how easy so much of it had been. "You would be a good mom."

"Thank you," Ashley said, beaming at the comment. "It's a long, long way off. But it's important to me. I would like to keep it in mind."

"Yeah?" Carly said, then nodded along. She realized she and Ashley were both silently checking out their options. To have kids or not to have kids? It would not be a deal breaker, not when they were still this unstable and fragile in their own lives. But it was something to consider. In the same way that their book tastes mattered for the immediate future, their long-term goals together would matter. This was a heavier weight than choosing *Treasure Island* or *Little*

Women. But it mattered. Carly knew that, eventually, she would have to make up her mind.

Just not tonight. She squeezed Ashley's hand and kissed her knuckles.

They kissed, their tongues barely touching, until they heard the phone go off on the nightstand. Ashley broke away, spilling Carly across the bed as she grabbed her device.

"Darren says yes," she said with a relieved smile. "I guess he was up all night playing video games. But yes, if we give him gas money, he'll drive us."

"Thank you," Carly said. "I really appreciate it."

Ashley nodded quietly and went to type a response back to him. Carly also grabbed her phone, sending her mother a brief message via email instead of texting about what to do for tomorrow with Richard. She was sure her mother would act indignant at first, only because it wasn't her idea, and eventually come around. When Ashley got off the phone, she sighed and dropped her head on the pillow.

"I'm exhausted."

"Come with me," Carly said.

"I am." Ashley flopped around in the bed, turning into the curve of Carly's body. "I would like to sleep, actually sleep with you now."

"No," Carly laughed, sliding an arm around Ashley. "As much as I also want that. I meant I want you to meet my aunt. Please? You'll like her. I like her. More than my mom, sometimes. She's better…easier."

"Shush," Ashley said. "I thought it was obvious that I was going to come along? What did you expect me to do? Drive you there, then turn around? Oh, Carly."

Carly worried her lip. That had been exactly what she thought. It was what Jillian did each time she dropped her off. So why wouldn't Ashley be the same way? Carly opened her mouth to explain, but Ashley shushed her again.

"Don't worry. It's late. You don't need to think about anything anymore. Because, of course, I'd love to meet Dorothy. Wouldn't miss it for the world."

CHAPTER 28

Darren picked them up in his black van. He came at nearly six in the morning, before anyone else in the house was up. Carly and Ashley snuck downstairs after they got his text message, so he didn't have to come to the door. As they tiptoed down the stairs without turning any lights on, Carly began to think the whole trip really was like a secret mission that needed to be done in the cover of darkness.

"Darren, this is Carly, Carly this is Darren," Ashley introduced as she stifled a yawn. "I think I need to reconsider my hate for coffee this morning."

"Hi again," Darren said, extending his hand. "It's nice to properly meet you, rather than sneaking around at night when you're with Ashley."

"Same," Carly said. She slipped her duffel bag in his trunk, along with Ashley's bag. The birds chirped mercilessly outside, which made both Carly and Ashley roll their eyes and groan as they headed into the backseat.

"If you don't mind," Darren said, as he slipped behind the wheel, "I think we may have to forgo the coffee until we hit the halfway mark. I want to try and make good time, so I can head back and still see Julia."

Carly raised a brow, and Ashley mouthed "girlfriend."

"Sure, Darren," Ashley said. "So long as you don't mind us taxicabbing you like this. Oh, and we will probably suck for conversation since we're going to sleep the whole way."

Darren laughed. "Oh, sweetheart. I'm used to this by now."

Carly woke up to Journey's "Don't Stop Believin'" blasting through the speakers.

"You are a terrible person, Darren," Ashley said, straightening up from the seat. She rubbed the sleep out of her eyes. "You have bad music taste. And you should feel bad."

Darren gave his sister the finger, which only made Ashley laugh. Carly yawned and tried to not wedge herself in between the sibling drama. Ashley noticed her hesitancy right away.

"Carly, this is what a real brother and sister look like. Sometimes, I think your relationship with Cyn is unhealthy it's so perfect."

"I don't have a brother, so how should I know?"

"*All* siblings need to fight. It's how you learn character development and problem solving."

"I can solve problems," Carly said. "And I have character."

"Yes, but you are a rare flower in a field of weeds. So many only children are forsaken because of their lack of social skills. Not that you're an only child. Close enough to it, anyway."

"Would you still like me anyway? If I was an only child?" Carly teased.

"Of course. But only because you have found my one weakness, Carly Rogers," Ashley said, as she leaned forward to peck Carly. "Pirates and swashbuckling. Oh my."

"I don't even want to ask," Darren said. He cranked up Journey on the radio. Ashley kicked his seat.

"No Journey or I crash this car," Ashley wailed.

"If I drive off a cliff, you do know that you're all dying too, right? Just so you know."

"Did you know that cliffhangers were actually called that because some authors would actually have their characters hang off cliffs in order to get people to read the next installment?" Ashley explained, much to Darren's chagrin.

"This is why taxicabs have a window between them. So they can keep the riffraff out," he said.

"Drive Jeeves. Just drive. And turn down the volume."

With another grumble, Darren did as he was asked, keeping the 1980s station at a lower volume. Carly took out her phone. She skimmed past some of her more recent messages to find several from Landon, updating her on the situation.

"How is Landon doing?" Ashley asked, with genuine interest in her voice.

"He's going to live with someone called Jacob now. At least, that's the plan after the moving today. The housing will be just temporary, until Jacob can hook him up with a better transgender housing network."

"Trans housing network?"

"Yeah, it's kind of like a linked system of people who pass around real estate listings, helping to find houses for people so they don't get kicked out. The landlord that screwed Landon over has been added to their list of 'do not rent' places. No one had come across him before. Landon figured that no news was good news. But hopefully people won't have to learn the hard way again. And Landon can find a place that has supported transgender people in the past."

"Kind of sounds like the underground railroad," Ashley commented. "Is Landon okay with being slotted around like this?"

"Oh, he's fine," Carly said. "He's always been strong like that. He really underestimates himself."

"Yeah, but it's healthy to have anger, too," Ashley said. "I was really surprised he wasn't angrier. I expected him to kick something. But he was practically zen."

"Oh, I think he is upset. But he's better at hiding it."

"Most men are," Darren said, jumping in. "Kind of conditioned from a young age. If you're really upset, you learn to ball it up until it comes out in a large amount. I suppose the same would be true for trans men, too. Right?"

"Probably. But is this why you have so much road rage?" Ashley asked.

Darren gave her the finger again.

"In all seriousness," Ashley said. "Landon's situation is hard. Very hard. He should be angrier."

"Yeah, but you do what you have to do to survive until people start to help you along," Darren added.

"I know. I've asked my mom countless times to look into some laws and to help me get some of them updated to better help transgender people. But she always skirts around the issue, not really wanting to bring it up. She says she's not that kind of lawyer, not criminal or real estate."

"What does she do?" Ashley asked.

"Family law, mostly."

"Ah, okay," Ashley murmured as if it all made sense. "I could give Landon the name of my storage company if he needs it. So much of the stuff from my old place is there. I'm really looking forward to the day when I no longer need it, truthfully. Landon could even toss some of it in with mine. I don't have that much—there's still room and we could split the rent."

Carly smiled. "Thank you. I will mention it to him."

Ashley waved her hand, issuing that it was not a problem. She leaned forward, touching the passenger side seat and smiling at Darren.

"Hey, Darren," she quipped.

"What? Ash, I can see your little maniacal grin form here."

"Can we stop? Please? I have to pee."

"And...?"

"I would like to get some food."

"And...?" Darren drew out, matching Ashley's smile in the rearview mirror.

"I would love to get you food too, I know, I know." Ashley turned and regarded Carly. "Do you want anything?"

"Coffee?"

"Right. Got it." Ashley dug through her pockets and pulled out a couple twenties, as they turned into a McDonald's parking lot. She wriggled in her seat, which probably had more to do with the fact that she had to pee than being excited for an Egg McMuffin. She wrote down Darren's order, along with Carly's, on her phone's notepad. "I'll be right back. Don't do anything I wouldn't do, guys."

When Ashley was gone, Darren turned to Carly with his eyes narrowed. "Okay. I'm glad we have a more formal setting to talk, Carly. Because I like you."

"Um," Carly said. "That's good to hear. I like you too, Darren."

"Always nice to hear, of course. But I have to ask; has Ashley told you what to do if she has a seizure?"

Carly swallowed. She shook her head.

"Thought so." Darren glanced into the McDonalds, before he turned back to Carly. "I'm going to tell you now. I know she's probably resistant to tell anyone what to do, because she wants to believe she's cured. And maybe that's true. It has been a year since her last seizure. But just in case, I want you to know. It's really a terrible feeling when you have no idea what's going on. Okay?"

"I don't want to see her as broken," Carly said before he could start. "I can't."

"I know that. No one wants to see anyone they love that way."

It was clear to Carly that he meant love as a byword, as something that was more pertinent in his own life and relationship than an extrapolation, or even observation, on Ashley and hers. But still, the word made her shiver.

"So," Darren went on, "as much as we love people and want to give them their independence, we're not islands. And it's really, really important to take care of people. This is something that you may need to know, however long you're going to be around. This whole seizure thing caught everyone by surprise. We don't want anything bad to happen. So please, just listen to me quickly."

Carly didn't know what to say. Why did this feel so much like a violation of privacy? As if Darren was telling Carly about Ashley's exes or her embarrassing childhood photos and not something that could potentially save her life. Carly kept feeling like this was a test, and either saying yes or no, would only lead to a failing grade. Saying yes meant that she violated trust, and Ashley's right of her own body. But saying no led her into a black spot in the family's eye, and a possible worst situation in the future. Carly fidgeted with her hands, thinking of what Landon said about sickness and health. Ashley wasn't broken, Carly knew. But Carly also knew that the world was hard, and life was fragile, and she wanted to support Ashley in whatever way she could.

Carly glanced back at the McDonalds and saw Ashley in the line. She was far back, probably another fifteen or twenty minutes until she returned.

"Okay," Carly said. "Yes, tell me. I want to know."

CHAPTER 29

Dorothy was waiting for them on one of her porch chairs by the time they arrived.

"Is that her?" Ashley asked.

"No, that is my rent-a-grandmother we keep on the porch. Of course that's her," Carly said with a smile.

"Oh, sassy, I like it. We've only been on the road for two hours and you've already changed so much." Ashley opened the van door and headed to the back for their bags before Carly could respond. With her backpack over her shoulder, Ashley waltzed back over to Darren by the driver's side.

"Thank you, Jeeves. I shall ring for you when I require your services again."

"Thank you, Darren," Carly said. "I really appreciate it."

"No problem, just behave this weekend. It looks like a real party central."

"You have no idea," Carly said, eliciting another couple of approving guffaws from Ashley. Darren nodded at her comment. His eyes flared slightly, as if he was trying to get her to remember their small conversation. *Don't forget*, Carly heard his voice in her ear. *Don't forget.*

Ashley and Carly took a step back, as Darren backed out of the driveway. Carly watched as he drove down the long road, until she couldn't see his car anymore. When she tossed her duffel bag on the porch, Ashley was already there, introducing herself to Dorothy.

Dorothy smiled up at Carly when she got close enough to hear.

"It's very nice to meet you, dear. I'm very excited Carly took me up on my offer to bunk one of her friends for the night."

"Aren't you cold, Dorothy?" Carly said. "It's a bit chilly out here, and you don't have shoes on."

Carly looked down at Dorothy's crocheted slippers she had made herself before the arthritis in her wrists got too much for her. There was a quilted blanket over her lap, which Carly was relieved to see. Dorothy waved her hands in the air, shooing away the concern.

"Pfft. I'm fine, dear." Dorothy wiggled her toes in her crocheted slippers. "Not like I'm going to die out here."

"Shush," Carly said. "I wasn't talking about that."

"Shush, yourself." Dorothy smiled. She regarded Ashley with curious, dark-blue eyes. "This one tells me she calls you Carly Rogers. Like its one word, it comes out of her mouth so fast."

Ashley chuckled. "Or like a pirate, you know."

"Ah, yes," Dorothy said, clutching Ashley's arms. Carly felt her heart swoon a little. Dorothy was already touching Ashley, clutching her like she did when she spoke animatedly about math, science, or the past. Ashley leaned against the railing around the wooden porch, grinning at Carly as if to boast that she had already, no matter how small, managed to win over Dorothy.

"As I was saying," Dorothy said. "I will die in this house like I was born in it. I'm practically the house itself. I still remember waking up early when I was in my teens and walking back to those plum and pecan trees. I filled up my skirt with fruit and nuts, and then hid them in my room. Every day, I would always walk back and forth and then hide my bounty for later."

"Why did need to hide it?"

"Wouldn't you? You must keep the good things inside, saving them for winter. I also had a lot of siblings who were nosy, you know. I had to seek out good hiding spots."

"I hear you," Ashley said. "I had a lot of brothers. I still have them, you know, but now I have them under control."

"Middle child?"

"Youngest, actually. They all want to take care of me."

"Luckily," Dorothy said. "I don't have that problem much anymore."

Dorothy gave Carly a small wink. Ashley sat on the porch railing, her gaze looking out toward the long fields. Most of the grass was green now, and many of the trees now bloomed. They couldn't see the plum or pecan trees from on the porch, but they could see the mountain ash and the cherry trees that lined the property and the highway. The dark-orange buds of the mountain ash tree were always Carly's favorite. She supposed, like her great-aunt, she kept time by watching the blossoms turn from dark red to orange, which signaled fall and Carly's upcoming birthday.

"So, that's enough small talk," Dorothy said. She shifted on her seat, falling slightly before she got up. While Carly rushed over to help, Ashley stayed still. She waited, just as Dorothy caught her balance again and then held onto Ashley's arm.

"You mind escorting me in?" Dorothy asked.

Ashley smiled, a proud boast on her face. "Dorothy, I thought you would never ask."

Ashley and Dorothy stayed in the living room, while Carly prepared lunch. She assembled sandwiches (of ham for Ashley and Dorothy and only cheese for Carly) and cut up some vegetables rather quickly. When she spotted a small Tupperware container filled with homemade oatmeal and chocolate chip cookies, Carly's smile grew. Carly made up one last plate, for dessert, and then began the rather arduous task of bringing in the meal from the kitchen. Ashley worked on setting up the coffee table and some TV trays, as Carly wandered back and forth.

Whenever Ashley wasn't leaning in close to hear Dorothy's opinions on the poet, P. K. Page, or something to do with biology, she was eyeballing the rest of the room. Ashley's gaze wandered from bookshelf to bookshelf, photo frame to diploma, each item evoking awe.

"You guys ready?" Carly asked, as she passed around glasses of lemonade.

"Yes, yes, of course." Dorothy pulled at the napkins on the table, and slid one over her lap. "I don't mean to be a nuisance, but could you make some tea, too?"

"Not at all." Carly glanced at Ashely, suggesting, "Cocoa for you?"

"Thank you. Sounds good."

"And I may as well make some coffee for me, while we're being decadent."

"I like your books, Dorothy," Ashley remarked, when Carly came back in. She handed out drinks and sat back down.

"Thank you, Carly," Dorothy said. "And thanks, too, Ashley. I'm pretty sure I've read them all."

"All of them? Every last one?"

Dorothy nodded, a smile on her face. "No story was too bad or too long. I like to finish what I start."

"I completely agree," Carly said. "I feel as if I abandon the characters if I do that."

"I'm impressed," Ashley said. "I think that's what my new life goal will be."

"To read all the books in the world?" Carly asked with a laugh. "I wouldn't put that past you."

"That's impossible. But I think I could try and read all the books in my house, whenever I get one again."

"What was your goal before that? I would hate to have so much sway I get you to change your path significantly."

Ashley laughed. "Don't worry. I sometimes make a lot of snap decisions."

"I hope Carly's not one," Dorothy said, raising an eyebrow as she ate her sandwich.

"No, ma'am, not at all." Ashley slid her hand toward Carly.

"So what was that goal, then? If I'm being too nosy though, please let me know. I don't want to turn into Jillian." Dorothy paused, considering something. "How is Jillian? With you two?"

"Um," Carly said, fumbling over her words. "I don't know, truthfully. I think she likes Ashley. But she never really asks about stuff like that."

"Did she ever ask before, though?" Ashley wondered.

Carly sighed. "Not really. My business is my business."

"Don't ask, don't tell," Ashley mumbled.

"Jillian is tough," Dorothy said, after a moment of thought. "She works very hard. But she needs to calm down, you know."

Carly nodded vigorously. She wanted to spill and talk about the whole ordeal the night before, but that seemed like too heavy a conversation for the nice meal they were having.

Dorothy turned to Ashley again. "So what was your former life goal, if I can still ask?"

"Of course," Ashley said. "I don't keep too many secrets. I used to want to build a house—from scratch. I wanted to plan out every last detail and build it to last. Raise my kids inside of it."

"That's still a worthy goal, you know."

"Nah, not with the housing crisis," Ashley said with a wave of her hand.

"You could flip a house, though. They have a show for that, right?" Dorothy asked.

"Yes," Carly said. "It's on after *Hoarders*."

"Oh my goodness, I love that show. The chaos inside those people's houses, it says so much about them. Says a lot about people in general, what they choose to keep and what they hold onto," Dorothy said. "But I digress. Yes, Ashley, you could flip a house."

"I used to think I'd get into renovating, sure. But it's not the same unless you build it from the ground up. Then you feel as if the house is yours, you know? Like how you must feel."

"Oh, sweetheart. I can't build. I can barely hold a nail and hammer, even before my arthritis. But when you live in a place long enough, and with someone you love, you change it. You can rewire the walls and rebuild the entrances with a family, easy as anything."

"Did you ever live with anyone?" Ashley asked.

"Oh, no. I can't stand people."

"But Carly?"

"Just Carly." Dorothy winked. "Everyone thought I was gay, you know," Dorothy added with another laugh.

"Oh, I do know."

"But really, I just don't like anyone. Never really did. And my siblings had all the kids, so why bother? I get to watch such beautiful boys and girls grow up in this world. I get to benefit from my sister's wonderful girls and then, whenever there is trouble in paradise, I can just send them home."

"Not that that ever happened with me, Dorothy," Carly teased. "Right?"

"No, dear," she said with a wry smile. "You are definitely a special case. You're the one who takes care of me."

Carly smiled, suddenly moved by the statement. She didn't let it linger too long. "Speaking of which," she said, rising to her feet. "I'm going to get more coffee. Anyone need refills?"

Ashley and Dorothy both shook their heads. As Carly ventured into the kitchen, both Ashley and Dorothy leaned toward one another, whispering carefully between them. Carly knew her name was on the tips of their tongues. As much as she wanted to have her ego stroked, she made her way to the coffee pot, added sugar to her drink, and tried to give them enough time alone before coming back.

"They called it a Boston marriage back in my day," Dorothy mentioned. "Ages ago."

"A Boston marriage?" Carly asked, sitting down again.

"Yes. It basically referred to two women who lived together and pooled their income. They were gay, basically, but people didn't think that happened back then. Women could get away with a lot more then, especially since most people thought women didn't enjoy sex."

"Well, it's a lot harder to enjoy sex when you don't like the other participant," Carly remarked, giving Ashley a wry smile.

"Indeed," Dorothy said.

"Did you know any women who were gay?" Ashley asked.

"Lots," Dorothy said. "There are some places that you go to when you're older where you start to notice people pairing up. You notice how close they are to one another at a table. There is a kind of intimacy that comes from living together, from being with someone, and it's written all over body language. You know, I used to play a game when I went out to eat. I would find people on dates and see who had been intimate with one another. Sometimes this game was a lot more interesting when the taboo around marriage was still there. But anyway," Dorothy smiled. "I could tell from the way the man still observed certain conventions, the way he spoke to her and handed her the menu. The way she held her body. It's better when you see someone walking together. You notice how their feet fall in line, how they hand one another their coats or hold the doors. When someone talks, how much they lean in. I swear, people who think they can hide who they date are wrong. It's always there, written on the skin."

Carly shifted in her seat, glancing at Ashley, who then burst out laughing.

"I'm sorry, Dorothy," Ashley said. "I meant to be more presentable."

"Sweetheart, I'm aware of what day and time it is. Don't be worried about this."

"No," Carly said, with a small laugh. She eyed Ashley. "I'm not worried about you at all."

"Jillian?"

"I can't live my life always being worried about her."

"No, you can't," Dorothy said, suddenly stern. Her stare lingered on Carly for a moment, before she suggested, "Does your work have an issue with this?"

Carly shrugged. "Probably not. And even if we were dating and they knew, so what? What's the worst that could happen?"

Carly's rhetorical question took on sudden weight. The worst had happened to Landon last night, and now Carly wasn't too sure if she could tempt fate with blasé statements like that. Before her anxiety took over, Ashley's hand slid over hers.

Dorothy smiled from across the table. "You take for granted that so often people don't want to see things," Dorothy said. "Especially things they don't understand."

"I know," Ashley said. "I'm never concerned. The people I have to impress I can fit onto a hand." As if to demonstrate, Ashley held up her hand and began to list her brothers, her father, and then Carly on each of her fingers.

"Well, you should use your other hand," Dorothy said. "Because I'm still here."

"Okay, okay," Ashley said. "So long as I don't have to start taking off my shoes and counting toes, I'm good."

"Even if you did, what's so wrong with that?"

"I don't like to let people's expectations hold me back," Ashley said. "It's a lot harder to live my life that way."

"Expectations are one thing," Dorothy said. "But people? Well, you can never have too many people that you care about. Right?"

"Bodies," Carly echoed, nodding along with a small tilt of her head, "and not ideals, right Dorothy?"

"Exactly."

When Ashley tilted her head, suddenly lost with the conversation, Carly explained Dorothy's words from before in better detail. Ashley nodded along, a small smile forming on the corner of her lips.

"I like that. I should keep it in mind."

"I wouldn't have gotten to be this old in a house by myself if I didn't do something right, I like to think," Dorothy said.

"I agree. And I think we should toast to that," Carly said, holding up her drink.

"To…love?" Ashley suggested.

"To homecomings," Dorothy corrected. "The best part of love is knowing when you can come home and who will be there for you."

Carly smiled, a small tinge of regret hurting her. Dorothy lived alone and had always lived alone. She spent so much time watching for intimacy in other people, but what about herself? Who came home for her? Dorothy's eyes seemed to catch her across the table, hinting subtly. Dorothy seemed to say, *don't you dare feel bad for me, especially when you are the answer.* Carly nodded, then brought her glass forward.

"To homecomings."

They all clinked their glasses as much as they could across the table. Dorothy couldn't quite reach so she simply said clink instead. Ashley laughed, and they all drank to the toast."

"I like you," Dorothy said. "You're nice and formal."

"Well, thanks. I try to get things right the first time," Ashley said.

"Even if you don't," Dorothy said, "there is no shame in second chances."

"Definitely," Ashley said. "I think I've taken a lot of them."

"Cookies?" Carly asked. She rose from the couch, and began to pass around the plate. She placed a couple oatmeal and raisin ones on her own plate, figuring that no one else but her would want them. She was surprised, as she worked her way around, that both Dorothy and Ashley cleaned the rest of them out. *Seems like we all have more in common than I thought.*

The idea made Carly smile. The rest of lunch was easy, like coming home.

CHAPTER 30

When Dorothy went upstairs for a nap, Carly and Ashley started cleaning duties. They did the dishes, with Carly set up to wash and Ashley to dry. They completed most of the lunch plates before Carly noticed the distinct slurping sound of the drain—followed by the dripping underneath the sink.

"Crap." Carly dried off her hands and opened the cupboard under the sink. The small bucket she had placed there earlier was now full, and spilling over inside.

"Crap," she said again. "I should have called the plumber."

Carly emptied the bucket into the sink. After the water went down the drain, water dripped down from the pipe and landed where the bucket once was.

Carly furrowed her brows as Ashley laughed. "Oh. Of course. I didn't think this through, did I?"

"I like it. Kind of speaks to the whole water cycle in nature."

Carly groaned. She placed the empty bucket back underneath the sink; a blush crept across her face. "Where is a phone book? I need to call a plumber."

"We have Google for that, dear."

Carly huffed again. Ashley took another step forward and touched Carly's cheek sympathetically.

"Don't worry, okay? We will figure that out later."

"I know what it is," Carly said. She struggled to explain the U shape pipe and how the mains around it were broken. Ashley nodded along.

"I can see as much. But I don't think a plumber is going to drop everything to come for a leaky pipe. He's probably already booked for today. We'll wait it out for now—and not dispose of the water in the bucket at the same place, okay?"

"Ugh," Carly said again. "I don't want to forget and leave Dorothy in a lurch."

"I understand." Ashley squeezed Carly's hands again, trying to calm her down. She moved her arms around Carly's waist and held her there. "I may know a thing or two. I'll look at it, but later, okay?"

"Since when were you a plumber?"

"Do I need to give you a job history?"

"I guess not. But right now I'm having a ton of fun imagining you as a renovator with your big tools. You know, kind of like that movie with Jennifer Tilly."

"Oh," Ashley sighed, squeezing her eyes shut. "No, no. None of that."

"Why not? I thought *Bound* was a cinematic masterpiece."

"Shush." Ashley pressed a finger to Carly's lips firmly. Ashley's skin was rough and smelled like the apple-scented dish soap they had been using. Carly pressed back into Ashley's lips, coaxing Ashley to deepen the kiss through opened mouths. When Ashley did, Carly nearly swooned. Ashley caressed her cheek, stepping closer and sliding their bodies together. This kiss wasn't an embrace like the ones they had shared around Dorothy or Ashley's brother. This was deep, secure. Carly didn't want to let go.

When Ashley pulled away, she grinned lazily. "Hey."

"Hey," Carly echoed. Her knees were weak. She turned to the counter, gripping the edge for strength.

Ashley glanced under the sink for inspection. After a few minutes of quiet assessment she clucked her tongue. "I see the issue. It's easy enough to fix, especially if your aunt has tools stored here somewhere. Maybe in the shed?"

"I've never really looked there. I figured there was no reason to."

"Okay, good to know. I can look later."

"Where exactly did you learn this?" Carly asked playfully. "Job histories aside."

"With tools and such? Well, before…all of this happened with me, I did have a car, you know. I had a nice car. She used to live in the garage, mostly, because you don't want to get something like that dirty."

"She?"

"Yes, all cars are women. That's why I'm really not surprised I turned out the way I did. I loved Tonka trucks from a young age, my dear."

"But you didn't have a Tonka truck, I hope," Carly said. "So what did you have?"

"Ford Mustang—in green. She was beautiful. I rode her all the time."

"How could you afford something like that?"

"Well, before my minimum wage days, I did have a good job, remember? I also bought her as a junker. Spent most of my time restoring her."

"That's amazing," Carly said, genuinely moved. She didn't even know how to pump gas. She was sure that she could figure it out—*how hard can it be, especially if I've watched Landon do it a million times?*—but the life under the hood of a car was just as mysterious as the life under her aunt's sink. There were too many pipes, too many nuts and bolts and levers of which she didn't quite grasp the function.

"Why don't I see you doing this anymore?" Carly asked, as Ashley began to place slow kisses on the side of her neck. When Ashley pulled away, Carly wished she had never opened her mouth. The ending of this story, and these questions, were always inevitable. Ashley didn't do that anymore because she got sick. She never gave up her hobbies willingly, Carly knew. Everything that made Ashley who she was now was a product of something else.

"I'm sorry," Carly said.

"No. Why would you be sorry? You're asking me a question," Ashley said, taking her hands in hers. "You're trying to get to know me."

"Yeah. Something like that."

"So now you know that story. I stopped working on my car because I couldn't drive. Because everyone was worried I'd have a seizure while I was underneath one."

"But you could still look at it. Look but don't drive, right?"

"We had to sell her to help pay for medical bills. I switched my old hobby for this one called *Warmachine*. That sounds far more badass."

"I'm sorry."

"No, no," Ashley said, holding up her hands. "You know, the one thing I didn't really do for my old car was her paint job. I was never good at painting. So, now I am. I had to learn from Darren and then fix all of the mistakes he made. But I was able to expand my skill set. I'm okay with this."

"I know, I'm just…"

"Stop being sorry, you ridiculous Carly Rogers," Ashley said. She took a step closer to Carly, wrapping her arms around her in a supportive, rather than seductive, embrace. "Don't ever feel sorry for me. I don't need—"

"I know, the pity."

"No, well, yes there is that. But the worry. I don't need the worry."

Carly ran her hands up Ashley's back, pressing her palms into her. It was hard to believe that someone as sturdy as Ashley, as warm as her, could possibly break. A ball of tension unleashed itself in her stomach. She closed her eyes, trying to push away what Darren had told her earlier. She tried to remove the protocols and what numbers to dial. She just wanted to hold Ashley, like they always did, and not worry that she could shatter. Carly felt Ashley's kips kissing the soft skin under her ear.

"I am healthy," Ashley whispered. "And you are healthy. There is nothing to feel sorry for."

"I know. I'm just…upset for you. That just sucks so much about your car."

"I will get it back again. There is a Buddhist saying that all desire leads to suffering. We must deal with impermanence. And yes, I know I'm not exactly a Buddhist or anything, but sometimes the armies in these games borrow eastern tropes. I found it incredibly helpful when I was able to work with my hands again. Nothing is permanent. We tend to think our bodies are, because so often, we live in a medical age where nothing is wrong with us. But our bodies will fail us. We will get sick. Nothing is permanent." Ashley leaned back so she could press another kiss on Carly's forehead. She curled some of Carly's dark hair around her ear. "I can't long for the past just because I lost my car. I will get another car, eventually, in the future."

"But what if…"

"What ifs make people so *tired*." Ashley kissed Carly softly, as she slid her hands around Carly's waist, then toward her thighs. "What ifs don't get us anywhere fun. And I like the time I spend with you."

"I like it, too." Carly opened her legs more, allowing Ashley to rub her through the fabric of her jeans Carly's mouth opened, her jaw slack with pleasure.

"And who knows?" Ashley said, her voice light. "Maybe I'll fall for a girl with a good car, and I can live vicariously through her."

Carly chuckled. Her eyes were still closed, focusing on Ashley's hands on her body. "Maybe? I guess that's not me then."

"Hey, no. You shouldn't worry about what you can't do, anymore than I should mourn what I used to be able to do."

"Oh, zen master," Carly said breathily. "Teach me the ways of your world."

Ashley's lips found the sensitive spot behind Carly's ear again. Ashley kissed, pressing her lips and tongue against the spot and making Carly's insides feel weak. She shifted on her feet, falling back into Ashley's body. As Ashley kissed, she moved her hands over Carly's thighs, up to the button on her pants, and began to undo it. Once free, she slid a hand inside.

"I don't…" Carly said, pulling away slightly. Her body wanted the touch, longed for it. But she glanced upstairs, her mouth formed in a tense smile. "What about…?"

"She's asleep," Ashley said. "She won't hear us. Moreover, I don't think she'll care."

"Yeah, maybe you're…" Carly stopped before she could finish.

Ashley's fingers found their way between the warmth of Carly's legs, touching the fabric of her panties with her index and middle finger. Ashley's thumb ran around the edge, and pushed back the fabric until she found her way inside. Carly made a small noise from the back of her throat, as Ashley's fingers found her clitoris.

"Oh." Carly pressed her lips together tightly, as if she was giving herself away. Ashley continued to caress the small bud, as if willing Carly to be more vocal.

"Oh—oh," Carly said, this time with a deep resonance in her voice. Ashley moved her body so that she could slide her fingers lower, coating them with Carly's wetness, and then rise back to rub against her again.

Ashley placed her mouth over Carly's neck whenever her fingers slid inside deeper, coaxing more movement out of Carly.

"Yes," Ashley said as she moved her fingers. "Yes, come on, Carly. Come for me."

The tension mounted inside of Carly. Ashley played in all the right ways, stroking her in a slow but persistent rhythm. The sensation of their hands on one another's bodies was still so new, so different, that Carly wondered if she could come standing up like this. Usually, she needed a mouth and a bed, a state of complete relaxation. But Ashley was able to get her going within a matter of seconds, and she didn't want it to end so soon.

"Ugh," Carly groaned. "Slow down."

"Yes?"

"Yes," Carly echoed. Ashley seemed to laugh into her neck, before her fingers slowed their pace. Ashley's hands moved up Carly's body, twisting her shirt and pulling it up. Carly's breasts, still in a bra, were exposed to the cool air, making her nipples even harder. Carly kept her eyes closed, only looking once to see Ashley's devious stare as she kissed her way down Carly's neck to her chest. Ashley slid out one of Carly's breasts, sucking the nipple.

"I want you," Carly gasped. "Come on. Let's go to the living room. The couch. Anywhere."

"No, no," Ashley said. She kissed Carly's neck, making her weak in her knees. Pliable. "Right here. Right here, Carly Rogers. I want to make you come."

"I don't think I can. Not like this."

"You can," Ashley insisted. "I had you close before. I just need you to relax. Come on. It's the first thing they teach you in school."

"That coming relaxes you?"

"That relaxation is good for your health." Ashley smiled. "I made the conclusion to coming all by myself."

"You're smart," Carly said, still teasing. She faced the window, pressing her ass into Ashley to tease and coax her. Ashley's hands slid between her legs again, pushing the rim of her jeans farther down her body.

"Come on," Ashley said. "You can do this. Relax."

Ashley stroked her fingers against Carly again, while she placed her lips on her neck. When Carly began to moan again, Ashley smiled against her skin. Carly lifted her shirt up each time it fell down. She liked the sensation of her breasts out, nipples exposed, and bouncing each time Ashley moved against her. The thought of being caught or being seen through the window was no longer nerve-racking to Carly; it became a motivator as she felt Ashley's fingers move her closer and closer to orgasm.

"Go," Carly urged now. "I'm almost."

Ashley moved fast, flicking her fingers as much as she could. She took her free hand toward Carly's face, along her chin, tilting their lips together. Carly's breasts bounced, as her breath became quicker, and her heart pounded in her chest. Carly moaned. Ashley went faster, faster, until—

"Fuck," Carly said. Her thighs opened with sudden invigoration and then nearly snapped shut around Ashley's fingers and wrist. Ashley paused, light laughter on her voice. Ashley did not move, except to rock Carly's body with her hips. Ashley held onto Carly's chin, as she continued to kiss her.

"See. Feel much better now?"

"Yes, I do," Carly said, as she caught her breath. Then she dropped to her knees in front of Ashley. "Now you're next."

A thud sounded from the bedroom upstairs.

"What was that?" Carly asked.

Ashley shrugged, as she slid her belt back into position. Her cheeks were flushed and part of her hair stuck to her forehead. Carly ran a hand over her own hair, fixing the few strands that had gotten out of place. They both paused, standing stock-still, as they heard another rattle followed by a thud.

"It's coming from Dorothy's bedroom," Carly said. "I'm going to go up and check on her."

"Do you need help?" Ashley asked.

Carly shook her head before she left the kitchen. She almost doubled back to get Ashley's help, especially given what she may find in Dorothy's room. She had heard her mother talk before about Dorothy falling out of bed and had warned Carly what to do if she ever broke her hip. They would need to call an ambulance, no question, because neither one of them could drive and there was no vehicle around. Carly hoped it wouldn't have to come to that, especially for her aunt's privacy sake.

She made her way to her aunt's room at the end of the hall. Carly listened carefully to the shallow sounds of breathing before she knocked.

"Dorothy?"

Nothing.

"Dorothy?"

Still nothing. Carly held her breath and took another step forward.

When she heard a faint snore from Dorothy, Carly let out a relieved breath.

"Dorothy?" Carly called again. She spotted a small bob of gray hair against the pillows. Blankets up to her neck. *Everything's fine. Don't even worry.* Carly turned around to go, only to step on a floorboard that let out a loud creak.

"Dear?"

"Yes, Dorothy. It's Carly. I heard a loud bang from downstairs," she tried to explain as she turned around.

Dorothy shifted slightly, but didn't move in the bed. She pushed down the sheets, exposing her tired face. Without her glasses and the clothing she usually wore, she looked so much smaller; much more fragile and weak.

"Are you okay?"

"Yes, yes, dear." Dorothy peered over the bed and pointed to something across the room. "Is it still there?"

Carly took a few steps closer to the direction Dorothy pointed. Around the large frame of the bed, Carly spotted a large anthology. The spine on the book was broken now, the glue falling off of it and onto the throw rug in large yellow pieces. Next to the anthology on the ground was a Bible that also used to sit on the small desk by the side of the room. A jug full of pens and pencils had also knocked over and scattered on the floor and underneath the throw rug beside her bed.

"Ah, okay. Sorry, Dorothy," Carly said. "False alarm. This is definitely what I heard downstairs. Nothing to write home about. I didn't mean to bug you."

"I could have told you that. My hips are still firmly attached to my body."

"Yes, so I can see."

Carly crouched down to clean up the mess, returning the books to the desk rather than the shelf they had fallen from. Carly was always amazed at how much her aunt's room resembled some of those illustrations she found whenever she flipped open books from the twentieth century, like *Little Women* or *Alice's Adventures in Wonderland*. The house was almost as old as those books, and so much of Dorothy's stuff seemed to come right out of that era. It was beautiful, as much as it was a reminder about how much time had passed.

"Are you okay?" Dorothy asked.

"Yes," Carly said, closing the book she found herself browsing through. "Just distracted. Sorry to disturb you." Carly wondered if she was missing something. The way Dorothy stared at her made her feel as if she was exposed, as if she had been caught in the act. Carly scanned the floor, to see if she had forgotten about any of the mess—then she looked at her jeans, hoping that she hadn't left her fly undone. She was fine. But the eyes on Dorothy, especially without her glasses, made her pause.

"I swear, sweetheart," Dorothy said. "I'm normally not this old. But I need to sleep again. Beauty rest."

"I know," Carly said. "Rest easy."

Carly nodded to Dorothy again just as she left the room. She pulled the door shut behind her, leaving it about an inch open, like before. Carly paused in the hallway again, holding her breath, and waited until she heard Dorothy's shallow breaths dip back into a sleeping rhythm. *Nothing's wrong,* Carly repeated to herself, and continued to repeat as she walked down the stairs.

"Hey," Carly greeted. "Crisis averted."

Ashley barely lifted her eyes from a piece of paper and her phone she held in her hand. "How was she?"

"Oh, fine. It was just a few books on her desk falling down."

"Out of nowhere?" Ashley asked. "Maybe the house has ghosts."

"Nah, it's just old, and Dorothy probably didn't put them back right. I cleaned up and checked on her. She's still sleeping now."

"I still think the house has ghosts," Ashley said, barley hiding her smile. She held up the piece of paper. "I found them writing poems."

Carly's eyes went wide. She recognized the small cue card she held—and her handing writing on it. "Where did you find that?"

"I was putting away some mugs, and this fell out of the cupboard," Ashley explained. She held the cue card behind her phone and showed Carly the screen. Google was pulled up, the first few lines of the stanza fed in. "And I've been searching. This isn't a quote, though it felt familiar. I think these ghosts are writing original works. And good works, too."

"'Yes," Carly confessed before she could be asked. "That's mine."

"I *thought* so." Ashley put her phone back into her pocket, but kept the cue card close. "My question is, why in the cupboard? I'm sure there are more poetic places than hiding inside an old blue mug. And why have you kept this talent from me?"

"Talent may be pushing it."

"I beg to differ. You are a poet—and a pirate. I like that kind of multiplicity in my women."

"Pfft. I'm not exactly your woman."

"Oh?" Ashley asked playfully. "What are you?"

"I'm your...girlfriend. Partner. We're equal, remember?"

"Ah, yes. But I don't know if I can compete with this poetry."

"Equal," Carly urged, still being playful. "But different. Does that make sense?"

"Yes, of course," Ashley said. She extended her hand in a delicate and polite manner, holding the cue card at the other end. "So can you explain this to me, more? In all seriousness."

Carly sighed, folding her arms over her chest. "It's stupid."

"I bet it's not. Come on, equal but different. Tell me," Ashley said, touching Carly at the side. "It's really good."

"Thanks. It's nothing, though. Just a kind of...game Dorothy and I do."

"Game?"

"I write something and then she writes something. We're kind of exchanging stanzas and observations. You heard her talk, right? She has these really interesting analogies and parallels. They work really well in poetry. I honestly forget how it started, but it's something we do. I like it."

"I do too," Ashley said honestly. She looked back down at the card, flipping it between her fingers. "So there is more than just this? It's not like a lone haiku?"

"No, there's more. We've been doing it since I've been coming here, since I was around twenty-one, maybe?"

"That's a couple of years now. What happens to all of this? Do you keep them?"

"I don't think so. Not really. We haven't been published or made a book of them or anything."

"Talk about impermanence. Maybe you should consider something more than just the act of creation."

Carly shrugged. "It's just a fun game."

"But games are good." Ashley paused. "You should know by now that I like games, even if you're not a chess master yet. And I like this poem, too. Can I keep it?"

"Sure," Carly said. "I'd like that actually."

Ashley smiled. She folded the piece of paper inside her palm and then shoved it in her jeans pocket, as she leaned in and planted a kiss on Carly's cheek.

"I fixed the sink, by the way."

"In that short time I was gone?"

Ashley nodded, her smugness showing. "It actually wasn't that hard. There was already a wrench down there to tighten the bolt. It barely involved anything at all. I'm really glad you didn't call a plumber."

"I won't need to anymore," Carly said. She crouched down by the sink and opened the door… No dripping. No nothing. Ashley crouched down next to her, putting a hand on her shoulder.

"Thank you. This is great."

"It was nothing, really."

"Apparently we both have hidden talents." Carly smiled, before she turned to Ashley again, kissing her deeply. Ashley placed a hand on Carly's cheek, deepening the kiss. The embrace went on a little longer, until Carly's legs began to hurt from crouching for too long.

"I like it here," Ashley stated when she pulled away. She looked up, examining the house, the backyard, everywhere else all around them. "It's a good place. Very home-like."

"Yes," Carly said, smiling weakly. "It is my home."

"More than your mother's place?" Ashley rolled her eyes, realizing how that was true. "More so than the apartment you got when you moved out? In Boston?"

Carly nodded. "Definitely."

"Then, thank you."

"For what?"

"Thank you for taking me home, Carly Rogers," Ashley said, as she placed her arms around Carly again. "I won't forget it."

Carly kissed Ashley; it was all she could do for some time. In the back of her mind, Carly repeated phrases of poetry that could describe this moment with Ashley. But she said nothing aloud and wrote nothing down. Carly merely held Ashley in her arms and tried to appreciate what she could of the moment, inside her small home away from home.

CHAPTER 31

After cleaning was done, they decided to watch a movie on Dorothy's old VCR.

"It really does feel as if I'm going back ten years every time I see you," Ashley remarked as she sat on the couch. "First we were sneaking out like kids, walking around and having no money, and then we had a sleepover with your friends. Now we're watching *Steel Magnolias* and probably are going to cry over Julia Roberts dying."

"Spoiler alert," Carly said. "I haven't seen this before."

"You have not been a girl, ever, then."

"Pfft." Carly got the button on the screen to glow green and clapped her hands together in success. "We also have *Mystic Pizza* and *Say Anything* if you prefer a change, Ashley Poindexter."

She laughed, a large smile on her face. "All end in the same way."

Carly raised an eyebrow until Ashley expanded, "Cheese."

"Then should we go for *Mystic Pizza*, so at least the cheese is appropriate?"

Ashley groaned from the couch. "Watch whatever you want, I'm just looking forward to getting to second base on the couch."

Carly went with her first inclination and slid in the VHS tape for *Steel Magnolias*. On the large couch, Ashley wrapped them both in a blanket. Before Dolly Parton even had a chance to get on screen, Ashley slid her hand around Carly's waist. And then up her shirt.

"Shush," Ashley said when Carly tried to joke around and call attention to Ashley's hand. "Movie is on. Very important stuff. I have to pay attention."

Carly teased Ashley with a kiss—that soon became a make out session. Somehow, Ashley managed to undo Carly's bra without touching the clasp. With a gasp, Carly pulled the bra off through one of her sleeves and then went back to kissing Ashley. Their passion soon cooled when Carly shivered, and Ashley tugged over more blankets to keep them warm.

"You are different here," Ashley declared during a lull in the film.

"What do you mean?"

"You're relaxed," she stated. "Happy."

"I'm not usually?"

"You're…a little uptight."

"I am *not*," Carly said, playfully swatting Ashley.

"Yeah, you are. Landon is nice about it because he's just as anxious about things—probably even more now that he's had his run in with the landlord from hell. So really, he's easy on you and understands what it's like to be afraid of everything, in an odd way. And even Cyn puts up with your anxiety without saying anything, because she utterly adores you. So no one really in your life tells you this. But you are a little uptight."

Carly looked down at the fraying edges of the blanket, feeling exposed. She didn't find the words hurtful or even overly honest. Ashley was like this all the time, calling her father old or Darren a bit dull. She didn't mean it maliciously; she was just illuminating foibles. But it still made Carly feel as if she had been hit in the stomach.

"I'm sorry," Carly said, sighing. "It's not my fault, you know."

"I never said it was your fault. I know you have a lot of reasons to be that way. And you do try to get better. You've probably developed a dozen coping strategies, like picking up almost any book ever and reading it, just to not be alone with your worrying thoughts. But you change when you're here. The past just kind of…" Ashley held up her hand, almost whimsically, motioning around the room, "disappears. You're yourself, Carly Rogers. And I happen to like that woman a lot."

"Do you now?"

"Yeah, yeah, I like this face," Ashley said, touching Carly's cheek. "I like these lips. I like the way you kiss with them." Ashley leaned in, planting a kiss to demonstrate her point. "I like this person. I like you."

The repeated words of like made Carly nervous—like sitting on a chair that was about to tip over at a moment's notice. Ashley made Carly think of her feelings deeper down, suppressed but almost at the surface. "Well, that's good," Carly said eventually. "Because I like you a lot, too. Even if you do make fun of me for being uptight."

"Pfft. If teasing works for kids on the playground, then it works for me too. Now shush. But we're missing the movie," Ashley insisted. "And I'd like to see where this goes."

Halfway through the film, Carly's phone nearly danced across the dark oak coffee table. When she picked it up, a short message from Landon followed.

I am stealing your little sister. She is the only other person I know who can have a full conversation with me in SpongeBob Squarepants quotations. And now, she is mine.

Carly laughed, showing the phone to Ashley before typing a quick reply.

Well, be sure to let me see her weekends and holidays. I will miss the kid, but so long as I know she's safe.

When Ashley peaked over Carly's shoulder, she also laughed at the text messages. "Well, I'm glad everyone's happy right now."

"Yeah," Carly said, snuggling closer to Ashley, though she knew she'd have to untangle herself soon. Dorothy usually only slept for a couple of hours in the afternoon, since her arthritis medication often made her drowsy. She would get up for dinner and in the summer, often spent most of her evenings on the porch reading or listening to the radio. Carly knew she would have to get dinner ready soon, but she was so warm and comfortable, she put her phone back on the coffee table and tried to forget for a bit.

"I like it here," Ashley declared after a few moments. "Everything here has a nice quality to it. Very old, rustic—but easy to fix. Even the plumbing's a breeze."

"This place is in dire need of a renovation. My mom hates it here for that reason alone."

"Sure, this place is a fixer upper, but that's easy enough to do. But do *you* like it here?"

"I thought you already had the answer to that?" Carly asked. "If I'm less anxious here, doesn't that mean it's better?"

"Perhaps. But I don't want to assume. And I think that has more to do with your aunt—or even, just not being around your mom as much than it does with antique windows."

Carly nodded, considering this. She eyed the old bookshelves, stuffed almost to the brim with the classics. From her vantage point on the couch, Carly saw books like *Moby Dick*, *Tess of d'Urbervilles*, and even some William Faulkner titles—all of which she had read and enjoyed immensely. But Carly also saw books she hadn't even cracked yet, like *Cymbeline*, *The Count of Monte Cristo*, *Jude the Obscure*—even a couple *Hardy Boys* mysteries. There were certainly enough books to keep her going for a long, long time.

"I like how antiquated it is here. Feels like we're in a simpler time, you know? My aunt still has a hand held mirror with a silver handle. That's incredible."

"Yeah, I get that. Kind of feels like being in a Dickens book, more often than not. But that doesn't necessarily mean that times were simpler."

"What do you mean?" Carly asked.

"I used to think a lot like that too, when I was in the hospital."

"How?"

"I used to want to go back in time. Revoke the internet, text messaging, and certainly commuting to work. I still wanted to be a contractor, but I wanted a simpler time of building, like back on a farm or working in the Old West. I wanted things to be easier like they used to be when I was a kid, when my parents were kids. So much of what happened to me, people attributed to stress. They were convinced that when my MRIs came back as something inconclusive, that I was surely the one that was at fault."

"That's ridiculous—"

"Sure, it's silly. But maybe stress was a part of it. So to avoid stress, I wanted to remove myself from the complicated life and have a simpler one. That was the allure of classic books when I started to read them, or even the historical and Regency romances. If Fabio could survive without running water and proper plumbing, and make it look good, then hey. Why not go back?"

"Okay. What's wrong with getting rid of stress that way? I sense a catch in your voice."

"There is always going to be stress," Ashley said. "The real trick is how you manage it."

"Like with your war gaming?"

"Yes, that certainly helped. My car did too, for the time I had her." Ashley paused, shifting to see Carly. "And your poems, too. I'm sure that helps you."

"I wish I could do more with it, though."

"Why can't you?"

Carly shrugged. "It feels like those verses are sort of stuck in time too, you know? What my aunt and I write only makes sense through context. It only makes sense in this room, and nowhere else. Sharing them would require my life story to have it make sense. And I'm not up to sharing that. Not with any more people, anyway."

"But I have one that will slip out."

"So maybe there is hope, then." Carly laughed.

On screen, Julia Roberts and Sally Field were talking complications during pregnancy, and whether or not Julia Robert's character would be able to survive. Carly sighed, realizing they were all talking about the same thing using different words and characters—strength, love, and leaving home. She felt comforted by that, even though it also made her sad.

"I guess it's sometimes hard to fathom what life will be like without certain crutches, you know?" Carly asked.

"We keep saying crutches like it's a bad thing to depend on something. Like it's a bad thing to be unable to walk on our own. We all *need* crutches. It just depends on what you call yours that matters. And I'd say that our vices—war gaming and poetry—are about as tame as they come."

"I guess so." Carly shrugged. Her eyes went back to the movie, where someone seemed to be teaching another character how to drive. She laughed. "You ever notice how big of a trope that is?"

"What?" Ashley asked.

"A significant other teaching their partner to drive. Even in *Say Anything*, Lloyd helps Diane Court learn how to drive. They have a scene of them going bumper to bumper in the roundabout on her street, which then cuts to them making out in the same car."

"It's just the sex appeal," Ashley said. "Just that alone, trust me."

"I guess, since a car is like a bed on wheels."

"It's a symbol of pride, too," Ashley said. Her face fell a little, but she did not linger in her loss. "It's also nice, showing someone something that you already know how to do. Helping them to become better, an adult, you know?"

"I know." Carly paused for a moment, remembering how her father taught her how to ride her bike. She had been so scared, so hesitant, that she made him promise to never take his hands off the back. Of course, he had, and when she looked back to tell him that she was perfectly fine by herself now, he was gone. She crashed and felt completely upset by his mistrust. She never got back on the bike until two weeks later, and by that time, she knew she could already go by herself. *That's the thing*, Carly realized at her young age. *You needed to have someone cradle you, until they suddenly dropped you, so you learned how to walk.* Breaking away from the proverbial nest was always like a kick in the stomach, but it was a kick you learned from. Carly wished that her father had been around to teach her how to drive, and not left it to her mother. But at least he was there for biking accidents, and her temper tantrums about them, before he was completely gone.

"I swear," Carly said, turning to Ashley again. "I think my mom deliberately kept me from learning how to drive some nights so I'd be there for Cyn. I don't regret it. But it's hard."

"And now Cyn has Landon," Ashley said.

"They're friends. I don't mind. It's not like I have to choose between them."

"But it's hard," Ashley nodded. "I can teach you, you know."

"What?"

"I can teach you how to drive."

"No, you can't. You don't have a license."

"But I used to have one." Ashley propped herself up with her arm and held Carly with the other. "It's not like they erased that part of my brain when they took it away. Come on, you know me. You saw me drive for the block and a half that I did with your sister and Landon."

"Yeah, but that was different."

"That was for someone else, yes," Ashley said. "I want to help *you* now."

"You already have. You're here, keeping me company."

Carly tried to snuggle close to Ashley, sealing away their worries with another kiss. But Ashley pulled away. "Carly Rogers."

"Ashley Poindexter."

"No time for jokes," Ashley said, placing a finger over Carly's lips again. "I'm serious. I want to teach you how to drive."

Carly sighed. "What good will it do? I don't have a car."

"But I know how to fix them."

Carly paused, looking away. She didn't want to force Ashley to do something that, from what she could tell, was annoying and hard. Jillian had always made such a big deal about going out to drive, how it was going to ruin her schedule and make her late for something. When Carly finally got her mother in the car, Jillian acted as if every small mistake would lead to ruin.

She wasn't like Dad at all, Carly thought suddenly. Dad's deception had been done for support. He kicked when no one was looking, so Carly could go out on her own. But her mother kicked Carly while she was looking, which only made her doubt. And doubt paralyzed Carly. It always had. She turned to face Ashley on the couch, who still smiled at her.

"I don't know…"

"Come on, you said it yourself," Ashley argued. "We're partners. Equal, but different."

"Yes, I did."

"So let me teach you. There are a million loopholes in any structure, a million ways to work around the system."

"Whose car do we use?"

"Landon's? Your mom's like before? It doesn't matter. Maybe even Darren would let me use his car."

"What if we get caught?"

"Landon could be there. Darren," Ashley said again. "We're not alone in this. There are people who could help us. We pretend they were teaching you. But they don't have to usurp the sex appeal from me."

Carly's chest tightened. Ashley by her side felt like too much, as if someone had finally noticed she was in the room and was caring. When she was a kid, she used to be so quiet. At school, Carly remembered holding her hand up inside the classroom for hours, waiting for someone to allow her to speak while everyone else talked over the teacher. Even at home, when Carly was a kid and her parents fought, she always felt as if she had to hold her hands up for years before people could see her. Before people noticed her. And with Brooklyn, the pseudo girlfriend and her first real love, it was even worse.

But Ashley looked right at her. Ashley took her hand in hers and held it next to her chest.

"Let me teach you," she asked again. "I want to, Carly. It's not a burden. It will be fun, really."

"And then?" Carly asked.

"And then," Ashley added, "let me help you escape. You deserve better than this. Let me show you that."

There was only a second pause before Carly threw her arms around Ashley. They pushed their bodies together on the couch, sighing softly into one another. Carly blinked away sudden tears that gathered in her eyes. It all seemed so stupid, so foolish. She had only known Ashley for a few months now, and they had barely begun their relationship. But she was so good to Carly, so supportive. Carly wanted to hold Ashley as she was, because in that moment, she knew that Ashley was utterly perfect for her.

"Oh, Carly Rogers."

"Ashley, Ashley Poindexter," Carly said, with a smile. Ashley pulled her back, kissing her mouth, and then rested their foreheads together.

"I love you," Carly said.

Ashley kissed Carly again, before she answered. "I love you, too."

CHAPTER 32

Work at Marshalls was often boring. Carly always seemed to be at cash, which meant she had to crawl out of bed just as the sun was coming up in order to make it to the store on time. But, for a while, Ashley was scheduled to work the same time she was. Those mornings were a lot easier to handle, and oftentimes, they spent the night together in order to make the experience of getting up early and getting to work slightly more bearable.

Ashley was mostly in the shoes department, but the staff was smartening up. As soon as most shift managers took notice that Ashley prospered much more when she was in menswear, she became a regular fixture in amongst paisley ties and Calvin Klein suits. Carly often looked up as she worked and watched as Ashley bounced back and forth between sections, her green collared shirt tied with her blue apron giving her away.

When a shoe needed a new tag or a bag of collared shirts were out of their packaging, Ashley would bring them up to the front, near cash, in order to use their tagging guns or refold the item.

"Afternoon, Carly Rogers."

"Afternoon, Ashley Poindexter."

The two of them would exchange a smile and a small nod before getting back to work. Since their pet names for one another were their actual names, no one ever noticed the difference in how they looked at one another, or even the traces of Ashley's hand on the small of Carly's back at cash, as they passed by one another. Though their full names seemed stilted in other people's mouths, when they talked to one another, it only seemed like the overzealous politeness that people use at work.

For lunch, the two of them would often trade or barter with other employees in order to have their break times line up. Since they were often in two completely different departments, this worked. When the two of them had finished *Treasure Island* together, they moved on to *Little Women*. After that, Carly had felt like a story with a happier ending, so they had gone to *Matilda* next, with the promise of finally reading an adult book in the following weeks. They had yet to pick what the next book would be, but since they were only halfway through *Matilda*, neither of them were worried. If any of the staff or managers asked what they were doing together, Carly often told them they were doing a book club.

"Really?" Suzanne, the day manager, said. She sat down at their table one afternoon, touching the older copy of *Matilda* they were using, with some of Quentin Blake's drawings still on the front. "Man, I remember reading this to my kid. This is a good idea, though, a book club. Nice to build team spirit. Is it just you two right now?"

"Yes," Carly said, realizing that perhaps some secrecy could have gone a long way. No one may have realized they were together, but if she and Ashley were just friends then that meant anyone could join their club. Carly gave Ashley an unsure look, just as Suzanne stood up.

"What's the next book?" Suzanne asked.

"I don't know," Ashley said. "We were thinking something that has a bad movie to go along with it. Maybe *Catch-22*?"

"You should do *The Fault in Our Stars*," Suzanne suggested, eyes wide. "My little girl is reading that now. Sounds really good. And the movie is on Netflix."

"Really?" Carly asked, scrunching her nose up and acting even more clueless. "Never heard of it. Who wrote it?"

"You know. John Green. Best seller. Cancer kids and a love story."

Carly and Ashley exchanged looks, feigning ignorance. "Nah, haven't heard of it."

"Well, you should get more people involved. They would want to do something like this," Suzanne said with another shake of her bracelets. When Amber, the young mother Carly befriended her first shift, walked into the back, Suzanne caught her attention.

"Would you like to join a book club?"

Amber, much to Carly's relief, laughed. "No, thanks. I'm busy enough as it is."

Suzanne was about to say something else, when the PA system announced a need for a manager to verify a price check. Suzanne sighed and ran her hands through her hair, shooting another look toward Carly and Ashley.

"Keep it in mind. I'll bring it up at the next staff meeting."

When Suzanne was gone, Carly sighed. "Oh, no."

"Don't worry. All we have to do is keep reading the same book, and no one will know the difference." Ashley pecked Carly on the cheek. "The eyes only see what they want to."

Carly laughed, only to look up and see Amber facing them. She held her cup of noodles in her arms, steam rising off of it.

"Did I hear what I thought I did earlier?" Amber asked.

Carly's eyes widened, and Ashley grabbed her hand under the table.

"What did you hear?" Ashley asked.

"Something about John Green? My kid's name is Alaska, after his book."

Carly let out a sigh of relief.

"Then yeah," Ashley added. "Suzanne is starting a book club. Just with John Green titles. You should talk to her about it."

"Neat," Amber said, sitting down with her lunch. "Well, in that case, it doesn't sound so bad at all."

Other times at work were not as easy as others. There were longer shifts over the weekends, which were exactly like the opening day, only with far less people to help out. Some days, Ashley and Carly wouldn't be on staff at the same time, and Carly wasn't quite sure what to do with herself. When Suzanne started to talk more about John Green, and the actress who played Hazel Grace in an upcoming movie, Carly found herself participating in the conversation. She reread *Looking for Alaska* with Amber a couple times during their shared shift, too. Carly began, ever so slowly, to open up more while at work whenever Ashley wasn't around. She would make friends, however incidental, and try not to hide so much behind her cash machine and then her books over lunch.

This was not the best job she had ever had. Not even close. She was almost working full time, but without any of the perks associated with it. But, Carly found herself liking it here. Even when Ashley wasn't around, everything else reminded Carly of Ashley. Sometimes, that was all she needed.

"Carly Rogers."

Carly looked up from her cash machine. It was close to the end of her shift, only another twenty minutes left. The younger high school kids arrived in for their afternoon shift and were already eager and opening up their till. Carly figured she may as well get ready to leave and had shut down before her manager had ordered her to. When she raised her eyes above the roll of dimes in her hands, Suzanne and Tim, both of the head managers, were staring back at her.

"Hi. Sorry," Carly apologized. She closed her till and moved her closed sign away. "I know I shouldn't have shut down yet. I still have some time."

Suzanne took a step forward and placed the sign back over Carly's station. A middle aged woman with a cart full of baby clothing huffed, as she moved her way back into line again. Andy, the teenage kid on staff, took her without his smile wavering.

"It's fine, really," Suzanne said. "We actually wanted to ask you to finish up here a bit early."

"Oh." Carly held her hands over the machine, a cold chill up her spine. "Is everything okay?"

"Yes, don't worry," Tim said with one of his big, gregarious grins. "Cash out, allow for Suzanne to sign off, and then see us in the back, okay?"

"Okay," Carly said again, her voice weak.

"Don't worry," Suzanne said. "It's nothing bad."

Carly maintained her composure until both of the managers walked away. They took forever to reach the back of the store, stopping several times to pick up broken merchandise along the way. *Fuck.* Carly knew that life in Marshalls was getting a bit too good to be true. She wondered if Ashley had been called in, and they were going to discuss their inappropriate relationship.

"Are you okay?" Andy asked.

"Fine. Just… Thanks for taking over."

"No problem." Andy paused, using the pricing gun while still staring at Carly. She didn't know him that well, but she wished he would stop staring.

"You're probably not in trouble," he said meekly.

"Oh, yeah? What makes you say that?"

"Because you're one of the fastest people on cash. I highly doubt Suzanne and Tim would come to get you and talk about anything bad. They're not going to fire you."

"Then what are they going to do?" Carly asked, her voice small. She was done cashing out her till now, though her movements were stiff. Andy had finished his own price check and was now making the woman with the baby clothing wait.

"I don't know. But trust me—you're probably one of the best workers here. You'll be fine."

He clapped her on the back, before walking back to his till. Carly knew he was just trying to help. And really, hearing that she was probably not going to be fired did help. But anxiety crept inside of her, and she teetered on the edge of full-blown panic. *Ashley, where are you?* Her cell phone was in her locker, and she knew she would have no time to call for a pep talk. This time, she had to do this alone.

Carly sighed, stepping down from the cashier's station, and began to walk toward the back.

CHAPTER 33

"And everything," Suzanne said, as she checked Carly's cash out log with the numbers on her computer screen, "seems to be perfectly in order. Yet another great shift on cash, Carly."

"Thanks."

Carly shifted on the plastic chair inside the head manager's work room. The back of Marshalls' storefront was usually very cramped. On one side of their thin walls, the shipment trucks backed up, and the men cursed as they unloaded the new material. On the other side, the lockers in the break room slammed above the din of workers' conversations. Carly crossed her legs, wishing again that she could have had her phone. There had to be at least two or three messages from Ashley waiting for her, now.

"What did you need to see me about?"

"Don't worry, Carly, we won't keep you too late," Tim said. His gray hair matched his tie pin, which shimmered under the light, as he folded his hands on top of the desk. He eyed Suzanne, allowing her to finish her sign-off on the computer system, before she turned around fully.

"This meeting, if it goes too long, you will be paid for," she said, marking it down into the computer system to allow Carly overtime. "But I don't suspect it will take much."

Carly nodded. She wanted to say something snarky like: *Hey, thank you for paying me a touch over minimum wage for maybe fifteen minutes,* but she couldn't move her mouth. She was worried they were being too generous with her now, because there would be no need to pay her in the future.

Not that losing her job, Carly knew, would be that big of a deal. During the short walk from cash, Carly had pretty much made peace with losing her job, if that was what it came to. *I can always find another one.* She didn't have huge bills. She wouldn't be homeless or lose too much time and money if she had to start all over again. The best part about her job and the minimum wage book club was Ashley—and Carly knew she already had her to herself.

"It's been nice training you," Tim said. "It's always good to see a new employee evolve into a good worker."

"Thank you," Carly said, still thinking of Ashley each time doubt trembled inside of her. "It's been a good job. Easy, and not too demanding."

"That's what we can tell," Suzanne said.

Carly worried she had said something wrong. She doubled back on her previous statement. "I mean, it's a good job. I'm glad I can do it properly. You know?"

Tim and Suzanne exchanged glances. Carly bit her lip again.

"Let's just cut to the chase, so you can get home," Tim said. "We're opening up a new regional office in the middle of the state. About an hour drive from here. In Woodstock or thereabouts. Are you familiar with the area?"

"Yes, actually," Carly said. "My great-aunt lives close by. My family visits her a lot. She's more in the wooded area surrounding the town, in the place that was developed in the 1900s."

"Ah, yes," Tim said, giving another exuberant look to Suzanne. "I know the area well, too. I have a cottage there."

"This is even better than we thought," Suzanne said, clapping her hands together in delight. "We were concerned before that you were getting too bored, too uninterested in the job because it wasn't difficult enough."

"Customers make it interesting," Carly said, with thin sarcasm in her voice. She noticed, ever so quickly, that Tim smiled at her small joke.

"We see your potential," Tim said. "But we also don't want to uproot you from a place that has always been your home. That you're comfortable with."

Carly nodded, unsure of the response expected from her. In spite of Tim's assurances, she felt horribly uncomfortable. But this wasn't quite like her last job, where the manager wouldn't take no for an answer, and she had to storm out one afternoon after he had cornered her in the stocking area. Tim and Suzanne were genuinely interested in her—but as a worker. The smiles they wore were too saccharine to be malicious. But how *were* Tim and Suzanne supposed to feel about her? They were her bosses. She hated it when people in power tried to appeal to her emotions, because they often had no idea what they were doing. It was one of the many reasons she had never told anyone about Ashley in the first place. At the end of the day, she got to go home and forget about work. Not try to forge relationships that were akin to awkward family reunions.

"I'm fine," Carly said. "Go on. I'm not quite sure what you're getting at, and I don't like to make assumptions."

"We want to promote you."

"Oh," Carly said, surprise in her voice. "Oh."

"The regional office is an hour or so away from here. The distance can seem intimidating, since it's not nearly as populated as this city. But there is another Marshalls store close by, one that will always need new sales reps. If you did end up taking this job in the regional office, and you did not like it, I could guarantee your old position again—at this or any of the Marshalls close by."

"We want to make sure you don't feel as if you are losing anything," Tim added. "Ultimately, you're doing us a favor either way. You work for us, but we also want to work with you."

"I don't know," Carly said. "I don't exactly feel as if I'm a good management choice."

"Oh, no, sorry," Suzanne said. She touched her chest, as if stifling a laugh at that thought. "We weren't thinking management. This is a regional office. You would be dealing with sales, but nothing like this." She used a finger to point all around them. Lockers slammed in the background and people cursed in English and in Spanish.

"What would I be doing?" Carly asked. She wanted to bite her lip and add a subclause to her remark: *Not that I'm taking the job.*

"A desk job, unfortunately," Tim said. "Not a lot of people like those. But it's better pay. Much better than what you're getting now. You would start small. We need a lot of proofreaders and copy editors, in addition to ad managers that can write bylines and pitches."

"You have demonstrated proficiency for reading, that's for sure," Suzanne said with a small wink.

"Okay."

"You're also good with numbers. There would be an opportunity to train you in the accounts department, as well."

"Okay," Carly said again, her voice deadpan.

Suzanne ruffled the papers on her desk. She pulled out a large blue folder with the Marshalls logo on it and handed it over. "This is the employment package. It should answer any questions you have about this."

Carly took the folder and was surprised by how heavy it was. Tim shifted in his seat.

"This is not a guaranteed job. We like to promote people from within, and we both think you're qualified. If you have two letters from us, you would have a better chance. But don't rush into this."

"Is there..." Carly asked, shifting in her seat. "A deadline?"

"Middle of September," Suzanne said. "You have lots of time."

Carly smiled and tried to nod. She folded the thick package under her arm. She eyed the calendar in the room and realized they were already halfway through July.

Carly suddenly felt the entire weight of her adult life, whatever small amount that could be, crash down on her. She still had debt to take care of, a shitty credit card she couldn't use without the bank freaking out. She still had this diploma, this degree that she had spent four years on without the slightest idea of what to do with it afterward. She still had a house she lived in, a bed she had had since she was fifteen.

I don't even know how to drive! Carly's mind reeled at this sudden revelation. This was all happening too fast. Her life had seemingly exploded in front of her, and she didn't even know what she really wanted to do *with* that life. What was her dream? What did she want to be when she grew up? She had been so content watching everyone else skate around in circles that she hadn't pointed any fingers at herself. She shifted in her chair, spotting the clock from across the room. It was already ten minutes past her typical departure time.

Tim followed her gaze. He stood.

"Take your time to think about this, Carly. We will be here if you have more questions."

"Yes. Please, sleep on it." Suzanne stood with Tim, folding her arms over her chest. She glanced at the calendar too, noticing the names written in small letters for the upcoming shifts. "If I remember correctly, you have something like four days off now. It's a nice break. Use it."

"I will," Carly said. She also stood, though her legs trembled. "Thank you."

"Not at all. Have a good night." Tim stepped forward and shook Carly's hand, along with Suzanne next.

Carly could barely lift her eyes from the floor when she walked out of the office. She slid her time card through the slot, and watched as it clocked her in fourteen minutes of overtime. She wondered how much that would be per hour and how much extra she made. Then she took her new package and shoved it into the bottom of her backpack, right next to her beat-up copy of *Matilda*.

So much for easy, happy endings.

Carly placed her keys on the front table and walked into the kitchen.

"Mom? Jill?" Carly called.

Nothing. Carly peered around the corner, checking for a sign of her mother's work. No file boxes or cell phones signaling she was working from home. That was probably a good sign. The credit card for grocery shopping was gone, so placing Jillian was easy after that. Carly walked up the stairs, two by two, and then stuck her head into Cynthia's room.

"Cyn?"

Nothing. Carly walked to her closest, opening up the doors a touch. The Rollerblades were gone.

You and Cyn running off together? Carly texted Landon.

When no response came, she figured that was an answer enough. Both Cyn and Landon really were running away together, or at least, skating at the local park for the afternoon. There was only Ashley left to consider.

Carly's stomach did a small flip-flop anytime she thought of calling her. Before she had been given the news by Tim and Suzanne, all Carly wanted to do was to curl up with Ashley and read. Now, she wanted to avoid her at all costs so no one would get hurt. She knew Ashley was too smart for that, though. If Carly called her, Ashley would see through her guise right away. She could sense that kind of thing. It probably came from so many years of practice in hospital beds. If Ashley couldn't figure out her own symptoms and where they came from, she would try to figure out people and how they felt.

Carly took her shoes off and hopped into her bed. She pulled the covers up all the way to her knees and held her phone in her hands. Her backpack was next to her on the too-large bed, taking up the normal space where Cyn or Ashley would go. The house was so quiet, almost ghostly. It never got this way, and Carly knew she should enjoy it. A year ago, she would have been overjoyed at having the space to herself. She would probably grab a snack, maybe watch a movie, or just sit alone in her bed and read until her peace was disturbed. *I thought you liked life like this,* Carly chastised herself. But something had happened in the past few months to wear down her resistance. And now, Carly sighed, because she found herself missing people in a way she didn't know how to. She found herself in a dilemma that she couldn't just ignore or solve by quitting. She didn't know what to do for the first time in her whole life, because her decision actually mattered.

Carly picked up her phone again and dialed Dorothy's number. She waited, the phone pressed to the tip of her ear, for her to pick up. She ran through all the possible things she could tell her aunt, and how exactly to phrase her solicitation for advice.

Dorothy, Carly imagined herself saying. *I'm in love. So completely and utterly in love, but I'm also so trapped. I want to leave, but I can't leave without taking her with me. But I can't leave without taking all of them with me, because I have already left so many times before. Because I already have a home, and while it's not perfect, it is mine. I grew up here…it's a part of me.*

Dorothy, Carly thought in her mind again. *I am so in love, but I am so in debt, too. I want to close myself away from the world. Give me another two years,* Carly begged again. *Give me another two years. I will go to work and come home every day. Be with Ashley, be with Cyn, be with Landon. I'll see you on the weekend, Aunt Dorothy. Please. Give me two more years before I have to decide.*

Carly flopped down on her bed again, the phone still ringing in her ear. She could swear that she felt time passing through each breath as she waited, considering all her options. But Dorothy never came to the phone. Carly didn't bother to leave a message when her machine finally picked up.

I am so in love, she thought again, running her hands through her hair. *But I must take her with me. I have to. We have to stay together, and I can't be the one to leave.*

Carly got up from her bed and began to write a small poem. A few lines, something she could send to Dorothy later on to summarize her feelings. When she finished her first draft, Carly began to rewrite it, removing the too jumbled words and run-on sentences that didn't make any sense. Poems were supposed to be sparse, delicate prose. They were supposed to be able to indicate, but not overwhelm emotion. On her phone, inside a blank text message, Carly transferred the stanza.

About two months, she thought when she was done. Sixty more days to decide.

Carly shoved the blue Marshalls folder under her bed with the rest of her library. When it was finally gone and hidden underneath like the monsters from her childhood, Carly texted Ashley.

Hey! Missed you today. So…when are you going to take me driving?

CHAPTER 34

Ashley insisted Saturday was the best day to drive. The weather was supposed to be perfect, though the July heat was nearly too much to bear. When Ashley, Carly, Landon, and Cynthia all drove out in Landon's car, the sun seemed to chase them, leaving beads of sweat on their foreheads, until they were safely under the bridge.

"Little piggy, little piggy," Cynthia joked. "Let me come in."

"That's not the right rhyme," Landon chastised, turning his strong hands against the wheel. "We're the three billy goats gruff, hanging out under a bridge. And *you're* the little troll."

"Pfft. I think I know my childhood rhymes."

"And I think I know little piggies." Landon pulled alongside the dirt pathway from the road, around some trees, before he put the car in park. They all undid their belts and began shifting roles outside the car. As they switched, Cynthia continued to go through some more fairy tales, discussing how each one was a derivative of each one of the Roller Derby girls' names.

"I was watching some old games on YouTube. Have you ever heard of the Grimm Girls? Fantastic team. All of their names ended up influencing fairy tales. That's how I know I'm right about the little pigs rhyme. There are a lot of girls on the team who are named Big Bad Wolf or something like that."

"All right, fair enough. But I think it's the other way around, Cyn," Landon said. "The Grimm Girls probably based their names on the tales, since they were written way back then. But hey, the culture can shift and change, so maybe things did happen your way."

Cynthia laughed. "I know the proper order, technically. But sometimes I like to imagine a world where the women came first and the men copied."

"That *is* how it went," Carly said. "The fairy tales are from old, wise women who told them orally. It's just that the history books remember men on paper. Women were always talking."

"*See?*" Cynthia said, leaning toward Landon.

Landon held up his arms to surrender. "Hey, little sister, I hear you. I'm also forgotten from history pages."

"I think," Ashley said, stepping ahead and holding her arms out. "That this can all be solved by agreeing we need new books. Better ones. Yeah?"

There was a resounding yes from the small crowd. Ashley's thin smile worked its way to the corners of her mouth, as she turned to Carly. "Now, excellent. You, Miss Jolly Rogers, I want behind the wheel."

The plan was for Carly to get used to the vehicle a little more, inside the closed lot under the bridge, before she would venture out on the road and then highway. She had only driven on the local roads once before, but Jillian had been a wreck the entire time, so Carly had forgotten all she'd learned. It had been over two years since she had even been in the driver's seat, so it would take some time to get reacquainted. Landon and Cynthia would stay out as Ashley taught Carly, until they headed toward the roads. That way, at least, Landon could say he was around and no one was technically breaking the law.

"We're acting like it's a police state," Ashley stated. "I'm sure no cop cars will even come by, and if they do, we're hardly their concern. Just a bunch of queers in a car, don't mind us."

Landon gave a forlorn sigh, but went along with the plan. "I know it's not a police state. It's just…difficult, you know? I don't want you guys getting hurt or caught."

"We'll be careful," Ashley said, placing a hand on Landon's shoulder. "Trust me. I will take good care of Carly Rogers."

"And remember," Carly said. "If we get caught and you're not around, then we can say you had no involvement whatsoever. For all you knew, you and Cyn were just skating merrily along, and us two little piggies stole your straw house."

"I like to think my car's stronger than straw, but I see your point." Landon turned to Cynthia, who was sitting on a small concrete slab and tying up her blades. Her Converse shoes were off to the side, next to her backpack full of leftover pizza and Gatorade. She had also brought a couple of bottles of water for everyone else, under Carly's insistence.

"And how are you holding up?" Landon asked.

"Great! I am Bait N. Switch now," Cynthia said. She rose up on her blades. "And I'm going to go off."

Cynthia took off in the roaring sound of wheels on concrete around the corner.

"Not by the hair on my chinny, chinny chin!" Landon shouted after her.

"Have fun!" Ashley said.

Landon extended his arm in a wave. Just barely audible to Carly, he called out, "If you need me, don't be afraid to holler."

"Yes, Big Bad Wolf. Hey now." Ashley took a step closer to Carly, placing a hand on her shoulder. She touched her chin, tilting it up. "It's driving. Not rocket science. You are already a star."

"Sure. Whatever you say."

"I'm being serious."

"Yeah, so was I." Carly heard the roar of Cynthia's Rollerblades in the hill, and Landon's questions and comments. The two of them were working on a routine, though Landon refused to wear skates himself. Other than the noise, and the overwhelmingly hot sun above them, Ashley and Carly were alone.

"Okay, fine," Carly said, then grasped the driver's side door handle. "I can't put this off anymore. Let's go."

Driving was a lot easier than Carly expected. Ashley kept her arm around her shoulder almost the entire time. She said it was mostly so she could view the driver's seat and to help point out what everything meant and how to move seamlessly between functions, but Carly knew that Ashley also just wanted to put her arm around her, too. Carly appreciated it, even allowing herself to smile between instructions.

"Turn the windshield wipers on," Ashley requested.

"But it's sunny."

"I know, but there will be a winter day where you will be stuck in a stupid storm."

"I wouldn't drive in a storm."

"Maybe, but sometimes you have to. And you need to know how to do several things at once. So humor me now. Turn on the windshield wipers."

Carly's stomach tightened again. *I know I can drive. I can turn, I can use the blinker, and I can park. Easily.* The two of them had driven by Landon a couple times now, under the bridge, just to show them all that she really could control the vehicle. But the turn signal had been one thing to master, and something hard for Carly. Touching a new item on the car filled her with a slow sensation of dread. As soon as she tried to reach out for it, she tapped the gas at the same time and shot the car forward. Easy to recover from, but it still made her feel like throwing up.

"Not too bad," Ashley said. "Just a little bumpy."

Carly laughed nervously. "Oh, man. I suck at coordination. I feel like you're asking me to rub my stomach and pat my head at the same time."

"I know you can do this."

"I know. Maybe I just won't drive in the rain."

"Carly," Ashley chastised. "Don't take the easy way out."

"I'm not stupid," Carly said, suddenly flustered.

"I know you're not. But the first time you do anything, you go absolutely bonkers. Just pretend you've always done it, so that way you don't need to scare yourself."

"What?" Carly said, turning toward Ashley. Ashley moved back to her original position in the seat, her belt tighter across her waist. Carly allowed the car to coast on the asphalt and concrete. The sound of cars nearby made her nervous, but she told herself to ignore them. "What do you mean I go absolutely bonkers?"

"The first time you do something, I said. Not all the time," Ashley corrected. "When you did cash for the first time, especially on opening day, you pretty much went mad."

"I did not."

Ashley opened her eyes, challenging. "I think I beg to differ."

"Okay, so maybe I was nervous. That was crowds, though. That wasn't me."

"It doesn't matter what it is, Carly. You're the only constant in those situations—and you are a nervous creature. You just are."

"I'm sorry."

"You're also highly aware of how nervous you are," Ashley said. She placed a hand on Carly's shoulder again. "I know you can do this. But the first time you do anything, you always think about all the possibilities—good and bad, but mostly bad—that could happen. You focus on the consequences and usually try to prepare a plan within a plan, ahead of time. That makes you nervous."

"Really?" Carly said, feeling exposed. She often did have plans within plans, especially related to driving. There had been too many times where she thought she was getting a ride home from her mother, only to have it revoked at the last minute because of a late meeting or client. It was another reason why Carly had learned to walk to everything; if her rides fell through, she always had her own way. "I never told you that."

"I can see it, though. I do the same thing, you know, with all the planning. I have to have that type of heightened nervous state when I play a game. I have to think through so many options."

"But that helps you win," Carly stated. "What's so bad about it if it helps?"

"You don't need that constant state of awareness in everyday life. It's like being on the edge of a chair that's about to fall."

Carly glanced back at the dirt path where they were previously, it led to the road. At the rate they were going, she'd never get on the road again. Rain or shine.

"Am I really that bad?"

"Yes and no," Ashley said. "I know you're not doing it on purpose. It just happens."

"It's just… I don't even know why I'm like this. I've always been."

"Shush. Not to silence you or anything. But there is no need to explain. I don't care."

Carly nodded. She let her hands slip to the bottom of the wheel and then put them up at ten and two again. She straightened her back, realizing the car was still coasting. She chastised herself for letting her guard down.

"That's one of those things," Ashley said.

"What things?" Carly asked.

"This." Ashley put her hands on the wheel, just above Carly's. "Go back to the way you were before. Lean back in the seat. Relax. You drive better when you keep your hands where they are."

Carly nodded. She attempted to affect a relaxed position, but she over thought it. Though she placed her hands back in the original position, at the bottom of the wheel, her back was tense.

"It's getting there," Ashley said. "But you'll need to work."

"Work at relaxing?"

"You know what I mean. Just shut down all the distractions. Focus on what you're doing. The thing with driving is that yes—it's dangerous. It's one of the most dangerous things you can do. That's why I'm not allowed on the roads."

"I don't know how this is supposed to make me feel better."

"It's dangerous," Ashley continued, "but there is nothing you can do to stop it. You can't make a plan within a plan, because there still will be someone like me on the road who could spaz out and hit you for no reason."

"Um. Oh."

"What I mean," Ashley went on, "is that you need to live in the moment. Just think about things how they are now. Pay attention to what's around you, but if you start to think ahead, you will lose the ability to react to something bad happening in front of you. If someone sprawls out in the middle of the road, but you're thinking two steps ahead, then you can't react. You can't just hit the brakes and save yourself."

Carly sighed, nodding along with this.

"You need to be able to anticipate, but also relax. Just drive. Eventually, you will get to your destination."

"Okay," Carly said. Already, her chest didn't feel as tight, and her breathing was less erratic. She turned the car around under the bridge and then began to coast back to where they began. "Car crashes aside. What else can I do here? How do I make things easier?"

"Take speed limit, for instance. It's there, but don't pay attention to the blind numbers of it. Blend into the road. If the limit is sixty and people around you are going seventy, then follow them. Don't be a slave to the rules, because you won't be able to react when someone changes them. *Everything* changes. The rules are nice, but they don't always fit."

"Don't fall for ideals," Carly said, thinking of Dorothy.

"*Yes*," Ashley said with recognition. "That is exactly what I mean."

"Okay," Carly said with a nod. She turned slightly, as if changing lanes, and used her turn signal to do so. Just when Ashley wasn't expecting it, Carly turned on the windshield wipers as she drove. She focused on the act of flipping the switch, her feet on the gas, and she felt a lot better.

"See?" Ashley said. "Nothing to it."

"And to think," Ashley joked when they had gone around the pavement a couple more laps, "the next step is the open road. Just like Kerouac."

"Yeah. Something like that."

A wave of sudden dread washed over Carly. Was it because they were going to go on the road next? She looked around the bridge, past the dirt path, and toward the yellow highway lines. No, Carly concluded. Driving didn't scare her that much anymore. She had hit the horn a couple times by accident, but she had managed to laugh those off. The thought of other cars on the road didn't scare her as much. She was still nervous, always wanting to get it right, but Ashley's presence did help immensely.

No, Carly realized, *it's not driving that bugs me.* It was what really did lay beyond them. She thought of the Marshalls package under her bed. She still hadn't told Ashley anything about it yet, because really, what could she say? Carly still hadn't made a decision and hated to see people upset for no reason. If she was going to ruin whatever comfortable feeling they had in their relationship, Carly wanted to be sure it was necessary. And she wasn't sure about that yet. Carly didn't know if Ashley was even aware of Marshall's new office, but since there was no one else vying for that job, Suzanne and Tim probably hadn't said anything. Carly was comforted by that, but she also knew that there would come a time when she and Ashley shared a shift. And Suzanne would make a remark, like she always did, and Carly's vow of silence on the issue would be over.

"Are you okay?" Ashley asked. "I don't think there's any reason to be embarrassed."

"What?"

"You looked a little pale there. I wanted you to be sure that I didn't care if you wanted to honk the horn all the time, it doesn't matter. Your driving was still pretty good. In fact, I really would say you're ready for the road."

Ashley smiled, placing a hand on Carly's shoulder. When Carly balked under the touch, Ashley withdrew. "But then again, maybe that's enough for today. I can take over, if you want. Drive you to a smaller, more deserted road. Maybe the same highway we came in on? Or, failing that, I could just get you to sit on my lap to make sure you really know what it's like from that perspective?"

Ashley smiled again, trying to assuage the situation. She seemed nervous too, as if she could sense a distance in Carly's voice and body language.

"No, no," Carly said. "Don't worry. It's fine. I was just thinking about work."

"Ah, the fun times at Marshalls. Maybe when you master this, you can pick me up from work? What do you say to being my chauffeur?"

"It's the least I could do," Carly said. "So when is your next shift?"

"Um. Tuesday, I think. I'm not too sure."

Ashley reached into her pocket, grabbing her phone to see her calendar. She held her phone in one hand, scrolling with her thumb, as she hissed in another breath and held her forehead with the other.

"Are you okay?" Carly asked. She narrowed her eyes, watching as Ashley's face twisted in pain. She had never acted like this before. As soon as Ashley noticed the attention, she tried to smile and pass it off.

"Sorry," she said. "It's nothing. I just think I'm getting a migraine."

"Oh." Carly drove them under the bridge and into the shade. *Maybe less light would help Ashley.* "There should be some Advil in my purse in the back if you need it. Getting some now before the migraine gets worse is good, right?"

"Indeed." Ashley still held her phone in her hand, browsing through her calendar. "Um… I think I was right. It's Tuesday at seven."

"AM or PM?"

"PM, actually. They only have me as backup for a couple of hours."

"Oh, okay." Carly's knuckles turned white as she gripped the wheel. The sick feeling came back to her stomach when glanced back over at Ashley, who was still holding her forehead. She hadn't bothered to grab Advil out of Carly's purse yet, as if she forgot.

"So, work?" Ashley said, hissing between touches of her head. "You were saying?"

"Um, yeah…" Carly kept exchanging furtive glances between Ashley and the road ahead. The car seemed to become a part of Carly now, easy to handle when she focused, but still foreign and distinct. She idled the car, hoping to turn to Ashley and actually tell her about Marshalls. But each time she caught a glimpse of her, Ashley seemed in more and more pain.

"Are you okay?" Carly asked again. Her voice was tight. "You really should get some pills. Here, let me."

Before Carly could dive into the back seat, she saw Ashley's hand tremble. Ashley tried to open her mouth, but closed it. Carly repeated her insistent cry. "Are you okay?"

"I'm just… Gah." Ashley's hands shook with more ferocity now. A small blink of panic crossed her face, before her entire body began to shake. Carly's eyes widened in horror, unable to grasp the situation beyond her own fear.

"Ashley!" Carly grabbed Ashley's hands only to feel them snap away from her. Carly's entire body became cold as she watched Ashley go into a seizure. *Darren, Darren. What did he say?* The instructions all came back to her in bits and pieces. Carly tried to turn Ashley over; she tried to position her body, but it shook too much.

Jumping ahead, Carly told herself. *You're jumping ahead. Slow down. Ashley depends on it.*

Carly got out of the car and tried to move toward her sister and Landon. Darren had told Carly how to position Ashley's body, but his last and final words on the subject had always been, *get her into position and then get to the hospital. Always go to the hospital, because as much as you want to help her, you can only do so much.*

Carly now felt the heavy pain of those words. There was nothing else she could do. All that she could do had been done—and the impossible steps needed to be taken now. They had to go to the hospital, but everything seemed so far away. She couldn't even see Landon or Cynthia. All she heard was the sound of skates.

"Landon," she screamed. There was no response. "Cynthia!"

Carly's voice was like a bad dream, one that she could not quite get to work, no matter how hard she yelled. She ran back over to the car and held her ear to Ashley's chest. She was breathing, but passed out. Her heart rate, always so kinetic, now seemed slow. The seizure was over. She was alive, Carly knew, but she still needed to fulfill the other half of Darren's instructions. *Get her to the hospital, as quick as you can.* Landon and Cynthia had gone too far. No one could help her.

Carly glanced at the wheel of the car. The huge vehicle didn't seem like a beast anymore. She couldn't second guess herself. She just had to act.

And if I fuck up, she told herself as she put the key in the ignition again, *then at least I'm heading toward a hospital.*

An almost blinding precision took over Carly, as she focused on her task ahead. All judgements, all fears, all worries from before faded away. All she knew was the road and how to get home again. She held Ashley's hand as she began to drive up the small dirt road and turned onto the town's main highway. She passed a big, blue sign that said, *Left Bank Hospital*, within minutes.

"Hold on, Ashley," Carly said, her voice shaky. "I'll be there soon."

CHAPTER 35

Carly paced the hallway of the hospital, her phone clutched in her hand. As soon as they arrived in the ER of the hospital, Ashley had been taken away, and Carly texted Darren, Landon, and Cynthia in short bursts.

Ashley had a seizure. I drove to the hospital. The one just outside the highway. Hurry, please. I'm sorry I took your car. I tried to call, but nothing came out. I'm sorry again. I'll pay for the cab.

Carly kept writing until her small series of messages began to feel like haikus. Landon wrote back first.

Okay, okay, Car. Yes, got it now. We're coming. Don't apologize, okay? You did the right thing.

I wish it was that easy.

When Landon stopped responding, Carly read over the messages again and again. *You did the right thing.* Her eyes lingered there the most, so she didn't have to doubt anything else. Ashley had been taken away twenty minutes ago. When Carly looked up, she saw Ashley again, this time being wheeled out on a gurney. She was as pale as the hospital sheet. IVs were in her arms, tubes in her nose. Her eyes were still closed.

A nurse approached Carly. She had dark-blue scrubs and dark skin. Her face was soft, kind. She spoke with sharp articulation, speaking fast, but with a sincerity Carly needed.

"Are you related? Can you give medical history?"

"Yes," Carly said and then paused, biting her lip. "No. I'm...I'm her... cousin. I know she's had seizures before."

"Epilepsy?"

"No idea." Carly blushed. She looked down at her phone again and held it up, as if it had all the answers. "I've called her brother. I let him know, but I think he may be at work. He hasn't responded yet. But h-he can answer your questions."

The nurse nodded and then turned her attention back to Ashley. Carly looked away as she called, knowing that staring at Ashley would only weaken her already crumbling foundations. *Why did I say cousin?* she asked herself. *This is Vermont. It's not like we're in the southern states and I could be thrown out just by looking...*

When another text message didn't rouse Darren, Carly called the number. He picked up the phone in a matter of seconds, his voice tense. "Carly? Why are you—"

"She had a seizure. At the hospital. I'm sorry. I tried..."

Darren sprang into action right away, his entire voice and demeanor changing. "Oh, okay. Which one?"

"Left Bank."

"How is she?"

Carly glanced over at Ashley, still unconscious and very pale. Darren understood the few seconds lag in her response. He sighed on the other end.

"On my way, Carly. Hold tight."

He hung up, though Carly still kept her phone to her ear, closing her eyes and letting it sink in. When she turned to find the nurse, a different, older one was in her place. Ashley was already gone, wheeled into a room down the hall. Carly felt her mouth go dry. She wanted to follow close by, but what else could she say? She had to wait.

She sat on the edge of a chair in the waiting room, her phone still in her hand, typing out the beats of longing and worry into a poem, so she could comprehend it all later on.

Darren filled out the paperwork when it came. Carly watched as he blasted through the forms next to her in the waiting room as if they were a prayer he had repeated. She figured that it was kind of like a prayer when you worked with insurance and had to take care of someone so much. You learn the billing information, policy numbers, and zip codes like mantras. You learn your sibling's middle names and blood types like hymns. Carly moved close to Darren on the blue hospital seats, hoping to know the answers for later. If there would be a later.

"This is probably not fatal, or even that critical," Darren said when he reached the end of the form. He folded it all on the clipboard, before handing it to a nurse who walked by. Carly had noted how calm he was for all of this. Focused, as if he was threading a needle, but calm. "It just looks bad on the surface, if you've never seen it before. She's probably fine."

"Probably," Carly repeated. She meant it to be a question but her voice would not cooperate.

"Probably," Darren repeated, nodding.

This word is another refrain, Carly thought. *Probably, maybe, hopefully, if we're lucky*, were all the choruses to this new place. She glanced around the waiting room, saw mothers with sick kids and even sicker kids. But no Landon or Cynthia yet. *Are they walking? Maybe they're walking…* Carly had a hard time imagining them finding a cab or any type of transportation where they were.

Darren was still in his work clothing. The dark-blue, collared shirt was untucked now, and his tie hung around his neck loosely. He ran his hands along his dark pants, touching his phone and checking messages, before he folded his arms over his chest.

"Your work is okay with you leaving?" Carly asked.

"Oh yeah. Family. Gotta go. But you. Man." Darren grinned. "You drove a fucking car. Nice one."

That grin, Carly shook her head. It ran in the family and still made her blush in spite of where they were. "Hah. It was a bad decision for a good cause."

"Amazing how fear kind of blinds all other worries, huh?"

"What?" Carly asked.

"Yeah," Darren reiterated with a sigh. "It's amazing. It's like your vision goes white, and you are entirely focused. The only other time I've been like that is when I play games."

"I've never been like that. Except for maybe…" Carly trailed off, not answering. She was thinking of poems, how she had already rendered this moment into a stanza itself.

Hospital lights shine on
Garbage pails that fill over,
Because throwing anything out
Is a threat. In case
It holds all the properties of life,
A magical cure, like an infomercial
That plays at three am. Patients keep
Books by their bedsides, with cracked spines,
Leftover like hallmark cards with stale
Hopes, lines, and good-byes.
Hospitals are waiting rooms where stories
Fester and bloom. One minute, then two—

Carly stopped herself. She turned to Darren and tried to smile. "I don't think I've ever felt that focused before. Not really."

"It's a good change, really. Even if it's not the best reason."

"But not fatal," Carly said again, "or critical, right?"

"Right." Darren nodded. "That's what I meant to say before. You drove here. That probably saved her. Sometimes, these things are nothing. Just a weird seizure. Other times, they're like ministrokes, and she needs to spend time in a hospital. The more time without medical contact, the worse it could possibly be. You drove her, Carly. You probably saved her. If she needed to be saved."

Carly wanted to scoff. Ashley Poindexter never needed to be saved. She was the strongest person that Carly had even known. She was the one who could fix pipes and read Hemingway, calm Carly down and then teach her how to drive.

But she was also human, and Carly needed to accept that, especially if Ashley was ever going to ask for help.

When Darren grew quiet again, Carly scanned the front doors of the hospital. As soon as she saw Cynthia's curly hair, she jumped up from the waiting area without a word, running over to Landon and Cyn with her arms wide.

"My car," Landon said, as he wrapped her into a bear hug. "Way to leave us out in the middle of nowhere."

"Sorry," Carly said. "I really am. I tried to call—"

"I'm teasing. I know where it is now and we're here. You did a great job, Carly. If only we could give you your license on this test alone."

"I wish," Carly said. "Thank you so much for coming... I mean, I know you had to, now that I have your car."

"Hey," Landon pulled her into another hug. "Wouldn't dream of it any other way."

Landon practically lifted Carly off the ground with his second bear hug. Cynthia was more reserved and needy as she approached Carly.

"You scared the shit out of me," Cynthia whispered. She still had her skates tied over her shoulders and hanging at the side of her body like her purse. Carly hugged Cynthia tightly, even though the blades dug into her shoulder a bit.

"I'm sorry, Cyn," Carly said. "I didn't mean to..."

"I know." Cynthia hugged her again, and with that, Carly knew she had been forgiven.

All three of them turned to where Darren had been sitting, only to find his spot empty. Carly panicked, searching for him in the crowd of people. When she caught sight of him talking to a stern-faced doctor holding a clipboard, Carly swallowed. A knot in her stomach formed again.

"That's him?" Landon asked. "Ashley's brother?"

"And her doctor?" Cynthia asked.

"Yes, I guess," Carly said. Cynthia tugged on her hand.

"She's fine, right? I mean, I think I've taken worse spills."

"Your wounds are on the outside," Landon said. "Easy to see. With the brain and especially things to do with chronic conditions, it's hard..."

Landon didn't bother to finish the sentence. No one made small talk or jokes. Carly wanted to explain more of what had happened, but no one was listening, either. Everyone's eyes moved to Darren as he talked with the doctor. Darren folded his arms across his chest, nodding along with what the doctor said. Watching as Darren's eyebrows furrowed, as if he didn't understand something, made her stomach twist even more. When the doctor left, he squeezed Darren's shoulder—and Darren seemed more troubled than ever.

"What's going on?" Landon asked. "I thought it was just a seizure?"

"I…" Carly said. "I don't know."

CHAPTER 36

"You can come see her," Darren said from the doorway. "She's more stable now."

Carly rose from the waiting room seat. She was no longer on the first floor ER, but on the second floor where Ashley had been moved. So far, only immediate family had been allowed inside. Most doctors and nurses would barely let more than two people in the room at once. Since Mike, Ashley's father, arrived an hour ago, Carly had been forced to wait her turn on the other side of the door. Now that Darren was giving up his spot, Carly felt her heart swell again.

"Thank you." Carly rose and walked toward the door. Darren waited, his hand clasped on the handle.

"Are you prepared?" he asked.

Carly was taken aback. Of course she was prepared. But something about Darren's gaze made her doubt herself. Landon and Cynthia had refused to leave when Carly told them to, but they were nowhere to be seen, wanting to give Ashley and her family some privacy. With her support network gone, the only strength Carly could muster was her sheer desire and love for Ashley.

"Yes, of course," she replied.

Darren nodded without adding anything else. And then Carly saw her, and realized that no, she wasn't prepared at all.

Ashley looked so small. Tubes and IVs covered her arms. A heart monitor beat slowly, displaying numbers on a side screen. Her blue gown made her skin look even paler. She was fine—logically, Carly knew all these things. But it was too much to see her like this. Ashley was okay...but so, so fragile.

Mike sat at one end of the bed, close to the heart monitor. He didn't hold his daughter's hand in his, but Carly could tell from the way he sat, he had at one point.

"Hi there," Mike said.

"Hi." Carly sat on the other side of the bed, looking at Ashley with a calm, yet pained expression. She fought the urge to ask Mike how he was. It didn't seem fitting anymore, or polite.

"I hear you drove her in," Mike stated.

Carly nodded.

"Which is even more impressive since you can't drive, right?"

Carly nodded again.

"Thank you," he said after some time. He still wore his work clothing like Darren. His gray hair was messed up, and his eyes were tired. But he smiled genuinely at her, and Carly did her best to smile back.

"Can I ask," Carly said, after a few tense moments, "what the doctor said?"

Mike took a while to gather his thoughts before speaking. "She had a seizure. It was pretty bad. She blacked out afterward, which is not uncommon. She was already a little dehydrated, and some of her electrolytes were imbalanced. She's resting now. It seems like a coma, and it is—but less permanent. There is really no other way to explain it. But she needs a lot of rest the next few days..."

Carly looked at Ashley. Her skin was almost as pale as the blue and white cotton sheets. Her arms were red where the IV had punctured her skin. As Mike continued to explain the nuances of what her condition now meant, Carly's mind wandered.

"Ashley will pull through in a little while, I'm sure," Mike added. His tone was hopeful, and that emotion alone knocked Carly's attention back into the present moment. "Her body has had quite a shock. A while ago, the doctor got her blood work back and there was no trace of her medication in her system. For a while now, it seems. Do you remember her stopping them?"

Carly tried to maintain composure. *She had pills?* Carly had never seen Ashley take anything, never saw anything pass her lips, ever. Even Darren, when he gave her the brief rundown of what to do in case of emergencies, never mentioned the pills. But then again, maybe he never had to. Maybe they were something that only Ashley had power over and had also stopped taking in order to not feel sick. If everyone watched you, day and night, waiting for you to break, then it was sometimes hard not to rebel against that in the smallest way possible even if it meant getting yourself sick again.

"No, I'm sorry. I don't remember any pills."

Mike seemed disappointed, but he nodded. "Either way, it's no one's fault. But at least now we can safely say that this is epilepsy, in combination with a few other issues."

Carly squeezed Ashley's hands. *You idiot, you should have taken your pills. You should have told me. You should have...* But she let the words slip away. Carly loved Ashley, in all of her wonderful faults. Carly held her hand, not thinking of the should haves or what ifs of this situation. She knew that would only lead to ruin. She held her hand and counted the heart rate monitors beeps alongside her own.

"Carly," Mike said.

"Yes?" Carly said, opening her eyes again.

"Are you okay? You've been through a lot."

"Not as much as her, not as much as you."

"I know," Mike said. "But you're here. You got her here. That deserves some credit. And some rest..."

Carly knew they were both trying to get her to leave. Visiting hours would be over, and only family could stay. Only family could know what was going on. Darren eyed her from the back of the room, nodding subtly. *Maybe,* she thought, Darren's small nod was his promise to her that he'd text her updates. *Maybe, maybe, maybe.* It was all another prayer. They would not know until later what had happened to Ashley

"They're just running tests now," Mike said, as if he heard the qualms in Carly's head. "She will be fine. Not going anywhere, which is its own blessing and curse."

"I wish I could have done something."

"Of course," Mike said. "We all do."

Carly looked back down at Ashley. She pressed a kiss to her forehead, feeling the hot surface of her skin, where the sun had touched her. Her body seemed so warm and feverish. She was getting help, Carly had to remind herself. No point in taking down notes to point out all that had gone wrong.

I'm sorry, Carly said to Ashley in her mind. *I'm so sorry*. She realized when she got up, that she was not apologizing for not doing something. She was apologizing for seeing her as sick.

Carly gazed at Ashley one final time, before she went out into the lobby again, her heart in her throat.

Coffee. Coffee fixes everything.

The first machine, just outside Ashley's hospital room on the second floor, would not work—no matter how many times she hit the buttons. She wanted to kick the machine she was so frustrated, until she finally gave up and hit cocoa. The machine spit out the hot chocolate and filled up Carly's small paper cup. She sighed, taking a small sip.

She walked down the hallways, trying to calm herself. She tried not to look into the other rooms when their doors were open, for fear of stumbling over something too private like she had before with Ashley and her brother.

When Carly turned a corner, she heard a familiar beat. *Cynthia's song.* One from a riot grrrl mix she played repetitively, especially when she was sad. Carly walked into the lobby, only to find Cynthia's Rollerblades tossed next to her mother's briefcase. Cynthia was curled up, half on the waiting room chair and half in her mother's lap, her head resting there as if it was a pillow.

"Mom?" Carly asked. "Mom, what on earth are you doing here?"

Jillian put down the book she was holding, and Carly saw her eyes were red, as if she had been crying. "I texted you," she said.

"Oh. I think my phone powered down. It's been a little crazy here."

"Here too, at least, with Richard and I." When Jillian shifted to stand, Cynthia crawled off her lap. Carly saw the tear stains on her cheeks then. Dread percolated in Carly's gut.

"What's going on?" Carly demanded. "How did you even know I was here?"

"Cynthia told me when I finally got a hold of her," Jillian explained.

Cynthia gave Carly a look, a small apology with her eyes. Nothing else was said. *Maybe she knows about Ashley now. Maybe now she understands I'm upset too.* But everything felt off. Her mom was angry, but also worried. She had never seen her this way before.

"What's going on?" Carly asked. "Please, tell me."

"Dorothy," Jillian said. "Richard and I went to see her this morning and…"

Jillian stopped midsentence, when Richard appeared by her side with a coffee in his hand. He looked tired and grave. He nodded to Carly, as he handed the coffee to Jillian and sat down next to Cynthia.

Then Carly knew. Carly knew before Jillian even bothered to open her mouth to tell her.

"Carly, I'm so sorry. I hate to have to tell you it this way, especially after what you went through. But Aunt Dorothy died last night. I'm so sorry."

CHAPTER 37

"Is that all you have?" Jillian's face was stern, her perfectly manicured eyebrows narrowed on her face. Carly noted, with some reservation, that there were bags under her mother's eyes that even makeup couldn't hide.

Cynthia lingered in the doorway of her room, her head down. She wore a black shirt and dark pants, which Carly eventually realized were jeans. *There's the problem*, Carly figured. Jillian can't handle her grief over Dorothy so she takes it out on Cynthia's clothing. No one said anything in the hallway for a long time, merely exchanged tense looks.

"That won't do for a funeral. Don't you have anything else?" Jillian finally asked, her voice thin.

"Hey, Cyn," Carly said. "You're about my size, right? And if not, I have belts. Come here and we'll pick you out something else, okay?"

Cynthia nodded, her eyes still down. She didn't say a thing as she walked across the hallway into Carly's room. Jillian's sharp inhalation of breath was broken by a slight quiver.

"Girls. I'll be in the car, okay? Come as quick as you can. God forbid we're late to her funeral."

Not like Dorothy would care all that much. But she knew she would do better than to voice her opinions. She gave her mother a nod and then disappeared into her room with Cynthia.

"Hey," Carly said softly. "I'm sorry about her."

"I don't know what her problem is," Cynthia said, twisted her fingers into her hair and then scoffed. Cynthia's hair had been straightened, begrudgingly, at the request of Jillian for the funeral. Carly knew how much Cynthia hated to fight her hair—but fighting with Jillian was always much worse.

"Here," Carly said, handing Cynthia some black dress pants that she used to wear in high school. "Try these."

Cynthia gave a weak smile before standing. She shifted around in the bedroom, not bothering to hide herself as she switched outfits. As Carly expected, the pants were a little big on Cynthia, but a belt could fix it just enough. She took down one of the black ones from her closet and handed it over.

"Was she always like this?" Cynthia asked, as she looped the belt around herself.

"Who? Mom?"

Cynthia nodded. "You know. When…your dad died."

"Ah." Carly paused and sat on her bed. She ran a hand through her hair and took a deep breath. It had only been a couple days since everyone found out about Dorothy, but they were long days that often stretched into the middle of the night and still felt like a blur. Jillian organized the funeral, went to see lawyers, and Richard made all their meals at home. Carly had been so busy with work and seeing Ashley during visiting hours (though she was drugged up and sleeping for most of them, and they had barely exchanged real words) that Carly had enough to do so her grief stayed at bay. For a time, at least. She was still grappling with the fact that they actually had to go to a funeral today. To think of her great-aunt's death as a reality, and not a future to be dreaded, was still working through Carly's mind. She could barely remember a month ago, when things were fine, and now Cynthia was asking her to think back to nearly ten years ago, when her own father had died.

"You were a baby. Well, not even a baby. Mom was still pregnant with you," Carly finally said. She crushed her eyes shut again and rubbed her temples, trying to place herself. Everything had been really similar to the way it was now. A lot of black, a lot of tension, but less Richard hanging around and making meals and more Davis, Cynthia's father trying to cheer everyone up with bad jokes and even worse casseroles. Davis' mother, Nadia, a great big woman with a booming voice, had come to stay with them during the funeral, because Jillian was so pregnant but still tried to do everything by herself. Even when she had warning labor pains and Braxton-Hicks contractions, Jillian still insisted on doing everything herself. All the time. So Nadia, mostly took Carly aside and read to her from her favorite books until the whole affair was over.

"It's all a blur, really." Carly shrugged. "You know. I'm starting to think that funerals are all the same."

"Sad?"

"Yeah. Sad and boring and…just a fucking waste of time." Carly rose from the bed suddenly, not wishing to linger anymore. "You ready, Cyn?"

Cynthia tried to laugh, but it came out like a small crack of breath. Carly's stomach dropped seeing her sister so upset and swooped over to her right away. "Shush. Cyn. It's okay. Davis is fine. I'm fine. We're all good here, okay?"

"I know," she said. "I just imagined what it was like for you."

"I'm fine. My dad died a long, long time ago. I barely remember it, really."

"No, but you were closer to Aunt D than anyone else."

Carly nodded her chin against Cynthia's too-straight hair. She missed the curls and could still smell the chemicals from the relaxer. She hated it, didn't know why Jillian had wanted Cynthia's hair so straight or why it really mattered. Carly felt a lot of things right then as she hugged Cynthia—worry over Ashley's future, their relationship, and anger at her mother for always making grief about her. Carly thought back to her father's life and how he was never around anyway, even before they divorced. He was always away at conferences and in hotels all across the country. Always calling them on a payphone or collect. It was only fitting that they got news of his death while he was away. Carly felt a lot of things in that moment, but not one of them was sadness. She still hadn't cried about her aunt. She had been too numb.

"I know. I miss Aunt D," Carly said, her voice sounding too far away. "But she always told me that—"

"Girls?" Jillian called from downstairs. "Richard's idling the car. Are you ready to go now?"

Carly let out a sigh. She hugged Cynthia tighter and then let her go. "Yeah, Mom. We'll be right there."

"What were you going to say?" Cynthia asked, turning to her.

"Oh?" Carly paused, checked her phone—still no messages from Darren about Ashley—and then shrugged. "Never mind. Let's just head out."

On the way to the funeral, Carly kept checking her phone. Darren had been texting her small updates as the time went on, letting her know the proper visiting hours and what Ashley's state was like. She had been awake, more or less, the past few days. But she was still tenuous, still not quite better. And Carly hadn't been able to talk to her and have a real conversation yet, which was killing her. Sometimes, Darren mentioned, after a seizure there could be some amnesia. *Nothing like the soap operas*, he assured Carly. Ashley would still remember who she was and usually what was going on, but she would be hazy and sort of blank for a while. She often forgot what happened leading up to a seizure and sometimes it took her a while to come back to her. *She'll still be in love with you, though,* Darren informed her. *That I don't think will change for quite some time.*

Carly closed her eyes and repeated those words in her head, even as her phone remained quiet. Richard drove the car slowly, as if he could feel the tension around everyone and was being extra gentle and attentive. Jillian was talking, and so was Cynthia, but Carly zoned out into another place.

Carly went over the funeral from her father in her mind, every so often, trying to recall and place herself inside a new arrangement. Things would be different, since she'd no longer be a surviving child, but rather a great-niece. But since Dorothy had very little family, and Jillian had spearheaded the entire organization, Carly knew they would have a prominent spot for the service. Jillian would give the eulogy. Carly resented that idea, but she was also relieved by it. As much as she knew she would have done a better job with remembering Dorothy through words, she also knew that Dorothy wouldn't have wanted her to dwell this way. *What would I even say in a eulogy?* Carly wondered. *Other than Dorothy was too poetic and special to die like this, from a simple cold that had turned to pneumonia and then dying in her sleep.* Dorothy was old, in pain, and this had been coming for a while. But it still didn't feel right. It would never feel right.

Carly remembered Dorothy telling her that the endings of the poems were always the hardest to write. *You always want to put a good word at the end, the right rhyme, the right rhythm.* And this day—this trip—and this car ride were all wrong to Carly. Not good at all, just a terrible ending all around. Carly knew that, like her father's funeral, she'd learn not to remember this aspect, but the better parts.

"And you, back there," Jillian's voice suddenly interrupted her thoughts. "Carly."

"What?"

"Oh, hello. So glad you've joined us. You're not even concerned with this at all."

A chill moved through Carly's spine at her mother's tone. "I'm concerned. Concerned about Dorothy."

"Then why have you been staring at your phone? Don't make me take it from you."

Carly's fingers tightened on the edge of her device. "You can't take things from me like that. I'm…not a child anymore."

"You act like it."

"Stop," Richard said, finally stepping in. "We're going to a funeral. I thought these were supposed to bring families together?"

Carly laughed. "You've got a lot to learn before you step in, then."

Jillian's eye narrowed. She didn't say a word, but Carly saw something inside her mother's gaze that she hadn't seen in a long time. Not since her father, Jordan's, funeral—more than grief, this was anger.

We were happy once, Carly thought. *With Davis and with Cynthia on the way.* They had practically been a Norman Rockwell painting then. But Jordan's death rocked through their house and made her mother angry and bitter. Even though she and Jordan had divorced years ago, Carly suspected that Jillian still loved Jordan. She had channeled that feeling into Davis and her new family, and did it well until Jordan's death. His passing was a crack in the illusion that was Jillian's life, and suddenly, as if overnight, she could no longer believe in love in the same way. She had become a workaholic then, taking everything on herself. Carly had always assumed that her mother had become worse when Carly came out as gay in her teenage years. But no, she realized now that her previous interpretation of events had been regular teenage narcissism. Her mother had started to go downhill around the time of Jordan's death; Carly just didn't have words, as a child, to put a name to the feeling the crept through the house. The marriage between her and Davis had been over then, too. Sure, Davis hung around for another couple years to try and give it another shot, but Carly's mother had shut down. Suddenly, Carly realized she had nothing to worry about with Richard anymore. He was a great guy and trying hard, but with this death to shake her up Jillian would remain angry and bitter and let no one else get close to her. Richard—like Steven, the rebound husband after Davis—was doomed.

After a moment, Carly sighed and tucked away her phone. She watched the houses pass by, before she saw the church and graveyard next to it. "If I know anything about Dorothy, she would think all of this ridiculous."

"What do you mean?" Jillian asked, her voice petulant but curious. "I got her favorite flowers. I know she kept reminding me how much she liked tiger lilies for this very occasion."

Carly laughed, because that probably was true. Dorothy liked to remind people of her mortality. But it was always in the abstract—*not ideals*, Carly remembered, *but bodies*. "She probably did that because we're all worm food for those flowers, though. Dorothy would have wanted us to think about the science behind all of this."

"Be nice," Jillian remarked with fervor in her voice.

"I am nice."

"Someone did just die," Cynthia added.

"I know. But funerals are always for the living. People cry during them because they mourn the last contact they had or last words said. Sometimes, in the best cases, funerals celebrate life. But not always. I'm sad, sure, but I'm also okay. Dorothy would have—"

"What, Carly?" Jillian asked. "What would she have wanted?"

Carly bit her lip. She knew that Dorothy would have wanted Carly to go to the hospital, to stay with Ashley, but that wasn't something she could say aloud. To remind everyone of the very real peril her girlfriend just went through, on a day they were supposed to be mourning the dead, was a no-no. Even as Carly felt her phone buzz in her pocket, she remained silent with her hands folded on her lap.

"She would have wanted us to be happy she lived so long," Carly said. "Not sad she died. It was a good life—and she lived it well."

Jillian glanced back at her in the rearview mirror. She breathed in and out deeply, then conceded. "Well, at least we can agree on something."

Carly let out a small smile. "Yeah, maybe we can agree on that."

Richard eyed her in the mirror. When Carly gave him a small nod, he seemed relieved. And she caught herself hoping he did stay around for a while. Out of all the men since Davis, he was the one Carly could put money on getting Jillian to open up again. *And if she did... Then maybe we could go back to the Norman Rockwell family. Maybe we could be happy again.*

Before Carly could entertain the thought very long, Richard pulled into the lot. Everyone else seemed to already be there. Carly could spot the people she only saw at her mother's weddings and now, family funerals. Everything seemed like one big show, but not a cool party like Dorothy would have wanted to send her into whatever afterlife. Carly's skin felt itchy just thinking of the ceremony, and she shivered as she stepped out into the summer sunlight. In a quick moment before Jillian could see, Carly looked down at her phone. A message from Darren stared up at her.

Ashley is awake and alert, all vital signs good. She's going to stay over for observation another night, but she can go home.

Oh thank God, Carly thought. She wanted to cry with relief. Luckily she was going to a place where tears wouldn't be too out of place. She felt Cynthia come by her side and take her wrist.

"You okay?"

"Yeah, I am. For the first time in a while."

"What happened?"

"Ashley...she's fine. She can go home soon."

"With you?"

Carly's face softened. She felt her eyes well up with tears. All she could do was nod for some time. "Yeah...with me."

Cynthia squeezed Carly's hand before she started to cry too. As if synchronized, they turned toward one another and hugged. Carly heard Richard and her mother's footsteps stop ahead of them, and turn around to wait until they were done. Carly could imagine her mother opening her mouth to yell at her, but then stop and wait as her children embraced.

"Ashley's okay," Carly said, letting out a slow sob. "Oh God, I'm so happy she's okay."

"Me too."

"Really?"

"Yes. Even if it means you abandon me with Mom, hah." Cynthia's laugh was a little strangled, but genuine from what Carly could tell.

"I'd never abandon you."

"Maybe…"

Carly didn't respond, only hugged Cynthia closer. As their embrace continued, the crying calmed. Whatever they mourned—maybe it was the same thing that Carly had come to realize about Davis and her mother—was resolved for now, at least.

"Has Mom told you yet?" Cynthia said, whispering into Carly's ear.

"What?"

"About the meeting yesterday?"

Carly let out a low sigh. The division of state had happened the day before, when Dorothy's will had been gone over. Carly had gone right from work to the hospital and then home, late enough to crawl into bed and get ready for the funeral. She had been avoiding her mother expertly.

"No."

"Oh." Cynthia paused. She pulled away from the hug slightly to glance at where Jillian and Richard were now embracing and crying. More people pooled around the front of the lot, and Carly knew they had to speak quickly. Carly recalled the way her mother had been acting all day; Carly had chalked it up to emotions because of the funeral, but it could have been something during the will and division of state. Her heart started to pound, suddenly worried that Dorothy had been carrying a deep secret.

"What's going on? Come on, Cyn, you're killing me."

Cyn nudged her slightly on the arm. "You get the house, Carly."

"What?"

"Dorothy's house. Mom was surprised but… I can't say I am."

The news washed over Carly. All the memories of the house came back, the conversations, the structure appearing like a ghost in her mind. *Not ideals*, she remembered in her aunt's voice, *just bodies*. Carly knew she had probably been given the house because it was the most useful thing Aunt Dorothy owned. More than that—Ashley was awake now, and able to come home. *And maybe she really can come home to me.*

"Girls," Jillian called. "We have to go. I hope you're ready."

Cynthia squeezed Carly's hand and then wiped away another tear.

"Yeah," they both said in unison, and walked together into the sea of people they had barely met until today. "We are."

When Carly walked inside the church, her eyes took a while to adjust to darkness inside from the sunlight outdoors. Once she did, and she saw the casket, she was no longer afraid.

Thanks, Aunt Dorothy. Good-bye.

CHAPTER 38

When Carly arrived at the hospital, Ashley was asleep. But Carly could see it was different. Ashley's face had more color now. She still looked small in the hospital gown and with tubes in her arms, but those had decreased in number. Carly pulled up the same chair she always sat in, trying to be careful as she scuffed it across the floor. Ashley's skin was no longer hot to the touch. She murmured in her sleep, turning over in bed, but not waking. Carly smiled. *You always slept like a rock, didn't you?*

Carly took out *Treasure Island* from her purse. At home, she had been rereading sections of it so it would remind her of Ashley and she could feel close to her again. Carly could pinpoint where she had been when she read certain scenes aloud, where Ashley's hand had been placed on her body, and whether or not they had kissed yet. This was really why Carly loved rereading books, because it was about the memory of reading as much as it was about the actual storyline itself.

Ashley still slept as Carly read silently. Her mind soon wandered away from the page, and the new place she had found herself. After the funeral, when everyone was back at their house for a light lunch. Her mother had finally broken the news about the house and the rest of the will to Carly. Jillian got most of Dorothy's liquid assets while Cynthia got antique Rollerblades that even Carly didn't know Dorothy had.

Jillian was distant as she reiterated the facts, and when Richard came up to them and laid a hand on Jillian's waist, Carly noticed her mother moved into the touch. Things were getting better, however slowly.

Carly had no idea what she would do with a house that big. Her mother had advised selling it, since it was already paid off and would yield a good price. But Carly wasn't sure about letting go of something that was so much a part of Dorothy. She wanted to talk to Ashley about it. She could trust her judgement.

An hour into the visit, Ashley still hadn't woken up from her nap yet. Carly rose to her feet, kissing Ashley's hand before she went for coffee. As she reached the doorway, a movement came from the bed.

"Carly Rogers?" Ashley said, her voice muffled. She rubbed her eyes and placed an arm behind her head. "Is that you?"

"Yes." Carly hadn't been called by her full name like this in what felt like a long time—and she cherished the sound. "I'm here now. Not going anywhere."

"Ah yes," Ashley said. "There's that enthusiasm I've been missing."

Carly wrapped her hand around Ashley's and grinned, Ashley was weak. Tired. Small creases formed around her eyes. Her fatigue weighed down the room.

"How are you feeling?" Carly asked.

"I'm in a hospital. That should be a feeling in and of itself."

"What's that like?"

"Trapped. Annoying. And tired, really tired."

"You're pretty much better now. That's what Darren tells me."

"And yet, they want to keep me here for observation. I guess I'm just too popular for my own good."

"You're a lot of things," Carly said. She meant the words to be playful, but Ashley's smile was barely there.

"Yeah, I suppose I am now." Her free hand went to her chin, as if she was thinking something over. She raised her eyebrows after a moment and shrugged. "I guess it's a fact that I do have epilepsy, right? No beating around the bush?"

"Um." Carly paused. She had been so consumed by Ashley just being okay that she hadn't stopped to think anything over in the bigger picture. "Maybe. I think, because of the medication"

"Ah. I guess you know about that now, right?"

Carly nodded mutely.

"Yep. No privacy. I figured as much."

"It's not like that. It's not like the NSA listening in on your phone calls."

"I know that," Ashley said, kissing Carly's hand. "But I wish I hadn't been an idiot about the pills in the first place."

"You weren't…." Carly started to argue and then stopped as she felt Ashley sigh against her fingers.

"Ugh," Ashley groaned. "Now I really can't drive. I'm never getting my license back."

"I know. That sucks. But apparently I may be your chauffeur a lot faster than we thought."

Ashley smiled and then burst out laughing. "Oh, man. I thought that was a dream! Darren told me you drove me to the hospital at like three in the morning, but I didn't believe him. That really is true?"

Carly nodded and shrugged her shoulders. "What can I say?"

"Badass. That's what you can say."

"Really, though, I know I should be happy," Ashley said after laughing. "At least I don't have some weird disease they can't diagnose. I'm just going to spaz out around bright colors and sounds. And they're going to lecture me about going to derbies."

Carly smiled. "You just need…"

"I know, I know. Pills. Fuck. Is there anything you *don't* know now?" Ashley smiled, but Carly could sense the pain in the response.

"I can tell you my medical history," Carly bargained. "Show me yours and I'll show you mine."

"Okay," Ashley said, sitting up with bright eyes. "I actually want to hear this. Gory details and all. It's only fair."

"I don't think I have much. I broke my toe when I was thirteen, while playing with Cynthia. Even then, she was causing bumps and bruises."

"What was she, like a baby?"

"About two years old. And then, when I was fifteen, I passed out in gym class from running a mile in heat. That was more the gym teacher's fault, I'm pretty sure."

"Probably. Gym class always felt like slow torture on most days."

"Oh, yeah," Carly agreed with a nod. "But I think that's it—as far as injuries go."

"Not fair. I want to know the little bits that you may be hiding."

"Oh?"

"Like…" Ashley said, her voice a little throaty. "First period?"

"Thirteen. Terrible. It was just after the toe incident, too. I hid it from my mom for like a year."

"How?"

She shrugged. "Bought my own pads. I finally told her one morning as I was leaving for school, when I was fourteen. I just didn't want to tell her before that. She doesn't exactly inspire girl talk."

"Fair enough." Ashley stared up at the ceiling considering all the information. "So really, no broken bones, huh? Nothing major?"

"Nope."

"Not even sprains?"

"Uh-huh."

"My God, you are a golden child."

Carly laughed as she squeezed Ashley's hand. "Ask something else and I'll tell you."

Ashley motioned for Carly to lean closer and then began to whisper. "First time you had sex?"

"Guy or girl?"

"Oh," Ashley said. "Now, we're interesting. Guy, then."

"Never. Not really. When I was fifteen I dated someone, and we both got off with one another, but I had to do the work, you know? I realized I didn't really like guys then."

"Pfft, who does?" Ashley joked. "With a woman, then?"

"I was sixteen. I would like to not reveal the name, for personal reasons."

"Okay," Ashley said, giving another nod. Carly thought from the way Ashley tipped her head that she knew who Carly was referring to. "What was it like?"

"Great," Carly said. "I was nervous, of course."

"Of course, it's you."

"But it was good. Her breasts were huge—and I remember that being a really, really scary thing to me. I didn't know where to put my hands and then where to touch. I didn't know if what felt good to me felt good to her. They always say that same sex relationships are easier because hey, you already have a body like that! So you should know where things go! But it's not like that. Not at all. Every body is so different."

"Don't I know it," Ashley said with a sigh. "But tell me more about the sex."

Carly laughed. "Well, I never came, but I got her off really easily."

"Mouth or hands?"

"Both. I was fingering her and using my tongue."

"Looks like you learned quickly, then." Ashley winked. "As much as I thank you for sharing, I'm sad now because I'm horny. And that's another thing about hospitals—you can't masturbate or your fucking heart monitors go off and they think you're dying."

Carly eyed the machine and then looked back at Ashley. "Personal experience?"

Ashley made a motion of zipping her lips. "I really think you know too much about me, so I'm keeping that answer to myself."

"Fair enough. But...Is that so bad? That I know a lot?"

"No," Ashley said genuinely. "I just wish I had been the one to tell you."

"I know," Carly said. "Me too."

They were quiet for a while before Ashley tugged on Carly's hand. She thought she was going to ask her another question. *Threesome? Personal favorite position?* Instead she pulled her close. They kissed, just a little, because if they kept going it felt like too much to handle. After almost losing her, and realizing the depth of her love, Carly couldn't handle so much touch. She could not handle that much reciprocated feeling—especially with a heart monitor next to them.

"What's up?" Ashley asked when she pulled away. Their heads still remained close, foreheads touching. "You're upset."

"I have been, yeah. I was really worried about you."

Ashley narrowed her eyes. "You should know I'm made of stronger stuff."

"I guess I should by now. I will keep it in mind."

"So what is it, then?" Ashley asked. Their eyes caught one another. "You can tell me, right?"

Carly's breath hitched in her throat. Her heart skipped a beat. And that's when she realized that Ashley already knew the answer, and was merely waiting for her to confess it.

"Dorothy died in her sleep—some complication with pneumonia. It was peaceful, really. Nothing to be upset about."

"A death is always upsetting" she said slowly. "No matter how well or how little you think you know someone. How long ago?"

"A while…" Carly said. She hoped that would be enough of a response, but Ashley raised her eyes to Carly. She narrowed them and squeezed her hand.

"I…uh," Carly said, stopping and restarting. "I went to her funeral yesterday. I was there…but I also wasn't there, you know? I didn't feel anything. Nothing like I was supposed to feel. Hell, Cyn and I cried before the service—not during it."

"What do you think you should have done?"

"I don't know. Made a bigger fuss? I was sad—don't get me wrong—I just… I know that's not what Dorothy would have wanted."

"Why not?"

"Because you should pick bodies over ideals. She was my aunt and I loved her. But she was not made for this type of mourning."

"Everyone's made for mourning."

"Not her… Not…like that. She was too good to be so simple. She…" Carly lost it then. For the second time in two days, she felt the sudden well of grief inside of her over Dorothy's death. She thought the small cry with Cynthia had been enough, but maybe that was mourning something else entirely. Now, inside Ashley's hospital room, she felt the emptiness, the blank space that Dorothy left. She would no longer have anyone to spend weekends with. She wouldn't have to trade her Saturday shifts, she wouldn't have to clean, and she wouldn't have anyone to write poetry with anymore. The good and the bad of that life and then just the boring bits of being at her house, all fell away. She would miss the conversation, the bickering over tea, and then the eerie quiet in the middle of the afternoon when Dorothy would sleep. She would miss everything, Carly realized, because time only ever went one way. Sometimes she could barely stand up without feeling the weight of all the decisions she had to make in order to keep moving forward. Sometimes, all Carly wanted to do was to stand still, because she thought that meant she could beat time. That nothing could happen around her. But it always moved. Things always changed. And Carly was suddenly so, so sick of everything moving on without her.

As Carly cried, Ashley held onto her hand and squeezed it at the right times, murmuring small encouraging words. It was small, but Carly thought it was enough. When Ashley expressed her own condolences, and her own personal mourning for Dorothy, Carly squeezed Ashley's hands in the same, small ways.

"I'm so sorry, Carly."

"Don't call me that."

"What? Carly?"

"Yeah," Carly said, wiping away a tear. She tried to take in a deep breath and smile. "I missed you calling me by my full name."

Ashley grinned. "Ah, Carly Rogers. I will use your full name so long as you're around to hear it."

"It's all I ask," Carly said, squeezing hands again.

"As much as I'm willing to comply to your needs, I sometimes think you should ask for more."

"What do you mean?"

"I…I wanted to avoid this." Ashley looked around and motioned to all the beeping equipment. The nurses' shoes scuffed up and down the hallway and added another din of white noise to the other hospital sounds.

"What? Me taking care of you?"

"Well, I was thinking I really wanted to avoid you driving without supervision—because really, how dangerous!"

Carly laughed. "Well, I figured since I was heading toward the hospital the worse couldn't possibly happen. With all the adrenaline pumping through my system, I figured I was like those supermoms who could lift cars up. Really, I was practically a superhero."

Ashley squeezed Carly's hand again. "We'd still better get you lessons. But you know what I mean, right? I didn't want this to happen. I didn't want my illness, whatever it is, to come in the way. I didn't want to scare you. Even if you are a superhero under all of your tight sweaters, I wanted to be the one to save you. Not the one to cause you to change."

"I'm not. It's not like that. Ever since I started that job, I've been changing. But that's not been you. Not entirely. I've just been realizing how much I gave up in order to come back here. In order to take care of other people."

"Cyn and your aunt?"

"No, my mom. And I can't do it anymore. She's left and gotten married so many times, but I thought I owed her something. Like I owed her to stay around…" Carly paused, putting her free hand to her mouth. "But it doesn't matter. It really doesn't. She has Richard, and I should have realized that sooner. I should have realized so many things sooner. I've just been thinking way too much while I'm here…"

"As if that's different from any other day," Ashley joked. She sat up in bed, her face serious again. She pushed her cords out of the way and took Carly's hand in hers. "What, my dear? What is your revelation?"

"That I love you. I want to be with you, and…" Carly trailed off, then took a deep breath. "Dorothy left me her house. Her will said something about how I had cleaned it so often I may as well get to keep the fruits of my labor. I didn't believe it…" Carly dug through her purse to find her phone. "Cyn sent me a picture of the will earlier today. I have it here if you want to see."

"I believe you," Ashley said. Her face softened. "Oh, trust me, I believe you. Even if I have just woken up like Sleeping Beauty and could be taken for any scam in the world."

"Oh, right. I'm sorry. I should let you rest. Do you need food?"

"No, I need you to tell me what's going on." Ashley asked, her face serious and playful at the same time.

"Well." Carly took a deep breath and tried to reorganize all her thoughts so they made sense again. "I suppose it's kind of like Godot, I mean. I think I realized that I was staying here like those men stayed on the stage, hoping for something better, hoping for something good to come along. Only it never does. The play always goes on and on, the same thing over and over again, but they never see Godot. They never meet Godot. He's an illusion, and you can't fall in love with myths. You have to fall in love with bodies." Carly laughed again. "I feel stupid not getting this until now. But there is so much homoerotic subtext in that play between Vladimir and Estragon. So. Much."

"Even I got that when I read it, and I'm not an English major." Ashley laughed again. "So that's really all it is? If you're making bad literary analogies and jokes about life, you can't feel that badly."

Carly laughed. "I do that, don't I?"

"And I tolerate it. By the way—did you bring me anything good to read?"

Carly moved slightly, letting go of Ashley's hand to pick up *Treasure Island*. She held it up with a smile.

"Excellent. Well done, Jolly Rogers," Ashley said, nodding and smiling. "An oldie but a goodie. Have you been reading it aloud?"

"Half and half. Depending on who was around and how I felt."

"No good. No wonder I've been having strange, pirate fantasy dreams that don't lead anywhere. We'll have to start from the beginning again."

"Well, fine, Ashley Poindexter."

Ashley smiled again. "There. I was waiting for it."

"What?"

"My name. You only use it when you're happy."

"I like the way it sounds in my mouth." Carly paused, and heard Ashley giggle again. "Wait, that didn't sound right."

"That sounded *perfect*," Ashley said. She kissed her cheek, before pulling back. "But tell me. Finish your story from before. If we don't wait for Godot, what do we do?"

"I'm moving," Carly said. "I have a house now. And a job, I think, with Marshalls. This is a little bit longer of a story, but it's easier to follow…"

Ashley nodded along as Carly began to explain the possible job at Marshalls. When Ashley had been in the hospital and Carly missed a shift, she worried that the job offer would be revoked. She had been shocked when Tim, one of the managers, had left her a heartfelt message on her machine, assuring her that not only was she a good worker—but to take the time she needed. She was most likely going to take the promotion, too, but only if Ashley came with her. Only if Ashley could still work, too. She wanted them to be together, if this was going to work. Vladimir could not leave Estragon, even if they could leave behind Godot.

"But…" Carly said. She wished that Ashley would help her out, but she no longer added commentary. She stared at Ashley, her eyes wide, waiting for Ashley to finish her story and give it the ending it needed.

"But," Ashley finally said. "Come on, Carly, you can do this. Ask me."

"If you already know what I'm going to say, then why should I?"

"Because I want to hear it from you."

"Come live with me," Carly said, sighing. "I want you, Ashley Poindexter, to live with me, Carly Rogers."

"Yes, Carly Jolly Rogers. I will go on whatever adventure you give to me. So long," Ashley said, kissing her knuckles and pointing to the book again, "as you start at the beginning."

Carly nodded. She got up from her spot by the bed and wrapped her arms around Ashley, touching her frail shoulders and kissing her cheek.

"I love you," she said.

"I love you too," Ashley reciprocated. When they pulled their faces back toward one another, their lips met. Small and chaste, the kiss seemed more restorative to Carly than to Ashley. Carly moved her palms down Ashley's small arms, being weary of the tubes and IV, until she sat back down on her chair. Both hands were on the bed, and for a while, they were both silent.

Then Ashley sighed. "Come on, you know how boring hospitals are."

"Yes, yes," Carly said. She picked up *Treasure Island* once again. She cracked open the first page, and with Ashley's hand in hers, began to read.

CHAPTER 39

"Hiya!" Cynthia jumped around the corner of the living room, Bubble Wrap firmly placed in her hands. She crinkled the edges. *Snap. Pop.* Her eyes widened with delight, especially as Landon jumped.

"Cyn!" Landon placed a hand over his chest. "You gotta warn a guy."

"That would defeat the purpose of the game." Cynthia unleashed another torrent of snapping and popping. When her Bubble Wrap ceased to produce sound, she glanced behind her. "Anymore, Ashley?"

"Oh no." Carly groaned. "You're in on this bizarre game, too?"

"What do you mean, bizarre?" Ashley rounded the corner from the hallway to the living area, her arms full of Bubble Wrap. Cynthia grabbed another sheet of it and started to snap it at Landon. Landon huffed, then paced over to Ashley to grab a sheet for himself. He and Cynthia then fought to the death. Or at least, that was what it looked like to Carly.

"I'm still not sure if I understand this game," Carly said. "But as long as my mugs don't break, then continue on for however long you want."

"What don't you understand?" Ashley asked. "It's the Wild West, gun-slinging, fun sound effects, without a weapon."

"So Landon and Cyn are…Bonnie and Clyde?"

"No!" Cynthia shouted. "Billy and the Kid."

"You mean Billy the Kid," Landon corrected, popping Bubble Wrap with emphasis. "He was one person."

"Oh. Well. We'll rewrite that part of history so he has a cool sidekick. Now draw, cowboy." Cynthia held up a sheet of Bubble Wrap around her fingers, pointed into guns. When Landon mirrored her action, they both started to count as they took steps away from one another. At five, they turned around and fired.

"I still don't understand how anyone wins," Carly said when Landon went down again.

"Oh, shush. Don't take everything so seriously." Ashley nudged Carly's shoulder, then clasped Bubble Wrap in her hands.

"Oh no," Carly groaned. But she wasn't upset; she could already feel the smile creeping on her face. She grabbed a section of Bubble Wrap from Ashley, then took a few steps back. She lamented the fact that there were still so, so many boxes to unpack and things to attend to in Dorothy's house for their move.

But if they couldn't have fun now, when could they?

"Five," Ashley declared. "Are you ready to draw?"

Carly nodded, followed by the snapping of Bubble Wrap. Ashley pretended to move as if a bullet went by her, then drew and fired her own "weapon." Before Carly knew it, everyone in the living room was running around and chasing one another, the sounds of popping only drowned out by laughter. By the time they ran out of Bubble Wrap, everyone was out of breath, and Landon's cheeks glowed red.

"Well," Landon said, as he flopped down on Dorothy's old couch. "That was fun, but I'm more out of shape than I thought."

"You need to skate with me. Easy solution," Cynthia said.

"Maybe. But I also think I should never, ever help anyone move again. So much work." Landon shook his head at all the half-empty boxes marked *FRAGILE* that snaked their way into the kitchen. There were still more in the truck in the driveway, plus all the stray bags and boxes that were in other rooms upstairs. Carly's head hurt just thinking about it all.

"You're telling me," she added. "I'm still in shock nothing broke from that long gunfight."

"Nah, everything's fine," Ashley said. "And really, this will all be done before you know it. But—I have to ask. You feel okay, Landon?"

"Yeah. Much better. Caught my breath, now." Landon smiled. "Why, though, Ashley? You seem to be planning something. "

"I might be." Ashley grinned. She extended her hand to Landon to help him up off the couch. "Nothing sinister, don't worry. I just need your help with the couch."

The move continued late into the evening. After the couch, Cynthia and Carly were assigned to organizational duties, putting away the contents of the million boxes holding everything that Ashley and Carly owned. Carly was floored at how much stuff they had—especially when combined with Ashley's other items from storage. While Carly and Ashley were moving in, they were also moving bits of Aunt Dorothy out. Jillian and Richard had been up earlier in the week to take out what keepsakes Jillian wanted. Afterward, Carly and Ashley were to discard or sell the furniture they didn't want or need.

"Her letters, books, and all sorts of stuff will take longer," Carly explained to Ashley and Landon when they were inside for a drink. "I know we'll probably need to get another truck, maybe even one of those junk bins you see on *Hoarders*. Or we could donate it all…"

"One moving day at a time, okay?" Landon said. "We'll take away whatever you give us and then dump it on your mom and Richard. Then, the rest of it… you'll forget. You'll learn to live with a bunch of papers and old books. Pretend you're in another era."

Carly smiled, liking the sound of that very much.

Landon slapped a friendly hand on Ashley's back, pointing to the old boxes that once held dishes. "We're taking those out."

"Yeah, yeah," Ashley said. "And then I think that's it."

Carly nodded. Once she and Cynthia had finished sweeping the floor, they moved on to food.

"The least I can do is feed you guys," Carly stated. She grabbed a couple of Cokes out of the fridge, along with ingredients for pita pizzas. "Not much, but it'll be something, right?"

"Feed us and leave us," Landon joked.

"You are welcome to visit, absolutely anytime," Carly said. "There is way too much of this house. Plenty of room."

"You'll find stuff to do with the space," Landon said. "Not that I wouldn't mind an occasional sleepover, for old time's sake."

"Oh yeah," Cynthia said. She checked her hip with Landon's, after sliding her pizza into the oven. "The rest of the time, you can hang out with me."

Landon nodded, rustling his hand through Cynthia's hair. He put the rest of the pizzas in the oven and then, without being prompted, began to set the table.

A sudden wave of nostalgia came over Carly. Landon had been at least half-right with his "feed us and leave us" comment. This really was a good-bye meal. Landon would come over for sleepovers, but it would be for old time's sake. Carly's chest tightened. She was so used to her life and her stuff being in one place. Moving always meant she had to untangle her life, and usually, surface memories at the same time. *Do I really want to let this all go?*

Then she saw Ashley across the room, and her mind cleared. This was exactly where she needed to be. Carly made her way over to Ashley's side of the kitchen, close to the fridge, where Ashley put her arm around her. They started their new jobs again in another week. Then, from there, who knew?

When the pizzas came out, Cynthia was the first to do the serving. She hummed that same song that always got caught in Carly's head as she did. No one seemed to mind.

"Well," Ashley said, as they all sat around the table. "It sort of feels like we need a toast…or something."

Everyone exchanged glances, expecting the next person to make the speech. To have the final words. Landon coughed, and finally raised his Coke in the air.

"I'm not one for words, but I think 'welcome home' is appropriate."

Carly smiled, and so did Ashley. They nodded, as everyone else raised their glasses in the air.

"Welcome home."

CHAPTER 40

"I'll be right back," Ashley said. "I just want to change."

Carly nodded, then sighed at more boxes. Cynthia and Landon had just left, but there was still so much more to do. "I'll get back to work in the kitchen."

"Don't work too hard now, okay?"

"Never," Carly teased. But left alone, she felt a small bud of anxiety creep back into her system, travel over her spine, and out through the hollow hallways of the house. Each time the floorboard creaked as Ashley went upstairs, she felt it in her bones, as if the house was a part of her, and Ashley walked around the chambers of her heart.

She got up from the table and began to clear the plates. She told herself she was being ridiculous. It was so weird, though, she knew. This was the first time she had been alone in this house. Really, alone at all in the past few weeks. She looked down at her hands, as if to be sure they were still there and not shaking. They were fine. She was fine. She took a step forward and began to run water for dishes, a task she knew so well at this point, she was sure she could do it without power, without light.

Out the window, she spotted the plum and pecan trees that were suddenly no longer full of blossoms. Pecans littered the ground, some of them growing moldy in the rain since Dorothy's death. She stood there and suddenly felt the loss she had yet to feel. She saw Dorothy, as a young woman, picking those pecans from the ground and eating them anyway, treating them, making pies. She saw her move back and forth from the tree to her home, from her job to work, and being happy. There was a simplicity to the way in which the fruit tree bloomed and then lost all it had ever held. But it was not quite a loss, Carly knew, because someone got something out of it. Every bud that grew and then died eventually turned into fruit. And someone came along, got that, and kept it as long as they needed.

Carly placed a hand over her mouth, holding her sob inside her chest.

When Ashley came back down, she didn't speak, didn't ask if she was okay. Ashley merely moved her arms around her shoulders, into a hug, and breathed quietly in her ear.

"It's okay, Carly," she said. "She would have loved it too."

Later that night, they unpacked the mugs. And that's when Carly saw it, the final stanza to their long standing poem. She took it out of the mug it was placed in and held it by the corners as she read it.

Love is the best story, I think.
Plato once said that our arms reach out
For the person on our back
Who has been split apart and sent away,
So we know how far to travel
So we know how long to wait
So we know that
When we find them again
They will know us better
Than we know our own names.
Plato once recorded,
Many old men, talking about love
But he missed the most important lesson:
The person reading the story,
The one who remembered it
Enough to write it down.
That is the best love story, I think.
Yes, the scribe, the one who lives alone
Is the one who knows love the most.
Fall for bodies, the scribe says
Not the ideals that Plato wished for.
Because the scribe gets nothing in the end
But a couple good last words.

When Ashley stepped into the kitchen, she held a box in her hands. As soon as she saw Carly, hunched over a small cue card, her face dropped.

"Is that...?"

"Yes," Carly said, holding it to her chest. She could still hear Dorothy's words in her ear. "The last one this time."

"Funny, because I found all the others," Ashley said. She held a small box in her hands.

"What?" Carly narrowed her eyes. "What do you mean?"

"Your aunt. She kept all the other cue cards full of poetry under her bed."

"I thought we threw them away?"

Ashley shook her head. She took another step closer, extending her arm to display the open shoebox filled to the brim with small cue cards with small handwriting and big, bold script. All the poems they had written, one stanza at a time, taking turns.

"I can't..." Carly held the small card to her chest, pressing it into her body as if she could absorb the ending. "I don't know what to say."

"You don't have to say anything. You don't have to do anything, either."

Ashley placed the shoebox on the table before she pulled Carly toward her. "In fact, if you wanted, we could add the last piece and forget about it. Or we could keep going."

Carly thought about both options for a long time. When she lifted her gaze, she met Ashley's stare, her blue eyes, and grin. And she already knew the next verse she wanted to write.

"Thank you," Carly said. It felt as if she was speaking to several people at once, and from the way that Ashley nodded, she seemed to understand.

"Yeah. Thank you."

Ashley's thumb continued to move back and forth across Carly's skin. Then, ever so slowly and with smiles on their faces, Carly pulled Ashley in for more.

About Eve Francis

Eve Francis's short stories have appeared in Wilde Magazine, The Fieldstone Review, Iris New Fiction, MicroHorror, and The Human Echoes Podcast. Romance and horror are her favourite genres to write in because everyone has felt love or fear in some form or another. She lives in Canada, where she often sleeps late, spends too much time online, and repeatedly watches old horror movies and *Orange Is The New Black*.

CONNECT WITH EVE FRANCIS:
Webseite: evefrancis.wordpress.com
Tumblr: paintitback.tumblr.com

Other Books from Ylva Publishing

www.ylva-publishing.com

Stowe Away

Blythe Rippon

ISBN: 978-3-95533- 523-6
Length: 279 pages (97,500 words)

Brilliant, awkward Samantha Latham couldn't wait to leave rural Stowe for an illustrious career in medicine. But when an unexpected call from a hospital forces Sam to move back home to care for her ailing mother, a life of boredom and isolation seems imminent—until a charming restaurant owner named Maria inspires Sam to rethink everything she knows about Stowe, success, and above all, love.

The Light of the World

Ellen Simpson

ISBN: 978-3-95533-507-6
Length: 357 pages (10,7000 words)

Confronted with a mystery upon her grandmother's death, Eva delves into the rich and complicated history of a woman who hid far more than a long-lost-love from the world. Darkness is lurking behind every corner, and someone is looking for the key to her grandmother's secrets; the light of the world.

The Sum of These Things

(A Story of Now Series – Book #2)

Emily O'Beirne

ISBN: 978-3-95533-471-0
Length: 396 pages (134,500 words)

This summer Claire has learned a few things already. Like falling for a girl is easy. Now comes the hard part, though: learning to trust. Then there's the question of what to do with her life. Claire's new job offers a potential future, but will her pushy mother like it? Now, the biggest lesson Claire must learn is to not let anything get in the way of her happiness. Especially herself.

Never-Tied Nora

(Girl Meets Girl Series – Book #1)

Cheyenne Blue

ISBN: 978-3-95533-451-2
Length: 131 pages (38,000 words)

Nora Kelly's London Irish family have only one rule when it comes to dating: Nora can date any woman she wants—as long as she's not a Flannery. The Kellys and the Flannerys have been feuding for generations, and time has not lessened the hatred.

But footloose Nora has just met the woman of her dreams, and suddenly commitment isn't a dirty word. Trouble is, Geraldine is a Flannery.

Coming from Ylva Publishing

www.ylva-publishing.com

The Space Between

Michelle L. Teichman

Life is easy for Harper, the most popular girl in her grade, until she meets Sarah, a friendless loner who only cares about art. Inexplicably, Harper can't stop thinking about her.

Unsure of her feelings for Harper, Sarah is afraid to act on what her heart is telling her. She can't believe Harper feels the same.

Can Harper and Sarah find a way to be together, or will fear keep them apart forever?

Ex-Wives of Dracula

Georgette Kaplan

Mindy's best friend, Lucia, has become a vampire. Every second Mindy spends with her she's in danger of becoming dinner. But Lucia needs help. To keep her alive they need fresh blood, and to cure her they have to kill the vampire that sired her. So why is it that Nosferatu, the cops, and the chance of becoming an unwilling blood donor don't scare Mindy half as much as the way she feels when Lucia looks at her?

Fragile
© 2016 by Eve Francis

ISBN: 978-3-95533-482-6

Also available as e-book.

Published by Ylva Publishing, legal entity of Ylva Verlag, e.Kfr.

Ylva Verlag, e.Kfr.
Owner: Astrid Ohletz
Am Kirschgarten 2
65830 Kriftel
Germany

www.ylva-publishing.com

First edition: 2016

Credits
Edited by CK King
Cover Design by Streetlight Graphics

www.ingramcontent.com/pod-product-compliance
Lightning Source LLC
Chambersburg PA
CBHW030933260626
47169CB00002B/461